NEW STORIES FROM THE MIDWEST 2016

NEW STORIES FROM THE MIDWEST 2016

LEE MARTIN
Guest Editor

JASON LEE BROWN AND SHANIE LATHAM
Series Editors

newamericanpress
Milwaukee, Wis. • Urbana, Ill.

n e w a m e r i c a n p r e s s

www.NewAmericanPress.com

Printed in the United States of America
ISBN 978-1-941561-06-5

For ordering information, please contact:
Ingram Book Group
One Ingram Blvd.
La Vergne, TN 37086
(800) 937-8000
orders@ingrambook.com

All stories reprinted by permission of the individual authors and/or publishers. Grateful acknowledgment is made to the journals and magazines where the stories first appeared:

"Grimace in the Burnt Black Hills" © 2012 by Thomas M. Atkinson. First published in *The Sun* issue 439 (July 2012). Reprinted by permission of the author.

"Forbearance" from *There's Something I Want You To Do: Stories* by Charles Baxter, Copyright © 2015 by Charles Baxter. Used by permission of Pantheon Books, an imprint of the Knopf Doubleday Publishing Group, a division of Penguin Random House LLC. All rights reserved. "Forbearance" first published in *Michigan Quarterly Review* (Spring 2013).

"Departures" © 2012 by Catherine Browder. First published in *Nimrod* vol. 44 issue no. 2 (June 2012). Reprinted by permission of the author.

"Upper Middle Class Houses" © 2012 by Claire Burgess. First published in *Third Coast* (Spring 2012). Reprinted by permission of the author.

"Chance" © 2012 by Peter Ho Davies. First published in *Glimmer Train Stories* #82 (February 2012) and then in *Bob Seger's House and Other Stories* from Wayne State University Press (May 2016). Reprinted by permission of the author.

"JadeDragon_77" © 2012 by Stephanie Dickinson. First published in *Weber* vol. 29, no. 1 (Fall 2012). Reprinted by permission of the author.

"All the Time in the World" © 2014 by Jack Driscoll. First published in *The Georgia Review* (Spring 2014). Reprinted by permission of the author.

"Three Summers" © 2013 by Nick Dybek. First published in *Ploughshares* (Fall 2013). Reprinted by permission of the author.

"Tosca" © 2012 by Stuart Dybek. First published in *Tin House* #54 (Winter 2012). Reprinted by permission of the author. "Tosca" also published in *Paper Lantern: Love Stories* published by Farrar, Straus and Giroux (2014).

for Jay

CONTENTS

* Winner of the inaugural Jay Prefontaine Fiction Prize

EDITORS' NOTE

NEW STORIES FROM THE MIDWEST 2016 showcases twenty-five stories set in the Midwest by midwestern and non-midwestern authors. The goals of *New Stories from the Midwest* are to celebrate an American region that is often ignored in discussions about distinctive regional literature and to demonstrate how the quality of fiction from and about the Midwest (Illinois, Indiana, Iowa, Kansas, Michigan, Minnesota, Missouri, Nebraska, North Dakota, Ohio, South Dakota, and Wisconsin) rivals that of any other region. To collect the stories, editors solicited via ads, flyers, letters, and e-mails for nominations from more than 300 magazines, literary journals, and small presses. We received more than 400 stories from more than 175 publications and editors. *New Stories from the Midwest 2016* contains stories published in 2012, 2013, and 2014 and by pure numbers was the most competitive volume to date. Readers narrowed nominations to sixty finalists, which were passed on to the guest editor, Lee Martin, who chose the twenty-five stories for inclusion. Thirty finalists stories are listed in the back of the book.

New Stories from the Midwest 2016 also includes the inaugural $100 Jay Prefontaine Fiction Prize, which is given to the best story in the volume as judged by an outside editor. The prize was named after writer Jay Prefontaine, who co-edited the first volume of *New Stories from the Midwest*. After reading all stories anonymously, this volume's judge, Randolph Thomas, whose short story collection *Dispensations* won the Many Voices Award from New Rivers Press, selected "The Lost Caves of St. Louis" by Anne Valente. Randolph Thomas said about the story, "Although there were many wonderful stories here (and amazingly varied in style, subject, and technique),

'The Caves of St. Louis' immediately blew me away. The voice—lyrical, scary, surprising—grabbed me and wouldn't let go. I loved reading the story, even though it was tragic, and I was sorry when it was over. It was beautifully, masterfully rendered."

— **Jason Lee Brown and Shanie Latham**
Series Editors

INTRODUCTION

I SPENT MY TEENAGE YEARS in the small town of Sumner, Illinois, a downstate town of around a thousand people. Before that, except for the six years my family spent in Oak Forest, a southern suburb of Chicago, where my mother taught third grade, I lived on a farm ten miles southwest of Sumner in Lukin Township. Out there in the country, we could get two television stations—WTVW in Evansville and WTHI in Terre Haute. Sometimes late at night, we could draw in snowy pictures from stations in Harrisburg, Champaign, Decatur, St. Louis, and Indianapolis. It was big news when Terre Haute added a second station, WTWO.

Our diversions were few. I was surrounded by people who worked hard: farmers and men who worked in the oil fields or at the refinery, or men and women who worked at the shoe factory, the garment factory, the poultry house. I grew up in a land of die cutters and welders and house painters and truck drivers and oil field roughnecks. This is all to say, I grew up in a time and a place where entertainment options were limited. We might catch a movie at the Arcadia Theatre in Olney, or the Avalon in Lawrenceville, or the Idaho in Sumner. We might go to a high school basketball game or to the championship wrestling matches at the National Guard Armory in Lawrenceville. And there were ham and bean suppers and fall festivals and county fairs, where folks could watch the demolition derby or the tractor pull or the harness races. At all of these gatherings and events, we did what we did best. We told stories.

My father or someone else would start in. "Did I ever tell you about . . . ?" There in the pool hall or the barber shop or the grain elevator or the gas station or the welding shop—there in the armory or the high school gym or in the grandstand at the fairgrounds or at the theatre before the show began—people would entertain themselves by telling stories. There were stories about love gone wrong, mistaken identity, questionable sanity, revenge, hunters and the hunted, legends of the supernatural and the haunted. There were stories that took place in the farm fields and the small towns and the steel mills of Gary and Hammond, where my father and uncle and other men had gone to work during the Great Depression. There were stories of the naive and the uninitiated paying their first visits to St. Louis, Indy, Chicago, Detroit. I sat in hayfields, on front porches, in people's kitchens, on car hoods, on upturned buckets and pop cases, on bleachers and church pews, and I listened to stories. Stories from the farms and the cities. Stories of what William Faulkner called "the human heart in conflict with itself."

Some misinformed folks will try to tell you nothing's going on out here in the Midwest, but Lord-a-mighty, just listen to the stories the writers in this anthology have come to tell—human stories about the urgent heart, which Faulkner said, ". . . alone can make good writing because only that is worth writing about, worth the agony and the sweat." Some of the writers represented here are native sons and daughters, and some are transplants who have taken root. Some of their stories come from Midwestern landscapes while some are set in other locales. All of these writers have some sort of connection to the Midwest, and all of them wrote stories that wouldn't let me go.

Isn't that what we're all looking for when we hear or read a good story? Aren't we wanting to inhabit it to the point that it becomes a part of us forever? From the Black Hills of South Dakota to the small Midwestern towns of Illinois and Missouri. From Ohio and Michigan to St. Louis and Kansas City. From Chicago to Minneapolis. From Nebraska to Wisconsin and Iowa. And those who migrate to California, Florida, Maine—or farther still, to Tuscany and Guatemala. All of these stories are memorable for what they have to show us about the come-and-go between people that presses on their hearts and on our own.

Characters journey through grief and the changes it brings in Lori Ostlund's "The Gap Year," Noley Reid's "A Purposeful

Violence," Charles Baxter's "Forebearance," and Anne Valente's "The Lost Caves of St. Louis."

Young people run up against the harsh realities of the adult world in Christine Sneed's "In the Bag," Baird Harper's "Patient History," Claire Burgess's "Upper Middle Class Houses," and John McNally's "The Magician."

The challenges and delights of time and space figure prominently in Josh Weil's "Long Bright Line" and Nick Dybek's "Three Summers."

Social issues speak to us in Joyce Carol Oates's "A Book of Martyrs" and Peter Ho Davies's "Chance."

Broken hearts and tattered lives seek rest in Stephanie Dickson's "JadeDragon_77," Theodore Wheeler's "On a Train from the Place Called Valentine," Devin Murphy's "Levi's Recession," Monica Fawn's, "Out of the Mouths of Babes," Emily Mitchell's "Three Marriages," Rebecca Makkai's "Dead Turtle," Stuart Dybek's "Tosca," and Thomas M. Atkinson's "Grimace in the Burnt Black Hills."

Families face obligations and compromises in Albert Goldbarth's "Two Brothers" and Catherine Browder's "Departures."

Young people try to imagine their futures in Jack Driscoll's "All the Time in the World," Abby Geni's "Dharma at the Gate," and Laura van den Berg's "Lessons."

At the end of Jack Driscoll's "All the Time in the World," the narrator says, "We are beautiful is what I think, travelers momentarily stranded inside the closed-off borderlands beyond which lie our future lives." All of the stories in this collection are in some way about characters longing to be whole even when that possibility—sometimes due to what life gives them and sometimes as a result of what they make for themselves—seems precarious indeed. They are all beautiful is what I think. I hope they live with you the way they have with me. All these stories from the Heartland, and from the heart.

— **Lee Martin**
Guest Editor

GRIMACE IN THE
BURNT BLACK HILLS

Thomas M. Atkinson

AFTER SIX STATES, 1,300 miles and almost 24 hours, the iron tang of blood and bleach still hadn't blown out of my truck. And that's saying something because since the fire I can't hardly smell dog shit if I step in it. About 350 miles back, when I crossed into South Dakota from Minnesota, I thought maybe I wasn't really smelling it, that it was just stuck in my head, caught behind the knife-slit nostrils in the nub that used to be my nose, like sometimes when you try to get to sleep and you think you hear music real low, so low you can't really make it out. I should have been halfway through Wyoming but I'd lost a lot of time stopping to put water in my leaking radiator. I pulled off I-90 into Rapid City as the sun was going down and ended up at a Family Thrift grocery store across some railroad tracks.

I parked at the back of the almost empty lot, a couple of rows from an old, shit-green International Harvester Travelall from back in the early '70s. There was an Indian guy in braids and a wifebeater sitting in the open passenger door and three or four kids bouncing around in the back seat. I could see him trying to check me out, but I put in some dark tint film on the windows a couple of years back and it was the best nine dollars I ever spent once I figured to work out the bubbles with the little squeegee before the water dried up. It's darker than what's legal back home, and one time a deputy stopped me on it. I'd seen him around, and he had a flaming baseball inked high on his arm, peeking out from under the short sleeve of his uniform, just like all the old high school ballplayers. After he got a good look at me, he put away his ticket book. He didn't even give me a warning, just said it was darker than what was legal.

Before heading into the store, I used the rearview mirror to draw on some eyebrows with the eyeliner pencil I shoplifted back in Ohio. I didn't *need* to shoplift it because I had a good job at Discount Tire working with Chief until not even two days ago, but it's hard enough looking like me without having to buy eyeliner from Mae, the big lesbian behind the counter at Dollar General, especially when your crazy mom is wandering the aisles yelling your name, and the way she calls "Paul" sounds just like a black crow cawing up in a dead tree. Mae's one of those lesbians that's big-boned and built like a man and you can't help wondering if she was supposed to be a man all along until her mom maybe took a fright when she was pregnant. She and Gwen have something going on, and while that probably means something to Mae, it doesn't mean shit to Gwen. Gwen will fuck just about anything whether it has a dick or not since she started smoking the meth. Hell, she might even fuck me if I caught her on her third bump and the lights weren't on, but I wouldn't because she's married to Chief and I've worked with him for almost four years. Until just yesterday, when I backed off a bottle jack when he was setting a jack-stand under a backhoe. He's up late every night chasing after Gwen, so he's always pissed off or hungover or both. And it all got worse when he had to send their little girl Amber up to live with his sister in Akron. He's not a real Indian like the one in the Travelall, I just named him that because he's got that thick black hair like lots of the Scots-Irish hilltrash that have been knocking around Ohio, Kentucky, and West Virginia where the Big Sandy meets the river for a couple three hundred years. Which I guess probably means chances are better than not that he *does* have a little Indian in him. That, and he had a shingle hatchet under the seat of his truck from when he used to be a roofer and whenever somebody pissed him off, he'd get it out and chop it in the air like a tomahawk. So I named him Chief, like how our boss Billy named me Grimace after that thing in the old

McDonald's commercials. I don't have enough left in the way of ears or a nose to hold up a pair of sunglasses, and the skin on my face is an angry purplish pink. Or maybe he named me Grimace because the scar tissue pulls my lips back so tight I can't keep them closed over my teeth unless I work at it, so I look like one of those screaming death's head tattoos. I don't guess it matters either way.

I'd said, "Ready?" and I thought he said, "Go." But when I let off the pressure, he screamed like I hadn't heard anywhere except inside my own skull, not since that big cook pot I was stirring blew up and covered my head in liquid fire. Maybe he said, "No." By the time I got that bottle jack pumped back up under the axle, there wasn't much left of that hand but stringy mash and some stuff you could still say was fingers.

He'd glared at me while he sucked air, and then he held the mess up in front of my face and said, "Well, it ain't going to tie *itself* off, motherfucker." I tied off his arm with my bootlace so he didn't bleed out and got him into my pickup. On the way to the emergency room at County, he cussed a lot at first, not at me, but just because he was in some serious pain, then he got quiet.

By the time we got to the entrance, his blood was dripping steady as a clock on my floorboards. He looked at that mess of hand and laughed, but not like he thought it was funny. He finally said, "Damn if you ever die before it's too late." Then he sighed and said, "But I guess you know that. Better than most anyone." Then he got out and went through the automatic doors, looking for all the world like he was holding a wet red shop rag. Between OSHA and workman's comp, Billy'd have to shitcan me either way. And while I counted Chief as a friend, I'm not sure that covered cutting somebody's hand off. He might come out in a day or two like nothing happened. Then again, he might come out and shove that stump up my ass. Hell if I wanted to stick around and find out.

I drove straight home, splashed some bleach and water around the passenger-side floorboards, got all my pills, my special soap and stuff, my cash stash, threw all my camping crap in the bed and latched the T-handle on the truck cap. It's not really a camper, just an old corrugated-aluminum cap as tall as the cab of the pickup, covering the bed. Not one of those nice fiberglass ones with a ladder rack and matching paint, but it has little sliding windows on either side, and I was glad I'd been too lazy to take it off for the summer. I told my mom I was going up to Hocking Hills for a long weekend of camping, but she was hypnotized by a woman selling loose gemstones on the Home Shopping Channel and just waved a goodbye. I didn't call Billy, and I damn sure didn't call Karl, my probation officer.

The eyebrows I drew made me look surprised. I still didn't have the hang of drawing on my own eyebrows, because my mom always does it for me every morning before work. At least she did. They were her idea. Somehow she got it in her head that the problem wasn't that my face was melted off, but that I didn't have eyebrows. She thought eyebrows would make me look more normal, and it seemed like a small thing to let her try. I'm not saying they don't look totally fake, because they do, but even fake, drawn-on eyebrows make you look more human than having none at all. And every morning when I got in to work, Chief would let me know how they turned out. Like he'd say, "You look angry," or "You look worried," or "You look sad." And I don't know how, but he was usually right, which meant my crazy mom must've known something when she drew them on, even though it wasn't like she asked me how I was feeling on any particular day. But now I looked surprised, and I didn't think I was.

I got my Flair Hair off the passenger-seat headrest. It was a joke present that Billy and Chief got me for my last birthday, a camouflage visor with spiky brown polyester hair sewn around the band, like something you'd buy your bald uncle for a laugh at Christmas. And Billy and Chief had a laugh when I put it on and wore it around the garage all day. But the thing was, the more I wore it, the more I didn't think it looked like fake polyester hair, and even if it did, fake hair was better than no hair, and if I adjusted it big and pulled it down low, it covered up a lot of territory. And you can even throw it right in the washing machine as long as you remember to get it out and hang it up to dry and don't throw it in the dryer on high heat like my mom did with the first one.

So looking surprised, with my country-ass camo visor and a full head of fake brown hair, I climbed out of my Ford. It was cool outside for early June, but I guess South Dakota isn't southern Ohio. The Indian gave me a head nod. He had a long nose and a strong chin, and he was probably my age but he seemed older. I nodded back without tipping my face toward the parking lot lights and headed to the store, my left boot flopping loose with every step. I wanted some tuna-fish pouches and white bread, some cheap, sweet cereal to eat dry, and some little cans of prune juice I didn't have to keep cold. I have to say, there's days those big Vicodin ES tabs are the only thing between me and kissing a train, but they plug you up something terrible. I don't take them like a pro football player or anything, but I wouldn't be here without them.

The store was blindingly bright, like all of them, and even though it was damn near empty, there were more Indians than I'd ever seen in one place in my life. Most of them were working there, running the registers and stocking produce, but there were a couple shopping too. I've gotten really good at avoiding folks, and not just by steering clear of places with lots of people, like the county fair I'd gone to for twenty-three years straight—ever since I was born—but by keeping the most distance between them and me. What that means in a grocery is taking the household-cleaning-products aisle straight to the back of the store. Or if someone's in that one, the greeting-card aisle, because those two are the least likely to have anyone in them. You might think the greeting-card aisle would be better because people are usually busy looking at the cards, which is true, but they're always in the mood to be extra polite, I guess because they're spending a few seconds of their day doing something nice for someone. They look up from the card they're reading to smile and say, "Pardon me!" and that's when I scare the hell out of them without even meaning to. And there's no card for that.

I was still hiking past all the laundry detergent when I thought I smelled cinnamon rolls fresh from the oven. I love cinnamon, and

I'm not sure why, because I didn't used to care much about it one way or the other. But since the accident, I love it about any way. I'll even stir it into a glass of cold milk with a little bit of sugar. Chief had a theory that since I can't smell too good, I can't taste too good either, and cinnamon is strong enough to get through. He might be right because I used to couldn't stand Vernor's ginger ale, and now I miss it already. I made my way to the bakery case at the end of the aisle. There was a pretty Indian girl behind the bakery case with dark eyes and a flat, oval face. The name tag on her white apron said "Betty," but Betty seemed like an old name for her. Her long black hair was tied back with a hairnet on top, and she was sliding a tray of iced cinnamon rolls the size of dinner plates into the glass case. There was another Indian girl in the back, working at a long stainless table, snapping plastic lids on disposable aluminum pans of something.

The key is to keep your head down but talk loud so they don't have to ask what you said. And that's what I did, "Can I get me one of those cinnamon rolls?"

And she said, "Just one?"

I couldn't tell if she was joking, but before I could answer, I heard a bunch of shoes squeaking on the waxed floor behind me, and she said, soft and sweet, "There's my babies." I looked up enough to see her looking past me with a small smile. Then she said, "Bert's on tonight. Bert don't like you hanging out in here."

Behind me, a man said, "Bert likes me."

And she said, "Not you hanging around. With the kids."

The man said, "His truck broke. Steam's just pouring right out."

She leaned down enough to look under my visor and said, "Mister? My old man says your truck's broke." Then she gave me a small smile too, and her black eyes weren't scared at all. The other girl was watching from the back with her hand over her mouth.

I looked over my shoulder, and it was the Indian from the parking lot and three little kids. It was two boys with long black hair who looked just like the dad and a girl with her mom's flat face, but with finer features. They wore jeans with the knees worn out and T-shirts with Saturday-morning-cartoon characters from before they were born. He said, "Your radiator probably blew." Then he shrugged his shoulders and said, "Maybe just a hose."

The younger boy was maybe five or six, and he looked at me and said, "You smell like medicine, Medicine Man." He wasn't being mean, just matter-of-fact.

But his mother, Betty behind the counter, was embarrassed enough to say, "Shhh."

I said, "No, it's OK. I do." I'm usually not so understanding. The last time somebody said that was this red-haired girl up in Chillicothe who let me fuck her for forty bucks. But only if I was behind her and she cried when I hitched up my jeans. She said I smelled like medicine, and I said she smelled like old cum and dirty ass and that was the end of that. And I'm not even sure she meant anything. Maybe it was all that crying.

But this kid didn't mean anything, just speaking the truth. I looked down at him and made a gesture I seem to make a lot, even when I'm alone, and I don't remember exactly when it started. I put an open palm up in front of my molten face and make a slow circle, which has come to mean, in my mind, *all of it.* "It's the soap. Special soap I have to use. It smells like medicine."

And like we were talking our own sign language, he nodded and made another gesture, like he was splashing water on his face in slow motion, "You sound like smoke."

I'd never thought of it that way, but I guess I did, kind of scratchy and low and thin from the scorching all the way down into my lungs. If smoke sounded like anything, I guess I was it.

His dad said, "Come on, I got a big flashlight."

I followed them down the greeting card aisle with my left boot flopping cadence. The boys were holding each of his hands and the little girl had two fingers hooked through a belt loop on his jeans.

His name was Edgar, and we were squatting in front of my truck. It was dark out now, but his flashlight was like staring into the sun.

The water we'd just poured in the radiator was running out like an open faucet.

He said, "If it's fixing to blow, that's when it'll do it, right when you shut it off and that fan stops blowing, cooling everything down."

I nodded. "Yep, when that water pump ain't moving shit around."

He tilted the flashlight up at me and said, "That's right. The heat builds up."

I shrugged. "I worked in a garage. Tires mostly."

He said, "No kidding? I got a tire question for you when we get this sorted."

I said, "That flashlight is like staring into the sun."

Edgar waved it side to side across the grill and said, "Two and a half million candle power." He turned it on his old Travelall. The doors were open, and all three kids were sleeping in the back seat like a pile of puppies. They groaned at the light and turned away. He said, "Sometimes the headlights go out if I hit a chuckhole. I just hang this out the window and it's daytime."

I said, "I bet."

And he said, "Sucks in the winter. We get bad winters. You get bad winters in O-hi-o?"

"How do you know I'm from Ohio?"

He laughed and pointed the flashlight at the license plate my forearm was resting on.

I said, "This winter was bad. Cold. Lot of snow. But most years go by and we don't get snow but one or two days."

He pointed the flashlight at the radiator, "That seam along the bottom pan is split. Not all the ways across. It needs resoldering." He rubbed his smooth chin and said, "There's two places that'll repair it, Dakota Radiator—three, four miles west—and Angel Brothers north of town. But I don't know either one'll get to it right off tomorrow, not on a Saturday." He thought about it for a minute and said, "But maybe. We can pull it right now. I got tools and I'm a pretty good tree mechanic. If you got it dropped off tomorrow early, fixed by, maybe, Monday afternoon? I got nothing to do till my old lady and her sister get off. Pass the time."

I said, "I got tools, but that's three days."

"Yep, that's three days. You got somewhere to be?"

I didn't, not really. I'd been thinking of heading to Portland, but I didn't really have a reason to go to Portland or anyone to see there. Karl and leaving the state and probation violation was all running around the back of my head, but truth be told, Karl's fat ass wouldn't even know to be looking for me until I didn't show up to report in three weeks, and I was five states past worrying about that anyway.

I said, "No, I got nowhere to be, but this is my camper. And I need to get some sleep."

Edgar walked around the side of my truck, and I followed him. He shined that flashlight through the little sliding window on the side of the cap. All my crap was in there, looking shabby in that bright, unforgiving light—a sleeping bag and a foam pad, a couple of spit-stained pillows, a black trash bag full of clothes, an empty cooler, a single-burner propane stove and cooking stuff, my dented toolbox, and a little square camp toilet the color of old mustard.

He said, "Nice setup. What's the floor?"

"Strand board. I cut it out with a jig saw to fit around the wheel wells."

He nodded, then looked to the store and back again, "Get your tools. I'm gonna talk to Bert." As he walked away he said, "Make sure no one steals my kids. I like them." Then he laughed and said, "Most of the time."

I had the top hose loose and was lying in the puddle of engine-warmed water with the flashlight and a screwdriver, working on the bottom one, when I heard soft footsteps close by.

I said, "Is that you?"

And a girl said, "No, it's me."

I scooted out far enough to shine the flashlight up at her. It was the girl from the back of the bakery, and before she could get her hand up, I saw she had a bad harelip, and not like the ones you usually see these days that you can hardly tell, but like one from the old days, like a piece of fishing line was pulling her lip up inside one nostril. But with her hand there covering it, I could tell right away it was Edgar's sister-in-law, because she looked just like the pretty girl behind the bakery case, if somebody took the pretty girl behind the bakery case out between the dumpsters and shot her in the mouth.

Her name tag said "Claire," and she shook her face behind her hand and said, "Don't." I put the flashlight back under the truck so she couldn't see me either, and she held up a white paper bag, "You forgot your cinnamon roll."

I laughed and said, "Yeah. I forgot to pay for it too."

She looked at her gym shoes, "It's OK. I get something free for my break." Then she jiggled one shoe and said, "I'm on break."

We sat down on a concrete parking block in the darkness between my truck and the Travelall of sleeping children, and she held on tight to the rolled top of the bag. My T-shirt was wet and I knew I probably smelled like whatever old antifreeze was still in there to leak out even though I couldn't smell it myself.

She pointed and said, "That's my niece and nephews. The oldest one is Chaske but we call him Charlie. He's eight. Then Clayton, you met Clay. He's six. And Winona. With an 'i.' She's four, but she's small for four. I'm Claire."

I said, "So Edgar's your . . . ?"

"Brother-in-law. He's good. He married my older sister, Betty." She tilted her head toward the store and said, "The pretty one."

"Well," I said, "You got the pretty name." And in the dim light of that dark parking lot, I saw her smile down at the bakery bag. Coming from anyone else it might've sounded like a line, but I'm not really in any position to use a line. I tried a couple of times at first, when I was really drunk, but then I'd catch sight of myself in the bar mirror behind all the liquor bottles and know exactly why the women found their ice cubes so damn fascinating.

She said, "Claire Kills Crow Indian."

And I said, "No lie? Claire Kill Crow Indian? That's your name?"

She nodded, "*Kills* Crow Indian."

I said, "Wow. That's the coolest name I have ever heard. How do you rate a badass name like that?"

She giggled behind her hand, "I guess one of your ancestors has to kill a Crow Indian. What's your name?"

And I said, "Paul. But everybody calls me Grimace. Everybody back home. After that thing in the old McDonald's commercials."

She sat quiet for a minute. I thought she was going to ask after my last name, but then she said, "That's not nice."

I shook my head. "I don't care." But I did. I always did.

She said, "Paul, are you hungry?"

I slapped my knees and said, "Am I hungry? Two gas station hot dogs in Iowa was a long way back."

She unrolled the bag and took out that cinnamon roll, and when I reached for it, she held it off to one side, "Your hands are dirty."

I held them up and said, "You can't even see my hands. Leastways whether they're dirty or not."

She said, "You think I don't know what they look like after working on a beater truck? Where you think I been my whole life?"

I thought about that before I said, "I don't know. I don't know where you've been my whole life." But I wished I did.

Then she pulled off a piece of that cinnamon roll and fed it to me. And I let her. I don't know why. I don't eat in front of anybody except my mom, on account of how hard it is to keep my lips closed. It's kind of a mess. And I can't feel if I got food stuck on me or not. But I sat there and chewed, and when I opened my mouth like a baby bird, Claire Kills Crow Indian was there to feed me. I pretended my face wasn't in the deep shade of that camo visor. And in those brief moments of forever, I forgot just who it was sitting on that concrete parking block.

I said, "Don't you want some?"

She said, "No. The diabetes runs in the family."

I didn't know if that meant she had it already, or that she didn't want to get it. But either way, working the bakery seemed like a tough gig.

And, like she read my mind, she said, "I know . . . a bakery." She shrugged. "Work's work."

I said, "You said a mouthful there." And as soon as I did, I wished I hadn't, because I didn't mean anything and I didn't want to make her feel bad about herself.

She sat upright and brushed at her apron, and said, "Here comes Edgar." She put the rest of the cinnamon roll in the bag and rolled the top down tight and handed it to me. "I got to get back anyway."

Edgar was there before I could think of anything to say, and he said, "Betty says time's up." Then he made a sound like a cracking whip and laughed.

As Claire walked off, she pointed to the Travelall full of kids and said, "For sure *somebody's* whipped."

Edgar laughed, and when she was out of earshot, he said, "That's my sister-in-law Claire, and she's got a mouth on her. Not as bad as her sister, but they both do. You wouldn't think so at first, 'cause she's so quiet. But she'll rip you a new one right quick if you cross her."

I said, "Claire Kills Crow Indian."

And Edgar said, "Yep, sometimes I think that Crow might've killed himself just to get some peace." Then he held both hands up in surrender, "But I never said that. Bert says you can leave your truck here until Monday. You can even sleep in it as long as you're gone while the store's open."

I thought about that and said, "Where am I going with no radiator?"

And Edgar said, "No, the truck can stay here. But *you* have to be gone during business hours. He don't like folks just hanging around. He doesn't even like me and the kids waiting for Betty and Claire, but I told him, I can't afford to be driving back and forth."

Bert probably didn't want me scaring away the paying customers, and I understood that. "What about the cops?"

Edgar said, "Well, I wouldn't build a campfire, but they won't bother you unless Bert tells them to."

That was a lot of daylight hours to be out walking around a strange city. Tomorrow was Saturday so maybe I could probably find an out-of-the-way table at a library. I didn't know about Sunday. I said, "Thanks. There a public library around?"

He said, "You'd better ask somebody that can read."

I couldn't tell if he was joking or not, then he smiled and said, "Claire'll know. She's always got a book in front of her face."

Between the two of us, it didn't take but twenty minutes to pull that radiator, and we put all of the bolts and clamps in a plastic cup from a gas station in Illinois.

Edgar pointed to the radiator I was holding and said, "Just slide it under the truck, and we'll run it over to Dakota in the morning."

I said, "You don't have to do that. I can walk it over there."

He shook his head, "No. We got to come by this way in the morning anyway. We're all going to see Crazy Horse."

I didn't know what he meant but I was too tired to ask. We took turns pouring water from my milk jug over each other's hands to wash off the worst of the grime.

I said, "Shit. We forgot your tire."

He waved me off and said, "It's been bleeding out for months. It'll wait till tomorrow. Get to rest."

After I climbed in over the tailgate and latched the cap window behind me, I opened the two sliders on the sides to get the cool breeze going through. I dry-swallowed a Vicodin because I'd poured out the warm pop for the parts cup and I wasn't betting the water left in the milk jug was still potable. I'd meant to get some pop and ice for the cooler but I forgot every time I stopped. With everything else pushed to one side, I rolled out the foam and my sleeping bag. The ointment I'm supposed to put on when I sleep was somewhere at the bottom of that trash bag of clothes, and finding it was more work than I had left in me. I stripped to my boxers and slid into the soft flannel lining of my sleeping bag. I eased down onto those pillows and set the bakery bag on my chest because I thought to have another bite or two, but I ended up just holding onto that rolled-up paper, falling asleep to the faint sweetness and sweat of Claire Kills Crow Indian caught in my head, not knowing if that's how she smelled or just how I wanted her to.

I dreamt the dream I dream a lot. Nothing really happens in it, and it changes from one night to the next, but it still bothers the hell out of me because it's the old me. I don't see myself, in a mirror or anything, but I just know it's me, the me from before the fire, the way you know stuff in dreams. I'm not even sure it's a dream. It might be shards of memories sharp as broken glass. Sometimes I'm at a dump Mexican restaurant back home I used to go to with my ex-girlfriend, and I'm eating cheese enchiladas and we're laughing about old joke that only meant something to the two of us. But it only meant something to us before the accident, before she saw me and moved down to Charlotte.

I woke up later, the white bag still clutched in my hands. Outside was dark and quiet, so quiet I could hear water running cold in a creek close by. But I wasn't sure if I was awake or just awake in a dream. Then I heard Claire whisper, "Good night, Paul." And a car door creaked shut. Edgar's old Travelall coughed to life and faded away down the road, towing me along into the cool mist of narcotic sleep.

The next morning I woke to the sound of scraping metal under the truck, and before I could wrestle my way out of my sleeping bag, Edgar peered in through the slider and tapped on the truck cap. It was cold enough to see his breath, but he only had on a canvas vest with burnt orange fleece on the inside and no shirt.

He said, "You awake in there? I'm gonna run this radiator over to Dakota. You get dressed and take care of your business. We'll be back in ten minutes to pick you up."

I was struggling with my jeans. "Hold on. I'll come with you." But his shadow was already gone. I pressed my face to the screen and said, "Where we going?" I saw Claire in the backseat squinting at me, with Winona dead asleep on her lap. Betty was up front filing her nails.

Edgar turned, holding my radiator up in front of him like a shield, and said, "Volksmarch. We're going to see Crazy Horse."

I didn't know what any of that meant, so I said, "That looks like a shield."

He looked down at the slate-gray radiator, "No, it's my breastplate."

He did a shuffling Indian dance and a sing-songy chant, and Betty stopped filing her nails long enough to lean out the window and yell, "Stop that, fool. You'll get us fired."

Claire cupped her hand over Winona's ear so as not to wake her and said, "They're usually prettier, with colored beads and bone hairpipe." While Edgar shoved the radiator in through the open tailgate window of the Travelall, Claire said, "Wear good socks and shoes. We're hiking."

Before he climbed in the driver's seat, Edgar said, "And we got food. Lots and lots of food. We got fry bread out the ass."

The boys laughed, and Betty said, "Edgar!"

And Claire said softly, "With butter and honey."

After they drove away, I thought about begging off, because I didn't know how I felt about Claire Kills Crow Indian seeing me up close in the harsh light of day. But I used the camp toilet and then gave myself a plain-water sponge bath crouched under the truck cap. I put on too much deodorant, clean clothes, and some thick socks, then slipped around into the cab to draw on my eyebrows and fix my Flair Hair. I was trying to find something to use for a lace on my left boot when I heard the Travelall pull in next to me.

When I climbed out, Edgar said, "Monday. Morning maybe. Early afternoon. C'mon." Then he turned and said, "You boys climb in the back-back."

Charlie and Clay scrambled over the back seat into the storage area behind it. Betty looked back at them over her shoulder and said, "Stay out of the food. And leave that rifle alone, unless you want to end up like Uncle Larry."

Claire opened the back door and, with little Winona still asleep on her lap, scooted across that wide bench seat. I thought she'd scoot all the way to the other side, but she didn't. She stopped right in the middle, with one gym shoe on either side of the transmission hump. She had on jeans and a white button-up blouse with no sleeves. With my head tucked down under my visor, I looked at the smooth skin of her upper arm. It looked like a lump of amber I had back home in a shoebox from when I was a kid. Or maybe it looked like melting butter and warm honey.

We drove south out of town and followed Route 16 southwest through the hills. Everything looked different out here, even the green and the sky. My part of Ohio is farmland butting into the foothills of the Appalachians, and when you get into the mountains proper, like over in West Virginia, they're nothing but up and down, old as time and bundled tight as cedar shingles wreathed in wood smoke. Out here everything was bigger and spread out, a lot of pine trees, and the grasslands were more of a sage green. We passed a sign for the Cosmos Mystery Area, and Charlie and Clay started bouncing in the back and begging to stop.

Edgar yelled, "We're going to Crazy Horse."

Winona woke up on Claire's lap. She stared at me for so long I finally looked out the window. She said, "Is that a mask?"

Charlie hooted from the back and yelled, "Winnie, you are such a retard. He's *burnt up.*"

I glanced at Winona and saw she was tearing up. I said, "It's kind of a mask. Just scar tissue."

Claire squeezed her tight and said, "Like Auntie's lip."

Winona hid her face in Claire's neck, and Claire cooed gentle nonsense to her, like you'd calm a horse. When that didn't work, she said, "Charlie, pass me that blue Tupperware."

Charlie handed it over the seat and said, "Can we have one?"

Betty said, "You boys had enough already. Both of you. You wait for lunch. Claire brought those for her friend."

When she peeled the cap back, I thought I almost smelled cooking oil, melted butter, and honey. And a little cinnamon. She tore off a little piece for Winona and passed me the bowl. "Try one."

I did. It was a lot like a funnel cake you'd get at the fair back home, but not so sweet. Winona watched me while she nibbled on hers.

Clay had his chin resting on the back of the bench seat. He said, "You like it?"

And I said, "Fried dough and sweet stuff, what's not to like?"

Clay closed one eye and said, "You like it with the cinnamon? She doesn't usually make 'em with cinnamon."

I pretended to think about it while Winona watched me. And then I said, "Yeah, I like it with cinnamon."

Clay nodded, "Me too."

Claire smiled and jiggled Winona on her lap.

Winona said, "I like your hair."

Edgar pulled in to a filling station and brought the Travelall to a rocking stop in front of the air compressor. I could hear Betty scrounging change in a quilted purse, and Charlie leaned over the seat and whispered, "Now's when he says, 'Twenty-five cents for air? Air ought to be free!'"

And he did.

We squatted on our heels looking at the tire. The boys stood behind us, still as small shadows.

Edgar said, "I already checked the valve stem and around the base."

I rubbed my hands around the tread, gentle as the nurse at the Burns Unit that changed my dressings.

Edgar said, "And I can't find a nail or nothing. I pulled it off and looked."

I looked at that rusted steel wheel and said, "Hmmm." Then I stood up and rooted through a trash can for an old coffee cup. I handed it to Charlie and said, "Go to the restroom and put a finger of hand soap in here and fill it up with hot water."

Charlie took off at a run and waddled back with the cup spilling over. He handed it to me and hunkered down, watching me stir the thick pink syrup, more soap than water. I figured that a "finger" of something must mean something different in South Dakota than it does in Ohio. I knelt down and said, "Now watch." I poured it slowly against the top of the wheel, where the steel meets the rubber, so it ran around both sides. Edgar and me and our shadows watched the tire, and after a long moment three different spots starting foaming with fine bubbles thick as shave cream.

Charlie said, "Cool!"

And I said, "Bead leak."

Edgar shook his head and said, "Damn. What'll that cost me?"

I shrugged and said, "Elbow grease and a couple of bucks. We'll peel off that tire, brush off all the rust, and paint the rim with this black shit. Comes in a little can with a brush in the cap."

Edgar said, "Good deal."

Clay put his open palms gently on my fake hair and whispered, "Medicine Man."

We passed some other roadside attractions gone to seed, the usual go-carts and fudge stands, and when I saw the signs for Mt. Rushmore, I said, "Mt. Rushmore? Like the big president heads?"

Edgar turned back over the seat and said, "Mt. Rushmore ain't shit." I heard Betty slap his leg, but he said, "Ain't *shit*. You know how big Crazy Horse is? All four of those old, dead white guys would fit in Crazy Horse's face with room to spare."

Charlie pounded on the back of the seat and yelled, "And Indians get in free!"

We did all get in free because the Travelall was full of Indians, and I guess they couldn't tell about me, or at least not enough to ask. We threaded our way through a gravel lot snowed over with people. Some were in their street clothes, like us, but most had on expensive hiking gear and weather-proof jackets and floppy hats, walking sticks that looked like ski poles and spun-aluminum water bottles. There were runners in shorts and women in stretch pants and seniors with their noses white with sunscreen. There were busloads of Japanese tour groups and two wannabe bikers on new Harleys, with their fat-assed, bottle-blonde wives on the back, none of them dirty or tattooed enough to be real bikers. Besides us, I didn't see many Indians.

Claire pointed to the Crazy Horse statue in the distance. She said, "I know it doesn't look like much, but he's still a couple of miles away."

Edgar said, "Boys, grab those two bags." He turned to me. "You're supposed to bring canned goods to donate."

Claire made a face and said, "For the poor Indians."

And Betty said, "We always bring something we like, 'cause chances are better than not some doctor's wife from Box Elder will drop them off at our trailer real soon."

Edgar frowned down at my left boot. "You won't get far like that. It's over six miles, and up the mountain is *tough*." He rummaged around in a cardboard box in the back of the Travelall and came out with a rawhide lace.

Charlie threw his arms up like a football referee after a touchdown and said, "Dad's magic box of junk!"

It was free to get in but three dollars to do the hike up to Crazy Horse, and after Edgar and I talked it out, I paid for everybody since they were nice enough to bring me along and feed me and cart my radiator around. Betty took Winona from Claire, and they disappeared up the trail ahead of us, trying to keep the boys in sight. The path wound through forest that was mostly pine, with a few trees that looked like birch but Claire said were quaking aspens.

She said, "I love that smell."

And I said, "I don't smell anything. But that doesn't mean much 'cause I can't smell shit if I step in it."

She said, "The pines, they're ponderosas. You can tell from the split orange bark. They smell like . . . "

But she didn't tell me what they smelled like. She asked if I couldn't smell on account of the fire. I thought she was asking because she wanted to know what happened. Most people do. It's the first thing they want to know. And the last. But I wanted to tell her, because I thought it was important she know the truth of it. I told her I wasn't saving babies from a burning daycare or old people from a nursing home. I told her I wasn't a soldier in the war or a fireman and I didn't get any medals. I told her the plain truth, that my Uncle Arnett was cooking meth in my mom's garage and he didn't know what he was doing. When he asked me to stir a pot while he ran to the feed store, I did, because I liked him, because when I was a kid he'd sneak me sips of some cheap Cincinnati beer as bright as pop and stick his false teeth out to make me laugh even though he wasn't near old enough to have false teeth. And whatever he'd poured in that pot right before he left wasn't quite the right thing. I guess it was close, only the one blows up and the other doesn't. The judge had a hard time looking at me, and he said, "Fate has dispensed some cruel justice. I do believe your punishment exceeds your crime." He gave me six years' probation, and the prosecutor didn't even argue.

Claire thought about all that, then she said, "What happened to your uncle?"

"He must've seen the fire trucks when he got back from the feed store, 'cause they never caught up with him. He burnt down our house, and we had to rent a single-wide. My mom brought me a 'Get Well' balloon to the Burns Unit she said was from him, but I don't think it was."

We walked along in silence on the quiet carpet of pine needles. Then she said, "I'm sorry."

I shrugged. "It doesn't matter."

But she knew the lie of it the same as me, because what she said was, "The boys called me War Hatchet Mouth. In school. Claire War Hatchet Mouth."

We'd caught up to the bikers, both in shiny black vests, talking drunk loud and tugging at their crotches while their wives sat on a log smoking cigarettes.

I heard one of the bikers say, "Shit. Burnt up like that, you can't tell they're not white."

I'd heard worse than that on my best day back home and didn't see any point in starting something. But then the other one, the one with the American flag bandana covering up his bald head, said, "Jesus, and look at the mouth on her." I turned and closed the distance fast, pulling off my Flair Hair, and when I got close enough for him to smell my breath, I said, "Tomorrow, I won't remember a goddamn thing about you. But I can guaran-fucking-tee, you won't forget me."

And I don't know how, but Edgar was there, and he was there with the biggest knife I ever saw. The blade wasn't wide or silver, but blue-black and long and thin, like it'd been honed on a whetstone for a hundred years' worth of gutting and skinning. He wasn't pointing it at anybody, or saying anything, but they all backed off down the path. I yelled, "Sweet dreams."

Edgar shook his head and said, "Come August, we'll be snowed over in those wannabe Sturgis assholes." He turned me up the path toward Claire while I snugged my Flair Hair back down. He tucked the knife away somewhere back down inside that vest and said, "Don't you carry knives in O-hi-o?"

I was going to tell him we carry folding knives, like a Buck, and guns, like the .38 I always kept in the dash box until Karl said I couldn't because it violated the terms of my probation. But I didn't tell him any of that. I just shook my head.

Claire told me not to turn around and look yet. She walked me through the crowd along the length of Crazy Horse's arm, all the way to the very end, to the tip of his pointing finger still hidden down there in the rock, waiting to come out.

Then she turned me around, and I rested against the chain-link fence, still puffing hard from the hike up. He was big, big as a mountain, strong and serious, staring off into the distance. And the hundreds of hikers, dressed in blues and reds and yellows, flowed from his neck like a beaded breastplate.

I said, "How big is he?"

And she said, "Just his face is almost ninety feet tall. When it's all done, him and his horse, it'll be over 550 feet high and almost 650 feet long."

I stared at the C shapes etched into his eyes and said, "What's he looking at?"

"The Black Hills. He said, 'My lands are where my dead lie buried.' Our land."

I squinted at the sun. "In what direction?"

She checked her shadow and said, "Southeast."

I shook my head. "Southeast? That's back home to Ohio."

She reached out her hand slowly, like I might be a strange dog, until her fingertips rested on my visor. She said, "Maybe. Or maybe that's just where you came from." Then she lifted off my Flair Hair and dropped it over the railing. We both watched it spiral away down the drill-scarred cliff.

She licked the pad of her thumb and started wiping away one of my eyebrows. "You know, nobody knows what Crazy Horse looked like. He never let anybody photograph him."

I said, "Me neither, 'cept for my mug shot and my driver's license." Then I looked at that giant rock face again and said, "So that's not even him?"

She rubbed away at my brow and said, "That's him on the inside."

She rooted in her bag for an old baby food jar filled with sage green jelly. She worked a dab into her palms and pressed them to my cheeks.

I said, "Is that sunscreen? I'm supposed to wear sunscreen, but I forgot."

"Yeah, it's like sunscreen." She sniffed the jar. "Indian sunscreen."

She painted more on my face, gently as brushing away an eyelash.

I tried to breathe deep. "Does it smell good?"

She smiled and nodded.

I took out my wallet and said, "I got a picture. From before."

She put her hand on that worn fold of leather in my palm. She said, "I never want to see it. Not ever." She wet her thumb again and worked at my other eyebrow. "That's not you."

When she was finished, she took me by the sleeve, and we headed back down the gentle slope of Crazy Horse's arm, the crowd parting before us like magic.

She ignored the staring people and said, "You're a strong man. You were strong to survive. You have to be strong to live."

I'd never thought of it that way before.

On the hike back through the pine forests, I said, "It smells like butterscotch!"

Claire smiled. "Yes, like warm butterscotch cookies fresh from the oven. That's the ponderosas." And when she smiled, I only saw her smile. And that twisted lip didn't mean a thing.

Back at the Travelall, we all drank cans of store-brand grape pop, and Claire and Betty fixed us Indian tacos, which were pretty much like regular tacos except with fry bread and hot beans from a thermos instead of tortillas and ground beef, with shredded lettuce and cheese and green chili sauce. I folded it like they did and turned away to take a bite.

When I turned back, Charlie shook his head in disgust and said, "You eat like my sister."

On the way back to Rapid City, with all three kids exhausted in the back-back and Claire next to me on the bench seat, I fell asleep against the window. I dreamt that dream again, but this time it was different. I was at the dump Mexican restaurant back home, but everyone was there. Chief was there, with Gwen and Amber and two hands. And Mae was there, and she was with Gwen too, but it was a different Gwen, thin and wasted, eyes as dark and wild as a raccoon with distemper. That Deputy was there too, the one with the flaming baseball inked high on his arm that stopped me about the window tint, but it wasn't a baseball, it was my head, screaming in the silence, and he's holding hands with the redhead from Chillicothe. I'm sitting with Claire and we're eating Indian tacos, and we're laughing at a joke, an inside joke, about the rare Flair Hair flying squirrel at Crazy Horse.

When I woke up, the dirt and sweat and grease of me had made a mottled print of my cheek on the sun-warmed window. And half-asleep, I studied that small map of an unforgiving land before I noticed that Claire Kills Crow Indian was holding my hand.

She whispered, "Are you awake?" And after I nodded, she said, "Will you do something for me?"

I hung my head and nodded again, "Anything. Just about anything."

She said, "Will you throw it away? The picture? From before?"

I took out my wallet and she turned her face away while I slipped it out from behind my driver's license. I held it, shielded in my palm, to look at it. It was worn at the corners and webbed with fine lines, a high-school-graduation picture of some good-looking kid, smiling, with wild brown hair going in every direction. There was something familiar about the eyes, but not much else. I cracked the window, and before I fed it out into the wind, Claire squeezed my hand. I let go, and the photograph fluttered away, a small thing caught in the slipstream of the old Travelall, carried higher and higher, to soar lost and alone above the burnt Black Hills.

FORBEARANCE

Charles Baxter

WHENEVER AMELIA GAZED at the olive trees in the yard, she could momentarily distract herself from the murderous poetry on the page in front of her.

Esto lavá çaso, metlichose çantolet íbsefelt sed syrt
Int çantolet ya élosete stnyt en, alardóowet arenti myrt.

Getting these lines into English was like trying to paint the sun blue. In several years as a translator, she'd never found another text so unmanageable. The poem was titled "Impossibility," and that's what it was. Each time she looked at the words, she felt as if she were having a stroke; she could feel her face getting numb and sagging on one side. Meanwhile, the ironic ticking of the wall clock marked the unproductive seconds as they shuffled past. The clock loved its job, even though the time it told was wildly inaccurate. The owner of this villa, a charming old Italian woman, had informed Amelia that the clock was senile and delusional like everyone else in the village and must never be adjusted. Adjusting it would hurt its feelings.

"That clock thinks it's on Mars," the old woman told Amelia in a conspiratorial whisper. "It tells you what time it is there. And *you*, an American, want to argue with it?"

The poem in front of Amelia on the desk had been written near the beginning of the nineteenth century, in an obscure Eastern European dialect combining the language of courtly love with warfare, with an additional admixture of *Liebestod*, called *mordmutt* in this dialect. The idioms of love and war should have blended together but didn't. In some not-so-subtle manner, the poet seemed to be threatening his beloved with mayhem if she refused to knuckle under to him. The language of these threats ("*Int cantolet ya célosete*," for example: "I could murder you with longing," or, more accurately, "My longing longs to murder"), inflated with metaphors and similes of baroque complication, was as gorgeous as an operatic aria sung by a charming baritone addressing a woman who was being flung around on stage and who wasn't allowed to open her mouth. *And it was all untranslatable!* You couldn't heat up soggy English verbs and nouns to a boil the way you could in this dialect, which actually had a word for love bites.

Amelia put down her pen and tapped her fingers. The decorative clock, painted green, was amused by her troubles. *There's a second of your life you'll never get back! And there*: there's another one! Too bad you're not on Mars like me. There's lots of time on Mars. We've got nothing but time here! Today is like yesterday! Always was!

With a tiny advance from a publisher and a six-week deadline, she felt like a caged animal hopping on electrified grates for the occasional food pellet. Her professional reputation was at stake: after this volume was published, she would probably be held up to ridicule in the *New York Review of Books* for her translation of this very poem. She could already see the adverb-adjective clusters: "discouragingly inept," "sadly inappropriate," "amusingly tin-eared." One of the few Americans who had any command of this dialect, she belonged to a tight little society full of backbiters. The other poems hadn't been terribly hard to translate, but so far this one had defeated her. *Let me murder you*, the poet demanded, *and we'll descend to the depths together/where darkness enfolds us in—what?—the richest watery silks./Down, down, to the obscurest nethermost regions,/where sea creatures writhe in amorous clutchings* . . .

Awful. The olive trees didn't care what she was doing, so she looked at them gratefully. Downstairs, her twenty-year-old son and his girlfriend were cooing endearments. Chirps. Impossible! Everything was impossible.

This particular afternoon, in the little Tuscan villa she had rented a month ago, Jack, her son, and Gwyneth, the girlfriend, were cooking up sausage lasagna. They cooed at each other after coaxing the pan into the oven. Over the noise of the clock, Amelia listened to their love noises. Here she was, enjoying the voyeurism of the middle-aged parent. After several minutes, she could hear them washing the ingredients for salad, speaking lovely birdsong Italian to each other. Through the years, Jack had spent so much time over here in boarding school that his Italian was better than his mother's. He didn't even have the trace of an American accent that Amelia had. Gwyneth, like Jack, was bilingual (her father was English and had married a local Italian), but she and Jack preferred Italian for their intimacies, as who would not?

The hour: too early for preparing dinner! What did those two scamps think they were up to? Gwyneth, beautiful and bossy in the Italian manner, though she was a blonde, held Amelia's lovesick son tightly in her grip; she gave orders to him followed by gropes and love rewards. They had met a mere three weeks ago. Love happened fast in this region, like a door slammed open. Amelia had seen those two trying to prepare dishes together while holding hands. Very touching, but comical.

She glanced at her watch: actually, the day was almost over, and the day's work was kaput, obliterated. She had struggled all afternoon on those stupidly impossible poetic lines full of masculine posturing, and now she had nothing. She felt word nausea coming on. The fraud police would be arriving at any minute.

The poet she was translating fancied himself a warrior type— aristocratic, arrogant, and proud. In one tiny corner of the world, mentioning his name—Imyar Sorovinct—would open doors and get you a free meal. But elsewhere, here in Italy and in the States, he was mostly unknown, except for the often-anthologized "I Give It All Up," his uncharacteristically detached and Zenlike deathbed poem. In midlife he'd presented himself in verse as a man supremely confident of his weapons, arrogantly imploring his beloved to join him in what he called "The Long Night." The particular line on which she had spent the last two hours contained consonant clusters that sounded like distant nocturnal battlefield explosions.

In real life, however, Sorovinct hadn't been a military man at all but a humble tailor of army uniforms, a maker of costumes, driven to poetic fantasies about the men who inhabited them. He cut and stitched, bent over, ruining his eyesight in the bad light and dreaming of heroism. To no one's surprise then or now, the poet had been unhappily married. Together, he and his wife had had a child who, as they said in those days, "never grew up." Cognitively, the son remained a child for all of his twenty-three years before his death by drowning.

Armored for sorrow, steeling my resolve, I sing/cry/proclaim (to) you our love-glue

In English, the vulgarity was shockingly nonsensical, and it missed the force of the verb in the original and suggested nothing of the poet's menace. "Love-glue"! "*Muttplitz*" in the dialect. What Walt Whitman meant when he used the word "adhesiveness." No real English word existed for it, thank God.

Downstairs, a cork came out of a wine bottle.

They were going to fall into bed and make love any minute now, those two kids. At least someone was having a good time. No point whatever in trying to stop them unless Amelia could appeal to Gwyneth's probably nonexistent Catholic morality. Should she mention the necessity of contraception? They'd just laugh. She came downstairs to see them pouring two glasses of the cheap blood-dark Chianti you could buy for almost nothing in this region. Just as if she weren't standing there, they raised the glasses to each other's lips.

Gwyneth's hard little face, bravely glassy-eyed, turned toward Amelia, and she smiled in the way that young people do when they know they've been dealt a good hand.

"Going out, darlings," Amelia said. "Just for a minute. Have to buy cigarettes. Be back soon."

"Well, don't be long," Gwyneth commanded with her charming Brit-Euro accent, putting the wine glass down on the counter and raising her finger in a comic admonitory fashion. "Food'll get cold. Hurry back." She leaned away from Jack for a moment so that he could admire her gaze upon him and her bella figura.

Jack, handsome in his khakis and soft blue shirt, turned toward his mother.

"Momma," he said, "what's this about cigarettes? You don't *smoke*."

"Well, guess what? It's a perfectly good time to start." She tried to straighten her hair, which probably looked witchy after so much futile desk work. "After a day like this one, I need a new affectation. I need to be *bad*. I need to be bad right now. If they're selling cigarettes, I'm buying them."

"Then you better buy a lighter and an ashtray too," her son reminded her.

She had leased an old Fiat from a man the villagers claimed was a part-time burglar. It was probably a stolen car. After starting the engine, she turned on the radio, hoping to hear Donizetti or Bellini, or at least *somebody*. Instead, they were playing Cher's "If I Could Turn Back Time," a mean-spirited irony considering how the day had gone. The gods laughed easily in the late afternoon, watching human futility fold up for the day. All poetry, good or bad, made the gods laugh. To the gods, poems were sour useless editorials, like bitchy letters to Santa. The Fiat coughed and hesitated as Amelia first passed by a vineyard, then, on the other side of the road, a painterly haystack. One old bespectacled man holding a walking stick ambled along the road, going in the opposite direction. He doffed his cap at her, and she waved at him. A single blue-flecked bird, chirping in Italian, flew overhead. But nature was unforgiving. The sun, lowering toward the west, recited one of the lines that Amelia couldn't translate: *Féyitçate fyr tristo, eertch tye mne muttplitz.*

By the time she reached the village, after negotiating three hairpin turns and avoiding death by collision from an errant truck out of whose way she had swerved in a last-minute effort to save her own life, she could feel the sweat in her palms oozing out onto the steering wheel. No water came from the fountain in the town square: the pump had been broken for weeks, and there was no money to fix it. The air smelled of burnt rope. A brownish liquid flowed in the gutter. She parked her car, turned off the ignition, and waited until the motor coughed and sputtered and dieseled its way into silence. An American couple sitting in the square's sidewalk café gazed at her with tourist interest, as if she were a quaint item of local color. Amelia hurried into the general store, where she was greeted by the owner, Sr. Travatini, a timid man who had a tendency to avoid her gaze; he was probably in love with her, or maybe he was planning on hiring someone to rob her.

"My dear Carlo," she said. "How are you? It's been a terrible day." Italian, with its languorous vowels, was sheer pleasure after a day's struggle with the Eastern European dialect.

"Yes," he said, looking out toward the village square and her car. "Yes, and the sun has passed its way through the sky once again. Things are not translating? Sometimes they do not. Sometimes they stubbornly stay what they are. I am sorry."

"No. Things are not translating. I need some cigarettes," she said.

"Ah, but you do not smoke." Everyone here kept track of everyone else's habits, and the villagers all knew her by now.

"After such a day as I have had, I think it would be a good time to learn."

He shrugged. "You are correct. As we get old, we need to acquire new vices. God will not be interested in us otherwise. We must wave our arms at Him to get his attention. It is the end of the day, so I will speak to you in confidence. I myself have attracted God's attention by acquiring a new . . . how do you say this in English? *Ragazza*."

"Girlfriend."

"Yes. I have acquired a new *girlfriend*. Perhaps I am being too bold in saying so." He stared at the cash register, harmlessly confabulating. The man was in his midfifties, and his pudgy wife, Claudia, dressed in black, sometimes lumbered into the store to do the accounts, and was known everywhere in the village for her terrible tongue lashings. Like Imyar Sorovinct, Carlo Travatini had earned a right to his fantasies. "My *girlfriend* loves me. And of course I adore her. She tells me that she admires my patience and my skill at lovemaking, despite my advanced years. The years give us older men a certain . . . technical skill. Forgive me for being so crude." Amelia shook her head, disclaiming any possible shock. "Why do I tell you this? I do so because our love, hers and mine, is an open secret. I will not, however, give you the young lady's name, because I should not wish to appear to be indiscreet. We Italians, you know, unlike the French, are not noted for our subtlety or discretion. We are announcers and are combustible. We announce first this, then that. In this announcing manner I have written poems for her, my *beloved*. Would you like to see my poems? They are of course not at the level of Montale, but . . ." He began to fumble into his pocket. Amelia stopped him in the midst of his harmless comic charade.

"No, thank you." More love poems! They came out of the woodwork everywhere and should be outlawed. There was far too much love, a worldwide glut of it. *What the world needs now*, she thought, *is much less love*. "How wonderful for you. But, please, no."

"All right. But I beg of you, do not mention the beautiful young woman to my wife, in case you should see her."

"I shall say nothing," Amelia told him. "What cigarettes do you have? I would like an Italian brand."

"Well, we have Marlboros. Sturdy cigarettes in a crushproof box. And L&M. That is a good brand also."

"Both American. No, I want an Italian cigarette."

"Well, let me see. I also have MS."

"MS?" She felt a moment of pity.

"Yes. MS. Of course. It is a brand of cigarette we have here. Monopoli di Stato. You should know that by now. Filtro? De Luxe? Or Blu?"

"Blu, please." He brought down a pack on which appeared, in rather large letters, the Italian phrase for *Smoking Kills*.

"You should not do this," he said, putting the cigarette pack into her hand with a tender gesture, brushing her fingers as he did so. "It is no way to get God's attention. You should get a *boy*friend, perhaps?"

"Also, I need some matches, please."

He reached under the counter and brought some out. He shook his head as she paid him for the cigarettes. "After all these years," he said, "I do not understand you Americans. Forgive me. I have been listening to the news on the radio just now. Iraq, Afghanistan. You are unexplainable, indefinable. So friendly and yet so warlike. This contradiction . . . I cannot understand it."

"Yes," Amelia said. "You are right. We are puzzling and incomprehensible. Thank you, my friend. Ciao."

"Ciao, Signora," he said, looking away from her again, down at his hands. "Grazie." What a sorrowful man, she thought, with his sorrow painstakingly narrated every day. You would never see such a man in the States. She had almost returned to the stolen Fiat when her Italian cell phone rang. When she answered, there was silence. She hung up.

The American couple waved her over. They were drinking wine.

"Hey there. Good afternoon," the man said in English with a slight Texas accent. "You care to join us?" He wore a Tyrolean hat, a blue shirt, a tan-colored sport coat, a string tie, and cowboy boots. His wife, deeply tanned, wearing a plain gray dress and a collection of thin gold bracelets that rattled like jail keys, smiled nervously upward at the sky, avoiding eye-contact. She had very expensive hair, Amelia noted, highlighted with blond streaks.

"How did you know I was an American?" Amelia asked.

"Aw, you look like one of us," the man told her. "It's a duck recognizing another duck." The wife nodded at the sky. Amelia felt all her strength leaving her body: she was heavily invested in appearing to be Italian or French, with a trace of beautiful haughtiness, or at least generically European, and if she could be exposed this easily by lunkheads, then her nationality might indeed be an essence that no role-playing could disguise. Being an American was a curse—you were so recognizable everywhere that your nationality was like a clown suit. Maybe Jack would escape it. She had come to think of her own countrymen as *them*. She shivered. After all her efforts, she was instantly identifiable and still looked like one of *them*. Fucking hell.

"Sorry," she said. "I have to get back. They've prepared lasagna," she said. "The kids."

"We're gonna be here in town for a few days," the man said, before gulping down half his glass of wine. "You just drop in on us any old time. We got ourselves that villa up the hill. There for the whole week."

"OK," she said, before waving goodbye to them.

On one of the hairpin turns on the way back, her phone rang again, and this time, when she answered it, the voice that came out—the connection was poor—sounded like her brother.

"Amelia?"

"Yes?" She held the cell phone in her left hand as she downshifted with her right. The steering wheel wobbled. "Jerry? Is that you, Jerry?"

"Yeah. Of course it's Jerry. Who'd you think it was?" Amelia let her foot off the clutch, and the car lurched into the lower gear. "Sorry. That was rude. I'm really sorry. I mean, we're on pins and needles here. I'm a damn mess, is what it is. Yvonne's a mess, too."

"What is it? What's going on?" There was another pause for the trans-Atlantic long distance or for her brother's hesitation. "Is it Catherine?"

"Yes, of course it's Catherine. She's taken a bad turn. The doctors have been saying that . . . actually, I don't really know *what* they've been saying. It's all a jumble to me. But like I say, she's worse. Now her kidneys aren't working. And that's on top of everything else. The pneumonia. But I'm not saying you should come here. I'm not saying that."

"Of course I'll come," Amelia said to her brother. "I'll be there as soon as possible."

"Thanks," he said. "We could use some bucking up." Amelia

heard another voice in the background, and then her brother said goodbye and broke off the connection.

As soon as she had parked outside the villa, she got out of the car, looked at the package of cigarettes in her hand, and went inside. The table had been set, and Gwyneth and Jack were waiting for her on the sofa, both of them beautiful and radiant. This world was paradise, after all, when your son and his girlfriend, healthy and in love with each other, cooked dinner for you inside a cool dark Italian villa, and you could worry all day about a line of poetry that you couldn't translate properly, and you could be annoyed by simpleton American tourists. To be bothered by trivialities was sheer heaven.

"Momma," Jack said. "What happened to you?"

"Your cousin Catherine's worse," Amelia said, tossing the cigarettes onto a side table, as if she'd never bought them. "I'm going to have to fly to Minneapolis. You two will have to hold down the fort here for a few days. Can you do that? I'll even leave you the Fiat if you drive me to the airport."

Jack nodded. Gwyneth rose and walked over to Amelia, taking her hand as if she were offering preliminary condolences. "Do you still want dinner?" she asked. The girl gave off a musky odor, and her face was slightly flushed and sleepy; naturally they'd had quick sex in Amelia's absence, and now they'd be soft and cuddly and compliant.

"Of course," Amelia said. "Of course, of course. And let's get drunk. OK? Are you willing to do that?"

They all laughed. Laughing, Jack asked, "So what's Catherine worse with?"

"She's dying," Amelia said. "She can't breathe. That's what she's worse with."

Although she loved him, of course, Amelia didn't like her brother very much, mostly because of his employment situation. He worked for a Minneapolis real-estate tycoon, Ben Schneiderman, a feral-looking man barely over five feet tall, whose customary expression—Amelia had met him once—was one of super-predatory avarice that mingled from time to time with his one other singular expression, massive sleepy indifference whenever matters of common human experience, those that were not for sale, were exposed to him. Schneiderman had run several newspapers into the ground, bought and sold a few major league teams, and built multiple granite-and-glass high rises and shopping malls. His wife, Bitsy Christianson, was a patron of the arts. Their personal website (and editorial sounding-board) was www.whatsittoyou.com. They owned eight or nine homes. Schneiderman had said many times that his motto was, "I never suffer. And neither should you." Jerry served as the primary consigliore for Schneiderman's various enterprises and spent much of his life in a private jet, scurrying from one financial brushfire to another. He negotiated, threatened, and placated. Amelia's brother was balding from all the stress and had taken to brushing his remaining hair, like tendrils or water weeds, across the top of his scalp.

And of course there was the other thing: Jerry supported his sister financially. Some of Schneiderman's money trickled down to her. He had paid for Jack's private schools in Switzerland and Italy. Her brother's charity was Amelia's safety net, along with alimony from Jack's father, and some part-time teaching. Well, no one's hands were clean.

But now, in the Saint Mary's Hospital's ICU, while Yvonne sat next to the bed holding her daughter's hand, Jerry leaned back against the window, and the blank stare on his face showed Amelia exactly how inwardly broken her brother actually was. She went up to him and hugged him and pecked him on the cheek and quickly did the same to Yvonne, whose eyes were tear-streaked. In the bed, her niece seemed to be gasping for breath. Another man was in the room, introduced to Amelia as the child's pediatrician, Dr. Elijah Jones, who wore rainbow suspenders with comic-book cartoon faces on them. Everybody thanked Amelia for coming.

"Anyone would have done it," she said. "You would have done it for me, if Jack, god forbid, got sick. Where's Gerald?" Gerald was Catherine's little brother.

"He's home with the babysitter," Jerry said, with a sigh. "The poor kid. We've been neglecting him. Can't be helped."

The pediatrician, after a few pleasantries, took Amelia aside down the hall and told her that her brother needed as much comfort and solace as she could give him, and that it was a good thing that she was there. He pulled off his glasses and cleaned the lenses with his Donald Duck necktie. He explained about the gradual impairment of Catherine's muscular control. She nodded. "You have to try to love everybody," the doctor said, embarrassed but also in earnest, as he smiled with deep sadness. "They all need it. All of them." When Amelia asked about the prognosis, the doctor shrugged. "Your brother and sister-in-law have been holding on. They're the ones I'm worried about. Your niece ... well, we're doing everything we can."

She left the hospital with her heart pounding.

So bleary with jet lag that she could not sleep or make any sense in conversation, and feeling that her brain was a haunted house in which bats flew randomly from one attic beam to another, Amelia found herself at two a.m. walking outside her hotel and then along the Mississippi River. Was there anything, anything at all, worse than the suffering of a child? Catherine had been a beautiful baby but had been sickly, and like Sorovinct's son, she had multiple afflictions that had prevented her from growing into adolescence. She had remained a child for her entire life. One time when Amelia had been visiting, Catherine had approached her with a calendar she'd made herself with a ruler and colored crayons. Two pages: the months of April and May. Her niece had listed a price for the calendars at the top: fifty cents for each page. Amelia had bought the two calendar months and taken them home and put them up on the refrigerator, only to discover that they were inaccurate and in some sense imaginary. Her niece had filled in the date boxes any way she wanted to. They were surrealist calendars, with dates that would never exist: Tuesday, May 14, 2011, for example. Wednesday, May 15. There would never be such days.

She had loved Catherine, and Catherine had been stalwart and seemingly brave in the face of all her physical and mental afflictions. Why should such a child suffer? Or any child? Sitting on a bench that looked out at the Stone Arch Bridge, Amelia thought of Ivan Karamazov speaking of the suffering of children and saying, "I don't understand anything, and I don't *want* to understand anything," and as the river flowed past her on its journey to the Gulf of Mexico, she leaned forward and put her head in her hands before straightening up again to wipe her face free of the tears that had accumulated there. Lucky me with my son Jack; lucky Jack with his girlfriend; lucky me, she thought, and if I could only share my luck with everybody, every living soul, I would.

She walked back to her hotel, trudged up to her room, undressed again, and put on her nightgown. Maybe this time she'd find·an hour or two of sleep. Almost as soon as her head touched the pillow, she entered a dream of astounding specificity: she was sitting in a slightly dingy living room in Eastern Europe, lit with four candles in pewter candleholders. To her left was a small sturdy wooden dinner table set for two, and in front of her was a fireplace in which the coals appeared to be dying. The room had a smoky and unclean smell. A mongrel dog sat to her right and barked once at her, as if the dream could now commence. It was like a film director shouting, "Action!" Amelia knew, without knowing how she knew, that she had found herself in Imyar Sorovinct's home and that the poet's wife stood off to her right, just out of sight, preparing a meal. In front of her, sitting in another chair, was Imyar Sorovinct.

The poet held himself up with straight soldierly posture, like a veteran in a wheelchair, but his face betrayed him: his left eye, lower than his right, looked at Amelia with patient compassion, while his right eye gazed on indifferently, as if two separate selves were housed within him. His uncombed hair rose wildly from the back of his scalp, and his large ears stuck out from his head like jug handles. He was a very homely man, after all. His hands trembled as they rested on his thighs. The expression on Sorovinct's face was one of scrupulous interest dimmed by time distance and dream distance, both of which were causing him to disintegrate. He had the weary expression of an old battlefield commander, even though he had never gone off to any war; his imagination had gone there instead.

Amelia waited for him to speak. When he said nothing, she told him, in his native dialect, "My name is Amelia, and I . . ."

"I know who you are," Sorovinct told her in perfect English. "You've been trying to translate 'Impossibility.' I know who you are very well."

"You do? Well. Then you know that I can't get anywhere with that poem."

"And you never will," Sorovinct told her. "You'll never get that one right. You'll just have to give it up."

"I hate to. I've spent so long on it."

"Well," Sorovinct said, rubbing his chin. "That's too bad. Just forget it." He picked up his book of poems from the floor and opened it in front of her. "There's something I want you to do," he said. He pointed at a page, where a poem entitled "Forbearance" appeared. "This is the poem you should be translating, not that other one. You'll translate this one in no time, believe me. Please just do what I ask. Also, and I don't mean to be rude, but it would be better if you did it right now."

The dog to Amelia's right barked twice, as if saying, "Cut! Print!"

She awoke and turned on the bedside light. It was four a.m. She went over to her suitcase, took out the volume of Sorovinct's poetry, and turned to the poem he had pointed to. After sitting down at the hotel room desk, she reached for her pen and translated the poem line by line, each line almost instantly suggesting its equivalent in English. She wrote out the translation on the hotel's stationery. The entire process took less than thirty minutes. The poem didn't really sound Sorovinct's characteristic note, but so what? She was under orders. When she returned to bed, the time was five minutes past five o'clock.

She had never seen a dog in a dream before. And the dream hadn't allowed her to say goodbye. Why was that?

*

At Catherine's memorial service, midway through, Amelia rose to speak, with the hotel stationery in her hand. Looking out at her family, she said, "I want to read a poem by Imyar Sorovinct. I've just translated it. It's called 'Forbearance.' I'm reading it in memory of Catherine." She lowered her head to recite, her voice trembling. "Forbearance," she began.

> *"Who is the child who stands beside this sea, wind-broken, wracked*
> *With spray that seems to paint his skin with heaven's tears?*
> *And who might be this man but the father of the boy, standing there*
> *In wrinkled clothes, holding a halo above the child to keep him dry*
> *Out of sorrow, out of love, at this abrupt and stony seashore*
> *Visited in autumnal days? This is the child who clutches at his father*
> *Who intercedes for him, this quiet, vested man guarding the boy*
> *From rain and spray. This is the child who does not speak,*
> *Who never speaks, who must be blessed. The gulls are circling.*
> *There is something patient in the waves that they both imitate,*
> *And it is in the rain and spray that one feels the power*
> *Of forbearance, in this autumnal drizzle*
> *Soaking the parent and his child, loving what is damaged*
> *And wholly theirs, held like a precious jewel*
> *Tightly, tightly, in their hands together."*

At the cemetery, in broad daylight, when it was her turn, she stabbed the shovel that had been handed to her into the pile of dirt, and, forcing the blade downward, scooped out a measure of clay and sand and soil. She carried the shovelful over to the gravesite and dropped it over Catherine's casket, on whose surface it made a hollow sound—like a groan from another world, mixed with the sound of her own grief. Then she seemed to wake up and heard the sounds of the others, and someone took her hand, and someone else took the shovel.

Twenty-four months later, Amelia found herself in Baltimore, sitting in a hotel lobby at a conference of translators. From the cocktail lounge came peals of alcoholic laughter, followed by jokes told in Polish, Russian, French. It was a habit of translators to speak in collage expressions in which three or four languages were mixed together. Ostentatious polyglots! As she waited for her friend to meet her—they had reservations at Baltimore's best seafood restaurant—she spied, across the lobby, Robert McGonigal, whom she thought of as the Old Translator. He sat slumped there in an ill-fitting suit, focused on the distance, rubbing his forehead above his massively overgrown eyebrows. He wore the thickest eyeglasses Amelia had ever seen, with lenses that made his eyes seem tiny. McGonigal's versions of *The Iliad*, *The Odyssey*, and *The Aeneid* were still being taught in colleges and universities everywhere, as were his translations of Pasternak, whom he had known personally. He had known everybody. But now he was sitting in a hotel lobby alone, wearing a facial expression that said, "I have seen it. You cannot surprise me."

She rose and walked over to where he was sitting. She wanted a blessing from the old man. Jack and Gwyneth were to be married in two months, in Italy. What would the future bring them? There had to be a blessing. McGonigal seemed to be gazing through space-time. Standing in front of him, Amelia introduced herself, and McGonigal nodded at her, as if she were a speck on eternity's wall. Nervously she prattled on, and as she heard more polyglot joking from the bar, she thought, *Well, I might as well tell him*, and somewhat against her better judgment, she related the story of her efforts to translate Sorovinct's "Impossibility."

"I couldn't do it," she said, and McGonigal gave an imperceptible nod. "It just wouldn't go. And then I went to bed, and Sorovinct appeared to me in a dream." McGonigal, startled, suddenly began to look at her closely. "I was in his house," she said. "His wife and dog were there too."

"What happened then?" McGonigal asked, his voice ancient and whispery.

"Well, he told me that I'd never get that poem right. He brought out his book of poems and pointed at another poem."

McGonigal's face took on an air of astonishment.

"And he said, 'This is the poem you must translate. This one you'll get in no time.'"

"So?"

"So I woke up," Amelia said, "and I translated the poem in half an hour."

"I am astonished," McGonigal said, struggling to get to his feet.

"Well, I . . ."

"I am astonished," McGonigal repeated. By now he was standing in front of her unsteadily, studying her carefully. He had taken Amelia's hand. "Are you seriously telling me . . ." He seemed momentarily incapable of speech. "Are you seriously telling me that that's the *first time* that such a thing has ever happened to you?"

"Well, yes."

"My dear," he said, his voice coming out of eternity. "Oh, my dear." He opened his mouth and exhaled, and his breath smelled of Catherine's grave, and then, as Amelia drew back, the grave started to laugh at her.

DEPARTURES

Catherine Browder

THE EXODUS TOOK PLACE during Alina Naroyan's first decade as an American. One by one her friends and countrymen left the apartments in Kansas City, some joining children in far-flung suburbs while Alina stayed put. She had no children, and her closest émigré relative lived in Texas. When he invited her to join his family, she considered it briefly and then refused. She'd never been dependent on anyone and couldn't imagine starting now. Besides, friends had warned her about Texas: *Don't go, Lina. It's too hot!* (As if it weren't miserable enough in Missouri!) Then a wave of new refugees swept into the apartment complex, and Alina thought she might drown.

First to go was a neighbor who'd attended Alina's citizenship party, a quiet woman with a sick husband. Alina had gone down to the entry to collect her mail and found Linda collecting hers. "We're moving," she whispered. "The end of the month."

"Where?" Alina asked. She had no sense of her adopted city and had never driven a car.

"Assisted living," said Linda soberly with a nod of the head. "A place in Independence. I need help with Frank."

Alina sorted through the pieces of this news bulletin. *Assisted living?* Linda explained. *Independence?* She thought it might have something to do with freedom, but from what? Again Linda explained. *Ah, that Independence!* Alina knew this to be the next town over, only a few miles east of where they stood, in the foyer of a declining brick building now infused with the spices of Africa.

Six months later Luba, who once lived upstairs, relocated downtown to a tall apartment building favored by retired Americans where, Luba pridefully pointed out, the language of choice was English. She was not saddened to see Luba go since Luba confronted her new life (her previous one, too, Alina guessed) with monumental scorn. Never a kind word from Luba, or a flicker of curiosity. Next, darling Nina, who'd become like a daughter, took her own little girl and went to live with a brother in Raytown.

But on the day Stella stopped by, bringing a container of borscht, Alina's heart sank.

"We've found a place," Stella said. "In Overland Park."

Kansas again. It was Stella who drove her to the Russian store or to the Price Chopper when it rained, also to the doctor's, even once to see the ballet perform the Nutcracker. Stella was now a nurse—in Kansas—and when she moved she would take an entire household with her. When that day arrived, Alina realized, she would be the only European left in the building.

After Stella's visit, Alina went to her bedroom and lay down. Her journey had taken her farther than she would ever have imagined. Too far, perhaps—from Baku by the sea to Moscow to the exact center of the United States, to a city she scarcely knew existed. Nowadays, when she opened the sliding door to her balcony, she could not hear a single word of English or Russian, Armenian or Azerbaijani for that matter. The area was no longer the comfortable hodgepodge it had once been. By 2007 and in her seventy-seventh year, she was the only one of her countrymen who remained in what she now thought of as Little Somalia. An Armenian forced to flee Azerbaijan for her life, Alina was again surrounded by Muslims, and she pondered whether her journey ought to continue.

In her former life she'd been a musician, the arc of her career utterly predictable. Her mother had been Alina's first piano teacher. Early on, the young family had moved from Yerevan, Armenia, to the neighboring Republic of Azerbaijan, so her father might teach at a better school. But that was in the old Soviet days when everything worked and anyone could safely live anywhere—before Gorbachev got it into his head to split the Union apart and The Trouble began.

After training in Moscow, she returned to the Music Institute in Baku as a piano instructor. Even then, Baku was one of the most secular and open Islamic societies, where music and opera and fine arts flourished, where visitors could find Persian carpets, caviar, and western theatre. She had accompanied several of the most prominent singers in the region, including mezzo-soprano Vera Ivanova. Then the great Portuguese soprano Pilar da Silva arrived as a visitor to the Music Institute, having left her own country during a time of distress, staying on to teach and perform and become one of Alina's closest friends. Alina was forty and still single when Vera introduced her to the tenor Bruno Dorn, son of a Russian father and Azeri mother, ten years Alina's senior, and divorced. Her brief marriage to Bruno stood out as the best decade of her life, until he'd died of an aneurysm—like Caruso—long before The Trouble forced her to flee. Even her good friends from student days had scattered: Natalia to Israel and Sonya off to Germany.

The knowledge that Azerbaijanis and Armenians had always fought lived on in one small ancestral pocket of her mind, even though she'd never been affected. She preferred to remember the good years of the Soviet Union when the government maintained order, ethnicity took a back seat, and people got on with their lives. Then came *perestroika* . . . . Why was it that after sixty years of civility the world went crazy?

When The Trouble first began, a sympathetic neighbor had told her, "They probably could care less about you. It's your apartment they're after." The same large apartment the government had granted her teacher father and she'd continued to live in after her parents' deaths. In those Soviet days, an apartment could remain in a family for perpetuity. The rent was not only low, but controlled. One evening she heard voices in the hallway and later began seeing the angry faces during the day. She'd spent most of her life in that temperate city on the Caspian but would never be considered a native. When ugly threats were slipped under her door, she packed two suitcases, all the goods she could carry, and all the mementoes worth saving. She carried her bags to her neighbor Nikolai's apartment, and he and his Russian wife took her in. A Tatar from Tajikistan, Nikolai was so fierce-looking no Azeri would bother him. Their blood lust was reserved for Armenians, not for Tatars or ethnic Russians. Alina had heard the screams in the night even before she fled.

"They" pounded on Nikolai's door while Alina hid in the closet. Someone must have seen her flee. The Tatar finally opened up, the chain still attached, while his wife cowered in the kitchen. *Are you crazy?* Alina heard his voice from the depths of the closet, behind the winter coats. *Are you nuts? I am here with my wife and you are upsetting her. I don't like that. So go away. And if you come back, you'll get this.* He shook a length of steel pipe. She knew this because he showed it to her later. She spent the daylight hours in the closet since "their" eyes and ears were everywhere, even in the apartment below.

Three days in the closet.

Alina slept on a bed of coats, a boot for a pillow. She did not move until the dead of night when she crept through the dark to the toilet and bathed her body with a cloth; for "they" were listening. After three days, an official arrived—sent by an influential cousin in Moscow. At dusk this official escorted her from Nikolai's apartment and drove her to the pier. He came with an official car and an official bodyguard and because he was an Azeri, no one dared to accost them. Her cousin had arranged passage on the night ship across the Caspian, and from there she traveled by train to Moscow.

Alina never saw Nikolai or his wife again, nor the Azeri official, and she owed them her life. Only later did she hear about the "massacres," passed on by word of mouth from one horrified Armenian to the next: someone had heard the BBC broadcast over a wireless, the mob that stormed a hospital in a northern city, tossing patients and babies out of windows. She'd always hoped it was only a rumor, but when she reached Kansas City and met other Armenian-Azerbaijanis, she learned it was true. It seemed so odd, shocking really, that her English teachers hadn't heard about the massacres. She asked her friend Jeanne-Marie about this omission. A Frenchwoman married to an American, Jeanne-Marie rolled her eyes and threw up her hands. "What do you expect, Lina? The Americans want that Caspian oil." Then the Bosnian horrors eclipsed anything that had occurred in distant Baku.

What made people so wicked? She'd lived peaceably among Azerbaijanis most of her life. If the Soviet Union were still intact, she would still be in the same apartment she'd lived in all her life, a woman with a good life and good work, with friends and pets. Instead she took her considerable savings and the support offered by the U.S. government, and left. Now all that remained of that life were a few photos hanging on her new walls and one album, her life condensed to what she could carry. As for the cats and piano . . . well, she'd had to leave them, and run.

She found the tired old upright at the City Union Thrift for $100, an inferior piano in need of new felts. When one runs for her life, she joked with Jeanne-Marie, one cannot bring along her baby grand. She located a tuner and put the instrument into passable shape so she could practice without cringing.

She'd even called the Conservatory of Music. They were polite, marginally interested, but alas, she knew, her English was not good enough, nor her credentials up to scratch. Besides, they'd just hired a flashy young pianist, a Van Cliburn finalist from the former Soviet Union. There would be room for only one "Russian" in this conservatory even though neither of them was Russian—the young prizewinner was an Uzbek.

The Garcias phoned to say they could not attend English School that night, or the night after. "So sorry, Alina. We'll pick you up next week." She accepted this as the price of being a passenger, of having no car in car-hungry America. A bus passed conveniently near the apartment, but after class she didn't want to wait on the Avenue in the dark. She did not like the look of the people loitering near the bus stop, so reluctantly she would forego English class for the week. Until she saw the taxi in the parking lot behind the building. For two days she went periodically to the landing to see if she could discover who in the building drove the cab.

On the third day of her vigil she saw below her a tall, lean Somali leaving the apartment where Stella's family once lived. He walked down the three concrete steps to the lot, and into the taxi. She followed quickly, tightening her brown wool cardigan around her. He'd just started the car when she waved at him. He flashed a friendly smile and rolled down the window.

"Yes, Madam." He turned off the engine and to her amazement climbed out of his cab

"I live in your building. Let me introduce myself." She held out her hand, and then quickly withdrew it. Was he one of those Muslims who still followed the old ways and did not shake hands? Probably. He had not stopped smiling, and she gazed at his perfect teeth.

"Miss Alina," he said and nodded his head in a little bow. "So happy to meet you. I am Abdi, and I have seen you before." He nodded his head again and placed his right hand over his heart.

"I had a question," she said and explained her transportation problem.

Yes, he knew where the school was. His wife Khalida attended the school some mornings, and Alina widened her eyes.

"Really?" she exclaimed, relieved to discover a wife. "I will stop by."

How serviceable and clear his English sounded. She had little trouble understanding him. It was her English that was fading from lack of use.

"This is business," she added, pointing to the taxi. "I will pay you."

He closed his eyes and waved his hand in front of his face as if swatting flies, his lips pursing. "I shall take you to school Monday, and I shall pick you up after." He bowed slightly. "We are neighbors . . . ."

On Saturday she prepared the walnut rolls, so popular with her American friends, carefully rolling the flour, adding the butter and sugar and chopped nuts. After baking, she wrapped them in foil and placed them in the fridge. On Sunday, she dressed carefully in a dark printed long-sleeved dress, a scarf at her throat, and went down to the landing to verify that Abdi's taxi was not in service but parked in the lot. There were, in fact, two taxis parked on the far side, and for a moment she felt perplexed. She had no idea which taxi was his, but taxis had become a cottage industry among the Somalis. She would have to risk it. She returned to her apartment and took the walnut rolls from the fridge, tightening the foil around the plate and took the stairs down to the apartment that had once been Stella's. She knocked and waited. She heard movement within and the piping voice of a child, but no one came to the door. Alina knocked louder. She heard a woman's voice trilling inside, two female voices in fact, and wondered which one was Abdi's wife. Perhaps there was also a mother. She knocked a third time but the voices carried on and then someone inside called out something but not in English and she called back, "It's Alina." All voices stopped.

The door flung open and there stood Abdi, smiling with his perfect teeth. He clasped his hands together and exclaimed, "Miss Alina! Welcome to my family." He stepped aside and ushered her in. She marveled at how tall he was, everything about him elongated and cylindrical, even his high forehead, and glossy black. A pleasant-looking man, perhaps in his thirties.

He said something speedily to the two women who appeared to be moving between kitchen and living room. "Our neighbor Bibi, and this is Khalida." He gestured toward an extremely young woman with enormous eyes, who stepped forward. "My wife," he added. She was dressed like all the women in her building—*hidden*, Alina thought—pulling a headscarf hastily around her face, more yards of colorful cloth draped over her body. When she stepped forward, Alina saw that she was hugely pregnant. Alina offered her the plate: "Russian pastries." Did this young woman speak English? Alina went on anyway. When she paused, Abdi interpreted, and the girl nodded, stepped forward and received the plate, then handed the plate to her friend, took both Alina's hands in hers and said,

"Thank you." At least Alina thought these were the words that came out. With Khalida speaking in Somali and Abdi in English, they asked her to sit. As she turned she saw for the first time the little girl hanging on to her father's pant leg.

"And this is little Fatima," Abdi said.

Alina bent down to greet her, and the child frowned and darted behind him, hiding her face in his leg.

Alina turned back to the lovely young woman. "And when is the baby due?"

She was prompt that first Monday—Jeanne-Marie was forever scolding her for being late—dressed and seated in her living room and fretful he may have forgotten. At 5:45, Abdi knocked on her door. "Miss Alina," he called. "Time for English."

The trip took less than five minutes, down Garfield to the Avenue, west passed the Paseo and the entrance to the highway, beside another clutch of grim public housing she never liked to pass on foot, over the bridge and another highway entrance—so many highways—and right again. The English School was housed in an old recreation and community center, built, she was told, by other immigrants, Italian stonemasons who'd once lived in the nearby buildings and attended the Catholic Church.

Abdi hopped out and opened the door. "I will be back at 9 p.m."

Throughout the evening she couldn't focus on the lesson, her thoughts drifting, worried that she might have to wait alone and forgotten in the dark. Yet when she left the building that evening, the taxi was parked at the curb. Her heart lifted in relief. She walked to the passenger side and tapped at the window. He was listening to the radio and waved, switching the radio off. He popped out, moved quickly around the front, and opened the front passenger door.

"Please," Alina implored. "No need to get out."

"But you are my guest."

She climbed in back, wondering if she should have gotten in front. That would alter the relationship, she thought, make it too personal. When they returned to the parking lot of their apartment building, she reached over the back seat. "I would like to pay you."

"No, no, no," he protested, his head wagging vehemently. "It is my pleasure to take you to school. Khalida used to go, you know, but now she is in her ninth month—not so good."

"But you are a businessman," she insisted. "And this is your business."

His head continued to shake, his hand flying up into that universal gesture of refusal. From her handbag Alina removed an envelope with a five-dollar bill inside and implored him to take it. The twin gestures of insistence and refusal threatened to lengthen out, and Alina placed the enveloped on the front seat. Abdi grabbed the envelope and swiftly tucked it inside her still open purse.

"Thank you," she said in surrender.

Abdi bowed his head. "You are always my guest."

The Garcias phoned Wednesday evening to tell her they would not be returning to school after all. They had good news: they were moving. *Carlos has found a good job!* How excited they were but sad to say good-bye. Cradling the phone after their call, Alina wondered if returning to the English School was something she needed to do. But where else could she shore up her disintegrating English? Where else would she see her friends? Now everyone in the apartment building was Somali, and a great sense of loneliness swept over her. Not that they weren't pleasant, as it turned out, but their children were so loud and numerous, playing ball outside her windows, calling and laughing and disturbing her peace. She would now have to approach Abdi and talk business this time. For a day she planned her English words carefully, picking and throwing out and choosing again the words that might appeal to a young father. She prepared a plateful of Russian pierogis, filled with potato and cabbage and butter, surrounded by a ring of Russian chocolate wrapped in colorful foil. As she descended the stairs to the ground floor, she coached herself: *this is business. Business!*

Every Monday and Thursday for a month Abdi took her to English School until Khalida had her baby. On that day a strange woman knocked on her door, wreathed in scarves and a long draping garment in a colorful print. If you could not discern a human shape, Alina thought, a face shone like a beacon.

"The baby has come," the woman said in a clear, scarcely accented English.

"Khalida and Abdi's baby?" Alina forced herself to look carefully at the woman's face. She appeared to be in her thirties. Her features were well proportioned, her eyes large and intelligent, her mouth trim, eyebrows plucked. She thought perhaps she'd seen this woman at English school. She felt certain this woman had been educated before she arrived in this country, unlike sweet Khalida.

"Yes. Abdi asked that I tell you he could not take you to class this evening."

Alina nodded. *Of course.* "What happy news! Is everyone well? The mother? The child?"

"I do not know," the woman said. "But we are hopeful. *Allah be praised.*"

The woman said her impeccable goodbyes and left. Allah be praised? A shiver ran along the skin of Alina's neck and scalp, and she felt besieged by the dismaying sense of isolation that now defined her days. Who was left but herself? What had once been laughingly referred to as Little Baku had changed so drastically it now replicated, in speech and look, the Horn of Africa.

"We've named him Hassan," Abdi said, as he drove Alina to English school the following week.

"And he is healthy?" Alina asked.

"Very. Strong lungs. Good stomach."

"And Khalida? She's well?"

"Hassan's mother is doing well."

What a curious way to refer to one's wife. She wondered if Khalida had been elevated in some manner, or simply redefined: the mother of a boy. A universal event, it seemed, since boys were assumed to be better. She'd never embraced the notion that the birth of a son should be more cause for celebration than a daughter. It didn't seem to matter in her expatriate community. Among her countrymen, daughters were equally plentiful and attentive (or inattentive) to their mothers, although this was not something she could speak to with any authority. She'd never dwelt on it, until recently, as the months and then years flew off the calendar and she found herself celebrating yet another birthday. A relic, that's what she was. She still dyed her hair, the preferred henna staining her hands. She still polished her nails and rouged her cheeks and surrounded herself with her younger Russian, Ukrainian, and Kazakh friends from English school. The young people had replaced the aging ones who'd moved to the suburbs and allowed themselves to grow old. Oh, so many she'd lost touch with!

But what should she give the baby? She asked Jeanne-Marie, who was never at a loss for an opinion. When she inquired, Jeanne-Marie shrugged in that peculiarly annoying Gallic manner with her face puckered, eyes fluttering shut, shoulders hunching. It wasn't like Jeanne-Marie to hold back. "Well, you can't very well give a doll."

Alina importuned the young Kazakhs to drive her to the Russian store. Here she bought the little Russian bear of carved wood, plus the metal top that spun when you pushed the plunger in the middle. There had been so few children in her life. Bruno had a daughter from his previous marriage, but the girl was grown by the time Bruno married Alina. She did not remember any Azeri customs for children, and the Armenian ones most certainly would not apply. So the wooden bear that "played" the wooden bells when you pulled the little string, plus the top—these would have to do. Alina wrapped the toys carefully in bright blue tissue paper and placed then in a gift bag that looked suspiciously like Christmas wrapping.

She waited another week before considering a visit to the young family, as much out of confusion as consideration. When, exactly, did Somali people call? Should she come into the busy apartment or deliver her gift from the threshold? The young family would likely have little rest with a crying infant in the house. Suddenly she remembered the little girl. Two toys for the baby boy and nothing for little Fatima? How unfair! She went to the dresser in her bedroom and pulled out the bottom drawer where she kept assorted trinkets and toys she'd picked up at the Russian store—hostess gifts, holiday gifts. She searched among the scarves and small decorative spoons until she found the little nested *matryoshka* doll: five dolls altogether, one inside the other. The main doll was too blonde and Slavic for Alina's taste, but she was beautifully decorated with a lovely red scarf and elaborate dress and apron painted over her round doll's body; and she wrapped it in a shard of yellow tissue. Then with wavering conviction, she went downstairs to Abdi's apartment and knocked on the door.

She was reminded of her first visit: she heard activity within but no one seemed to acknowledge the door. She knocked louder, fearful she might wake the babe. There was still no answer. She would try once again and then leave, giving her gift to Abdi when she saw him next. The door suddenly flung open, startling her, and the woman who had come to announce the baby's birth stood there like a solemn and burnished gatekeeper. Then the stern expression vanished, and the woman smiled. "Ah, it's you! Please come in."

She took Alina by the arm, raising her voice to speak to someone in another room, and then insisted that Alina take a seat. It hadn't occurred to her that Abdi would probably be working. She heard voices in the bedroom, and then Khalida and the baby emerged. Alina rose to greet them, the other woman translating for the new mother. How beautiful the little boy was, so small and perfect, his eyes sleepy.

"He has just finished his dinner," the tall woman said. "But Khalida wanted you to meet him."

Alina glanced around the living room: only two chairs and a misshapen coffee table, with numerous large cushions on the carpeted floor. The two women insisted that she sit down again, in the plumper of the two chairs. She recognized the imperatives of their hospitality because they so much resembled her own. Before she sat she held up the holiday bag. "There are two gifts for Hassan . . . and one for your daughter."

The neighbor translated for Khalida and took the handle of the bag out of Alina outstretched hand. Khalida thanked her and bowed her head. The reception of the gifts struck Alina as strangely solemn, as if to trill or titter over the gift might demean it, and their appreciation, and she felt moved by their gravitas. The tall woman disappeared into the galley kitchen with the gift bag, leaving Alina alone with mother and babies. Alina admired the baby again and spoke to the little girl, knowing whatever she said would be lost on Khalida. When the older woman returned, she was carrying a tray of tea.

Several weeks after little Hassan's birth, Luba called to inform her that space was opening up in her building downtown. Luba arranged to pick her up for a visit and sat beside Alina as she filled in the forms. There was a waiting list, the manager regretted to inform her. The Barbican apartments were very popular with retirees, but she was certainly qualified and would be considered. Alina returned home feeling neither encouraged nor rejected. Whatever would happen would happen. What else could one do? In the meantime, she lived as she had always lived: reading, playing her thrift store piano, attending English school, watching Russian-language videos, and spending an inordinate amount of time on the phone. Yet whenever she paused to rest, the young Somali family crept into her mind.

For eight months her days stretched out into a predictability that had begun to make her feel stale, even elderly. In one bleak and heavy moment she contemplated a return to Moscow, then chided herself. *Lina, you are an American now. Your life is here.* Abdi continued to drive her to English school Monday and Thursday evenings (her favorite hours of the week); on Fridays she walked to the neighborhood grocery, unless her Kazakh friends drove her to the Price Chopper; once a month she had lunch with Jeanne-Marie (but Jeanne-Marie was as prickly these days as Luba); and every Saturday she gave Nina's daughter a piano lesson. She had placed a notice by the mailboxes that she was available to teach piano, but no one called or came to her door. It wasn't that she needed the money.

She'd clung to her savings, and there was the reliable monthly SSI check, reserved for elderly refugees. Still she would have liked to teach someone in this new country the music she loved.

In March the Barbican apartments phoned: a one-bedroom had opened up on the third floor. Small but nice, if she was still interested. It would be available in a matter of weeks. Luba came to fetch her, and Alina viewed the rooms, the clean and carpeted corridors, the light and well-appointed ground floor lounge where one could sit and read the newspapers and watch television and visit with neighbors. It reminded her of a hotel lobby, which gave her a vacant feeling, but it was safe, if one wanted to leave one's apartment but not the building. Nonresidents had to pass through a security door that was carefully monitored. Luba took her arm and escorted her to the end of the third floor hallway. Arranged here was sitting area with a small, white wrought iron table and two matching chairs, wall to ceiling windows and large potted plants, overlooking a tree-lined street.

"Every floor has one," Luba said, indicating the small café table and chairs. "Nice and bright, you can have a picnic."

Alina glanced at her old friend. It wasn't like Luba to promote and applaud. Alina would have expected her to fault the sitting area for being too small or the potted palm for being too large. "And you like it here?" Alina asked.

"I do. Not perfect, but better than where you are. Everyone speaks English, you know." Luba gave her a superior look, and Alina knew what she was implying. The reminder strengthened her resolve, which had continued to waver. Unfortunately, the Barbican apartment was in all ways smaller than her current place, and a quarter of the size of her Baku home, but who could have everything?

"Lina, you can walk to the opera," Luba declared. "Even the ballet!"

She signed the agreement under Luba's approving eyes but when she returned to the old place, her heart rose up in rebellion. How could she leave? The last twenty years of her life had been one departure after another. How can one live in this way? Her eyes traveled the walls hung with paintings she'd found at the City Union thrift, the rugs she'd purchased from the Russian store, the framed photos from Baku—Bruno, Vera, even Pilar. She had acquired chairs, tables, even a daybed. Secondhand, to be sure, but they were hers. She would never be able to squeeze it all in. Then the old apartment seemed to swell with seventeen years of memories. How could she bundle her American life up once more and squeeze it into an even smaller space? She walked to the upright piano and touched it. It would come with her, of course, since she had gone to the trouble of restoring it and couldn't live without it. She sat down at the instrument, stretched her fingers, and began a Chopin nocturne.

She would manage, she counseled herself as she leaned into the keyboard. She had always managed. She would pare down. She had survived once before, twice if she included the decision to leave Moscow after her escape from Baku. Friends here had asked why she'd left Russia. Why indeed? Because she was an impatient and independent woman and could not bear to rely on her cousin's family. Because she had her own career and way of living, and it was not theirs. Because she was only sixty at the time and everything still seemed possible, and what was possible in America, with proffered American support, seemed far better and less cramped than anything in Moscow in its newly diminished condition, its post-Soviet confusion. Sonya had moved to Germany, after all. And Natalia had immigrated to Israel, so why not Alina Naroyan? Yes, in 1991 everything still seemed possible and interesting and adventuresome!

Alina finished the Nocturne and rested her fingers over the keys. She walked into the small dining room adjacent the kitchen and then into the spare bedroom, cataloguing what would come with her and what she must give away. She thought suddenly of Abdi and Khalida's sparsely furnished place and began to make a mental list. They must be the first to choose.

She couldn't bear to watch as Abdi and his two friends maneuvered the piano across the living room. A headache set in. She'd just had it tuned, and after the move she would have to tune it again. Abdi arranged for the truck, but the men were taxi drivers, not movers, and their struggle was too painful to bear. When the instrument passed through the door, lumbering slowly on its misshapen wheels, she fled into the back room and stared out the window.

Her friends had rallied: the young Kazakhs with a different truck, Nina and her brother in a large SUV, even Jeanne-Marie's husband with his minivan. Not much remained now except some clothing in a suitcase, a few toiletries, a teakettle and cup, and the bed she intended to leave behind. The piano had been the last significant piece of furniture. Abdi and Khalida had taken a small side table, a dresser, two rugs, and a chair—thrillingly received them, she had to admit, and this had given her unexpected pleasure. The Kazakhs had taken another chair and rug, a few paintings. Abdi would drive her to the Barbican apartment to supervise the placement of the piano, but for the moment, she could not watch. The instrument rumbled toward the stairs, and she felt the accumulated years move with it.

Exhausted, Alina stood among the boxes filling the new apartment, her temper short, pointing nervously here and there. At least the piano was in its appointed space. Before he left, Abdi turned to her and flashed his astonishing smile.

"Miss Alina, would you like a beautiful ride in the country? Khalida and I would like to thank you for the furnishings. And Khalida wants to have a picnic."

"Now?" she asked in amazement. It was April and cold.

He ignored her astonishment and went on. They would drive out to a special place friends had told him about. Had she been to Kansas?

Well, of course! One could not live on the Missouri side and not at some point visit the Kansas suburbs, with its Russian store and half her friends. She wouldn't have minded living there herself, except she did not drive. And since there were few buses and no streetcars or trains, what was the point? She'd never even seen a taxi.

"But this is further," he told her. "Far out in the countryside. We will wait until the weather warms."

At last, on a morning in late May with wavering sunshine and a brisk breeze, Abdi and his family, packed into the taxi, arrived at the Barbican apartments at ten. Alina had dressed warmly just in case: a sweater and a light coat and scarf.

"You will sit in front, please, Miss Alina," Abdi announced. Khalida was sitting in the backseat with the babies.

Once she was settled, her container of walnut rolls and pierogis and chocolate at her feet, Abdi turned to her and announced with a grin, "Now you are riding shotgun."

She wasn't sure she'd heard him correctly. "What is this? 'Riding shotgun'?"

"It means to sit in the seat where you are now. Beside the driver."

"But what does it mean?"

He shrugged. "Who knows? An American told me. In a taxi almost nobody rides shotgun." He laughed at some joke unavailable to her.

He drove them through the city and onto the highway, traveling the edge of the metropolitan area, then onto the Interstate and at last beyond the suburbs. She had never been this far west before. They traveled for over an hour, nearly two, and then at an exchange with scarcely anything to see but farmland and one vast gas station on a corner, he drove away from the busy road and along a smaller one. She felt as if the car was plunging between rows of sprouting grain, with no idea what was growing there. She had spent her life in cities and scarcely noticed the road signs, observing only an amazing number of unknown birds flying over the fields or perched on the wires. One large bird circled in the distance.

"Look, Miss Alina," Abdi pointed. "An eagle!"

He declared this with such authority that Alina let her gaze linger. But the bird was black against the sun. She couldn't discern any features familiar to her from paintings and posters—the talons, the beak, the stern eyes, and white head. Alina shrugged.

"So, Miss Alina. How is your new apartment?"

"So-so," she said, not wishing to sound too pleased. "Smaller, you know. But my countrywomen live there. Two of them."

Abdi nodded approvingly. "That's good. Like family. Now you can speak your language."

Not exactly like family, she thought. She would never wish to consider Luba *family*.

"It's for older people. Retired people."

"Ah, and no kids. No noise." He threw back his head and chuckled.

She glanced at him as he shared her news with Khalida. She did not tell him she felt safer there, with its elaborate security system. Nor did she wish to say there were white people like herself. It would not do to explain that the gulf between them was too vast—a woman with an austere European education, who loved Dumas and Tolstoy, played Mozart and Beethoven, and watched the Bolshoi on faded VCRs. She did not wish to say she was not interested in these fluid, undisciplined people who cooked at 10 at night and let their many children stay up until all hours or play on the grass in front of her apartment. When the first wave of Somalis arrived, a noisy family moved in above her, waking her at all hours. She did not wish to reveal that once, in frustration and fury, she had banged a broom handle against her ceiling and screamed in Russian, *What's the matter with you people? Are you animals?*

She'd grown fond of Abdi and his family. He had helped her— a single woman frequently in need of help. Nor could she bring herself to say the word—*old*—or any of its English variations. She had held *old* at bay for so long until this last move, which was at last an acknowledgment: The Barbican Apartments were only for retirees. For *old* people—and now in her eightieth year she ought to be allowed to enjoy safety and quiet, oughtn't she?

"How did you come here?" he asked, the question popping up unexpectedly.

"How? By airplane of course."

He burst out laughing, as if she'd made a joke. "No. I meant the reason."

"Ah, well, that is a long story . . . I couldn't stay any more in Baku. Everything changed. A new government, you see. It wasn't safe for me."

He nodded and said something to Khalida, who looked at Alina with her deep and sympathetic eyes. He didn't ask why and she was glad. She wasn't sure her English was up to it.

"And you?" she asked. She did not usually ask questions, fearful she wouldn't understand the answers. It was so much better to talk. That way she could practice her English. But nowadays Jeanne-Marie told her she was always interrupting, never letting anyone speak. *Why are you so chatty, Lina? It's like you never want to hear an answer. And whenever anyone tries to speak, you walk right over them with your busy tongue!* But Jeanne-Marie was a talker herself. How many times had they found themselves in dueling conversations?

"You, too?" she asked him.

"Yes, we too. No government. Nothing. Like you, not safe."

She wanted to hear the rest and waited, but Abdi turned and spoke to his wife, then announced, "We are almost there."

Abdi lowered his window. The draft made Alina shudder and she asked him to raise it up, please. "Yes, in a moment. But smell the air, Miss Alina. First smell."

"Drafts are not healthy," she said, instantly regretting the overbearing tone. At one time or another, non-Russian friends had registered a complaint against this imperious tone, as if it were a national flaw. Even Jeanne-Marie. Alina bridled at the memory. *As if a Frenchwoman has any right to chide a Russian for haughtiness!*

Abdi laughed gently and raised the window except for one inch. "OK?" he inquired and reluctantly she agreed since she couldn't actually feel any wind.

"It doesn't smell the same," he said. "It smells like the earth and the sea."

"The sea? How can it? Kansas is one thousand miles from the sea."

"I smell the sea," he insisted with a laugh.

They entered a small town, drove through it and out again. The name sounded peculiar when he pronounced it. *Strong City?* Ahead, another sign rose up, and she peered at it.

> *Tall Grass Prairie National Preserve.*
> *One Mile.*

She understood the first four words although they did not congeal into a single meaning. Abdi drove slowly as if he were looking for something. There was a bend off the road and here he pulled the taxi in and stopped.

"Picnic!" he announced and pointed again. Around them was a tiny roadside park with a few tables, none of them shaded by trees. Tiny saplings struggled beside two tables, as if someone had considered the need for future shelter. The place was so empty it felt desolate. Who would choose to eat in such an exposed place? All around the small park grass rippled across a treeless landscape, the land rising and falling in gentle swells. Abdi climbed out first and stretched, prodding his family until they all clamored out, and the little girl squealed her pleasure.

"Where are we?" Alina asked.

"I'm not sure, but it's nice, isn't it?"

Khalida appropriated the nearest table and was uncovering and removing the contents of a large food hamper, arranging containers across the picnic table. The little girl helped while the baby, slung across Khalida's back, slept contentedly.

Who could possibly enjoy a place whose name they didn't know? Alina found it unsettling, but Abdi was in no way unsettled and lifted his face into the breeze, holding a bowl for his wife while saying something in Somali to his daughter. Khalida seemed equally unalarmed. For an instant Alina wondered if they were completely daft. Then the spurt of anger vanished, as if it had only been a bird, flying overhead. Its swift departure made her feel strangely light-headed.

"You see?" Abdi let his arms sweep outward, encompassing the landscape. "Like the ocean. When I was a boy we would go to the ocean, walk along the edge of the water, tossing sticks, tossing stones, finding little crawling animals in shells. The family would come. Watch the sunrise. Sometimes the water would climb up. Other times it rippled and waved like the grass there." He pointed again, outward and beyond, and then shrugged.

"Everything falls apart. No government, no presidents, no help. Little boys like me carrying guns from one hidden man to another, from one small army to another. My father works to keep us together. Mother tries to save us all, but it is no use. We lose one, we lose another, and then we lose Father. Those of us who can run away to Kenya."

Alina held her breath. He had never spoken about himself, and she suddenly wished he would say more. An unfamiliar sorrow swelled inside her. Where was his family now? Had he met Khalida here or in one of those disheartening camps she'd heard about? But how do you ask such a thing, especially when there are two beautiful children and a happy father nearby? Khalida seemed so content organizing the picnic, placing carefully wrapped parcels on the wood table, laughing as she weighted the paper plates and napkins with condiments so the wind would not whisk them away. The baby began to fuss, and she reached one arm around and gently bounced him back to sleep.

A breeze passed over, and Alina removed her scarf. How unlike her, to want to feel the wind brush her face and hair? She couldn't explain this feeling. In this open, uncluttered place the wind belonged, running over the undulating land like an animal.

"Look, Miss Alina. Look at the grass move. Isn't it like your Caspian Sea?"

She gazed out and saw the grass change color as the wind tossed it, just as she had once watched from the embankment as the wind riffled the waves in the bay, changing the color of the water from green to gray to foamy white.

"I like this Kansas!" Abdi announced. "I like its ocean grass."

Khalida was speaking to them, supplicating, her graceful arms escaping the gauzy layers of her blouse, moving in rhythm to the dancing grain. Abdi answered his wife and laughed.

"Eat, Miss Alina! My Khalida says you must eat."

UPPER MIDDLE CLASS HOUSES

Claire Burgess

AT FOURTEEN, YOU ARE AN EXPERT on the insides of upper middle class houses. The sectional sofas, the glass coffee tables, the natural color palettes, those entertainment units with the doors that slide out and hide the TV like that's not what everyone's in the room for anyway. You can walk into a kitchen and find the silverware drawer on the first try, almost always next to the sink, the most accessible drawer in the highest-traffic area of the kitchen. You know which doors lead where even when they are closed and you've never been on the other side of them. You are also an expert at hiding places. The shoe boxes, the sock drawers, the backs of closets, under mattresses, beneath loose carpet: this is where you find the old love letters, the firearms, the porno magazines. These are the things you are most interested in, the hidden things. Especially the magazines.

Yes, you do wonder if this is normal. You suspect that you are creepy. You are also concerned that your interest in looking at naked ladies makes you a lesbian, but you don't think so. First of all, you like looking at naked men, too. And second, the way you look at the women is with a clinical, educational gaze, sometimes with a spark of amusement at the scenery or props. (But admit it, when you imagine yourself in their places, spread-out and airbrushed on a million magazine pages, you get a thrill deep in the cup of your hips, a buzz there like a wasp slowly waking.)

It started a year ago and innocently, the slow advance into the bedrooms of the parents you babysit for. At first you would just stand in every room and observe the furniture, the layout, the knickknacks and photographs, interested and excited by the knowledge of these places you weren't supposed to go. You liked passing a house on the way to school and knowing that inside the cabinet to the left of the sink, there was a stack of blue bowls. You enjoyed seeing one window lit up at night and knowing it was the study, which had a sagging futon and a reprinted painting of a Rocky Mountain vista and the entire series of *Cheers* on home-recorded VHS. And then you started pushing deeper, hesitantly opening jewelry boxes and dresser drawers. You never took anything—just looked. You started discovering more things, secret things. You knew a bottle of gin was hidden behind the linens in the Parkers' hall closet. You knew Mrs. Stadler had a cache of romance novels in a file box behind her shoes. You knew the Monroes had one more birth certificate on file than they did children. You knew Mr. Aronson had a desk drawer filled with framed pictures of a woman, all of them turned face down. All these things just whet your appetite. And then you started to find the sex things.

If it wasn't for this part of babysitting, you would probably just work at frozen yogurt stands like most of your friends. But you love the thrill of sneaking into someone else's bedroom and standing in that private space, opening their drawers and touching their underwear. Not in a creepy way—it's not like you sniff the underwear and get off on it. What you love is the knowledge that they don't have, the knowledge that they will come home and never know you were there looking through their things, never know you have seen what you've seen. You especially like seeing the adults in public afterward and knowing that they have silk boxers on underneath their clothes, or a lace negligee of sea-foam green, or the bra with leopard spots, or the briefs with the light bulb printed over the crotch and *Turn Me On* stretched across the back. You have found vibrators of various shapes and colors, dildos slipped inside socks and once inside a riding boot. You have found thigh-highs and garter belts; crotch-less panties, probably gifted as a bachelorette gag and never used—or maybe they were used, but only because they happened to be a gift (they would never have bought them otherwise), but boy how they love them now. In the Kirkpatricks' closet, you found a full-body cow costume with removable udders right over the private parts, but you didn't know if that was for sexual purposes or for ease of urination during costume parties. Not all of the homes held these treasures, of course. Sometimes, there was nothing more illicit than a tube of KY Jelly in the nightstand. But every time you are referred to a new house, you hope.

Then, one Saturday in May, you babysit for the Mayfields, who you have been referred to by the Walkers, the Walkers who have two nasty little goblins, two and six years old, and whose silk blindfolds and fuzzy handcuffs you found in a nondescript shoebox at the top of their bedroom closet months ago. The Mayfields' house is so newly constructed that the grass out front still shows its square grid marks. It is a hot day, and you are aware of your long, willowy legs below you after your mother drops you off, the loose way you move your hips, the light sheen of sweat on your inner thighs as you walk up the Mayfields' driveway. You are a good girl; this is why you are a babysitter in high demand. You sing in the church choir; you pull your hair back neatly; you wear pristine white sneakers. Sometimes, you see yourself from some objective viewpoint outside your body and try to imagine how other people see you. What do they think when they pass you on the street and say, "Good morning?" How do they perceive your lanky form, your opaque unsurpassable skin that they cannot see inside, that they know nothing about except what they can tell by your fresh face, your neat clothes? Well, one thing they can tell for sure is that you're hot.

You knock on the door at 10 a.m. to keep the children for the day. An attractive blonde woman answers the door, says "Thanks for coming! The Walkers speak so highly of you!" Just like that, an exclamation point explicit at the end of each sentence. You stick out your hand, say "Nice to meet you," but the woman says, "Nonsense!" with another exclamation mark, and pulls you into a hug. She smells like the tissue paper lingerie stores wrap your panties in.

Mrs. Mayfield is a tiny woman but has somehow pushed out twins. As you follow her into the living room, you imagine her body with a double-wide baby bump protruding from the front of it. You wonder how she stayed upright. You imagine her waddling around in a near-backbend for the last couple months of her pregnancy just to maintain her center of balance. Your own mother is pregnant with a child she insists is not an accident, a little brother who will graduate high school when your parents are almost sixty, for whom you will be more of an aunt than a sister. You imagine Mrs. Mayfield sweating and grunting and cussing as she pushes out one baby and then another, and it makes you smile.

The twins are fraternal, a boy and a girl, two years old, and they sit in the middle of the beige living room carpet banging colored blocks together. Both of them have short, wispy blond hair and neither looks at you when Mrs. Mayfield introduces them. You are glad to find out they don't have matching names like Reginald and Regina or Samuel and Samantha and are instead named Caitlin and Thomas. You kneel next to them and make yourself smile at them, the "I like babies" smile that you're supposed to use with children. Your braces were just taken off earlier this week, and you are still unused to the feel of your lips pulling smoothly across your teeth. You find yourself licking them a lot, which your mother tells you looks disturbing.

"Well, hello," you say to the twins, making sure not to lick your teeth at them. "Pleasure to meet you." The girl turns to you and hands you a yellow block that has just been in her mouth. "Thanks," you say, pretending to be grateful.

The Mayfields are going to an afternoon wedding the next town over and don't know what time they'll be back. "You never know when these receptions will end!" Mrs. Mayfield says. "Open bar, you know!" She shows you the list of emergency numbers and the directions on naptime and bedtime—your two favorite times of day. She shows you the twins' lunch of turkey dogs and green beans and instructs you to cut the dogs into bite-sized pieces and then cut the bite-sized pieces in half. For dinner, she leaves twenty dollars on the counter for pizza, which she also instructs you to cut into bite-sized pieces.

"We usually try to be healthier," she explains, "but we wanted to make it as easy as possible for you! You can order anything on the pizza, except sausage! What do they put in that?"

When Mr. Mayfield comes down in his suit, he shakes your hand curtly instead of hugging, which is fine by you. He has the sort of close-cropped hair that's always styled with a wet comb, parted on the side. His tie is tied into a small, perfect triangle, pulled closely to the neck. He looks like the kind of guy with a secret porn stash—the hard-core kind, with penetration. You smile at him sweetly.

"Our cell phone numbers are on the fridge!" Mrs. Mayfield says as her husband hurries her out the door, muttering things about being late. "OK!" you yell after her, imitating her exclamations. "Don't worry about us! Have a nice time!"

Their sporty family-sized van pulls out of the driveway, and you stand in the living room doorway and scan the perimeter for suspiciously placed teddy bears or plastic-y potted plants or non-functioning air purifiers—all prime disguises for nanny cams. There's just no trust these days. When you are satisfied that there are none, you stare at the twins. You get good money from babysitting so you pretend to like kids, but you really don't. Kids freak you out, these little goblin creatures with their short arms and legs, and their heads too big for their bodies, and food always smeared around their mouths and on their clothes. You don't like the way they look at you. Their eyes all animal and expectant. You never know what to say to them.

The goblin twins notice you watching and look at you. You look back at them. You look at each other.

With kids, you try to be as quiet and still and boring as possible so they don't start playing with you. You learned this the hard way, when you were too nice to a three-year-old and she kept bringing you empty cups from her miniature toy kitchen and expecting you to pretend to drink them while you were trying to watch one of the TV shows your parents had forbidden because "the teenagers climb in and out of each other's windows like they're revolving doors," which didn't set a good example.

"Proceed," you say to the goblins. You smile without licking your teeth and back slowly from the room.

You head straight for the pantry for a preliminary overview of the Mayfields' foodstuffs. You always hope for some new food you've never tried when you open the cabinets, something other than the carrot sticks your parents have at home, and the crackers with the seeds on them that always fall off into your hair before they make it to your mouth. You hope for potato chips, sleeves of cookies, full-fat mega-butter popcorn, cereal with marshmallows in it, anything covered in chocolate, anything involving cheese powder. The Mayfield's pantry, however, is stocked with canned vegetables, pasta, oatmeal, and rice cakes. The only moderately unhealthy thing is craisins, which are only unhealthy because eating too many can give you the runs. You frown at the shelves and move on to the freezer. All the way in the back, you find a carton of cookie dough ice cream. That will do. You earmark it in your mind for your naptime snack. Sometimes, you like to make yourself wait for things. If you anticipate it long enough, everything is more exciting. This applies to everything: food, birthdays, vacations, and orgasms.

You are not supposed to know that about the last of these. Two years ago, your parents made you go to the church's abstinence camp called *Save Yourself and Be Saved!* where you learned about how touching yourself is a sin (oops) and were forced to sign a chastity contract with God and place it in a floral-print heart-shaped box under the proud gazes of your parents and the pastor.

The best babysitting gigs are the ones where the family has movie channels that your parents do not have and would never let you watch anyway if they did have them, what with the un-dubbed cuss words and drug use and un-censored sex scenes showing the women's breasts and the men's butts. Of course, you can only watch these things when the goblins are young enough not to notice and not to be able to rat you out to their parents. At two years old, you judge that these are young enough.

The twins are still peacefully mouthing their blocks, and you locate the remote tucked beside the flat-screen TV and discover, to your immense pleasure, that the Mayfields have digital cable, and the kind where you can record TV shows and watch them later. You immediately go through their saved programs, hoping for something illicit. It appears that Mrs. Mayfield likes moving medical dramas and Mr. Mayfield enjoys hard-boiled crime shows. Typical. They also have a backlog of educational children's cartoons. Then, as you scroll farther down, you discover with a thrill that someone has a taste for soft-core porn. It is in clear view on the DVR menu, where Mrs. Mayfield can easily find it, not hidden at all. Maybe they watch it together, you consider. You imagine them putting the twins to bed at night, settling down on the cream-colored leather couch, selecting some soft-core to unwind and get in the mood. They keep the volume low so the children don't hear. Mrs. Mayfield's eyes are rapt and glossy on the bodies on the TV as her manicured hand slides onto Mr. Mayfield's crotch. Mr. Mayfield lets out a low, involuntary grunt as she slips her hand into his slacks and cups his testicles.

Last night, Carter Dobbs picked you up and took you to a movie. An early movie—5:30. Your parents had set your curfew at 9:00 and demanded to see the ticket stubs when you returned. They had also insisted on meeting Carter's parents before they let you start to date him, so your mother had invited the Dobbses over for Sunday brunch last month and you and Carter had sat rigidly on the couch with two feet separating you and your hands folded in your laps as your parents laughed politely at each other's jokes and asked each other questions about their occupations and what churches they go to. The consensus: they like each other, and you and Carter are allowed to go on one date a week. Last night, you bought tickets to a romantic comedy (rated PG-13, no R movies till you're seventeen), tore them in half, and got back in Carter's second-hand Volvo to drive to the Sack and make out.

The Sack is an empty cul-de-sac out on Lakeshore, past the Wal-Mart and the Home Depot, out on an emptied stretch of road between the town and the golf course. You all supposed that the Sack had been intended as part of a new housing development that never got finished. You could see where they had once cleared the trees from the radius of low growth that spread around the paved circle before the tall screens of dense pines closed in. There were no lights in the Sack, which made it perfect for stargazing and intimate liaisons. It also made it so you could see headlights coming far down the road and be prepared in case it was cops.

Carter parked and the two of you sat on the hood of his car listening to the plinking of the engine and smoking a joint he had stolen from his older brother. When you lay back on the hood, the stars were amazingly bright and Carter said, "It's like being inside a planetarium." Then you leaned over the top of him, replacing the stars with your face, and asked him the leading question: "Are my eyes like the stars?" He provided the correct answer, and then you made out. Your lungs had that full, floating feeling that they get when you smoke, and when you let him touch your boobs it felt like they were pumped up and buoyant like pool floaties, pulling you upward, floating you on the air. You made sure to make the appropriate sounds when he pinched your nipples and sucked on your neck, and you even let him put his hand down your pants. It excited you to have your shirt pushed up and your breasts out like that in the open air. You imagined shadowed people watching from the trees and arched your back upwards like you had seen in movies. If Carter had remembered to leave the radio on in his car, it would have been perfect. But you stopped him before he took your pants off.

You eye the goblins, who are paying no attention to the TV, and choose one of the movies that has already been watched so as to not leave a trace. You aren't going to watch it right there in front of the children. You just want a preview. Something to tide you over till naptime. You select one called *2001: A Sex Odyssey*, with a description reading: "Lost in space, a man and woman must procreate to save Earth." To your knowledge, this has little to nothing in common with the plot of the original movie, but you select it anyway. A parental control screen pops up asking for the four-digit passcode, and you roll your eyes. These are always either 0000 or 9999. Sometimes 1234. Easy-peasy. But none of these work. The Mayfields have a better system than most. You try several more combinations until you get nervous that the parental controls might have some sort of mechanism that locks you out if you get it wrong too many times, and how would you explain that to the Mayfields? You give up and choose one of Mrs. Mayfield's medical dramas instead. The especially graphic ones are almost as good as watching sex.

The morning goes well. The twins play peacefully on the floor, only occasionally bothering you with toys and requests for milk or juice. You watch people get rolled into the ER with unlikely injuries— industrial piping thrust through their abdomens, pizza cutters lodged in their skulls. You watch the surgery scenes with the most interest, where they show simulated shots of opened abdomens, blood welling in the incisions, like digging somewhere with a high water table, before it is siphoned away with a vacuum instrument like the dentist uses to suck spit from your cheeks. In elementary school, when you found out the human body was seventy percent water you took it literally. You imagined your insides were a fleshy fish tank full of floating organs. You wondered how they didn't get tangled when you moved. Now, of course, you know better.

After you feed the children their green beans and their turkey dogs cut into half-moons—both of which they indiscriminately cover in ketchup, ignoring their silverware and eating with their fingers—you set them down for their nap and give them ten minutes to fall asleep before you turn on the TV. You are going to take another crack at the code. You grab a spoon and the carton of ice cream from the kitchen and try a few more combinations before chickening out again and selecting an artsy French film instead, the kind that sometimes shows dick. You mute the TV so as to not wake the goblins and fast-forward until you find a sex scene. The French protagonist is lying in the long grass beside a road with an American soldier on top of her, staring into her eyes and moving slowly in and out of her as if he's doing pushups. In the wide shot, you can see the man's ass flexing with each slow thrust. In the medium shot, the French girl's small breasts are visible, the skin undulating slightly like a waterbed as the man becomes more vigorous. In the tight shot, all you can see is the profiles of their faces, their lips open, their eyes staring intensely. They seem very serious, their movements very intentional. They say non sequiturs to each other in very calm voices as they do this. "It was a blue vase," the yellow subtitles say. "Were you sad?" the subtitles say. "No," the subtitles say.

You eat a few spoonfuls of ice cream, still too hard to really scoop, then pause the movie, which doesn't show anything you haven't already seen, and abscond to Mr. and Mrs. Mayfield's bedroom. You have high hopes, judging by their well-protected DVR collection. It burns you up that you couldn't figure out the code. But upon entering their bedroom, the deep burgundy bedspread, tasseled throw pillows, and dark wood furniture are promising. On the long, hip-high dresser, a wedding photo sits in preeminence over the other photos of family and vacations and the twins fresh out of the womb, wrapped in pink and blue hospital blankets so only their squinty purple faces show. Above the dresser, a large mirror hangs. It occurs to you that the mirror directly faces the bed, which is bad Zen, but maybe Mr. and Mrs. Mayfield did that on purpose to be able to watch themselves have sex. You crawl into the center of the bed to check out the view, and sure enough, you can see your whole body from any point on the bed. You bounce up and down on your knees for a moment. Kinky.

You then commence your search for illicit paraphernalia. Since the Mayfields have pornos in clear view on their DVR, you suspect that Mr. Mayfield is able to keep his magazines somewhere normally too accessible, like his sock drawer. But there is nothing there except socks. And nothing in the other drawers either. You check Mrs. Mayfield's panty drawer, thinking the porn is maybe her thing, that happens sometimes, but there is nothing there but panties. You think you are on to something when you open the wicker box beside the toilet in the master bath and see magazines peeking out from under the toilet paper and tampon boxes, but they're only things like *Home and Garden* and *Sports Illustrated*— and not even the swimsuit issue. The shoeboxes in the closet and under the bed hold shoes or receipts or old photos, nothing special. *They had presented so well!* you think, disappointed. And then you open the last shoebox of a stack of four at the bottom of the closet, hoping for sex devices, explicit love letters, anything. Inside are more photos.

You find a vagina, up-close, spread. It's shaved or waxed, and the lobes of it are deep red and shiny. You gasp, unprepared despite what you hoped to find inside. The shock of it is like looking up from a book and finding someone watching you. But you grab the box anyway and take the whole thing to the bed. You remove the photos carefully, one by one, spreading them in front of you in the order that they came out of the box so you can return them exactly as they were. You are good at this, memorizing the placement of things, erasing all traces of your passage.

The second picture is of breasts, the small, outward-pointing kind. The third is a man's penis gripped in a female hand. By the fourth, you have figured out for certain that these pictures are of the Mayfields themselves. You can tell by the burgundy bedspread underneath the body in the fourth picture, which is a point-of-view shot taken from the man's perspective of Mrs. Mayfield bent over the edge of the bed and Mr. Mayfield doing her from behind. You peer down at the bedspread you are presently sitting on and a small jolt shoots through your stomach like static electricity. You lay out a few more photos from the box, placing them carefully like tarot cards. This is more than you had ever expected or intended to find. The thrill of trespassing is magnificent. Your senses are heightened; you are aware of every movement, every sound in the house, even as you stare intently into the photographs.

Most of the photos don't include their faces. You wonder if this was on purpose or just because they were taken from so close-up that they had to choose between getting the face or the good bits in the frame. There are a few photos taken in the mirror to get full-body shots, but that's it. Somehow, it doesn't seem right to not have the faces. Without them, the pictures become anonymous, more like the diagrams of the human body in biology textbooks than the women posing in the *Playboys* and *Penthouses*. You want to see what Mrs. Mayfield's face looks like with her eyes closed and mouth open. You want to see Mr. Mayfield slack-jawed and red-cheeked. You want a video. You want more.

At this point, your heightened senses catch movement out of the corner of your eye, just a dark flicker outside the crack of the door. Your head flies up like a triggered net trap. You can feel your cheeks burning red like someone put a lit flashlight inside your mouth. There is nothing in the door, no face watching you, but you shovel the photos quickly into the box, probably out of order, toss it into the closet, and creep slowly to the door anyway, peering furtively into the hall. The door to the children's room, which you were sure you closed, is open. You walk as quickly and silently as you can and look inside to find the boy's bed empty, the bumpers still in place on the sides. Now you run through the entryway and dining room into the living room, and there stands the child, in the middle of the carpet, safe, peering up at the television screen on which the image of the French girl and American soldier having sex is frozen. The boy is not wearing clothes.

You grab for the remote and turn off the TV, erasing the image of the American soldier's bare ass. The child turns to you and smiles.

"What are you doing?" you say to the child. His response is to giggle and toddle toward you till he bumps against your legs, at which point he starts grabbing at your thighs, trying to crawl his way into your arms. You don't help him. You look down at him and are uncomfortably aware of his little penis bumping against your bare shin. It makes you feel like a perv, your awareness of it, hanging there like a snail without a shell. An image of his father's hardened penis flashes through your brain.

"*Where are your clothes?*" you hiss, wanting to find them and get them back on him as soon as possible.

"Took them off," the child says.

"I can see that." Your voice has a frantic edge to it. "Let's go find them, 'kay?"

You lead the boy back in the direction of his room by the hand, not wanting to pick him up when he's like that, him giggling the whole time. You locate his clothes at the foot of his bumpered twin bed, suspecting he must have escaped via the unguarded end of the bed. The girl child is sitting up in bed now, and seeing her brother naked, she starts taking off her clothes, too. She pulls up her shirt, revealing small androgynous nipples.

"No, no, no, no, no," you say, letting go of the boy's hand to pull her shirt back down. "Not funny," you say. "Big girls wear clothes," you say. When the girl's shirt stays down, you put the boy's clothes back on and re-tuck them both into bed. This time, you stand there with your hands on your hips until they are definitely asleep.

When you return to the living room, the ice cream you forgot to return to the freezer is melted into a creamy moat around the corners and the carton is getting soggy. You put it back in its spot at the back of the freezer, yank off a handful of paper towels to clean up the ring of condensation on the side table, and find you're too afraid to finish watching the French film. You wonder if you've ruined the boy with that one image of artsy sex. Instead, you return to the medical show and watch some more organs get placed in metal, kidney-shaped dishes, on mute.

After naptime, you take the children into the backyard to play. They dig holes in the ground with red and blue plastic shovels, and you wonder what they are looking for or if they just like digging holes. You are afraid that if you let your eyes off them for a minute, they'll start taking off their clothes again, this time in full view of the neighboring yards. So you watch them as the boy continues digging and the girl toddles off to find fallen twigs and pull up handfuls of grass, which she then deposits in the boy's hole, which he then covers with soil, hiding it in the ground. *Teamwork*, you think. *I hope I don't have to bathe them*, you think. You would have to take their clothes off. You decide wet wipes will do. You thank God that they are already potty trained.

Later in the afternoon, after cleaning the dirt from their hands, from under their black nails small as fish scales, you sit them in front of the TV and turn on a cartoon. You have decided to not even watch the medical show in front of them, afraid of them seeing the blood, the strange and gruesome rashes, the clean iodine-swiped incisions, the rubbery pull of skin spread with forceps. You watch a cartoon in which a little girl asks questions to the children through the screen and waits for them to respond, which these children don't, and when the gaps of silence start to get to you, the cartoon face's eyes blinking at you in expectation, you locate a *Cosmo* in the mail on the dining room table and settle down on the couch to read it. You flip to the sex advice column and read about women whose men want them to role play, but it makes them uncomfortable; women whose men want them to have a threesome, even if it's with another man; women considering plastic surgery. The general advice is always: *Trust is key. Communication is key. Sex is fun! Have fun with it.*

This is all well and good, but really you need a *Cosmo Girl*, or an older sister. You have been scrutinizing the diagrams on instructions in tampon boxes to try to get the layout of your insides. You know how to work a tampon, of course; you got your period a year and a half ago, before which you had asked your girlfriends naïve questions about menstruation like, "How do you tell when it's going to happen? Does it feel like you have to pee?" But you want to know exactly where Carter's penis will go, how it will fit in there, how close it will get to your uterus, that organ you had never felt until it cramped like a loose fist suddenly closed.

You accidentally overheard your parents having sex the other week, your mom five months pregnant. It made your stomach feel like it was bobbing in the water you used to imagine filled your insides, and then a huge wave had just come and drowned it. You tried not to imagine it—your father and mother having sex, and how close—you can't even say it—how close *it* would come to the baby, which actually *was* floating around inside your mother, in a sack of amniotic fluid. You know this from the movie the school nurse shows every year before prom, the one that shows pregnancy from conception to birth, playing suspenseful space-adventure music as the sperm swim up the vaginal canal and burrow into the translucent skin of the egg, and some sort of pan flute world music during the horrendous, bloody birth. Yes, it showed the entire birth, head cresting and all, and the nurse would say, "You don't want to look at it, do you? It's ugly, isn't it? Think about that on prom night," and while everyone else put their hands over their eyes or laid their heads on their desks, you stared horrified, enthralled, as the woman's vagina stretched like a rubber band and the baby's dark-haired head crowned in a way that reminded you, for some reason, of a solar eclipse. It seemed impossible that that was you once, coming from there, covered in goo, mucusy plugs having to be sucked from your throat and nostrils. You and Carter would use protection when you finally did it, for sure. You wonder if the fetus of your little brother could feel the movement when your parents did it, if his curled body got ebbed up and down on amniotic shockwaves.

The goblins are giggling, but you ignore them and flip to the article on six new ways to please your man. When the giggling escalates, it becomes apparent they are up to something, and you look up from the magazine to find the boy and girl with their tongues stuck out of their mouths, tense and pointed at the tip. And then they touch their tongues together. And then they giggle.

They do this several more times while you are frozen in horror. Many things run through your mind, the first of which is *How do I make it stop*; the second, *Is this my fault*; the last, *Is this my problem?* It is innocent, of course. They don't know what they're doing. They probably saw their parents frenching and got the idea from them. Is this the age when they start exploring their bodies? This is normal. Is this normal? Do you have to report this to their parents? Should you intervene?

You watch the flexed muscles of their tongues pointed at each other like fingers, green and orange from the Jell-O cups they had for snack, as they once more make contact, and then you spring into action. You drive yourself between them, saying, yelling, "No! No! Good boys and girls don't do that! Germs! Yucky! Germs!" It occurs to you that this is perhaps why their mother speaks in exclamations, in a perpetual state of panic by default. When it appears they have stopped, you sit backwards and remove your hands from their shoulders. You stare at them for another few seconds to make sure they're finished, their eyes too big for their heads blinking at you, and then you say, "Good children," and return to the couch.

As soon as you sit down, they lunge at each other and do it again.

This time you fly between them and grab their thrust-out tongues, pinching them between your thumb and the knuckle of your index finger with each hand. They squeal simultaneously, but you don't let go. You hold their tongues, firm, not trying to hurt them—but maybe hurting them—and look into each of their wide blue eyes as you say, forcefully, "No! You hear me? No. Don't do that. Tongues are for keeping in your mouths."

The boy starts crying first, and then the girl joins in, their wails muffled by the tongues still pulled from their mouths in your fingers.

"Are you done?" you say to them. "Nod if you aren't going to do that anymore." They both nod through their tears. You let them go.

One of them, the girl, hits you in the shoulder with her miniscule but dense fist, and you don't stop her. You sit on the floor with them as they cry, and there is a feeling in your chest cavity, that water in your abdomen swollen to flood level. You can hear it inside the swirl of your ear—the rushing of a river.

But no, you know better. That sound is the sound of your own blood.

The children are starting to quiet down. You rub their backs softly. You say, "Hey, it's OK. Don't cry. Just don't do that again. It's OK."

You play with them for the remainder of the night, sitting on the floor until your legs fall asleep and your butt goes numb, afraid to leave them even to go to the couch. Then you order the pizza—no sausage—for dinner, cut it into bite-sized pieces, and watch them put the pieces in their dark mouths with their messy fingers covered in tomato sauce and saliva. It's like watching animals eat, this is. The children unaware of table manners and the proper use of silverware. But when you eat your own slice, you pick it up with your hands and take large, messy bites, wipe your mouth with the back of your hand, lick your fingers clean.

After cleaning their faces and helping them brush their miniature teeth with their miniature toothbrushes, you read the children a book, sitting in the rocking chair between their beds. They both hug you when you tuck them in, and you find yourself smiling at them. You feel a swelling in you of something like protectiveness, like your lungs are an airplane life vest that someone's just inflated. It is an uncomfortable feeling, not quite pleasant, but you allow it to happen.

You wait till their breathing is steady and slow, and then you return to their parents' room to try to replace the photos into their previous order. You fan them in front of you again, trying to remember your progression of discovery—the vagina, the penis, then the breasts; or the vagina, the breasts, and then the penis? This time, when you look at them spread out on the bed, you see the way Mr. Mayfield's dark, curly leg hair gradually fades out at the thighs, leaving them a pale, vulnerable white like the belly of a frog. You see how Mrs. Mayfield's hips and stomach are emblazoned with pink stretch marks, thin and branching like maps of deltas where they meet the sea, like she is emptying into something. You pick them up gingerly by the corners as you re-order them, and that's when you see the next picture, the one you hadn't had time to see before.

It's the husband's face, just like you thought you wanted to see. It is taken from the wife's perspective, of her husband above her, the ceiling fan motionless behind his head off-center in the bottom left corner of the frame. His face is caught in what looks like mid-orgasm, looking straight at the camera. His eyes are wide open, his brows raised, his mouth limply parted. The expression is one of surprise pain. You have seen it before in movies watched on other televisions, on the faces of people who have just been shot through the head, before the blood starts running in their eyes and they slide down the wall; on the faces of soldiers whose legs have been blasted out beneath them; on horror movie victims who have just been gutted, their insides falling in wet ropes to their knees. You read once in a magazine from the bathroom of another house that the French call orgasms *la petite mort*—the little death. Looking at Mr. Mayfield's eyes, open and lit up with emptiness—looking not at the camera but past it, past Mrs. Mayfield, past the burgundy bedspread—that suddenly makes sense. You can't tell if he is seeing something somewhere else, something only visible for that moment, caught and forgotten between the raptured flutter of eyelids, or if he is seeing nothing at all.

You don't want to look at the photos anymore. You pack them carefully, one by one, back into the box in the order they came out. You replace the shoebox exactly where it was when you found it, under three other shoeboxes in the closet, the side with the shoe size facing out. You should look in on the children, make sure they're safe in bed. Yes, that's what you'll do.

On your way out, you smooth the bedspread. Straighten a photo. Close the door.

CHANCE

Peter Ho Davies

THERE WAS A CHANCE the baby was normal. There was a chance the baby was not.

Fetus, he told himself.

There was a chance the fetus was normal. There was a chance that it was not.

She, he told himself. That was the result of one of the tests on the fetus.

There was a chance that she was normal. There was a chance that she was not.

Jesus.

No one could tell them the exact odds, but there was a small chance the baby was normal. A tiny chance. BB-sized. No bigger than a bean. And there was a large chance she was not. A full-grown, adult-sized chance. Big as a whale, big as a house.

"Stretch marks," his wife said, gazing at the pregnant women across the waiting room like distant mountains. "That's what I used to be afraid of."

The chances of what was wrong with the baby being wrong with the baby had been a million to one.

Before the test.

Except there was still that tiny chance it was wrong.

A million to one was a figure of speech, he knew. The condition was so rare there were no reliable statistics. It was so rare the genetic counselor hesitated to put a number on it. *But if you press me.* Fifty or sixty cases world-wide. Ever. So rare that even after a positive test the doctors couldn't be sure the baby had it. But they thought so.

He was a writer now, this father, but he had studied physics once—the science of the unimaginably vast and the unimaginably small, as one of his professors boasted—and still the numbers meant nothing to him. Unimaginable. He didn't like that word—as a writer, had a professional dislike of it. Sometimes, he wondered if the baby would grow up to be a scientist. If the baby might make sense of the numbers. What would the baby say in his place, what would the baby decide?

The list of things the baby might have was four pages long. Single-spaced. The list was not numbered. When he cried and stared at it, blurred, it looked like poetry, free verse. Short lines, long lines, run-on lines. He couldn't make any more sense of it than language poetry. He would start to read, and a page in, or less, his mind would drift. Perhaps the baby would be a poet. He felt proud of himself that he wanted the baby to be smarter than him, better than him.

There was a chance the baby would be a poet or a scientist. There was a chance it would die in the womb, live a few hours or days or months in pain. Unimaginable pain.

It was June. The due date was December 7th. "A date which will live in infancy," they'd joked.

Then it was July.

"Chances are, it's not hereditary," the genetic counselor counseled them. She deftly drew the elongated chromosomes upside down on a pad between them. "More likely a spontaneous mutation. A random copying error during meiosis—cell division."

He nodded rapidly. He wanted to tell her he used to be a scientist.

"A freak," he agreed, and her face, radiant with concern, flickered.

"Just bad luck," she said with the infinite care of diagnosis. "Very bad luck."

There was a day care center down the street. He jogged past it every day. The kids in the little playground. They'd thought it would be convenient, his wife and he. *Lucky*, they'd said.

They'd been used to thinking of themselves as lucky, until a couple of years earlier. They'd just bought their first house, taken a week to unpack, hung the last pictures, shelved the last books, gone away for the weekend. A pipe had burst, a $1.99 plastic tube running into the base of the toilet tank. When they came home, water was running from the light fixture onto the dining table, like a fountain. Water was running down the bulging walls, it was running *behind* the paint like veins. For days they watched dark brown seams spread across the ceiling.

He'd felt like it was God's fault. He'd felt as if it had been hubris to buy a house. It was the worst thing that had ever happened to them in their life together. And yet months later, when they had a much nicer house, they'd kidded each other, *Thank God for insurance.*

They had wanted the house to start a family. They had worried about a child drawing on the bright new walls.

He didn't fault God for the baby. He didn't believe in Him. Couldn't imagine Him. The numbers were too big. They dwarfed God.

They couldn't know—no one could—so they decided, this mother and father. Someone had to and, in the absence of God, it was them. They waited as long as they could. They waited for more tests. They waited with hope, but not hope of good news. The later tests couldn't refute the old ones. The best the new tests could do was confirm the worst. So that is what they found themselves hoping for, as they held hands. The worst.

"Do you ever wish we hadn't done any tests?" he asked her and she squeezed his hand so tightly he felt the bones must fuse.

The tests were inconclusive.

So they had decided anyway.

And that was all months ago. The baby would have been born by now. They'd have taken the baby home from the hospital by now. The baby's grandparents would have visited by now. The baby would be smiling by now.

Months ago. They were licking their wounds. They were gardening for the first time in their lives, the sunlight heavy on their shoulders and necks. They were starting to tell people they might try again—trying out the idea of trying again, the words ashy on their tongues. They told their friends, the ones who, even though they knew the truth, said encouraging things like, "So-and-so had a miscarriage; they tried again."

Once, in bed, in the dark, his wife had whispered to him, "I *wish* we'd had a miscarriage."

It was just a thing people did, he knew. By the kind of chance he was growing numb to, the rhetorical figure was known as *meiosis*. Calling one thing something else, something safer. It made his wife furious, but to him it seemed only human, as if the events, the circumstances, so rare, so unheard of, shouldn't have a name. Perhaps in ten years, he thought, it's what we'll say. "We had a miscarriage." It seemed so easy to spare themselves explaining it again, over and over. Perhaps it was what they'd even say to another child, if they had another child. And then he knew it *was* what they'd say, because how could you say what really happened to a child, your own child. If you had another child.

Cars with pro-life bumper stickers were everywhere on the roads that election year. *93% of women regret their abortion. If Mary was Pro-Choice there'd be no Christmas. What part of Thou Shalt Not Kill don't you understand?* His wife tailed one to a convenience store, followed the driver, a woman, inside. "I wanted to tell her how she made me feel. I was going to, and then I saw her at the register. Know what she was buying? Lotto tickets." They laughed until they cried.

The next week he saw one that read, *The Number of the Beast? 50 Million Abortions*, and found himself, despite himself, coldly comforted. For once the numbers seemed with him.

"Will you write about it?" his wife asked. It was his way of making sense. "You can, if you want."

But he didn't know how to make a story of it. The odds were too long. The case too special. "People would only believe it if it was true."

"Non-fiction, then."

He shook his head so slightly it felt like a shiver. "It's too shameful," he whispered. "Not *that*," he called after her. "Too shameful to be this unlucky, I mean."

He stared at the white of the walls. Ashamed, and ashamed of his own shame.

If he ever did write the story, he thought, there was a chance that it would be true, a chance that it would be not. A story, at least, could be both.

He rejoined his poker game. Not a game of chance, he knew. But now when he lost a hand, the winner apologized: *Bad beat, man.* The next week, he started playing online. He had always been a good player—good with numbers from his physics days—but he played badly now. Drew to inside straights, chased cards. He figured he was due some luck. But when he told his wife, when she saw the bills, she said, "You think that'd make up for it? You think that'd make it better?" And he quit. But he could tell she thought they were due something too.

There was a chance the baby was normal, he told himself. There was a chance the baby was not.

Even now they didn't know for sure. But they could if they wanted. Somebody did, somebody somewhere in a white coat, in a lab. There had been more tests. Afterwards. *Post-*. Finally, the definitive tests could be done. They had agreed to them. *If it helps science, they said. If it might help other parents some day. If some good could come out of this.* There were results to these tests and they were conclusive. And they were out there in some file, just waiting to be asked for. "Whenever you want to know, or never," the genetic counselor told them.

Were they those "other" parents now? Was it "some day"?

They talked about trying again, but they didn't. Trying again, she said, just didn't feel like anything they'd ever tried before. Instead, they talked about the results, whether they wanted them. They couldn't decide about the results. They could decide about the baby, but they couldn't decide about the results. It felt like a cruelty that the results existed. It felt like someone out there with a gun. They had agreed about everything, but now, sometimes, they disagreed.

She wanted the results, and he didn't, just as once and for a year or two she'd wanted a child and he hadn't. Perhaps she thought he'd come around again.

"Someone knows," she said. "Some doctor, some technician. If they know I want to know." It was the same argument she'd used when talking about finding out the baby's sex. It had made sense to him then.

"I can't bear it," she said. "The not knowing. How can you bear it?"

He had been a scientist. Could have been one. It was the path not taken. At parties he used to joke that he was a "lapsed" physicist: *a bit like being a lapsed Catholic. They still feel guilt; I still feel gravity.* All he remembered of his physics now was the uncertainty principle, and the famous thought experiment about Schrödinger's cat. The cat in a box with a vial of poison. The poison to be released by a random radioactive decay. According to the physics the decay might or might not have happened until the physicist looked in the box. Only then, only when observed, would the cat be finally either dead or alive. He was thinking, of course, of the baby in the box. Wriggling. Squirming. Heart racing. The gray, grainy baby from the ultrasound that his wife still had somewhere in the house, not exactly hidden away, but put somewhere he wouldn't stumble upon, somewhere he'd have to ask her where it was, as if she were protecting it from him. When he imagined having sex with his wife again, he pictured the milky ghost of his penis, entering her swirling, snowy womb as if on the monitor at the doctor's office. It looked very cold in there.

He thought of the results. If they got them the baby would be normal, or the baby would not. Issue settled. But he couldn't do it, couldn't ask for the tests.

All he could think of was the old physics line:

How can you know the fate of Schrödinger's cat without looking in the box?

Throw it in the river. If it floats, the cat's a witch.

He wanted that box to stay shut.

"But why?" his wife implored.

He couldn't tell her.

Why, why, why, like steps, receding.

Not because if the baby was normal, it would make things worse (though it would).

But because, even if the baby wasn't, it wouldn't make things better. He didn't *want* to be relieved of this shame, when it was all he could feel, all he was allowed to. All he had left to remember her by.

That was why.

Because the baby was already dead.

There was a chance the baby was normal. There was a chance—tiny and miraculous—that they had killed their baby.

Here was a thing about numbers, he thought for years after. The chance of a flipped coin coming up heads a hundred times is a half times a half times a half one hundred times. Astronomical. But on one flip, the first or the hundredth, the chances of heads are still just 50-50. The coin doesn't care how it's fallen ninety-nine times before. The coin doesn't give a fuck. That's what it is to be random. That's what chance is.

JADEDRAGON_77

Stephanie Dickinson

IF I HEAR THE SONG in my running dreams, then I fly, or I lift the ceiling and take off through it. When I hear the song awake I know something is about to happen. My eardrums tickle. Suddenly the sleep music stops and the door opens part way. Here in the dormitory at Crippled Children's Hospital and School there aren't any locks. It's Saturday and I'm in my nightgown. I sit up on my bed and dig my fingers into my calves that feel spongy, not like the strong legs I used to tap dance with.

"Is Rose about?" a guy's voice asks. "I'm her brother Wiley." He pushes the door in all the way and stands next to Rose's desk rubbing his hands together. The fringes of his suede jacket look frozen as icicles. He's tall.

"She's in the hospital with chicken pox," I say, reaching for my wheelchair parked beside the bed. "Quarantined."

The hospital is in another building separate from the school dormitory. Rose has multiple sclerosis and we've roomed together since the eighth grade and now we're juniors. There's not a kinder or smarter person on Earth. It must have been because she was born on the Reservation that she'd missed her chickenpox vaccination.

"You're Jana, right?" he asks the air. Unless he comes in farther he can't see me.

"Wrong. I'm 77." I glance over at the empty bed across the stretch of gray-pink flecked linoleum where strewn clothes look like they're trying to run away. The floor seeps heat no matter how cold the room is. Like summer in Destoroyah not winter in Sioux

Falls, South Dakota. My alter ego is JadeDragon_77, a female warrior from the Temple of Godzilla. I love Godzilla movies.

He chuckles, walking deeper into the messy room and finding out for himself Rose isn't there. Snow is melting from his silver-tipped boots, drooling puddles on the linoleum. He glances in my direction and then does a double take. His mouth falls open. I'm wearing a red sleeveless nightgown that pictures a smiling cat and the words Hello Kitty. It doesn't look that bad. It hits just below the knee. His jacket's sleeves smell like they're thawing. Rose told everyone for months he was coming. Everyone knows how proud she is of her brother graduating from law school at the University of Wyoming. Big shit Wiley who didn't show up for Thanksgiving or Christmas or her birthday. They forgive him for everything because his fiancée was abducted from a mall parking lot and killed. But that was years ago. Wiley is the first Barking Moose to finish high school, college, then law school. By this time next year Rose will be the second Barking Moose to graduate from high school. I'm usually the smartest person in every gathering. That's why I know better than to put in hours studying. Why I read only what interests me. They scraped Crippled Children's faculty from the bottom of South Dakota's pedagogic barrel: geriatric substitute teachers and PE coaches dismissed for cause from regular schools.

"Well, aren't you going to ask how your sister is?" I say.

He pulls the tie out of his ponytail and shakes his hair free, like a black horse stumbling up rimrock, finding its footing, then banding it back up again. His eyes are the same as Rose's, without pupils or irises, just solid black suns that could heat whatever they looked at. Like the strike and slam of black flint.

"How is she?" he asks, craning to look at the pyramid of Coke cans taped together to resemble the great pyramid in the Valley of Kings. Then he seems to be studying me. "Rose told me about you." His glance of a second ago turns into a staring contest. Who will blink first? "My sister said you were very pretty."

I wonder how he heard that since he never visits or calls. I drop my legs over the side of the bed. My nightie bunches up and I notice him noticing the dirty bottoms of my feet. Check out the linoleum floor if you wonder why. I need to transfer into my chair but that's my business how I get from bed into my wheelchair. I don't want to do it in front of him. He slips his hand into his jean pocket and digs for keys. "Can you show me where the hospital is?" he asks. My cheeks burn and I tell him I have to get dressed first. He can ask one of the aides to show him or he can wait outside in the hall.

After I've changed into my JadeDragon_77 T-shirt and jeans, I roll out barefoot into the hall and find Wiley waiting. He knows from being around his sister how to walk alongside a wheelchair girl and not push in a bum's rush. I lead him through the tunnel that intersects the physical therapy rooms and the hospital facility. There's the click of Canadian canes, the thump of crutches. The parallel bars they torture you on. As long as you can walk, no matter if you do it like a crab, you're better off. No thank you. I sit in a wheelchair and move myself along with my feet. I hate wearing socks and shoes, but in winter when I go outside I compromise and wear clogs.

"Hey 77," the physical therapist Wesley Snobel says to me, smiling. He seems to be on his way to the soda machine in the hospital lobby. A large-bodied, square-headed man with brown eyes and frame glasses, a goofy grin takes up most of his lower face. "I missed you in Wednesday's gym class." Well, I sure didn't miss him or the class where they make gimps play ping pong or badminton. The A.B. aides have to run all over for the balls and birdies. "Remember, 77, if you want to graduate with your class, physical education is mandatory."

I roll my eyes.

He gives Wiley Barking Moose the once over and waits expecting me to make an introduction. If he expects that, he'll have a long wait. I roll into the hospital lobby where Eleanor Peglog sits at reception. Wiley follows. Wesley Snobel must put two and two together and at least come up with five. "Oh, you must be one of

Rose's relatives," he lights up, "but sorry you won't be able to see her. Chicken pox is a communicable disease. There are students around here who might not survive a bout of it." Then he gives me a meaningful look and addresses himself again to Wiley. "Mrs. Peglog will tell you the same thing. We take extreme care. Our students come first. And, 77, put some shoes on."

We enter the butter-pat-sized lobby of the twenty-bed hospital that adjoins Crippled Children's school. Mrs. Pegleg wearing her purple eye shadow and candy striper uniform queens the security desk. She reminds me a little of my other icon Tammy Faye Baker of the PTL (Praise the Lord) Club. Wiley explains who he is and how he wants to visit his sister.

"No can do, Mister Barking Moose. Rose is in quarantine. Absolutely no visitors," she says, batting her eyelashes like mascara-drenched spiders. I think of Godzilla vs. Hedorah. The alien Hedorah evolves into an amphibian and his gigantic tongue licks the pollution from the air. He fattens on plastic bags and sludge. Mrs. Peglog and Wesley Snobel remind me of the poisonous emissions of Hedorah.

"What a drag," Wiley says, reaching into his jacket for gum and offers me something fruit-striped. I fold a stick into my mouth. "I'm sorry for waking you," he apologizes, then takes hold of the grip bars on my chair and pushes me down the hall, hurtling me along. I thought he knew better. You couldn't count on people. Like Rose couldn't count on Wiley. The only thing you can do with people is trick them. When we reach the elevator he lets go of my chair. From the side his jaw juts. Like the photograph of Crazy Horse on his pinto, his nose high and sharp.

"Would you mind taking me to Dunkin Donuts?" I ask. "I like the coffee there with real cream." That is what they cleared off the Cheyenne and Crow and Oglala Sioux to build.

The elevator opens and he pushes me inside. He hesitates. "I don't know where Dunkin Donuts is. And you'd have to put socks on and get a coat if I said yes. Really, I need to get going."

"Well, where are you going?"

He looks like he's deciding whether to answer. The horses are stumbling on the rimrock. "Near Pipestone. I have a cabin there. I'm going to hole up for a month and study for my bar exam."

"You mean if they'd let us in to see Rose this is all the longer you would stay? She thought she could count on you for Thanksgiving." I push the hair out of my face. "I need to get going too. But I never get to go anywhere!"

He takes the gum out of his mouth and balls it into the wrapper and looks for a wastebasket, then apologizes for being in a hurry. "How old are you?"

I shrug. "How old are you?"

"Twenty-six," he answers.

"I'm sixteen."

His eyes spark, but deep inside like flints striking. Like you could fall a long way into them before you hit bottom. "You have to get your coat, 77. It's about ten degrees outside."

Sixteen is the age of consent in South Dakota. At sixteen you can drop out of high school. You can marry. I don't bother with the sign-out sheet next to the front door.

Wind blows across the crusts of old snow in the parking lot. All the dirty snow reminds me of how my eyes roll back when I'm asleep, and because the muscles in my lids don't work properly they can't close all the way. It is how the dead sleep. And I imagine when Godzilla dozes his eyes roll back like milk buckets. Wiley pushes me in my wheelchair to the oldest Ford pickup in the lot. The hood must have been replaced because it's yellow while the rest of the truck is a deep indigo blue. The fenders and grill and headlight caps shine. I like that. How people care for their things means a great deal to me. He opens the passenger's door then lifts me into the cab. I don't feel him brace himself or stagger. I smell clay and scrub-brush. In the side mirror I watch him roll my chair around to the back and lift it. He doesn't slam or bounce it. Two feathers hang from Wiley's rearview, one black, one grayish white. Instead of butts there are jellybeans in the ashtray. There's more smell of sage.

"Take a left on red, and Dunkin Donuts is on the right," I tell him. We pull into the only available space between a police cruiser and a tow truck. A cop sits in the passenger's seat and you can hear the radio crackling. Another policeman lumbers out of Dunkin Donuts. He's bald as a door knob and carrying two coffees and a donut bag along with his fat-ass citation book. His stomach wraps over his belt while he gives Wiley the twice over. The cop's eyebrows lift as he hurries over to circle around the blue Ford checking out its yellow hood, the University of Wyoming sticker, and finally the bed of the truck. Spotting the wheelchair, he really gawks. This time at me. I pretend to pick my nose. "Geez, that's quite a sight!" he bellows to his partner. Wiley grips the steering wheel, the nerve in his cheek twitching. The clouds have turned to dirty soapsuds and dishrags. I tell Wiley I changed my mind about going inside. I don't want the cops to bother him. The police in South Dakota don't like Indians. You'd think it was their people who got corralled into reservations.

"OK," Wiley says, tapping the dash, "so if you don't want coffee I'll take you back to Crippled Children's." His fingers remind me of creek water and smoke since they don't stay long in one place. But his eyes do. They keep looking at my face. I want him to think I'm pretty. People always tell me I am, but who believes them. They patronize.

I stare back at him. "You promised you'd take me for a ride. Are you really going to Pipestone?"

He watches the cop taking down his license tags. "No, Crooks, South Dakota. If you blink you miss it."

"I want to go too."

"I can't take you out on the highway," he says.

"Yes, you can. How far is it from here?"

"An hour."

"You mean you can't take an hour out of your life to drive me there and take another hour to drive me back? Rose would want me to see your house so I can tell her about it. I bet your sister never visited it." I look down at my hands, and then up at him as if beseeching, although JadeDragon_77 would never beseech or beg or say the bad word "please." The real bad word is "MD." Muscular Dystrophy. Onset in childhood. Muscle wasting. Shortened life span. Loss of ability to walk. The bad word is "Father." Who suffered from invisible MD, never telling my mother until he had to—the day I was diagnosed.

He makes a turn in the seat, reaches into the ashtray for the red jellybeans, offers me some. I take two. I like him. "Listen, I usually don't carry passengers. I brought you here because it's not far."

"Why? Because you were driving around while your fiancée got killed?"

There's a flash of lightning in his face, a clenching of his jaw. "I guess my sister told you that."

"No, she didn't," I lie. "I read minds."

"So you're clairvoyant?"

"I am."

But I'm not and Rose didn't tell me much because that subject is off-limits. I only know Wiley gave a friend of his a ride somewhere and when his fiancée finished shopping he wasn't there to pick her up. That's when the man stepped out of his nothingness and pulled his knife and forced her into his car.

The snow is about to fall into the noon twilight and stir up the wind. The sky holds its breath. I feel free in Wiley's truck, being this high up, the wheels under me. I like how he drives, his left boot stepping on the clutch, his right hand shifting. First, second, third gear. He never pops the clutch. I show Wiley a photograph of my family. It just happened to be forgotten in my jacket pocket. We're stopped at a red light in a tiny town. A grain elevator and a beer tavern, a four-way stop sign. There's my parents. My black-haired brothers look almost as Lakota as Wiley except they're seated on a couch surrounded by pale blue carpet instead of stuck in a camper heated by propane. "Was this you?" he asks, pointing to the unsmiling girl sitting on the carpet. "You were a prim little thing." I chuckle.

The little town disappears and we drive into more country. The early afternoon light is sinking into the ramshackle fields. Soon dark will creep up from the ditches. Winter light is more vivid than summer light. It knows when it's about to die. The heater doesn't work well and the windshield keeps icing over. The temperature must be dropping.

"How many kids are you eventually going to have, Wiley?" I ask.

"Zero," he tells me and then pulls over onto the shoulder and gets out with the ice scraper to clear the windshield wipers. His breath is white when he jumps back inside. "Remember I almost was married," he says, his strong jaw clenching, "and I won't go near that again." He owns a little house in the woods where South Dakota almost becomes Minnesota. He and his fiancée Liliane bought it when they were in college with leftover student aid money. An eyesore, they'd worked hard fixing it up. They never lived in it together. His fiancée was killed the summer after their junior year. At first he thought she'd come back, that she'd just forgotten herself and somehow disappeared. He hoped, prayed to his ancestors for Liliane to still be alive. Then police revealed that a man's face captured by mall security cameras the afternoon she vanished was of a recently paroled sex offender. Video showed the man lighting a new cigarette from the old one like the cigarette was his air and he had to keep one going to breathe. Joe Hawk. Age 40. His jerky hands, his entire body had a confused, startled look. Joe Hawk denied having anything to do with Liliane. There was no real evidence. The police questioned whether Liliane was even dead. Wiley drank too much after that. Then one day while driving his Toyota he was broadsided by a woman living in her car with her vodka bottle and eighty-year-old mother. She'd barreled through the red light into him. "They were homeless. I wanted to hate them. I hated everyone for a while," he admitted. "But that crash woke me up. Hating only hurts the hater."

"Yesterday I hated my father, but most days I don't." When he asks me why I hate my father I shrug, changing the subject. "Does your gas gauge work? It says Empty. It has the whole time we've been driving. And the clock says 10:10. Is that the last time you bought gas?"

He laughs and I like his face even better. "Yes, it always reads Empty. We have plenty of gas to reach Crooks. There's an old guy who runs a gas station. I like to give him business."

If we run out of gas, that wouldn't be so bad. When I see the first snowflakes drifting down like torn Kleenex I scoot against the door and roll down the window to catch them. Cold soft. I taste it from my cupped hand. "Want some?" I ask him, extending my hand.

"You shouldn't be asking that of grown men, 77," he says, the laugh disappearing,

"You're putting on a disapproval face," I tell him. "Draggy teachers always wear them." I lean my head farther and farther out the window and wait for him to tell me to roll it up but he doesn't. I look into the side mirror wondering how my wheelchair is faring with cold falling through its spokes. The chair has powers. It doesn't exhale atomic fire like Godzilla, although its hide is tough and snakes can't swallow it. And it's like a horse too. The wheelchair wants to be cared for and remembers mistreatment. Here the cab's seat smells like brown leaves lying on damp earth streaked with clay. I roll the window up on my own.

"Your face is Lakota you know." He keeps looking at me, even the angles of his cheeks.

"What's it to you?" I say, feeling goosebumps in my stomach.

"It isn't anything to me. But you look like Liliane."

Like the dead girl who was native. I've always been told I look Indian by white people. But I don't, not really. Not my cheekbones or the color of my skin. I have brown almost black hair and brown, almond-shaped eyes. And I can't smile so I look solemn. Some of the kids think I'm stuck up. "Does your radio work?" I ask. It would be nice to watch the trees and fences go by and listen to music. The light might fade into the roofs of barns and the abandoned orchards in time to drums.

When he answers me his eyes are black snowflakes melting in the windshield. "It does but I like to hear myself think. I like to hear the thoughts of whatever is around me." Then almost as an afterthought he adds, "It took a year before Liliane's body was found by a boy digging for arrowheads."

Her death stayed silent like those of goats and sheep and cows. Her bones marked by a hunting knife and teeth. The hunger of small animals. I'm wondering about Joe Hawk and what happened to him after Liliane's body was found. The kind of stuff Wiley thinks seems to have a good deal to do with either his fiancée or his bar examination and how he expects to practice as a legal aid lawyer too. He studied on a scholarship set aside for a Lakota Sioux. He made his peace with Liliane's spirit. Do I know the Lakota have the shortest life expectancy of any peoples in the world? When native women go missing the authorities don't really look for them. Liliane would want him to help their tribe. He's going to pass the bar exam for her. That's one more reason he's going into the woods—to study and meditate. I'd like to make each moment I live in expand.

Is he trying to hear my thoughts? Probably not. He's not thinking about me at all. And why should he? I'm a kid. His sister's age. He's tolerating me like an older brother does. There's a funny light coming from the stubble poking through the old snow and from the farmhouses that look like no one has ever lived in them. I light a cigarette. A Virginia Slim or Virginia Slimes as I like to call them. They are the brand of cigarettes Godzilla smokes. I crack the window.

Wiley's head jerks to look at me. "What are you doing?"

"Relaxing."

"Put that thing out. That's death you've got in your mouth. Are you crazy?"

I toss the cigarette out watching it spark behind the truck. I think he cares about me like a little sister. He might not let Rose smoke either.

"You're quite the rebel," Wiley remarks, lifting his eyes into the rear view. "Liliane was too." He reaches into his jellybean ashtray and chooses the black licorice ones. He tells me nothing happened to Joe Hawk because the trail went cold after a year. The police even questioned him. Wiley took a lie detector test and passed. He took time off before law school to dig into the sex offender's past, following him around to bars and shopping malls, to rivers and fish houses. He had to let it go. Joe Hawk was part Oglala but never lived on the Res. Instead his white mother took care of him and still does. Wiley came to understand the sex offense on Joe Hawk's record came from his having had relations at age seventeen with his fifteen year old girlfriend. The rest of his trouble came from drugs. If Joe Hawk didn't do it, whoever killed Liliane was still out there.

Wiley reaches for a bottle of water, offers me a swallow. I take the bottle, swigging. "Do you mind me asking why you can't walk?" he asks.

I cough on a mouthful of water and a black jellybean. "Sure, I mind. Why would you think I wouldn't?"

"Because you look tough. Mysterious. Like the trees."

I wanted to ask what Liliane was like but he spoiled it with the same old question. The one everyone asks, although I like being compared to trees.

"I've got muscular dystrophy," I say, pressing my thumb into the cold of the window. "My father gave it to me although I don't blame him."

It was me not smiling that finally woke Richard, my father, up. I remember being ten years old in my camel-colored pleated skirt seated on the floor with legs to the side, as if riding the carpet side-saddle. The Siamese Sasha lies against my leg. For a moment the photographer focuses on me and the cat. He tells us we both have bewitching eyes. Ten is a peculiar age, awkward, but I had those long slanting lids and dark brown irises staring out so solemnly. A cat-girl. Behind me the stupid flocked Christmas tree and the blue stars and red satin covered balls. OK let's all smile. Big smile on the count of three. "Cheese, say cheese," the photographer commanded. I could see him thinking he'd have to get the cat of a girl to smile, to stop staring at him with those slow river eyes; she knew he needed get to his next house, his next appointment. Just get her to smile, like her two brothers Steve and Christian, honor society boys in cable-knit sweaters, like Sharon, the gap-toothed younger sister, grinning ear-to-ear. "Jana, would you look this way and say cheese." Maybe my eyes flashed, irritated because I was smiling, at least I thought I was. I could feel it in my cheeks and chin. He wanted me to show teeth. "Spaghetti, Jana, relax. Think spaghetti and say cheese." I was looking his way, and then I said cheese but the word didn't turn my mouth into white teeth. My father, sitting on the couch next to my mother, looked at me. In that moment he knew I had it. Earlier I'd seen him trip going up the steps into the living room. His leg gave out, then he immediately righted himself. I tore that photograph of my Christmas family into many pieces; I tore up the fireplace burning its gas log, the eggnog and fruitcake, a can of Redi-Whip, the ruby red goblets. I reminded my father of a Siamese cat too. I had the secret in me like he had it in him. I tore up the handsome father seated next to my fine-boned mother, who wore a turquoise skirt and cashmere sweater her lover had given her. I tore her up too. I tore up the tinsel tree with blue bulbs.

Crooks, South Dakota. Finally we're in Wiley's town, what there is of it. Chuck's Hideaway and the U.S. Post Office share space with a Happy Chef café. Snow is starting to blow sideways across the highway. We turn into Buck's Filling Station & Snacks where a haywagon collapses next to the storefront. The one Phillips 66 pump is fat and round and the sign says ADD $2 TO EVERY GALLON. Wiley gets out of the truck, walks with his arms straight down and close to his sides, his hands clenched. The wind takes the store's screen door and slams it.

I roll my window down when an old man shuffles out wearing a shabby brown cap with earflaps. "Sorry, partner, they retired me," he says. "Phillips 66 won't deliver gas. Nothing in the pump, Wiley." The old man's lip wrinkles, showing creases like a farmer's hands. "Maybe I've got one can of gas I can give you. I'll siphon it from my station wagon." Old Buck does his best but the gas in his car doesn't fill a quarter of the red can. Wiley thinks that might be enough to get us to his place Then he'll hitchhike to Pipestone and fill two cans. "You kids be careful," Buck says, holding onto Wiley's door. "There's a blizzard coming. It's about on top of us."

A blizzard. I'm thrilled. The wind blows even harder once we're back out on the two-lane highway and rattles the truck. It takes both of Wiley's hands to keep the vehicle on the road. The snow gives off a peculiar yellow color. It pings against the truck. All at once, everything blurs. Goes white. A white-out, the clouds spewing snow. The wind vulture starts to sing. Wiley hits his high beams. "OK, 77, you're my navigator. We're about a half mile from the turnoff for my place. I can't see the road. If you spot the ditch getting close call out. We're running on fumes. Let's hope we make it."

Sure, let's hope.

In the blowing snow the telephone lines strung between poles start to swing. Like jump ropes. I was good in elementary school at double jump rope. Skip. Hop. I liked the sound of rope smacking the ground. Another blast of wind shakes the truck. The windows vibrate. Wiley works the clutch, shifts us into high gear, and tries to ride it out. I tried to ride it out too when I started to fall down in seventh grade. I kept getting up. Are you all right, Miss Genevieve asked. I didn't answer. Another wind blast rocks us and the truck starts to sputter. We're going to try coasting. Gradually, we lose speed. We make the turn onto a gravel road. Barely. Then gravel catches the tires. Wiley steers us toward the shoulder. The truck is wounded. We stop.

"We're less than a quarter mile from my place," Wiley says in a rushed voice. "We can't stay here. We'll freeze. I'm going to carry you." There's fear in his voice, something I haven't heard before. He'll carry me on his back. I can hang on, can't I? Sure, I can hang on, but it will be easier to push me. Just get my wheelchair out of the back. I can help with my feet. The wheels will stick in the snow. No, you have to take my wheelchair or else leave me here. "Look your socks are so thin as to be nonexistent," he says. We argue. I don't want to be without my chair. If there's enough road I'll make it.

"That's not a warm coat. You're going to wear my hat." He buttons my suede jacket, and then he reaches behind the seat for a bag that holds old clothes. Stuff he donates to the Res. He ties a spare, long-sleeved shirt around my neck like a muffler and pulls a stocking hat on my head. I watch him tie another shirt around his neck and put on gloves.

"Try to keep your head down when the wind hits." He shoulders his door open.

It takes all of him to keep it ajar and slide himself out. I think of Crazy Horse. A Sioux too. I strap my purse over my shoulder. I feel happy. Far away from the house where I grew up. I don't see Wiley until the passenger's door swings wide and he jams my wheelchair against the seat. Somehow I slide out and he catches me and I land in my chair. The bite of the wind takes hold. My next breath is pulled from my nose. JadeDragon_77, a female warrior from the Temple of Godzilla, arrives. He pushes me into the stinging needles. I pull with my feet while snow flies into my mouth, sticks its fingers up my nose. I almost can't breathe. The chair sticks, won't move. I try to help more with my feet, but they're far away. I kick at the snow. I can't feel my feet. The wheels of my chair keep getting stuck in the snow. He's shouting into the wind of white ravens. "Not much farther! Doing OK?"

I'm trembling like the day I couldn't climb the stairs to my tap dance class. More white ravens. I hear wings beating and in the snow are the steps to Mr. Sells' practice room. He lived in a big old Victorian house in Pierre with a flight of stairs, and then a curve and up another flight. Beautiful wooden banisters carved with ring-necked pheasants, the state bird. My mother signed me up for ballet and tap lessons. That was before the X-link dominant gene derailed my future. I had just seen my first Godzilla movie.

Another shock of wind. I can't see anything. I can hear Mr. Sells talking about living in Paris or Barcelona, how soon he wanted to fly away, migrate to a soulful alive city. Pierre was isolated. Backwards. He filled his house with antiques and chairs you didn't dare sit in because the French Revolution was about to break out when they were built and the wood had rotted into green worms. And he had photographs of the most interesting woman in the world. Her face perched on the wall like a garishly feathered bird. Her eyes were mouths. Her lips looked as if glass had ripped them. She posed in a coat of leopard spots and walked two leopards on leashes. Mr. Sells wanted to live grand like that, but he'd studied dance at the University of South Dakota. He gave dance lessons in his mother's house. Her clutter everywhere except the practice room with its pristine floor.

The snow burns and in the wind Mrs. Sells' doilies and salt and pepper shakers tumble. I can't see. I don't know if we're moving, but I'm trying to help. My eyes tear and my lashes freeze together. Mr. Sells keeps calling from inside the wind. Gay and very nice, he's in his tap shoes on the hardwood floor buffed to a blond gloss. The snow hisses, "Slide leg forward, drop heel." Intermediate tap. Mostly white girls. I stand by the one Sioux girl who's been adopted by a wealthy couple. I stare at us in the mirror and see girls more alike than different. Then I'm at the bottom of the steps again. Class has already started. I grasp the banister to climb the stairs that a year ago I didn't have to think about. I shake, each step makes my legs quiver. Shaking, I hang on, and then lift my leg with my hands and set my foot on the next step. Mr. Sells has already closed the door; the taps are sliding over the floor, like tiny hammers, hitting hitting.

"77!" someone shouts.

Last stretch. He carries me through the snow into the gingerbread house.

Wiley's long fingers massage like they are soothing hungry spots. He's kneeling next to the couch and my feet are in his hands. My teeth chatter. He keeps rubbing my feet. I don't feel them. A candle is the only light and shadows left by other people creep over the ceiling. Wind howls. I still have feet. I just can't feel them, and then I do. He's staring over my head at the wind. The snow hitting the house sounds like rocks.

Wiley lets go of my feet. He stands. "This is what happens to a bad idea, 77. It gets worse. I knew I shouldn't have brought you along."

Where is it? I don't see it. He didn't abandon my chair, did he? Please. I lift my head. My wheelchair is next to the couch. Safe. He walks into the next room and comes back with blankets. He wraps me in one, covers me in another. I still feel the bitter cold. The candle's flame shivers.

"Can you feel your toes yet?" he asks, worried. "I've started a fire in the stove. I'm going to have to cut more wood to get us through the night. Then I'll make some tea." Smoke from burning wood fills the room. Through the haze the knotty pine walls look on. It feels like the dark eyes of deer are staring. Wiley's searching for a blanket to wrap himself in. He has to keep feeding the fire. "You could be frostbitten," he tells me when he returns.

I think about my feet in his hands.

He pulls a little table over and sets the cups down. There are fruits and vegetables painted on the pot. He seats himself in my wheelchair and we drink tea that tastes like rainwater. I know at this moment that I want him to love me. We stare at each other. Without saying anything we're playing the silence game. Who will look away first? The candle flickers in his face. A wick in each eye. "You're the first girl since Liliane in this house," he informs me, beckoning by not moving at all.

I can almost touch the little picture inside the frame on the end table. The murdered Lakota girl with dark mournful snowdrifts for eyes. The cold is too cold. Snow keeps rattling the windows. The wood-burning stove burns hot only for a few minutes. Like its smoke could curl down our throats and choke us, yet leave us ice-covered. My body shakes, the thin blankets aren't warm enough. He sits on the floor wrapped in a blanket with his back against the couch. I could touch his hair. Outside is the frozen world without leaves; the trees creak like attic stairs. Outside Godzilla fights the Snow Behemoth.

He hunches his shoulders and makes a pallet on the floor. "Are you cold, Jana? I like that name better than 77."

"Please, I'm freezing." I ask him to lie next to me on the couch I'm so cold. Please. Will it hurt for him to put his arms around me? I turn my back to him and he fits himself against me. He takes me in his arms. We lie against each other fully clothed holding the other's body heat close. Later, I'll remember dreaming of snow and Mr. Sells and the snow hitting like tiny hammers. I'll shake in Wiley's arms as Mr. Sells has me sit; he'll sense my whole body trembling and my fingers looking for a hand railing, a wall, anything. He wants to call a doctor. No doctor. No doctor. I'll be all right. I slip off my flats and wiggle my foot into my tap shoes. Wiley breathes on the back of my neck, buries his nose in my hair. I'm a cold pane of glass iced over and where he breathes the ice melts. The snow is angry and I like it howling.

"If we take our clothes off we'll be warmer," I stammer, rolling over to face him. He pushes the hair out of my eyes, brushes my cheek with his knuckles, and tells me it's not a good idea. I'm a kid and he's a man. "I am expected to live only six more years," I say with a catch in my throat. "I heard the doctor tell that to my mom. They're my six years and I'll never do anything again I don't want to. But I want good things to happen too." I want him to kiss me, more than I want to wake up in the morning. More than I want to walk again. I breathe in his skin's smell of sagebrush. Won't you take me far away from the world?

"Sleep, Jana. Just sleep. I don't want you to come to harm."

"But I'm already harmed." I think of his fiancée's killer Joe Hawk, his footsteps in the snow. The bringer of harm. Then, miraculously, his footsteps shuffle away. I listen, following them into the snow, the footsteps dragging something. The Big Dipper is spilling tiny drops of snow onto me, tickling my belly.

"You just don't want to kiss me because I'm a gimp," I accuse. Then I feel his lips on mine. Like a place you're ready to be stranded forever.

When he stops kissing me, he strokes my hair. "I think you're beautiful. But you're too young. Now go to sleep."

South Dakota, the law says the age of consent is 16 and that's not exactly my age. When he asked me how old I am I lied. I'm fifteen going on sixteen.

I'll know later what I don't know now. I'll wake up, the wind still blowing, the twilight of day without sun, a day of eclipse. Wiley's not beside me. He's out in the storm cutting wood. I'll need to pee, to wash, I'll need to eat. He's pushed my wheelchair against the couch. I'll roll into the kitchen, reach up and open one of the cupboards. I'll pull the silverware drawer and use a wooden spatula to push down some noodles. Finding a spoon of butter, I'll fry the butter and mix in the noodles. Lots of pepper, it'll be good. The package cost 65 cents. I'll wheel into the bathroom. One of those old tubs with black-pink tile. I'll turn on the taps and wash my face with the last of the cold water in the pipes. I'll brush my hair with Wiley's brush and imagine JadeDragon's green horse with a long mane of cornsilk, a braid of green from her chin, her neck longer than a horse's but shorter than a giraffe's. It will be hard to turn around in the bathroom. Yet I won't want to leave ever. Wiley calls my name. Jana. I'll roll toward him, toward my name. He's at the door. His arms full. He needs me to open it. The knob takes a long time to turn, but I get it open. He carries in an armload of wood; wood chips settle in his loose hair that falls over his shoulder. Maybe I'll say, "My clothes are dirty. Can I wear some of yours?" He'll try the noodle gunk. "This tastes good. So you can cook." He points to an upright closet. It latches with brass. I choose a silk shirt, white and brown like a leopard only striped. I ask if he has any jeans. Of course he does, except he's 6 feet tall, and I'm 5 feet two. But that doesn't count anymore, because he'll never see me standing up. This is perfect, a blizzard, snowed in. I'll think of it always as Godzilla's blizzard.

After two days, a pure white morning appears. Silence. Everywhere drifts of snow and Wiley's gingerbread house half-buried. A grove of pines and oaks. A little brown driveway. I'll see the house in daylight. A pale tangerine. I'll recognize the police when they show up. The very policeman who bought coffee a million years ago in Dunkin Donuts. The one with a door knob for a head. The cruiser's red police bubble will bleed into the snow. They'll come to arrest Wiley. For kidnapping. You likely escaped a bad fate, the wind will say. Look what happened to Liliane. You're crazy, I'll curse the wind. I'll see Wiley in handcuffs.

I'll fight to free him. I'll swear leaving Crippled Children's was all my idea. Godzilla with the help of JadeDragon_77 will get the charges dropped. But I'll never see Wiley again.

JadeDragon's theme song likes to play in my sleep; a music that is almost beyond hearing from a sound track found in Destoroyah. It's a song that sounds like the sun and moon are shining at the same time or a watery melody that guitarfish thrum.

ALL THE TIME IN THE WORLD

Jack Driscoll

MY FATHER'S NAME IS BRADLEY CHICKY. He who fanned fifteen consecutive batters to win the 1989 Division II high school state championship. A spider-arm southpaw submariner whose full-ride scholarships mark this town's first ever Big League prospect.

Except that it's the new millennium, the year 2004, and so long gone are those glory days that just this morning he gripped the baseball's tight red seams in the double hook of his prosthetic to demonstrate how to throw "No, not a downer, a sinker," as he said. "And here, like this for a heater, like this for a splitter, OK? Got that?" As if right out of left field, the blue, mid-November twilight snow falling, I'd decided to try out for some latter-day version of *A League of Their Own.*

No matter the weather he'll sometimes play catch in the backyard with his girlfriend Lyndel, who stops by certain evenings after work. If I decide to hike those couple miles instead of riding the school bus, there they are when I get home, two silhouettes in the semi-dark. She hasn't spent the night, nor he at her place, and I assume it's for my sake that they're taking things slow. We're up to twice each week that the three of us sit down to dinner, the extra leaf just recently reinserted into the dining room table. She might, as he maintains, *be* a dynamite Chef Boyardee, but bite-wise I take maybe one or two and, blank-faced, lower my fork to the plate, and excuse myself without a single word. They haven't yet, but if either of them attempts to coerce me back I swear I'll yank that new linen tablecloth from underneath the serving platters and silverware, the ceramic gravy boat and those oversize glasses of ice water, like some irate and vengeful magician.

He says to give her a chance, she's a good sport, spirited. A real game-changer is how he puts it, a welcome addition. Plus she's plenty smart, he says, reads a ton, and has a two-year degree in health and fitness from the local community college. "In time you'll grow to like her, Sam," he says.

"Right," I say.

But nothing deters his enthusiasm, her painted fingernails flashing signs and my father bent over at the waist and staring in as she squats and rocks back on her heels, her ass mere inches from the half-frozen ground, a Detroit Tigers ball cap worn backward, as if that's cool. Sometimes she takes off the catcher's mitt and warms both hands in her armpits. Shrugs and shivers and yet acts as if this is the most fun she's had in decades. Home plate is maybe fifteen yards from where, in full windup, he releases the ball, every pitch a slow looping change-up though he claims that some scout's speed gun once clocked him at 101 mph. Other times he'll practice his pickoff move, his sneaky slide step. All of it, under our current circumstances, about a bazillion light years removed from the majors.

Anyway, Lyndel teaches Pilates and yoga at Go Figure, so *hers* is pretty much perfect in that camo sports bra and short-shorts getup she occasionally wears, a shiny silver bracelet on each wrist like handcuffs. Standing straight-legged she can touch both elbows to the floor, fingers folded like she's praying, and then hold that pose before tucking under herself as if she might push all the way up past her own backside, like something out of a Chinese circus. She's twenty-six. Seven years younger than my father and a full eight years older than my mom was when she had me—Samantha Ann. Or, as that sheriff's department deputy I hand my urine sample to every other Saturday afternoon always singsongs, "Sam Chicky, Sam Chicky," like he's propositioning some teenage junkie slut, which so isn't me.

I mean, against the odds I'm holding it together, doing my best, resisting every temptation, and avoiding lockup by side-sailing as fast and far away from the local pot and meth heads as possible. Staying clean. And stripped naked not a single body piercing or the fancy needlework of some butt-crack tattoo. No hickeys either, ditto the eyeliner, and the sad fact is that foreplay thus far pretty much constitutes locking fingers with a guy.

But just one time, when Deputy Dildo orders me to empty my pockets and sweatshirt pouch, I imagine, among my personal and lawful contents, that I had nerve enough to plant a couple of Trojan Ultra Thins. Packets I could then flip right onto the counter. Free samples from the Journey Church for safe, underage sex is what I'd offer up, an inside joke with me and my best friend Allison. Maybe bat my eyes and nod toward the empty holding cell, the stripped-down cot, but like my father reminds me, "Zip it. Keep your motor mouth shut and your thoughts to yourself." To ensure that I arrive there on time he's the one who chaperones me and then waits outside in his pickup, where he rolls down the window and leans his head against the seat rest, his hook visoring above his already closed eyes, and says, as I exit, "Remember, no attitude, right? Do you hear me? No bullshit this time."

My official guilty-as-charged? Random theft and alcohol. As in every morning before school, my father in the shower, I'd refill the same juice box with straight Bombay Sapphire from my secret survival stash in my closet. And from which, during third-hour phys ed, I'd sip between sets of stomach crunches and jumping jacks, and the one time I puked the gym teacher thought it was food poisoning or the flu and called my father at work to come pick me up.

I haven't lapsed in almost three months and counting, and the NO ENTRY sign on my bedroom door I removed voluntarily. Not that he'd walk in unannounced one way or the other. It's the tone, as my father says, the negative message it sends. Sort of like how I used to gnaw on ballpoint after ballpoint until the spring and the ink erupted inside my mouth. Now I take notes instead, and my grades, as of just last week, they're back up again above average. Nothing *Quiz Bowl* or *Odyssey of the Mind*. Nothing, as my teachers make clear, that even approximates my full potential, though so far no backslide either, and so no more hassles and scare tactics from the school principal and guidance counselor about having to repeat the year.

But three sheets flapping I'll shoplift almost anything spur of the moment. A silk blouse, more booze, Elmer's and Magic Markers to uncap and sniff all day. Rubber cement. Model airplane glue. Bottles of syrupy Robitussin as chasers. Once, a chew toy and a couple packs of liver chips, plus a Basenji pup to feed them to. Scooped up in broad daylight from Spoiled Brats, our Front Street pet shop that's likely, like so many of the town's landmark mom and pops, to turn belly up, the census here being in perpetual long-term freefall.

I named the pooch Ty Cobb, for my father's all-time favorite ballplayer. An innocent, warm-blooded addition to the household that we could love and care for together and spoil rotten in my mom's absence. We'd never had a pet. Not so much as a goldfish or gerbil, and when my father, bleary-eyed, home finally at the tail-end of another fifty-hour work week at the foundry, offered his dead hand to be licked and sniffed, the puppy peed right there on the living room carpet. "I'll clean it up," I said, and, the first words out his mouth, "Why didn't you just leave our names and phone number and address? And hand over a note saying, BEWARE: KLEPTOMANIAC ON THE PREMISES."

"Maybe I bought him," I said. "Did you ever consider that?" And he said back, "Tell it to the judge," and then he threatened to press charges himself and wave bye-bye as the juvenile delinquent facility van pulled away. He'd had it, he said. "Enough is enough, Sam. The dog's got papers, a high-dollar price tag, and there's no buying you out of this. Not after the fact, and I don't even want to. Listen: this isn't kid's stuff anymore, an impoundment or rescue mutt; we're talking a felony offense. Do you understand what that means, the possible consequences? Trust me, you've just taken on way more than you ever bargained for. And God forbid that I lose you, too."

He sat me down at the kitchen table and coached me, sentence by sentence, as I composed what sounded to my ears like a heartfelt letter of apology and remorse. Still woozy and half hungover, I took a while to get the words "appealing for clemency" unslurred, but the cops, they'd already been summoned anyway, a good hour in advance of that written admission of guilt. The final period, the sincerely yours, the scribbled, almost illegible, back-slanting left-handed signature I'd sometimes practice in the back row of every class to annihilate another wasted few seconds of mandatory school time—all of it made little difference.

"She does it for attention." That's what the first Family Services social worker—young and nervous and strictly by the numbers—concluded. A rookie, as my father insists. Limited. Right or wrong she attributed such aberrant behavior to my mom's midnight departure eight months earlier, and my on-the-rebound father still somewhat tilty in *his* thinking. Like I told her, he and I, we do our best to tune each other out, and, whenever possible, communicate telepathically, or in single-word sentences. *Sorry* is not among them, except, I guess, whenever I attempt to decipher the Morse code of his hook tap-tapping on the Naugahyde couch cushion as he watches the History Channel or *60 Minutes* with the sound off.

Around Lyndel I'm occasionally more forthcoming, and way less inclined to play the victim, the angry, uppity, unstable, at-risk, insolent, wayward, and all-mixed-up crazy child—"the offending minor," as the juvenile court judge referred to me. I'm also less inclined to lay the blame so directly on my parents, or on anyone else for that matter. And for sure *not* on Lyndel, who I first off figured for a ditz I could easily despise, my every silent glare announcing, "I can wait you out. This is not your house. There is no later on, no better tomorrows here. This is who we are. Leave now."

Truth told she's OK, with no grubbing up or big sister stupid stuff. No offers of a free radical jazzercise class or any personal trainer tips to improve my bust line or ease the pain of those killer premenstrual cramps and spasms. And her laugh . . . it's eerie-weird in the extreme, like a fun gene long dormant from this dysfunctional family. Zero rug rats and never married. When I finally asked her what's the deal anyway—my father chasing after the young stuff—she said, her jeans low-slung, her hair blue-black and shiny, "Lyndel, not Lolita." Which I didn't get, but I winced when she added, "Your dad is a good man at a bad time and half out of his mind with worry over you."

I'm fifteen, and by far the tallest girl in the entire school. At twelve I stood an even six feet in my mom's high heels and magenta lipstick and had a premonition of myself as Miss Michigan turned runway supermodel and swinging five-hundred-dollar handbags. Leggy and gray-eyed like my father and, reformed or not, I don't for one second assume that I'm the only guilty party here whenever he asks, all pissed off and judgmental, "How brainless can you be?"—and I, too, lose all composure and fire right back. Exactly like my mom used to do, the same zinger about how he'd forfeited a life of fame and fortune—and, as she said, for what . . . one goddamn dark night of the soul's idea of a joke?

"Beyond belief," is how she'd phrase it, and my standing comeback was, "Yeah, remember that?"

"Every day," he says. "Every last painful detail." He means the homemade guillotine, and that forged steel doorframe he hauled out of the county dump. Pulleys and half a dozen oblong window weights, and the side-by-side outhouse shitter holes sawed crosswise and hinged like a double yoke to fit those frail, pale, aristocratic necks of Louis XVI and Marie Antoinette. A last-ditch, hands-on world history show-and-tell he brainstormed to salvage a final passing grade so he could graduate and they could flee to Florida or Arizona or Texas: no hitters, perfect games, a College World Series MVP ring, and trophies enough to fill a hallway of polished glass cases. Jerseys and scorecards and pennant flags to autograph. And so my mom, already pregnant with me, could follow the team bus in that white Mustang convertible she imagined was already theirs, and think about the sprawling brick ranch or split-level they'd buy, the backyard in-ground swimming pool with its rainbow of underwater lights, and a trampoline. And eggs any style.

All of which sure beat, she said, slow-dying here in this squatty, spawned-out, northern Michigan toss-pot of a town where they married anyhow, for better or for worse, and honeymooned in a cheap rustic cabin just a few miles south. And where some twisted turn of fate determined that I, too, would be born and raised.

"Let it rest," my father would say, his name stitched in red cursive above his work-shirt pocket. "Good God Almighty, do we always have to end up at the same damn crash site?" My mom, each and every time she'd wig out or fly into overwind—didn't really matter anymore what for—insisted that the moment was forever fixed in her memory. The bedroom walls, they're so tin-can thin that I've awakened nights to screams unlike anything you've ever heard unless, as she'd say, you've witnessed close up a human arm lopped clean off below the elbow in a public school classroom.

You couldn't make it up, that's what the local newscasts reported as far across the Big Lake as lacrosse and Fargo. Freak of freaks. Grimmer than grim and referring to him, all six-foot-six, as the next Big Unit but with his career closed out just like that. "You don't want to hear this," they said, as if it might incite or traumatize young athletes everywhere, and then they provided a graphic play-by-play anyway. The teacher present—"My God, the magnitude," the news anchors intoned in hushed voices—his teammates and his teenage fiancée all gathered for the execution, laughing and hooting and slapping him on the back, and then, as if in stop-time, looking on in horror.

They mentioned how he'd done his homework. His stand-up easel and flip chart and a dean's-list gabble of gruesome facts about the French Revolution: how king and queen were beheaded separately in 1793, his Majesty in January and she in October, a child bride, barely fourteen when they tied the royal knot.

"Jail bait," my mom—her baby bump already showing—interrupted. "Cradle robber." And my father explaining, to her and to everyone, that if he could have he'd have spared the queen's life and maybe changed the violent course of history. But this was now or never and all that mattered was to pass the class, a measly C-minus their gateway to the future, and what was theirs right there for the taking.

"And Jesus Christ from there the hell on," my mom said, and wherever he'd found the mannequins, the padded church kneeler, was beyond hers or anyone's comprehension. Not to mention those flowing indigo robes. Coconuts for heads, faces sand-papered smooth and spray-painted white and pasty like a geisha's, and which, on this day two centuries later, would tumble and roll together—their carved pink lips barely parted, blindfolds refused and their doomed eyes neither closed nor staring downward in disgrace but rather looking straight ahead.

By all accounts they were still crazy about each other, my father ad-libbed, as if the case for true love at any age might invalidate all those trumped-up and treasonous charges. They admitted to nothing, he said, and right to the bitter end remained poised and silent, resilient and unafraid.

Then came a drum roll, and that honed and weighted industrial paper cutter blade way too heavy for a single release lever and a makeshift shear pin. But even at that, as my mom calculates, what were the odds, the prospects of such an ungodly, unforgiving physics, that it would snap full force exactly as my father reached in to straighten those two wavy white wigs borrowed from the drama club.

Family Services social worker number two—older, seasoned, the pack's dominant jackal with the focused determination of breaking through to me alive in her eyes. A veteran, according to my father, a prime time, no-nonsense professional. They've talked, and a few times all three of us together. He says for me to pay attention, that this one knows her stuff—a warning that she's seen it all, every defiant cocky-young headstrong screw-up like yours truly. Her square, Army-green coffee mug says SPEAK YOUR MIND, but whenever I offer an opinion she wide-eyes me with the emptiest, most remote and dismissive stare in creation. Glowers like she can see right through me from the onset to the absolute end of my socially impaired and substandard existence. Nods. Clenches up. Says stuff like, "So." Says, "Uh-huh. Fair enough, though the victims of much greater calamities cope and move on, don't they?" Always slams on the brakes with some loaded, instant override question like that. Then says, "Go on, please." As in, "Sing it again, Sam, and let's see where *this* next burnout version of reality leads us, shall we?"

And against which we somehow forge our slow way hourward. It's all part of the guilty plea, and of me being perceived not as some dangerous criminal but rather as not really giving a shit. Even wanting to get caught red-handed, making a desperate appeal for help—denials and anger issues and the like. So mostly I just tuck in, nod and grimace and gut-roll through every session. I close my eyes. With my finest fakery I stammer and bite my lip and sometimes cry because it's a thin ledge I'm walking—that's the message loud and clear—and the falloff rate for girls my age is nothing to frigging underestimate. I'm good at this: hand tremors and hyperventilating on demand. Within seconds I can double my pulse rate and begin to run a fever. Wicked sweats and hiccups, and the whole act so convincing that I once said "Hollywood" when she asked about potential career tracks, and she didn't for one dense second even catch the irony. Talk about a movie set on Venus or Mars.

Her name's Ms. Foisie. Early-forty-something, springy strawberry-blonde locks drawn back into a ponytail. Perfume so thick that you enter the room and *boom*, a giant blast of Chocolate Daisy or Autumn Snakeroot explodes straight up through your nostrils, and those eyes, I swear, wide-spaced and lobelia blue, and her pupils black as dahlias. Feather earrings to top it off. I've never admitted as much, but it's enough to get a person high. For that initial full hour of "getting to know me," I kept scanning the room for bumblebees and hummingbirds. A praying mantis, maybe, and the featured talk that day all about my parents and the recklessness of teenage sex and marriage. "You do," she said, "understand what I'm telling you, correct?"

I nodded. "The basic thrust," I said, and she said, "Which is?" and I said, "Things happen. Things buzz"—but hey, not to worry, no lick and stick from where I rest my weary bones and noggin. And look, no engagement rock, and that I was *still* patiently waiting to go all wild and wet in my dreams. It's why my father reams me out about the wisecracking. A curse or spell, he says, but pure reflex is what it actually is, totally spontaneous and, come on, only meant as a joke. All in good fun, woman to woman to possibly lighten the psychic load just a little, and her husband and two sons smiling sideways at me from out of that fancy, gold-leafed photo on her desk.

Allison says no sweat. Says, "Remember, we're good." Says, "Hey, guess what?" and we simultaneously flip each other off. This goes back to the carnival fortune-teller two summers ago, who held my hand and explained the length of a woman's middle finger predicts her future. I'd be some modern-day Egyptian queen, all satin clad, dripping rubies and sapphires, ruddering down the Nile at twilight while dining with sheiks or whatever, instead of serving breakfast for minimum wage at our local Denny's.

I whirled around in a full circle on my tiptoes right outside the gypsy tent with its heavy canvas flaps and burning candles and Mason jars of giant scorpions and smiling horseshoe bats in formaldehyde. I said, "Holy rip-shit," confirming that wherever in the hemispheres the spirit took us was where *we* were headed, nonstop into the slipstream of epic romance and greatness and maybe even a blockbuster feature-length film or two, with Oscars and Golden Globes. And so we made that pact to go and go as we sashayed arm in arm in our skintight miniskirts and flip-flops through the slowly rising mist of the midway—what my mom called the land of stuffed lions and lambs and that prized oversized panda she insisted nobody ever won: "Nobody, Sam. Remember that. Above all else remember that when the fairyland dream smoke clears, women like us, like you and me, we always, every single solitary time, wake up elsewhere. And that other life we wanted so badly? The one back *there*? It's nothing more than a mirage, the simple-sad story of our botched and misguided lives."

What I now believe is that the price of my father trying and trying to prove my mother wrong about him actually made her love him less. The ring toss, that pyramid of milk bottles that never wobbled or fell and, in her eyes rendered him a mere figment of his former self.

The postmark on her last few letters is from Kenosha. They're addressed to me and me alone, and to my knowledge she's made no other human contact hereabouts. I could lie, tell my father, "Mom asked about you. How you were doing." But what she's conveyed thus far is this: That in her new job she individually hand-wraps brandy-soaked chocolates in a warehouse where they pipe in *Peter and the Wolf*, and musicals like *The Sound of Music*, and Judy Garland's "Over the Rainbow."

I've thought for the millionth time, "Just hop a Trailways, Sam," and it would have long ago been a done deal had she ever once offered to take me with her. Or had she, after the fact, dropped the slightest hint that the choice was mine, legal or otherwise. Or that of course she wants me to move out there or, bare minimum, come visit for an extended stay—though yes, it's too late for this Thanksgiving, but consider Christmas as a possibility, OK?

She says the Salvation Army ringers are already at it with their handbells and hanging red coin kettles. And the tree on top of the water tower is decorated with ten thousand translucent stars, a galaxy of tiny blue spires aglow in the night sky. If only she had a balcony or fire escape, she thinks, she could see the display from her single-occupancy efficiency apartment. It's small, of course, but with a TV and microwave and mini-fridge.

She says, "Can you imagine it, a town with prehistoric sturgeon in the rivers? Caviar!" she says. And a brand new Grand Union that hires the blind as greeters, as well as to stand at the head of every other aisle to offer toothpicks and so much free sample food that it's impossible for anyone to go hungry. So far not word one about another man in her life, though that's how she's ended up where she has, morose and alone, lost to us. That's the part I hate her for and refuse to forgive. Except that I haven't, against my father's will and certainty, ruled out entirely that she still might rally like someone suddenly waking from a decade-long coma and remembering her husband's name, the address and phone number where she used to live. Or like the mute who picks up a smoky cat's-eye marble or piece of mica, holds it to the sun, and begins to lip-sync some long-forgotten serenade about leaving and love—and then just dodges the holy, haphazard hell right out of there and straight for home.

Instead, she claims that the haloed prison lights she drives by some nights remind her how lucky she is to be so free and alive. Though possibly it's a lunatic asylum, she can't be positive—the grilled windows and the like—but either way it's just another case in point, as my father would argue, to fortify his position against her return.

That's true. It's like she's writing from a land so foreign and far-flung I had to locate it on our Rand-McNally atlas just to remind myself she's only in Wisconsin: a straight shot north through the U.P. and then, at any given junction or crossroads, just hang a louie and hold that sightline all the way to the horizon.

What's clear to everyone is that if she hadn't in fits and flashes beat it out of here so often we'd *already* be on our way to rescue her, whispering, "Where are you, where are you?" and then begging her back. First time she fled was on foot, and my father found her shivering in the pre-dawn just blocks away, silent and shamefaced, her eyes closed like she'd been slapped. And then him leading her by the hand, slowly past the neighbors' houses, up our porch stairs with the dying potted spider plants, and back inside. Once a regular homebody, she began disappearing, no telling when or where to, a half mile or so beyond the town's outskirts to begin with, and later stranded out by the I-75 motor lodge where that grid of high-tension wires crackles and hums. And that was followed not long after by collect calls from Menominee and Battle Creek, though never before had she crossed state lines or stayed gone for more than a day or two, a week at most. But this time, come spring, it'll mark a calendar year—and by then, according to my father, she'll have forfeited all rights, including visitation privileges.

He says about having filed for divorce, "How wrong you are. We've done everything we can. Everything humanly possible, Sam. There's no turning back, not anymore, and your mother and me, we've *already* gone our separate ways. No other alternative exists, and for sure no coping or compromising away what she *imagined* and believed back then should've been our lives going forward."

What *I* imagine is her vanishing, not for months or even years, but forever. And the only photograph in my possession, that grainy, 8 x 10 black-and-white my father secretly snapped of her—like some private eye, while she stood staring skyward in the storm-light as it massed and rumbled like a tide directly toward her: the air electrified and a giant monochrome shadow eclipsing those endless windswept alfalfa fields—the entire silvery span of them— and her head flung back and her arms outstretched as if, as he reported it back then, she was waiting to be abducted by aliens.

"It's who she is," he said. "A human lost and found and lost, and, for good measure, gone, and gone lost yet again. Elsewhere—that's the direction she's always been headed in. The sequel to the sequel to the sequel, Sam. Look," he said, as he handed the photo to me. "Look at this. Look closely and tell me honestly that you or anyone can conceive for her a happier outcome."

Ms. Foisie agrees. As she's said repeatedly, "Let's let the credits roll, shall we?" Her take is that my mom suffers from a chronic case of arrested development, the defections so numerous that even I had to admit that I'd lost count. But hope, nonetheless, springs eternal, right? "And she is, after all," I've continued to argue, "still my mom. Is she not?" And Ms. Foisie's standard comeback is, "Yes, she who has self-destructively turned your lives into a charade," implying furthermore that she'd turned me into my own worst enemy.

I suppose I could have revealed, but wouldn't ever to the likes of her, how some nights my mom would sit on the end of my bed and patiently cast whichever hand shadows I requested, animal or reptile or insect. Rabbits, dragonflies, camels and storks and pelicans. Sometimes that scary profile of a crocodile, her index and middle fingers slowly scissoring up and down, while that raised knuckle of an eye socket floated across the calm, imaginary white water of my bedroom wall. How it was me who held the flashlight, who aimed the beam as if it were a magic lantern. How it took two hands and all *ten* fluttery fingers for her to simulate the erratic nose-diving flights of those swallows that nested in the rafters of our unused woodshed. And how one time my mom said, right out of the blue, "No, your father *can't* do this." Which was exactly what I'd been wondering. And then, turning to look at me, she speculated that if his double hook was diamond-tipped he'd score each windowpane and tap out a thousand perfect pinpoints to let in the moon and the starlight.

My father calls it the best Christmas present ever, that I've been taken off probation for good behavior. Or possibly, as Allison speculates, the judge was doubling down on my redemption in this, the season of miracles. Either way, as of this weekend, this very Friday night, I've been rewarded with an 11:00 p.m. curfew. "On the dot and not a second later," my father said, and if the roads start to get bad I'm to head home immediately. They already almost are, though suddenly it seems like we've got all the time in the world.

Because Allison has graduated from learner's permit to driver's license, we're sitting on the front bumper of her parents' second car, a dented, high-mileage Oldsmobile Custom Cruiser, recently tuned-up and with four new snow tires. Plus a first-aid kit and emergency roadside flares—all fizz without the firecracker—stashed in the trunk.

The early pardon calls for a celebration. As Allison says, "Out the door and on the loose like old times. Only better," and I agree wholeheartedly now that we're much older, wiser, and wily, and have wrangled a set of wheels and a full tank of gas, notwithstanding that there's absolutely nowhere to go in weather like this. It's why we're bundled up against the freezing cold, scarves and hats and a Hudson Bay blanket around our skinny shoulders like a double cape, and the snow slow but steady-falling, giant feathery flakes—a scrim half obscuring the lights of the town below us, the abandoned gravel pits with the rusted-out derricks and the limestone quarry beyond. The only color is the blurry, rectangular, neon-red Dairy Queen sign. Otherwise, everything's white, the pines and Doug firs on the steep downward slant ghosting over, and the foundry smokestack—though we can't see it—like a vertical ice tunnel into the sky.

Months. That's how much winter's ahead. And yet there's not a single county plow taking notice. And no wind at all, and even when we strain to hear that unmistakable shrill whine of transport trailers out on the interstate, we can't. Everything's quiet, the loudest sound anywhere the tips of our two cigarettes burning back with each next inhale.

We've been parked for maybe half an hour at this scenic, no-name lovers' lane overlook, but of course no one other than us is about. No jocks on the prowl, but girls like us, we take it on faith that some night hence we will draw them out of their small-town, shit-box lives in droves and teach them how to love us. How to kiss and kiss us all over until their lips and tongues go numb. How to follow the sway of our hips gliding us like phantoms across dream fields so vast that even a search party of thousands couldn't detect a single trace.

Instead, here we are, waylaid in the panorama of so much emptiness that Allison tilts her head heavenward. She says, "Hey, Sam, we gotta go," but even so she leans back against the hood and closes her eyes and remains silent. The snow sticks to her long lashes like tiny white wings; her face is almost luminous. We are beautiful is what I think, travelers momentarily stranded inside the closed-off borderlands beyond which lie our future lives. I imagine my father standing and staring out the living room window, conjuring a blizzard, and how the winter roads will begin to narrow, and the Black Creek Bridge we have to cross to get back, always the first to ice over. He'll switch the porch light on, and the TV weather station. He'll call Allison's house to see if we're there, the car's colossal ass-end fishtailed safely up the gradual incline of their driveway.

And I imagine my mom, listening to that din of voices inside her head, the fade-ins and fade-outs, the New Year almost upon us, and my overdue trip to visit her never taken, the intervals apart growing longer and longer by the day.

"Look," I say: the moon is almost full, and for those delayed few seconds before the snow falls harder into the dark, the disappearing landscape turns purplish blue. "Like a dying spotlight," I say, and this is a pageant, a dance we do while opening the car doors and sliding in. The engine catches on the very first try, the wipers clearing the windshield with one wide swoop. We're ready to launch, and the Olds is no longer a car, as Allison says. It's a catamaran, and the roads are rivers. You can see in the low beams how slowly we're drifting over the snow, leaving no wake. No stars to follow home, though for now, for this night, it is where we're headed.

THREE SUMMERS

Nick Dybek

THE SPRING I TURNED TEN my father told me we'd be spending a month in Maine with old friends.

"They have a daughter who's a little older than you, Josh. And it's time I taught you to fish," he said. "You remember the Izelins don't you?"

I didn't, not exactly. They'd stayed with us for a night when I was three or four. I remembered a silver Chevette with a New York license plate at the end of our driveway, a pair of giant, torn sneakers by the door. That was it. Roy was a professor of ornithology at the University of Buffalo. Jan was a pharmacist. But I knew them only as voices on the phone and as players in my parents' stories, stories that usually began, "Once, before you were born . . ."

Before I was born my father had served in the Peace Corps with Roy in Indonesia, and a few years later they overlapped at Duke. By the time I dropped into the world, my parents had jobs at a college in Clarinda, Nebraska. My mother was a musicologist, and at nine I could identify most of the piano works of Erik Satie by ear. My father was a James Agee scholar, and so devoted to the man that he often read aloud from *Let Us Now Praise Famous Men* before dinner.

We lived on the literal edge of town. Behind our house there was nothing but fields, and fields, and fields. Exile was the word my mother used to describe it. But it wasn't exile to me. It was all I knew. I knew the evenings my father and I played catch in the soft grass behind our house. I knew that as the sun went down I'd look up to see his arm stretching into the twilight, the ball vanishing in the darkness and reappearing above my glove. I knew that we would continue until, across the field in the half dark, my father looked like a shadow and I could only listen for the pop of ball to glove. The summer I met the Izelins my parents had just begun to take the faint shapes of people.

Roy Izelin stood on the front porch of the summerhouse. As we pulled into the driveway in the convertible my father had rented at the airport, Roy gestured at the house with both arms, as if conducting an orchestra. My father bounded out of the car. Roy kissed my mother on the mouth. The air was cool and thin.

"I remember this guy," Roy said, looking down at me through green-tinted glasses. "You remember me?"

I shook my head and Roy mimicked. His ponytail followed, as if it were a snake he'd charmed. "Jacko," he said. "Look at this place, will you? I'm almost too excited." Roy grabbed a handful of his pants at the groin and shook it at my father. My father grabbed the crotch of his own pants, laughing, and my mother began to laugh too.

"Goddamn, it is. Man oh man, Roy, where did you find this fucking place?"

The house made an impression, I had to admit: the paint the color of a storm, the second-story windows gabled like heavy-lidded eyes, the bracketing under the porch like crooked teeth.

"Do some exploring. This is your vacation too," my mother said. I'd hauled her suitcase onto the porch, and as she bent to lift it the sun shone through the curtain of her hair.

There was a girl in the backyard with a book in her lap and two horse-shaped barrettes in her hair. She wore a western shirt belted at the waist like a dress.

"I'm Carol," she said, without looking up. "But don't tell me who you are."

"Why not?"

"You could be the Jordans' kid," she said. "But you could be anybody. You could be William Kidd. You could be William H. Bonnie."

"Who?"

"They're outlaws. Killers."

"I've never killed anyone."

"That's what you say," Carol said, letting the book slide from her lap as she got to her feet. Her ankles were caked in mud. Her eyes were green. "That's what Captain Kidd said too, but when it was time to bury his treasure, he'd anchor his pirate ship and row to shore on a boat with one of his men. He'd have that poor sucker help him dig a hole, and then he'd cut his throat right there."

"Obviously," I said. "So only he'd know where the treasure was."

"Follow me," she said. She took the back steps in two leaping strides and slipped into the house, emerging a moment later with an empty coffee mug. She ran into the woods behind the house and I followed. Leaves and twigs rustled and snapped under her feet; it sounded as if the ground were on fire.

The woods ended abruptly at a ledge before the line of high tide. The beach below was littered with bouquets of seaweed. Black rocks crusted with barnacles jutted from the mud. Carol slipped off her sandals and walked to the water, bare feet pressing little stamps. She dipped the cup in the surf and held it out to me with both hands.

"Don't be afraid," she said.

"I'm not drinking that," I said.

"Good idea." She nodded as if I'd finally done something smart. "Saltwater will drive you crazy. In the old days, sailors, especially pirates, used to get so thirsty that sometimes they'd forget that." She grabbed a handful of hair on either side of her face and let her feet sink into the mud. She opened her mouth and eyes wide. "They hallucinated," she said. "And do you know what they always saw? Millions of bats. With leathery wings and little red eyes and little bat claws. They thought they were drowning in bats."

"They all saw the same thing?" I asked.

"Maybe not always. You tell me. I'll pretend I see it too."

When I didn't answer, Carol pulled her feet from the mud and began to pick her way over the rocks toward the ledge. The thought of returning to the house alone, of unpacking my bag and lying down in a new bed made my chest tight.

"What about a giant squid," I said.

Carol glanced back over her shoulder.

"Is that what the sailors saw?"

"It could be," she said.

"A giant squid with a hundred tentacles and a hundred eyes on each?" It just came out like that. I didn't recognize what I was saying. "Did you see the car we drove up in? We could pretend it's a ship."

Carol turned and took a step back toward the water. She tapped one finger on her chin. "All right," she said. "But I'm captain."

That entire afternoon we fought the squid. It attacked suddenly, tentacles sending up great jets of spray. The deck pitched and we tumbled across. I could see our reflections—soaking wet and exhausted, yet brave—in each of its hundred eyes. The hull buckled, the engine quit fighting, but we didn't, and, at last, the squid reared its flame-shaped head from beneath the waves. Its true eye was the size of the boat and blue as the water. Carol hurled a harpoon, a desperate and perfect shot. Jets of black ink blasted across the deck as the squid howled an almost human cry of pain, then sank, fatally wounded, one tentacle slithering down the bow.

In the month that the six of us shared that house, my father took me fishing once. We sat side by side, our feet dangling from the edge of a pier. He held the rod loosely with one hand and squeezed the bridge of his nose with the other. After an hour without a bite, he said, "We'd better head in. We'll try it again tomorrow."

When we returned to the house, Roy was in the backyard bumping a volleyball into the air, his ponytail crawling down his back. "Shhh," my father whispered. Then he ran at Roy, shouting

Hai-ya, tackling him around the waist, heaving until they fell to the ground, laughing.

They laughed that whole summer. Constant laughter like a sticky film on the endless stories the four of them told about four other people also named Roy, Jan, Jack, and Sarah. Jan driving my mother to the hospital in the middle of the night because she'd fallen on her face trying to walk the length of the porch on her hands, a cigarette in her mouth. A good mutual friend who'd kidnapped his own son because he was certain his ex-wife was brainwashing him, who'd showed up in Durham, looking to trade mescaline for a place to hide. Roy and my father driving through pouring rain to a farmhouse famous for the best marijuana in North Carolina, grown by a farmer willing to trade weed for books by Anaïs Nin. The road flooded and they stumbled the final mile over muddy fields, passing a bottle and shouting the lyrics to "Desolation Row" to keep warm.

"And after all that," my father said, "that farmer hands us a bag of hay. Hay! I could have fucking killed him."

"You should have fucking killed him," my mother said.

At night, they steamed clams and mussels, and the unfamiliar smells wafted through the big rooms. They drank beer as they cooked and wine during dinner, and after dinner Jan would fetch a cocktail shaker that rattled deep into night. Roy's high-pitched voice whirred like a dentist's drill. My mother swore. My father *sang*. I remember very little about Jan Izelin except that a nervous laugh followed everything she said like walky-talky static. I'd lie in bed and wait for the crescendo from the living room, the voices, the laughter, the music on the stereo. Louder and louder, until goodnights were said and doors banged shut and suddenly it was quiet enough again to hear the rumble of waves on the beach.

In the mornings, despite their swollen eyes, my mother still sliced half a banana for my cereal; my father still slid the newspaper to me across the breakfast table. But there was something different about the way they spoke. A tone of voice I recognized from when students called our house in Clarinda—impatient, dismissive.

"Look at it out there," my father said one morning. "There's some serious freedom out there. Why don't you go find it?"

Was that why I spent every moment I could with Carol? Together, we became navigators of the South Pacific. Horse trainers in Wyoming. Scientists on the moon. It was up to me to decide the game, and as the days wore on I got better at it. I had to, because any time I asked Carol what her school was like, her town, her friends, she'd flatten me with a bored expression and refuse to answer, as if guarding her real life. And any time I said, "Why don't you pick the game," she only shrugged, as if she were guarding her imagination too.

Luckily my imagination had a lot to work with. The downstairs of the house—the dining room, the kitchen, the bedrooms where my parents and the Izelins slept—was well kept, but the upstairs was shabby and neglected. To me, the peeling wallpaper and splintering floorboards were mysterious and new. The opposite of the off-white drywall of our ranch home in Clarinda, of our neighborhood with its carpets of bright sod. We ran through those hallways and threw open the doors. One door was locked.

"There must be a key," Carol said. She pressed her ear to the wood. She peered into the keyhole. "I can't tell. Can you see anything?"

I nudged her over with my shoulder, blinked into the keyhole and shook my head.

We raced down the rest of the hall, darting in and out of the rooms. Some rooms were empty, some decorated like shrines to old lives. Twin beds strapped down by moth-eaten orange blankets. Two swords crossed above a doorway. A series of posters advertising The Grand Dubrovnik Hotel. Framed maps of coastlines, intricate as treetops. An old-fashioned scale like I'd seen at the doctor's office. We were archaeologists sifting through the ruins, trying to piece together a lost civilization.

"This was a pirate's house," Carol said. "It must have been."

And one afternoon, when we pulled the clothes out of a battered dresser, hat by hat, mitten by mitten, we found a map hidden in the bottom drawer beneath a tattered black cardigan.

"Hold one side, put your knees on it," Carol said. Together, we spread the scroll across the floor. The paper was bright blue and penciled with geometric shapes.

"It's this house," Carol pronounced after a moment. "The blueprints."

There was the front door, the front hall leading into the living room, behind the living room the kitchen, off the kitchen the first floor bathroom, the distance from one room to the next spanned by squares of a faint grid. Seeing the mathematics behind it only seemed to further the mystery of the place.

"This is us." Carol pointed. "Right? But what about this?"

She pointed to another room. In the center of the square was a smaller square. Carol traced it with one finger.

"It must be the locked room. And that, my friend, is a treasure chest if I've ever seen one. Doesn't that look like a treasure chest to you?"

At dinner, while our parents sat at the table, we sat beneath it, hiding out. We heard the rap and rattle of plates and bottles. Someone overturned an ashtray and gray snow fell from the table's edge. I'd learned to stop paying attention, to let myself believe they were playing games not so different from ours. But it didn't always work. That night my father said, "You're right, Roy. You're completely fucking right. What *did* happen?" He was drunk—I could tell the signs by then—his words coming at half speed and double volume. It must be true, he said. Somewhere along the way, and he didn't know where, that was the hard part, but somewhere, he'd screwed up big. He must have, he said, if it had led him to a second-rate school that treated him to a windowless office in a building surrounded by a grid of asphalt, grass, parking lot, field. If it had led him to Clarinda, to neighbors he both pitied and resented and a basement that flooded and smelled like a body. This was all wrong.

Someone was swirling a drink, the ice chiming.

"Well," Roy said. "Serves you right for dedicating your life to James Fucking Agee. Anyone could have told you that."

"*That* was a guy who could drink," my father said.

"He could. But if you were going to slave over a drunk, why not me?" As if on command the adults laughed. I strayed too close to Roy's foot. He bent under the table and yanked me up into the light.

"Here, here, look at these stowaways." He drum-rolled the table with his palms.

"What have these stowaways been up to?"

"Pirating," Carol said.

"Bravo to that." Roy began to clap and the rest of the adults joined in. "Élan, that takes some true élan. What are your pirating plans? Treasure, death, what?"

"Still deciding," Carol said.

"It's just you don't look so piratey," Roy said. "What about an eye patch, a parrot, some venereals, at least?"

"We've got a map," she said.

Roy led another round of applause. "A map. We've got to see it."

I knew Carol kept it folded in her back pocket. I'd already dreamt up a story for the map, and I could feel Roy's questions wiping away the trap doors and moss-covered tombs.

"Actually, it's a secret map," I said.

"We don't have secrets," Roy said. "Not between us. Let's see."

Carol handed Roy the map. He swept the plates in front of him aside and unfolded it across the dinner table. He made a show of studying it carefully. "Hmm, yes, I see, yes, interesting," he said.

I watched Carol watching him. Smiling. "Well?" she said.

"Come here, and I'll show you," Roy said. "You see this room here, and there's this square, here. I bet that's your treasure."

Carol rolled her eyes. "We know *that* already."

This brought the adults to hysterics.

"OK, OK," Roy said. "I figured you did, but look at the size of that square. You know, when I was living in Scotland as a kid, I went to stay with an uncle one summer, and he had a room like that. There was a chest in that room so big that it could never fit through the door. It was built in the room, built to never leave. That might be what we're dealing with here."

"What was in it?" Carol asked.

"That's a secret."

"You just said there were no secrets."

"You have an uncle in Scotland?" my mother said, giggling.

"Well, I *might*," Roy said, and in the laughter that followed I snatched the map from the table and dragged Carol away.

We returned to the house the next summer. My father rented another convertible and once we'd parked in the gravel drive I leapt out. I found Carol at the edge of the water, digging up the shore. Her arms were sleeved in mud. There was no wind to soften the smell of brine and seaweed.

"I'm glad you finally got here," she said. "You can help me."

"Help you play in the mud?"

"I'm looking. I've been thinking about this all year, about what you and I should do."

If said by the right person, no words are more powerful than "you and I."

"We should find that key," she said, using a filthy finger to push hair over one of her ears. "So we can get into that room. So we can see what's in that chest."

"You think the key's out here?" I asked.

"Maybe," Carol said, without looking up. "Are you going to help me or not?"

We'd all left the last summer, hugging and throwing bags into the convertible and saying how we'd return the next year and do it all again, and I'd stayed up nights that winter sketching out new planets. I'd dreamt of racing lava as I'd waded through knee-high Nebraska snow. I'd fled across the prairie, an Indian chased by cowboys.

I was young enough to think that it was possible for things to be exactly the same, but my parents should have known better.

"Why didn't you tell us you were coming alone?" my mother asked Roy that evening. She stood at the kitchen sink, filling the slate-colored steamer pot. Roy was bent over a cutting board, the knife clicking fast as a sewing machine.

"I didn't come alone," he said. "In fact, I brought an entire case of northern Rhône, and Carol's somewhere too."

"Why didn't you tell us *Jan* wasn't coming?" my father asked.

"I don't know. I should have." Roy ran his finger along the broad side of the knife, wiping garlic off the blade. "But the better question is why didn't she tell me she was leaving?"

My parents shared glances and a few shards of conversation about how maybe this wasn't a good idea anymore. But there was something irresistible about Roy, maybe even more so after he lost Jan. Sometimes self-destruction looks just like self-confidence, and Roy seemed invulnerable.

In fact, with Jan gone, my parents and Roy receded further into the distance. They stayed up deep into the night and slept off most of the days. In the mornings, I'd come downstairs to find the house deserted; the dining-room table littered with bottles; the ashtrays overflowing and the air stuffed with smoke.

The late nights that, the first year, had been so confusing began to seem almost funny. My father, his glasses dirty, his hair gray at the temples, lolling his head from side to side, raising a glass of Canadian Club in a toast "to the cocksuckers of Bali." My mother, wearing the ancient cardigan we'd nicknamed the Brandenburger, laughing so hard that she poured an entire glass of wine into her lap.

Then one night we were joined by a woman with deeply tanned skin and a smoky voice. She wore her dark hair pulled back and there was a mole or sore at the corner of her mouth that she'd tried to cover with lipstick. "I'm Margaret, Roy's friend," she said. "Which one of you is Carol?" We just looked at her. "I'm only joking," she said. "You're very beautiful, Carol."

Carol glared at Roy through dinner, but his attention was on Margaret. He twirled his fork and served the spaghetti. He twisted the wine bottle up in his napkin like a waiter when he refilled her glass.

Later, when Carol and I were playing Scrabble in my bedroom, music began to blare from the living room. We crept to the top of the stairs, and from there we could see the four of them dancing. My mother's head on my father's shoulder. Roy and Margaret, swaying, his hands clasped at the small of her back. His eyes closed and jaw clenched, as if it took a great force to will them shut.

"Why don't we camp out in one of the empty rooms tonight?" I asked. "There's a ton of extra pillows and blankets." The ballad ended. Before he let go, Roy lowered his lips to Margaret's brown shoulder.

Later that night, I turned out the light and lay down in the darkness. There was a ridge of shadow maybe half a foot away. There was the sigh and faint heat of Carol's breath.

"If anything goes wrong in the night just wake me up," I said. "If the pirates who lived here come back or something." I'd meant it as a joke, a jab at the year before.

"The pirates are downstairs already, don't you hear them?" she said.

"Where's your mom?" I asked.

"In New Jersey with Clark. He helps run a plastic cup company. What kind of person would want to do that? Anyway, she moved to New Jersey with him months ago."

"You stayed with your dad?"

"I had school. That's what I told her. But is it so crazy that I wanted to stay with him? Is she going to argue with me about that?"

"She shouldn't."

"Or maybe she should. I don't know. My dad's always saying he's sorry, he's sorry. I found him asleep in the car one morning. One night the police dropped him off."

"What will you do?"

"I'll probably have to move to Clark's in the fall. But I wanted to come here for the summer. I had to really beg for that."

"Really?"

"Well," she said. "I want to see what's in that chest before I die."

"What do you think is in it?" I asked.

"It could be anything. It could be a whale."

"A whale would be too big."

"A baby whale, or whale bones."

"Do you really believe that?"

"You're ruining it, Josh," she said. "Stop ruining it, OK?"

For the rest of the summer we searched for the key. We hunted through the shed out back, peering between the rusty spokes of old bicycles. We crawled into the shade under the front porch and found nothing but the gray skeletons of birds and one bright blue feather, which I saved. We emptied out the closets and rooted in the pockets of heavy winter jackets. We pawed through the paste of old leaves in the gutters.

Back in Clarinda that fall, my parents barely mentioned the Izelins. Sometimes the phone would ring late and I'd hear my father clomp down the stairs and answer (not in the voice from Maine but in his real voice). "No, Roy. I wasn't asleep yet. What's on your mind? Just slow down. We can talk, I've got time."

One night, as my parents were cooking dinner, my father said, "He wants the three of us to buy that place. Can you imagine that?"

"My god, what did you say?"

"Well, I couldn't just tell him he was crazy, could I? I wonder if we should even go back at all."

It was a question my parents discussed often that year. One evening in February my mother said, "You won't believe who called today—*Jan*, saying that Carol told her we were going back, saying she just wanted to make sure before she says yes."

My father raised his eyebrows and said nothing. Roy continued to call and my parents continued to debate, and finally they turned to me and asked, "Do *you* want to go back to Maine next summer?"

I'd turned twelve that year. I'd joined the basketball team. I'd learned how to play "Lithium" by Nirvana on the guitar, and I'd already had my first kiss with a girl who played clarinet in the school orchestra.

Carol was on the front porch when we arrived. Her hair was cut short. She wore pleated khaki shorts and sunglasses on top of her head. She was taller, much taller.

"Oh my god," she said, as she hugged me.

"How was your year?" I asked.

"It's good to see you."

As my parents lugged in their bags, I sat down on the porch next to her.

"What do you want to do?" I asked.

"I have homework," she said. "That's how stupid this new school is. Other than that it's up to you."

"You sound different," I said.

"That must be New Jersey. I don't notice the accent anymore. I wish I did but I don't."

As always, I didn't know what to make of Carol, but Roy was worse than expected. His belly looked bigger, his neck fleshier, but his legs—poking out of boxer shorts as he sleepily ground coffee—seemed too thin to support his body.

And almost immediately I could see why my parents had been hesitant to come. In Nebraska my father could shake his head at Roy, pity him, laugh at him. But in Maine my father was powerless, roaring drunk by the end of dinner. As my mother cleared the table, Roy yelled, "Polish Fire Drill," and he and my father took off, tearing through the house, laughing furiously. They discovered the rooms upstairs, just as Carol and I had two years before. One night, they tossed the doctor's scale out of the second-story window, and it lay on the lawn for days, a mess of weights and pulleys. It was Carol who cleaned it up, Carol who helped Roy into bed that night and the next night. Pouring him a glass of water, rattling aspirin from a bottle on the bedside table.

When she wasn't taking care of Roy, Carol spent her time just as she'd promised, reading *Jane Eyre*, *Wuthering Heights*, and *Lord of the Flies*. The sun boiled away the days. By dusk, there was nothing left but heat, and the air felt thick as seawater. At night I would follow her on long walks through the woods.

These journeys turned into dares. How far could we go into the forest? Until the waves no longer sounded and the insects seemed to rise up. It was frightening, all that blackness and buzz. I could hear Carol's steps get fast and her breathing shallow, but I was always the one to suggest turning back. I was happy to, because only then—when it was just the two of us picking our way toward the glowing windows—did I feel I could talk to her.

"You know, I almost called you last fall, in November," she said one night. "Would that have been strange?"

"Did something happen?" I asked.

"Not really. Someone kicked in Clark's basement windows. I cut my foot on the broken glass. My mother thought I did it on purpose. Then we both cried for hours."

"How did you get her to let you come back?"

"That was easy. I told her this is the only place I don't think about dying all the time."

Our footsteps crunched in the dark.

"I just told her that," Carol said. "I don't really think about dying all the time."

"What do you think about?" I asked.

"My mother says I need to stop pretending that nothing's changed, because everything has, and that's life. She says some people never stop believing in the past. Do you think I've changed? Since you've known me?"

"I'd say yes."

"I knew you did. I can always see it on your face when you get here. It's nice actually."

"Have I changed?"

She laughed. "No," she said. "Not really. Don't worry, though. There's time."

But there wasn't. A few nights later I was awoken by shouts from the yard. The air was doused with fog, but from my window I could pick out the shapes of Roy and my father. Each held a sword pulled from the wall upstairs. The enormous moon seemed to be held in place by a string of cloud.

"Avast, lover," I heard my father say.

"You mean lubber," Roy said. "Prepare for a keel haul under me big balls."

They rushed at each other. The swords gleamed and clinked as they passed like jousters. My father stumbled a few steps and sat down, laughing hysterically. I heard the back door open and crack shut. "OK, enough of that," my mother said. "I wasn't serious about a duel."

But Roy and my father ignored her and began the dance again, rushing, shouting. This time my father dropped his sword and went down, howling. My mother ran out and reached for his bleeding hand.

"What the hell is wrong with you?" she said.

"He's a scurvy dog. That's what's wrong with him," Roy said.

By the time I got downstairs there was a trail of blood through the kitchen, yards of paper towel and the beginning of a debate about the emergency room. My father stood, bleeding into the sink, looking more sober, more embarrassed than I'd ever seen him.

He wore the same expression the next afternoon as my mother asked me to have a seat in the living room. She said she was sorry, but it was best for everyone if we left. It wasn't anyone's fault, she said, and it had been fun—no one was saying that it hadn't. She addressed everything to Roy because my father—holding his bandaged hand above his head—had apparently already agreed.

Roy stared at the floor, looking a million years old. They were all too embarrassed to say much else, so my mother turned to me.

"Why don't you get packed up," she said.

"I should tell Carol," I said.

"Please do," Roy said, tilting up his tired eyes. "I have to call her mother."

I didn't have to tell her. I'd seen her at the top of the stairs, listening. Just where we'd stood the summer before, watching Roy dance with that woman. I imagined Carol and me dancing. I imagined her returning home to New Jersey, her feet bleeding on a white rug in her bedroom.

I looked for the blue feather I'd taken from under the porch the year before. I dug through the dresser where we'd found the map, tied a scarf around my head, and stuck the feather behind it. I found a fedora that looked enough like a cowboy hat, tied another scarf into a holster, bent a wire hanger into a pistol.

I stood in the doorway of Carol's room. Her eyes were red. She sat with her arms around one knee. I drew back the arrow on an invisible bow.

"Come on," she said, laughing and crying at the same time. "What is this?"

"Run," I said.

She tied on the holster, drew the coat hanger and pointed it at me. "You run," she said.

She chased me through the halls all the way back to Nebraska. I licked at the flint of an arrowhead as I waded through a cold white river, slid on my belly through tall grass, under the enormous heads of buffalo and a sky knotted with clouds. Across the prairie, I saw her silhouette, dark except for one silver glint as she pulled a key from a tangle of dry weeds.

Then we were back in the house, racing down the hall to the door. Carol's hair was long, and she wore horse-shaped barrettes. Jan was downstairs rattling a cocktail shaker, laughing with Roy and my mother and father.

The key rattled too, but the lock finally turned. As the door swung free, light poured into the dark hall. No one had been in the room for years and it was as if all the light had been saved up.

The chest inside was mammoth. Built from dark wood, it was unadorned except for a keyhole. Carol stood in front of it, arms outspread as if she might rise off the floor. The chest was wider than her wingspan. The sunlight rolled over the rounded top and struck her hair. She turned the key and heaved it open.

"It's full of water," she said.

She dove in headfirst and after a moment I followed, swimming through a shoal of black fish to the bottom of an ocean. Carol's hair streamed like flame. We exchanged messages in bubbles of air. We took giant steps along the seafloor, weaving between stingrays, kicking up showers of sand, until we found another chest crusted in barnacles. We pried the second chest open too: inside there was another shimmering pool. She took my hand and dove again through cold currents. We emerged above a reef lit up like a city. Another chest filled with water. We continued, to another chest and another. Down and down and down until, from the living room, I heard my mother calling my name.

Soon after, I was on my way to the airport, and soon after that, I was in high school. And soon after that, the friends I'd played pick-up basketball with were tuning muscle cars and I'd begun to feel angry and alone. My parents, with all of their social realist literature and Ravel, had made me an outsider in my own hometown, had left me no choice but to look at my classmates with a mixture of jealousy and contempt. When I left Clarinda, I went straight to San Francisco and stayed on after college and planned never to leave. I guess it should have been no surprise that Carol would wind up there too. It should have been no surprise to hear her voice on my machine one evening after work, but it was.

We got together at a bar in the Mission. We hadn't seen each other in over ten years, and I can't say I would have recognized her if we'd passed on the street. She was thin and sort of Nordic-looking with teeth like Liv Ullmann's. She took my hand and led me upstairs to a lounge with leather chairs where it was stifling hot and loud. She spoke fast and had a nervous way of laughing, just like her mother. Roy, she told me, had quit drinking years ago, he'd just retired and was working on restoring a little cottage on Owasco Lake. She'd spent two years at Tufts before an anxiety attack drove her out west. She loved San Francisco. She was taking a poetry class at City Lights and learning to sail at the marina and feeling much better. She was still working on her degree and just waiting for credits to transfer and temping in the meantime as the receptionist at a bank.

"And your parents?" she asked.

"Nearly retired. I think they're happy," which I said automatically because I could still never think of them as anything other than happy.

"You know," she said, "Those were some bad years for me. I never really thanked you. I must have been so self-absorbed. Were they bad for you?"

"No," I said. "They weren't bad. I even miss them sometimes."

"I don't, but you know what I was thinking the other day after I called? I'll never have another friend like that. All of a sudden, it's too late."

The music went up and we had to lean close to each other's ear to be heard. I caught every third word about a therapist in Boston, about an old boyfriend. I could tell she was missing much of what I was saying, though much of what I was saying wasn't important. Eventually, she said that she had friends to meet and that I should come too, and I told her that I had friends to meet as well, even though I didn't.

Really, I was just tired. I'd taken a job teaching history at a junior high school in Oakland. Each morning, I stood in line for the metal detector behind shoving eighth graders, cleaning the change from my pockets. Each day, I came home with stacks of crumpled notebook paper to read, already so exhausted that my teeth hurt.

We promised to call, but I knew that I probably wouldn't see her again. There are only so many people you can have in your life, and three summers spent together half a lifetime before just wasn't enough. I walked home thinking this but also imagining—it just came to me, I couldn't shake the image—that I'd climb the dark stairs to my apartment and twist the sticky lock and shoulder open the heavy door to find her there, waiting.

TOSCA

Stuart Dybek

READY!

Aim!

On command the firing squad aims at the man backed against a full-length mirror. The mirror once hung in a bedroom, but now it's cracked and propped against a dumpster in an alley. The condemned man has refused the customary last cigarette but accepted as a hood the black slip that was carelessly tossed over a corner of the mirror's frame. The slip still smells faintly of a familiar fragrance.

Through his rifle sight, each sweating, squinting soldier in the squad can see his own cracked reflection aiming back at him.

Also in the line of fire is a phantasmal reflection of the surprised woman whose slip now serves as a hood (a hood that hides less from the eyes looking out than from those looking in). She's been caught dressing, or undressing, and presses her hands to her breasts in an attempt to conceal her nakedness.

The moment between commands seems suspended to the soldiers and to the hooded man. The soldiers could be compared to sprinters poised straining in the blocks, listening for the starter's gun, though, of course, when the shot is finally fired, it's their fingers on the triggers. The hooded man also listens for the shot even though he knows he'll be dead before he hears it. I've never been conscripted to serve in a firing squad or condemned to stand facing death—at least, not any more than we all are—but in high school I once qualified for the state finals in the high hurdles, and

I know that between the "Aim" command and the shot there's time for a story.

Were this a film, there'd be time for searching close-ups of each soldier's face as he waits for the irreversible order, time for the close-ups to morph into a montage of images flashing back through the lives of the soldiers, scenes with comrades in bars, brothels, et cetera, until one of the squad—a scholarly looking myopic corporal—finds himself a boy again, humming beside a pond, holding, instead of a rifle, a dip net and a Mason jar.

There's a common myth that a drowning man sees his life pass before his eyes. Each soldier taking aim imagines that beneath the hood the condemned man is flashing through his memory. It's a way in which the senses flee the body, a flight into the only dimension where escape is still possible: time. Rather than a lush dissolve into a Proustian madeleine moment, escape is desperate—the plunge through duration in "An Occurrence at Owl Creek Bridge," or through a time warp as in "The Secret Miracle," Borges's *ficción* in which a playwright in Nazi-occupied Prague faces a firing squad.

In this fiction, set in an anonymous dead-end alley, the reflection of a woman, all the more beautiful for being ghostly, has surfaced from the depths of a bedroom mirror. The soldiers in the firing squad, who can see her, conclude that she is a projection of the hooded man's memory and that her flickering appearance is a measure of how intensely she is being recalled. Beneath the hood, the man must be recalling a room in summer where her bare body is reflected beside his, her blonde-streaked hair cropped short, both of them tan, lean, still young. The mirror is unblemished as if it, too, is young.

"Look," she whispers, "us."

Was it then he told her that their reflection at that moment was what he'd choose to be his last glimpse of life?

Each soldier is asking himself: Given a choice, what would I ask for *my* last glimpse of life to be?

But actually, the hooded man never would have said something so mawkishly melodramatic. As for having the unspoken thought, Well, so shoot me, he thinks.

Back from netting tadpoles, the scholarly corporal, sweating behind his rifle again, imagines that rather than recalling random times in bars, brothels, et cetera, the hooded man is revisiting all the rooms in which he undressed the woman in the mirror.

One room faces the L tracks. The yellow windows of a night train stream across the bedroom mirror. After the train is gone, the empty station seems illuminated by the pink-shaded bed lamp left burning as he removes her clothes. Beneath the tracks there's a dark street of jewelry shops, their display windows stripped and grated. Above each shop, behind carbonized panes, the torches of lapidaries working late ignite with the gemstone glows of hydrogen, butane, and acetylene. Her breasts lift as she unclasps a necklace, which spills from her cupped hand into an empty wineglass beside the bed. Pearls, pinkish in the light, brim over like froth. A train is coming from the other direction.

In the attic she calls his tree house, the bed faces the only window, a skylight. The mirror is less a reflection than a view out across whitewashed floorboards to a peeling white chair draped with her clothes and streaked by diffused green light shafting through the leafy canopy. The shade of light changes with the colors of thinning maples. At night, the stars through bare branches make it seem, she says, as if they lie beneath the lens of a great telescope. Naked under a feather tick, they close their eyes on a canopy of constellations light-years away and open them on a film of first snow. Daylight glints through the tracks of starlings.

In a stone cottage near Lucca, rented from a beekeeper, they hear their first nightingale. They hear it only once, though perhaps it sings while they sleep. At twilight, the rhapsodic push-pull of an accordion floats from the surrounding lemon grove. To follow it seems intrusive, so they never see who's playing, but on a morning hike, they come upon a peeling white chair weathered beneath a lemon tree. When he sits down, she raises her skirt and straddles him. The accordion recital always ends on the same elusive melody. They agree it's from an opera, as they agreed the birdcall had to be a nightingale's, but they can't identify the opera. It's Puccini, he says, which reminds her they have yet to visit Puccini's house in Lucca. Tomorrow, he promises.

Recognize it—the aria playing even now, the clarinet, a nightingale amid twittering sparrows.

Sparrows twitter in the alley from power lines, rain gutters, and the tar-paper garage roofs onto which old ladies in black toss bread crusts, and this entire time the aria has been playing in the background. Not pumped from an accordion, probably it's a classical radio station floating from an open window, or maybe some opera buff—every neighborhood no matter how shabby has one—is playing the same aria over, each time by a different tenor—Pavarotti, Domingo, Caruso—on his antiquated stereo.

The clarinet introduces the aria's melody and the tenor echoes it as if in a duet with the woodwinds. *E lucevan le stelle, he sings: And the stars were shining. Ed olezzava la terra: And the scent of earth was fresh* . . .

Stridea l'uscio dell'orto,
e un passo sfiorava la rena.
Entrava ella, fragrante,
mi cadea fra le braccia . . .

The garden gate creaked, and a step brushed the sand. She entered, fragrant, and fell into my arms . . .

Admittedly, "*E lucevan le stelle*" is a predictable choice for an execution—so predictable that one might imagine the aria itself is what drew this motley firing squad with their unnecessarily fixed bayonets and uniforms as dusty as the sparrows brawling over bread crusts.

Doesn't the soldiers' appearance, from their unpolished boots to the hair scruffing out from beneath their shakos, verge on the theatrical, as if a costume designer modeled them on Goya's soldiers in *The Disasters of War*? A role in the firing squad doesn't require acting; their costumes act for them. They are anonymous extras, grunts willing to do the dirty work if allowed to be part of the spectacle. Grunts don't sing. In fact, the corporal will be disciplined for his ad-libbed humming by the pond. They march—*trudge* is more accurate—from opera to opera hoping to be rewarded with a chorus, a chance to emote, to leave onstage some lyrical record of their existence beyond the brutal percussion of a final volley. But their role has always been to stand complacently mute. This season alone they've made the rounds from *Carmen* to *Il Trovatore*, and when the classics are exhausted then it's on to something new.

There are always roles for them, and the promise of more to come. In Moscow, a young composer whose grandfather disappeared during Stalin's purges labors over *The Sentence*—an opera he imagines Shostakovich might have written, which opens with Fyodor Dostoyevsky, five days past his twenty-eighth birthday, facing the firing squad of the Tsar. Four thousand three hundred miles away, in Kalamazoo, Michigan, an assistant professor a few years out of Oberlin who has been awarded his first commission, for an opera based on Norman Mailer's *The Executioner's Song*, has just sung "Froggy Went A-Courtin'" to his three-year-old daughter. She's fallen asleep repeating, *Without my uncle Rat's consent, I would not marry the president,* and now the house is quiet, and he softly plinks on her toy piano the motif that will climax in Gary Gilmore's final aria.

And here in the alley, the firing squad fresh from Granada in 1937, where they gunned down Federico García Lorca in Osvaldo Golijov's opera *Ainadamar*, has followed the nightingale call of "*E lucevan le stelle*" and stands taking aim at a man hooded in a slip.

If you're not an opera buff, you need to know that "*E lucevan le stelle*" is from the third act of *Tosca*. Mario Cavaradossi, a painter and revolutionary, has been tortured by Baron Scarpia, the lecherous, tyrannical chief of Rome's secret police, and waits to be shot at dawn. Cavaradossi's final thoughts are of his beloved Tosca. He bribes the jailer to bring him pen and paper so that he can write her a farewell, and then, overcome by memories, stops writing and sings his beautiful aria, a showstopper that brings audiences to applause and shouts of *Bravo!* before the performance can continue. Besides the sheer beauty of its music, the aria is a quintessential operatic moment, a moment both natural and credible—no small feat for opera—in which a written message cannot adequately convey the emotion and the drama soars to its only possible expression: song.

She entered, fragrant, and fell into my arms, oh! sweet kisses, oh! lingering caresses. Trembling, I unveiled her beauty, the hero sings—in Italian, of course. But in American opera houses subtitles have become accepted. *My dream of love has vanished forever, my time is running out, and even as I die hopelessly, I have never loved life more.*

That final phrase about loving life, *Non ho amato mai tanto la vita,* always reminds me of Ren. He was the first of three friends of mine who have said, over the years, that he was living his life like an opera.

We were both nineteen when we met, that day Ren stopped to listen to me playing for pocket change before the Wilson L station and proposed a trade—his Kawasaki 250 with its rebuilt engine for my Leblanc clarinet. Usually I played at L stops with Archie, a blind accordion player, but it was thundering and Archie hadn't shown. I thought Ren was putting me on. When I asked why he'd trade a motorcycle for a clarinet, he answered: Who loves life more, the guy on the Outer Drive riding without a helmet, squinting into the wind, doing seventy in and out of traffic, or the guy with his eyes closed playing "Moonglow"?

Depends how you measure loving life, I said.

Against oblivion, Ren said, then laughed as if amused by his own pretension, a reflex of his that would become familiar. A licorice stick travels light, he explained, and he was planning to leave for Italy, where, if Fellini films could be believed, they definitely loved life more. He'd had a flash of inspiration watching me, a vision of himself tooting "Three Coins in the Fountain" by the Trevi Fountain and hordes of tourists in coin-tossing mode filling his clarinet case with cash. He'd rebuilt the 250cc engine— he could fix anything, he bragged—and even offered a warranty: he'd keep the bike perfectly tuned if I gave him clarinet lessons.

A week later, we were roommates, trading off who got the couch and who got the Murphy bed and sharing the rent on my Rogers Park kitchenette. From the start, his quip about loving life set the tone. The commonplace trivia from our lives became the measure in an existential competition. If I ordered beer and Ren had wine, it was evidence he loved life more. If he played the Stones and I followed with Billie Holiday, it argued my greater love of life.

The university we attended had a center in Rome, and Ren and I planned to room together there in our junior semester abroad. Neither of us had been to Europe. A few weeks before our departure, at a drunken party, Ren introduced me to Iris O'Brien. He introduced her as the Goddess O'Iris, which didn't seem an exaggeration at the time. He assured me there was no "chemistry" between them. Lack of chemistry wasn't my experience with Iris O'Brien. In a state that even in retrospect still feels more like delirium than like a college crush, I decided to cancel my trip so that once Ren left, Iris could move in. I'd never lived with a girlfriend before.

When I told Ren I wasn't going, he said, I suppose you think that giving up Europe for a woman means you win?

Iris isn't part of the game, I said, and when I failed to laugh at my own phony, offended honor, Ren did so for me—uproariously.

Living with Iris O'Brien lasted almost as long as the Kawasaki continued to run, about a month. Although Ren and I hadn't kept in touch, I figured that if he wouldn't return my clarinet, he'd at least fix the bike once he got back. But when the semester ended, he stayed in Europe.

From a mutual friend who had also gone to Rome, I heard Ren had dropped out. He spent his time playing my clarinet at fountains across the city, and he fell in love, not with a woman, but with opera. That surprised me, as the love of jazz that Ren and I shared seemed, for some reason, to require us to despise opera. With the money he'd made playing arias on the street, he bought a junked Moto Guzzi, rebuilt it, and took off on an odyssey of visiting opera houses across Italy.

That spring I got an airmail letter without a return address. The note scrawled on the back of a postcard of the Trevi Fountain read: *Leaving for Vienna. Ah! Vienna! Non ho amato mai tanto la vita—Never have I loved life more. Living it like an opera—well, an opera buffa—so, tell the Goddess O'Iris, come bless me.*

It was the last I ever heard from him.

I didn't catch the allusion to *Tosca* in Ren's note until years later when I was enrolled in graduate school at NYU. I was seeing a woman named Clair who had ducked out of a downpour into the cab I drove part-time. Nothing serious, we'd agreed, an agreement I kept reminding myself to honor. Clair modeled to pay the bills— underwear her specialty. She'd come to New York from North Dakota in order to break into musical theater and was an ensemble member of Cahoots, a fledgling theater on Bank Street, which billed itself as a fusion between cabaret and performance art. Cahoots was funded in part by an angel, an anonymous financier whom Clair was also sleeping with. Through Clair, I met Emil, the founder and artistic director of Cahoots, and the two of them, flush with complimentary tickets, became my tutors in opera.

Their friendship went back to their student days at Juilliard, where Emil had been regarded as a can't-miss talent until he'd become involved in what Clair called "Fire Island Coke Chic." She'd been Emil's guest at a few of the parties he frequented, including a legendary night when he sang "Somewhere (There's a Place for Us)" with Leonard Bernstein at the piano. Clair worried that Emil's addiction to male dancers was more self-destructive than the drugs.

Emil worked as a singing waiter at Le Figaro Café, a coffeehouse in the Village with marble-top tables and a Medusa-hosed Italian espresso machine that resembled a rocket crossed with a basilica. Each steamed demitasse sounded like a moon launch and the waiters, singing a cappella, were all chronically hoarse. Emil felt even more contempt toward his job than Clair had for modeling. The one night he allowed us to stop in for coffee, Emil sang "Una furtiva lagrima," the famous aria from *The Elixir of Love.*

His voice issued with an unforgettable purity that seemed at odds with the man mopping sweat, his Italian punctuated by gestures larger than life. The room, even the espresso machine, fell silent.

In the opera, that aria is sung by Nemorino, a peasant who has spent his last cent on an elixir he hopes will make the wealthy woman he loves love him in return. Nemorino sees a tear on her cheek and takes it as a sign that the magic is working. Watching Emil sing his proverbial heart out at a coffeehouse, Clair, too, looked about to cry. He's singing for us, she said. Until that moment, I hadn't recognized the obvious: she'd been in love with Emil since Juilliard—years of loving the impossible.

Emil's voice rose to the climax and Clair mouthed the aria's last line to me in English, *I could die! Yes, I could die of love*, while Emil held the final *amor* on an inexhaustible breath.

The espresso machine all but levitated on a cushion of steam, and patrons sprang to a standing ovation that ended abruptly when Emil, oblivious to the blood drooling onto his white apron from the left nostril of his coke-crusted nose, flipped them off as if conducting music only he could hear.

After Figaro's became the third job Emil lost that year, Clair decided to risk desperate measures. Emil was broke. His doomed flings with danseurs had left him without an apartment of his own. The actors in Cahoots had grown openly critical of his leadership. Refusing to crash with increasingly disillusioned friends, Emil slept at the theater, whose heat was turned off between performances.

He's out of control, we're watching slo-mo suicide, Clair said, enlisting me in a small group of theater people for an intervention. It was an era in New York when the craze for interventions seemed in direct proportion to the sale of coke. Emil regarded interventions as a form of theater below contempt. To avoid his suspicion, Clair planned for it to take place at the private cast party following the opening of the show Emil had worked obsessively over—a takeoff on *The Elixir of Love*.

In the Donizetti opera, Dr. Dulcamara, a salesman of quack remedies, arrives in a small Basque town and encounters

Nemorino, who requests a potion of the kind that Tristan used to win Isolde. Dulcamara sells him an elixir that's nothing more than wine.

In Emil's script, the town is Winesburg, Ohio, an all-American community of secret lusts and repressed passion. The townsfolk sing of their need for a potion to release them from lives of quiet desperation. Emil played the traveling salesman—not Dr. Dulcamara, but Willy Loman. As Willy sings his aria "Placebo," sexually explicit ads for merchandise flash across a screen, attracting the townsfolk. They mob Nemorino, and the bottle of bogus elixir is torn from hand to hand. Its mere touch has them writhing lewdly, unbuttoning their clothes, and when the bottle breaks they try to lap elixir from the stage, pleading for more, threatening to hang Willy Loman by his tie if he doesn't deliver.

Willy finds a wine bottle beside a drunk, comatose and sprawled against a dumpster. As scripted, the bottle is half filled with wine, and Emil is only to simulate urinating into it. But that night, onstage, he drained the bottle, unzipped his trousers, and, in view of the audience, pissed.

"Here's your elixir of love!" he shouted, raising the bottle triumphantly as he stepped back into the town square.

The script has the townsfolk passing the elixir, slugging it down, and falling madly, indiscriminately in love. Willy demands to be paid, and they rough him up instead. The play was to end with the battered salesman suffering a heart attack as an orgy swirls around him. In an aria sung with his dying breath, he wonders if he's spent his moneygrubbing life unwittingly pissing away magic.

Script notwithstanding, opening night was pure improv, pure pandemonium. When the actors realized Emil had actually given them piss to drink, the beating they gave him in return wasn't simulated, either. Emil fought back until, struck with the bottle, he spit out pieces of tooth, then leaped from the stage, ran down the center aisle, and out of the theater. The audience thought it was the best part of the show.

The cast party went on backstage without Emil. Stunned and

dejected, the actors knew it was the end of Cahoots and on that final evening clung to each other's company. Around midnight, Clair pressed me into a corner to say, You don't belong at this wake. We stood kissing, and then she gently pushed me away and whispered, Go. One word, perfectly timed to say what we had avoided saying aloud, but both knew: whatever was between us had run its course. Instead of goodbye, I said what I'd told her after our first night together and had repeated like an incantation each time since: Thank you.

Emil showed up as I was leaving. He still wore his bloodied salesman's tie. His swollen lip could have used stitches, but he managed to swig from a bottle of vodka.

Drunk on your own piss? asked Glen, who'd played Nemorino and had thrown the first punch onstage.

Shhh, no need for more, Clair said. She took Emil's arm as if to guide him. Sit down with us, she told him. Emil shook off her hand. Judas, he said, and Clair recoiled as if stung.

Keeping a choke hold on the bottle, Emil climbed up on a chair.

I've come to say I'm sorry, he announced, and to resign as your artistic director. I guessed you all might still be hanging around, given that without Cahoots none of you has anywhere else to perform.

Clair, blotting her smeared makeup, began to sob quietly, hopelessly, as a child cries. Emil continued as if, like so much else between them, it were a duet. Sweat streaked his forehead as it did when he sang.

Did you think I didn't know about the pathetic little drama you'd planned for me tonight by way of celebration? he asked. So, yes, I'm sorry, sorry to deprive you of the cheesy thrill of your judgmental psycho-dabbling. But then what better than your dabbling as actors to prepare you to dabble in others' lives? Was it so threatening to encounter someone willing to risk it all, working without a net, living an opera as if it's life, which sometimes— tonight, for instance—apparently means being condemned to live life as if it's a fucking opera?

*

The last friend of mine to say he was living life like an opera was Cole.

He said it during a call to wish me a happy birthday, one of those confiding phone conversations we'd have after being out of touch—not unusual for a friendship that went back decades to when we were in high school. Twenty years earlier, Cole had beat me in the state finals, setting a high school record for the high hurdles. We were workout buddies the summer between high school and college, which was also the summer I worked downtown at a vintage jazz record shop. Cole would stop by to spin records while I closed up. He'd been named for Coleman Hawkins and could play Hawkins's famous tenor solo from "Body and Soul" note for note on the piano. Cole played the organ each Sunday at the Light of Deliverance, one of the oldest African-American churches on the South Side. His grandfather was the minister. I'd close the record shop and we'd jog through downtown to a park with a track beside the lake, and after running, we'd swim while the lights of the Gold Coast replaced a lingering dusk. His grandfather owned a cabin on Deep Lake in northern Michigan, and Cole invited me up to fish before he left for Temple on a track scholarship. It was the first of our many fishing trips over the years to come.

Cole lived in Detroit now, near the neighborhood of the '67 riots, where he'd helped establish the charter school that he'd written a book about. He'd spent the last four years as a community organizer and was preparing to run for public office. When he'd married Amina, a Liberian professor who had sought political asylum, "Body and Soul" was woven into the recitation of their vows. The wedding party wore dashikis, including me, the only white groomsman.

He called on my birthday—our birthdays were days apart—to invite me up to Deep Lake to fish one last time. His grandfather had died years earlier and the family had decided to sell the cabin. When I asked how things were going, Cole paused, then said, I'm living my life like an opera. I knew he was speaking in code, something so uncharacteristic of him that it caught me by surprise.

I waited for him to elaborate. Before the silence got embarrassing, he changed the subject.

We'd always fished after Labor Day when the summer people were gone. By then evenings were cool enough for a jacket. The woods ringing the lake were already rusting, the other cottages shuttered, the silence audible. Outboard engines were prohibited on Deep Lake, although the small trolling motor on the minister's old wooden rowboat was legal. Cole fished walleye as his grandfather had taught: at night—some nights under a spangle of Milky Way, on others in the path of the moon, but also on nights so dark that out on the middle of the lake you could lose your sense of direction.

The night was dark like that. There was no dock light to guide us back, but the tubed stereo that had belonged to his grandfather glowed on the screened porch. Cole's grandfather had had theories about fishing and music: one was that walleyes rose to saxophones. His jazz collection was still there, some of the same albums I'd sold in the record shop when I was eighteen. We chose *Ballads* by Ben Webster. The notes slurred across the water as I rowed out to the deep spot in the middle. Cole lowered the anchor, though it couldn't touch bottom. I cracked the seal on a fifth of Jameson and passed it to Cole; tradition demanded that I arrive with a bottle. We'd had a lot of conversations over the years, waiting for the fish to bite.

I been staying at the cabin since we last talked, Cole said.

What's going on? I asked.

Remember I told you I was living life like an opera? You didn't say boo, but I figured you got my meaning, seeing you'd used the phrase yourself. Never know who's listening in. Cole laughed as if kidding, but, given the surveillance on Martin Luther King, Jr., he worried about wiretaps.

Cole, I said, I *never* used that phrase.

Where do you think I got it? he asked.

Not from me.

Maybe you forgot saying it, he said, maybe you finally forgot who you said it about. Anyway, whoever said it, I'm at a fundraiser in Ann Arbor, everyone dressed so they can wear running shoes except for a woman I can't help noticing. You know me, it's not like I'm looking—just the opposite—there's always someone on the make if you're looking. She's out of *Vogue*. I hate misogynist rap, man, but plead guilty to thinking: rich bitch—which I regret when she comes up with my book and a serious camera that can't hide something vulnerable about her. Photojournalist, her card reads, and could she take one of me signing my book, and I say, sure, if she promises not to steal my soul, and she smiles and asks if she can make a donation to the school, and how could she get involved beyond just giving money, and where's my next talk, and do I have time for a drink? Two weeks later at a conference in D.C. she's there with Wizards tickets. And this time I go—we go to the game. In Boston it's the symphony, in Philly I show her places I lived in college and take her to the Clef, where 'Trane played, and in New York we go to the Met. I'd never been to an opera; we go three nights in a row. Was I happy—happiness isn't even the question. Remember running a race—thirteen-point-seven-nine seconds you've lived for, and when the gun finally fires and you're running, you disappear—like playing music those few times when you're more the music than you? She could make that happen again. One night, I'm home working late, Mina's already asleep, and the phone in my office rings. I'd never given her that unlisted home number. You need to help me, she says, and the line goes dead. Phone rings again. Where are you? I ask. Trapped in a car at the edge, she says. Her calls keep getting dropped, her voice is slurred: Come get me before I'm washed away. I keep asking her, Where are you? Finally she says: Jupiter Beach—I drove to see the hurricane. I say, You're a thousand miles away. The phone goes dead, rings, and Mina asks, Who keeps calling this time of night? She's in her nightgown, leaning in the doorway for I don't know how long. Too long for lies. I answer the phone, but no one's there.

She have a husband? Mina asks. You got to call him now.

The business card from Ann Arbor has private numbers she listed on the back, one with a Florida area code. A man answers, gives his name. I say, You don't know me, but I'm calling about an emergency, your wife's in the storm in a car somewhere on Jupiter Beach.

I know you, he says. I know you only too well. Don't worry, she doesn't tell me names, I don't ask, but I know you.

Mina presses speakerphone.

You teach tango or Mandarin or yoga or murderers to write poetry, film the accounts of torture victims, rescue greyhounds. I know the things you do, the righteous things you say, and I know you couldn't take your eyes off her the first time you saw her, and how that made you realize you'd been living a life in which you'd learned to look away. And like a miracle she's looking back, and you wonder what's the scent of a woman like that, and not long after— everything's happening so fast—you ask, What do you want? and she says, To leave the world behind together, and you think beauty like hers must come with the magic to allow what you couldn't ordinarily do, places you couldn't go, a life you'd dreamed when you were young. But now, just as suddenly, she can destroy you by falling from the ledge she's calling from, or falling asleep forever in the hotel room where she's lost count of the pills. She's talking crazy since she's stopped taking the meds you never noticed, and when she said she loved you, that was craziness, too—you're a symptom of her illness. So you called me, not to save her, but yourself, and it's me who knows where she goes when she gets like this, and I'll go, as I do every time, to save her, calm and comfort her, bring her home, because I love her, I was born to, I'll always love her, and you're only a shadow. I've learned to ignore shadows. She made you feel alive; now you're a ghost. Go. Don't call again.

I told you on the phone, Cole said, that I was living my life like an opera, but he's the one who sang the aria.

FIRE!

A borrowed flat above a plumbing store whose back windows look out on a yard of stockpiled toilets filled with unflushed rain. Four a.m., still a little drunk from a wake at an Irish bar, they smell bread baking. Someone's in the room, she whispers. It's only the mirror, he tells her. She strips off her slip, tosses it over the shadowy reflection, and then follows the scent to the open front windows. A ghost, she says as if sighing. Below a vaporous streetlamp, in the doorway of a darkened bakery, a baker in white, hair and skin dusted with flour, leans smoking.

FIRE!

A bedroom lit by fireflies, one phosphorescent above the bed, another blinking in the mirror as if captured in a jar. The window open on the scent of rain-bearded lilacs. When the shards of a wind chime suspended in a corner tingle, it means a bat swoops through the dark. Flick on the bed lamp and the bat will vanish.

FIRE! DAMN YOU! FIRE!

Whom to identify with at this moment—who is more real—Caruso, whose unmistakable, ghostly, 78-rpm voice carries over the ramparts where sparrows twitter, or Mario Cavaradossi?

Or perhaps with an extra in the firing squad, who—once Tosca flings herself from the parapet—will be free to march off for a beer at the bar around the corner, and why not, he was only following the orders barked out by the captain of the guard, who was just doing what the director demanded, who was in turn under the command of Giacomo Puccini.

Or with the hooded man, his mind lit by a firefly as he tries to recall a room he once attempted to memorize when it became increasingly clear to him that he would soon be banished.

FIRE! I AM GIVING YOU A DIRECT ORDER.

How heavy their extended rifles have become. The barrels teeter and dip, and seem to be growing like Pinocchio's nose, although it's common knowledge that rifles don't lie. Still, just to hold one steady and true requires all the strength and concentration a man can summon.

Turn on the bed lamp the better to illuminate the target. On some nights the silk shade suggests the color of lilacs and on others of areolas. See, the bat has vanished, which doesn't mean it wasn't there.

FIRE! OR YOU'LL ALL BE SHOT!

The lamp rests on a nightstand with a single drawer in which she keeps lotions and elixirs and stashes the dreams she records on blue airmail stationery when they wake her in the night—an unbound nocturnal diary. She blushed when she told him the dream in which she made love with the devil. He liked to do what you like to do to me—what *we* like, she said.

In the cracked mirror each member of the squad sees himself aiming at himself. Only a moment has passed since the "Aim" command, but to the members of the squad it seems they've stood with finger ready on their triggers, peering down their sights, for so long that they've become confused as to who are the originals and who are the reflections. After the ragged discharge, when the smoke has cleared, who will be left standing and who will be shattered into shards?

PLEASE, FIRE!

I can't wait like this any longer.

Non ho amato mai tanto la vita.

DHARMA AT THE GATE

Abby Geni

LUCY WAKES UP WITH HIS SMELL ON HER CLOTHES. Before school she packs herself a lunch, putting in extra food for him—he will not bring anything from home, and she can't abide his habit of getting by on nothing but sodas and candy bars from the vending machines. It is not yet dawn when she hurries to her car, the frost crackling beneath her feet. She has to leave early and detour south along the highway to pick him up. Xavier is already waiting outside the house when Lucy gets there. Despite the cold, he has no coat; he leans against a tree, posing for her, his ears and nose charred red by the chill. He climbs into the car and kisses her wildly, as though he has been drowning without her presence in the long hours of the morning.

On the way to school they fight. It is the same argument as usual—Lucy has been applying to colleges, and Xavier needs to be reassured, over and over, that she will not go far, that she will not forget him. He himself has no use for higher education. He will go into his father's garage and work as a mechanic, make a good living. By the time she pulls into the high school parking lot, Lucy is exhausted. The weight on her shoulders is exquisitely familiar, bearing down on her as they walk together across the sweeping lawns. Xavier holds her hand, fondling her fingers. He murmurs that she is beautiful, his little porcelain doll.

As always, Lucy meets him before second period, after third period, before fifth period. He is present for her even during her classes. They pass back and forth their own private notebook—an ordinary-looking spiral-bound thing, into which they can scribble letters to each other while appearing to take notes on trigonometry or Aristotle. In the hallways, they exchange wet kisses. Xavier often grabs her in a muffling embrace, going on long beyond the bounds of what is normal, as people dart around them like water streaming around a stone. They eat lunch together on the scrubbed, windswept grass in front of the school. Xavier takes what Lucy has brought him, thanking her absently, as he might thank a benevolent mother for doing exactly what is expected of her. They take sips from her juice box, share bites of the same apple. During recess, whatever the weather, the high school empties onto the grounds, students picnicking wherever they can find room. Xavier likes to observe his peers in the manner of an anthropologist, droning on about the social forces that cause the cheerleaders to laugh almost spontaneously, or the stoners to gather in front of the gas station across the street, marking their separation from the rest of the herd.

Lucy eats quietly. She can predict how Xavier will respond at any given moment. She knows when he's in a prideful mood and might be offended if she offered him her scarf, though the sky is an icy slate and snow has begun to fall in downy tufts. She knows when he will curl up and doze off in her lap, weary from a long night of video games in his house with no curfew. She knows that when lunch is over, he will insist on throwing away their garbage alone, chivalrously braving the stink of the cans and the presence of the pigeons and squirrels that hover possessively around what they perceive to be their own territory.

On the way to her next class, Lucy tugs their special notebook out of her backpack, wondering what on earth she will find to write in response to the letter he has scrawled there. Xavier will be waiting for the notebook after seventh period, with his haunted, adoring face. She is no longer amazed at how he can consume her entire day, though they do not have one class in common. People often ask about him, how he's been lately, what the two of them did last weekend. Lucy and Xavier have been a couple so long—

four years now, since they were freshmen—that no one can imagine them apart. No one knows anything about her except that she belongs to Xavier. Once, in health class, as the teacher rolled a condom onto a banana and explained its function, Lucy got the giggles, imagining Xavier as her own personal condom, a barrier that surrounds her completely, keeping the rest of the world at a distance. She has no particular friends anymore. Nobody would know to ask about her dog, about the trails she has been blazing in the woods on the edge of town, about her father, now permanently in a wheelchair. Instead they ask about her boyfriend, and Lucy smiles brightly and says that all is well. People glance at the back of her hand, where Xavier has inked a heart, or at her jeans, where he penned his name along the seam, and she sees them roll their eyes, smirking.

After school she drives him home. Snow has begun to fall in earnest, the whirling flakes blurring the horizon line. Xavier dozes in the passenger's seat, now and then coming to and remarking that she really ought to get the car cleaned—every seat is coated in golden fur, the back windows smeared with dog snot. Lucy acquiesces mildly, though like most dog owners she knows there isn't much point in cleaning a space that will be dirtied again the second the animal returns to it. She watches Xavier slouch up the walk to his house. The place has a distinctly unloved air, the bushes half-dead, the screens caked with dirt. Lucy has never been allowed inside, not once—the father is a dangerous drunk, the mother a cipher. The house has the same ramshackle, uncared-for aspect as Xavier himself, with his falling-apart jeans and his hair in an unwashed tousle. Lucy waves him inside, wishing, not for the first time, that he would be mowed down by a bus. A car accident. A plane crash. Something sudden, painless, and unexpected, as though God himself had reached down and rubbed her boyfriend out of existence with a big pink eraser. What a blessing it would be, after four long years—her entire high school career—to have Xavier out of her life, gone entirely, and to know that it was not her fault.

*

The blizzard continues into the evening, and by morning all of Ohio is swallowed up in white. Lucy bounces with anxiety beside the radio until they announce that school is canceled. Her parents are already gone—they navigated the snowy roads early that morning to take her father for a check-up. Lucy wraps herself up in sweaters and gloves. Her dog is planted by the front door, beating his tail against the hat-stand and moaning with anticipation. Lucy takes him to the arboretum. The walk is over a mile long, and soon she is loosening her coat, sweating beneath her layers. During the storm last night, sleet fell and froze, so that the surface of the snow is crusted and cracking. Lucy leaves cavernous footprints. Dharma skids and slips over the uneven surface, falling through with a startled yip. At the arboretum she lets him off leash, and he pelts away between the trees, kicking up a sparkling wake. Lucy follows him down the slope and scrambles over the frozen stream, making her way to her favorite log, where she can sit and let the stillness settle over her. Branches droop, their weight doubled by a coating of ice. Here and there, snow topples off a twig, landing in a floury explosion. In the distance, the dog is barking. Every so often he appears at the top of the hill, his tongue hanging ecstatically out of the side of his mouth. When Lucy smiles at him, he takes off again, whimpering with joy.

Dharma came to her six years ago. He was technically a birthday present—she had always begged for a dog—but even then, at eleven years old, Lucy knew better. For the first time, the doctors were certain that her father would have to spend at least some of his days in a wheelchair. The house was in an uproar: ramps to be built, the bedroom moved downstairs, the kitchen remodeled so that coffee cups and plates would be easily accessible. Lucy learned to lock the bathroom door when she showered, so the workmen would not barge in on her accidentally. She learned to do her homework at the library, where it was quiet, no hammering, no phone ringing off the hook. She learned not to ask her mother for anything—there was too much going on for Lucy to have a new backpack or a friend over, thank you very much. Even the dog was more a present for her father than herself. Her father was querulous, nervous, ashamed; he did not meet Lucy's eye for months, struggling around in his wheelchair, hollering for help from the bathroom, where he was stuck between the tub and the sink again. He no longer felt himself to be the head of the household, the protector. Lucy was not told any of this, of course. She was told that the dog was her own gift, a combination birthday present and a thank-you for her patience and understanding. But she saw how her father nodded approvingly when Dharma barked at the mailman—how her mother smiled, watching her father—and she knew who was really being appeased.

None of that mattered after the first few days. It was love from the beginning. Dharma followed her from room to room, laying his head on her knee. He clambered into the empty space beside her in bed, his body burning like a coal. He whined when she left for school. When she wasn't paying attention, he would rush up behind her, a chew toy in his mouth, and bash into the back of her knees, hooking one paw around her ankle. Dharma was a font of unintentional humor. He howled along with distant sirens. He charged around the house at top speed and, unaccustomed to the hardwood floors, skidded full-tilt into walls. Lucy was almost embarrassed by how fond she was of him. She had never been one of those girls, cooing with delight over kittens or sketching deformed horses in the margins of her homework. But this was something else. Every day after school, she linked a leash around his neck and walked for hours. In the rain he would dance in the brimming gutters. In the spring they made tracks together across deserted parks. Eventually Lucy discovered the arboretum, and the two of them tried in vain to map the network of trails that wound among the trees, Dharma ducking under twining creepers, chasing the moths that hovered in the watery light.

At last the dog bounds down the hill, panting and shuddering. He has worn himself out. Lucy scratches his head, and within minutes he is curled up in the snow, a red-gold bundle of fur, his nose tucked beneath his tail, in what Lucy likes to call his Dead Dog

Impression—so deeply asleep that he can scarcely be bothered to breathe. She plans to stay in the arboretum as long as she can stand the cold. Already her feet are numb. Clouds loom in the western sky, dark and smoky. The pine trees shake snow off their branches. The boulders are spangled with icicles. Dharma snores quietly, and Lucy's mind empties out as though someone has pulled the plug from a drain. For a while she is able to contain the easy silence of the forest. One of her history teachers—a man who quite clearly regretted never chucking his career and heading off to be a yogi in India—once spent a lesson on the rudiments of meditation. Lucy never mastered it; her mind is always crowded with Xavier. Sometimes she feels as though she has a double brain, her own thoughts bouncing around in a sea of his. She carries him with her. But in this place, if she sits still long enough, she can finally let him go. The sun emerges from between the clouds, and the snow gleams painfully. Bright whorls dance across the forest floor—and yet the light gives no warmth. Lucy is freezing. Her calves are buried in snow. Still, she can bear it a little longer. She takes a deep breath and closes her eyes.

Back at the house, her cell phone is waiting. As a rule, Lucy does not bring it with her to the woods. The trees block any semblance of service, giving her an excuse to render herself, while there, temporarily untethered. Three voice mails have accumulated in her absence. She glares at the tiny screen as she towels off the dog's feet. Dharma flings himself gratefully into his kennel, where he will sleep for the rest of the afternoon. Lucy putters around, opening the fridge and arranging the leaves of the plants on the countertop. She refreshes the water in Dharma's bowl and stares out the window, waiting in vain for her parents to come home.

At last she can put it off no longer. All three messages are from Xavier, of course. The first is a cheerful hello, isn't it awesome about school being canceled, so sad that he won't see her today. He misses her. Give him a call when she climbs out of bed. Lucy sighs and skips to the next message, which contains a note of anxiety. Xavier's voice spools out, filling the sunlit kitchen. Is she still in bed? She must really need her sleep, hah hah. He's a little worried though— could she call, just so he knows that she's all right, that her house didn't lose power or anything? Lucy rolls her eyes. She is accustomed to that particular plea, the *are-you-OK?* gambit. By the third message, Xavier's tone is annoyed. Lucy lays her head in her hands. The implication is clear: *he* celebrated their day off by telephoning her immediately whereas *she* has left him in a state of bewildered abandonment. He says in a crisp voice that they need to talk about the college thing again. Where exactly is she thinking of applying? He's been doing some research. Call him as soon as possible, please. He sounds like a guidance counselor reprimanding a wayward student.

Helplessly, Lucy dials his number. She bites her lip as she listens to it ring.

Xavier has tried to kill himself three times. This is the secret that she keeps for him. His first attempt happened early in their relationship; he went into his garage and endeavored to hang himself from the rafters. He told Lucy afterward that he did it because his father smacked him around and broke his computer. Xavier spent that night lying awake in his bedroom, gazing at the ceiling, and by morning he was nearly out of his mind. The rope was there in the corner of the garage, flung carelessly across a heap of tools. Xavier got it over the beam on the third try. He wound the knot with precise care and climbed onto the sagging hood of his father's old Ford. Then he stepped into space. But the rope was ancient and rotten. Xavier felt a blinding pain in his throat—there was an explosion of dust—and with a groan the noose snapped clean through. He landed on the floor in a daze, perfectly intact; but Lucy knew something was wrong as soon as she saw him the following morning. He was as pale as a vampire, his brow clammy, his voice a faltering whisper. After burying himself in her arms, he tugged his collar back to show her the scar, a livid red rope burn that has since dimmed to papery brown.

The second time was different. Xavier took all the pills from his mother's medicine chest and swallowed them ceremoniously, one by one. He and Lucy had been dating for over a year, but she was out of town at the time; her parents took her to Canada for the Christmas holiday, to visit old family friends and wander the quaint little tourist-trap shops. Lucy did not find out what had happened until she returned. Xavier went to bed, delirious from all the medicine in his bloodstream. But after a few hours he woke with his belly on fire. He spent the rest of the night vomiting into the toilet, shuddering on the bathroom tile, and trying not to wake his father. By dawn he had thrown up everything. He took the next few days to convalesce, and by the time Lucy came back he was marginally better—he looked as though he'd aged a few years, but he was well enough to gobble down the soup and crackers she brought for him.

The third incident, according to Xavier, was more of an accident than anything else. Lucy privately disagrees, believing that accidents involve things like misplacing your wallet or tripping on the stairs, rather than self-mutilation. One day in chemistry class, Xavier lost his temper and punched a hole through the window. The story is famous now around the school. His experiment wasn't working right. One of the chemicals they'd been given was labeled incorrectly. The teacher, pausing at Xavier's desk on her way around the room, chided him for not following directions. Xavier responded by shouting that no one else was doing any better and he was tired of being picked on. When she threatened to keep him after class, he stormed to the window and glared out. (Though she wasn't there, Lucy can picture it vividly: Xavier eyeing his own reflection, a caged bird challenging the rival that flickers in and out of the mirror.) He breathed through his teeth. His cheeks flamed. The classroom grew still around him, everyone riveted in gruesome anticipation. At last, almost as an afterthought, Xavier hauled off and socked the glass. Blood dripped onto the pavement three stories below. His forearm was studded with icy shards. People screamed and bolted. One of the girls fainted dead away.

Lucy picked Xavier up at the hospital that evening, his arm swathed in a wad of bandages. On the way back to his house, she pulled into the deserted parking lot of a strip mall, and they sat for hours in the shadowy darkness, Xavier crying, Lucy insisting that it was time for her to tell someone; she had been aching to tell someone. But Xavier begged her not to. If anyone knew—Lucy's parents, the guidance counselors—he would be removed from his home and placed in the foster care system. There had been a scare, apparently, back in elementary school, when he had to stay away from the house for a few nights, all his things packed in a plastic garbage bag. He did not wish to repeat the experience. He could be taken out of their school permanently, away from Lucy herself— just saying it aloud made him look terrified and desperate. Lucy was in over her head. She promised not to tell. She promised and promised again, Xavier pulling the words out of her like a mantra, like a magical incantation.

During the long months of the winter, Lucy works on her college essays. Downstairs the fire crackles, and periodically she hears her father grunt at the newspaper. The smell of woodsmoke drifts up the stairs. The dog lies by her feet, drooling into her socks.

His name, Lucy writes, *had already been given to him when we got him from the animal shelter. I remember I tried to change it to something dumb and girly, like Socks or Fido, but now I'm glad my dog wouldn't let me. Many parts of his personality were already there at the beginning. It is difficult to explain what it means to me to have a dog . . .*

Lucy has been lying to Xavier. They agreed that she would only look at colleges in their immediate area. She knows his litany so well that she could say it with him, word for word: he will visit on weekends, on holidays, and if one of them gets a crush on somebody else, he will uproot himself and move to be with her. But Lucy has requested applications for schools in California, Alaska, and Maine—as far from Ohio as possible. She has been thumbing through pictures of ocean vistas, half-concealed in mist. She imagines walking with her dog beneath redwood trees so tall that the canopy might as well be another planet. She will buy a pair of hiking boots. She will let Dharma chase seals down the rocky coastline, climb over glaciers, charge through swamps. It is all a dream, of course. She throws these enticing applications away as soon as they arrive, hiding the evidence—it is enough of a rebellion just to have looked at them.

Seated before the computer, she chews her fingernails, and Dharma glances up hopefully at the cessation of clatter from the keyboard. Lucy reaches down absently and scratches his ears. What she wants to say about him drifts tantalizingly at the back of her mind. There is something important here. In her anthropology class, she once read that dogs and humans co-evolved, creating a relationship that stands in stark opposition to the normal pattern of domestication. In every other case, as people brought animals into their sphere (to use them as workers, food, protection, or transportation) the animals' brains would gradually change. Over the millennia, horses lost a significant portion of their frontal lobe—the decision-making sector—as this side of things was relegated to their masters.

But in the case of dogs, the situation is different. Humans and canines *both* changed. In their domestication, dogs became permanent puppies, never fully maturing as they would in the wild. They did not need to mature; their owners would tell them what to do and care for them. People, however, also lost a portion of their brains—a section that had to do with the emotional experience. Part of the human capacity to have feelings disappeared, surrendered to their canine companions.

Lucy sits up straight again, and Dharma, recognizing the signs, gloomily retires to the corner beneath the desk.

Without my dog, Lucy writes, *I would not know how to feel certain things. Without him, I do not believe that I would ever feel joy.*

She tumbled into her relationship with Xavier almost accidentally. At the age of fourteen, she liked a boy in her Spanish class, kissed him once or twice behind the bleachers, and before she knew it,

Xavier was head-over-heels in love, planning already to marry her, picking out baby names. It happened so fast that it made her head spin. Lucy was flattered; she could not get her bearings. She had never expected to be adored so entirely. Xavier gazed into her small, freckled face as though he had been blind before the sight of her. He treated her like his own personal gift, something he had always waited for and deserved, now finally delivered to him.

At first Lucy had been proud to have a real boyfriend, holding hands in the movie theatre, falling down the rabbit hole of delirious make-out sessions, her friends cornering her in the hallways to demand all the details. She spent hours chatting with Xavier, sprawled across her parents' bed, the phone crooked beneath her shoulder, one ear slowly going numb. She listened to tales of his alcoholic father, of beatings and neglect. She told him about her own father, his many surgeries. Her father was in and out of the hospital then, her mother half-mad with worry, ferrying him to and fro, on the phone with specialists day and night. Xavier said it made them more alike. They were both abandoned children, nearly orphaned—and though Lucy knew, even then, that their situations were not at all analogous, she agreed just to please him. But she did not love him—had never loved him—had never yet loved anyone.

Soon he began to want to have sex. Lucy refused, surprising both of them with her firmness. It is the only place (she sometimes thinks, in particularly low moments) where she has been able to hold her own. Xavier whined and pleaded. After a year of dating, in a burst of annoyance, he even told his buddies that they had done it. Lucy was relieved by this, rather than angry, since it took some of the pressure off. At least he would be able to brag and swagger. At least he would not be able to complain about her to anyone. Every now and then, as the months passed, he would try again to win her over with his powers of persuasion, and Lucy would disingenuously agree to it all without once changing her mind. Yes, they had done everything else, so this last barrier scarcely mattered. Yes, where love was involved, it probably wasn't a sin. His genitalia struck her as faintly floral, the bi-lobed bud at the top, the strong pink stem, the bulb of the scrotum, all matted with rooty hairs. Lucy was able to please him well enough. Sometimes she even wanted to go ahead and cross that final threshold. But still she held her ground. It was the one blessing of those ubiquitous health classes: the phrase "I'm not ready" had become a powerful weapon, three words that were not to be argued with or comprehended, only obeyed. Lucy was not ready; every so often she would say it again, and Xavier would have to acquiesce.

Over the winter holidays, Lucy and her family load their gear into the car and spend a weekend touring the state, scoping out colleges. The trip is hard on all of them. Her mother is a nervous driver, her knuckles white on the steering wheel as she negotiates around trucks and copes with potholes. Her father fidgets and grumbles in the passenger's seat. Dharma, who generally loves a good long ride in the car, becomes nauseated after so many days of travel and sits moaning with his head in Lucy's lap, occasionally passing gas so foul that the whole family has to roll down the windows, despite the drizzle outside.

On each campus, Lucy gazes up at the ivy-colored dorms and the imposing pillars of English halls and theatre buildings. She watches the students hurrying by her, wearing ripped hoodies and hand-knitted scarves, their hair still mussed from sleep. She sits in on a few classes, her eyes lowered to her desk, expecting at any moment to be called out as a fraud. She makes sure to telephone Xavier every night, aware that he will be waiting anxiously. Her parents, on this trip, seem to fade almost into shadows. Her father's difficulties worsen in unfamiliar settings. The car makes his back ache, and he has trouble getting any rest on the cots the colleges provide for their prospective students. Her mother is in constant attendance on him, her usual solicitousness increasing to almost saint-like proportions. When they return home at last, Lucy watches her mother lean over the passenger's seat, her face filled with gracious consideration, every particle of her being alive to her husband's discomfort—and Lucy feels an odd shiver, as though she herself is in danger. Something in her mother's posture reminds her of her own way of moving. That delicate sway of the neck. The shoulders bent in sympathy and concern.

Spring comes in with a thunderclap, bringing days of lashing rain. Undaunted, Lucy and the dog take longer walks than before, crossing to the very edge of the arboretum, where the woods open unexpectedly into a genteel golf course. Lucy gets the sniffles from tramping around in a downpour. Dharma shakes himself dry in the living room, sending out silvery cascades of water. Crocuses shove their determined heads through the soil. Mist curdles out of the gutters. Lucy walks along the highway into unfamiliar neighborhoods. Sometimes she feels like she is disappearing, a sensation that is reinforced when she and the dog reach the very outskirts of her hometown, staring together down a dirt road that caps a hill and vanishes from sight. Sometimes she loses her way, wandering helplessly down side streets, unable to navigate in the hazy evening. Street lamps shine between the trees, the glow echoing off the branches in concentric circles, so that the bulbs appear to be wreathed in haloes. Lucy rarely makes it home before dark.

She and Xavier have been fighting worse than ever. First he accused her of scoring too well on her SATs; then he accused her of looking down on him because he had no desire for a college degree. How will it be, he shouted, when they are married and have kids who watch and learn from their parents' attitudes? Will she continue her snobbish, self-absorbed behavior then, or will she be able to consider the greater good? Sometimes, during these squabbles, Lucy will literally begin to pass out, so wearied by his circular logic that her eyes grow heavy. Xavier's "accidents" have become more frequent as well. He kicked the wall at his father's shop and busted his toe, limping around for the next few weeks. (Lucy took it upon herself to drive him everywhere he needed to go.) He bruised his elbow in gym class, falling against the mirror and leaving a flower-shaped series of cracks in the glass, the petals expanding outward in a glittering ring.

One day, while he and Lucy are on their way outside for lunch, Xavier pauses by the vending machine. As Lucy watches, he grows increasingly frustrated. The mechanism spits his money out, then jams, so his treat dangles tantalizingly over the void. Xavier shakes the machine and swears at it. Finally he punches the plating, hard enough to leave a dent. Lucy looks wildly around for a security guard, but as a rule there is never one nearby in a crisis. Xavier leads her outside to a sheltered spot beneath a tree, waving his candy triumphantly, as though he has just pulled Excalibur from the anvil. Before long, however, his hand begins to swell. The knuckle blooms into a taut purple grape.

At the hospital, the doctors tell him that he broke the vein, not the bone. As long as he is careful not to hit anything else, it will heal on its own. For weeks, Xavier walks around with his knuckle swollen, unable to hold a pencil or make a fist. Even after the vein returns to a normal size, the bruise remains, like a splotch of violet paint on the back of his hand.

At last Lucy's acceptance letters begin to arrive—big, fat packets from schools all over Ohio. Her parents are overjoyed. Lucy is a little startled by their enthusiasm, unaccustomed to having their full attention. Her father claps her on the back, his weary eyes watering. Her mother pulls her into an impromptu waltz around the living room, keeping time in a jubilant hum. Even Xavier gets into the swing of things. He is proud of his brilliant girlfriend. He is gentle with her, forgiving. He comes over whenever he can get away from the garage, poring through her letters and playing with the dog. (Xavier once had a dog himself and likes to wax poetic about how close they were. "When we're married, we'll have a whole bunch," he says, and Lucy's mother, overhearing, smiles indulgently.) At school, no one can talk about anything else. People throw their arms around each other in the hallways, squealing with delight, or burst into tears in the student lounge because they were rejected from their first choice.

Lucy finds herself somewhat numb. Her hopes for college were modest all along: the chance to take a few classes Xavier might not approve of; the chance, perhaps, to make a friend. It has been a light for her at the end of a long, dim tunnel. But now she can picture herself there in earnest: Xavier walking her to class and back again, lurking outside her dorm, and sharing her bed whenever her roommate is away. "Yes, that's me and my bodyguard," she will say to her teachers, to her new classmates, who will give her the pitying, bewildered look she is accustomed to and turn away.

In the last week of school, Xavier disappears. Lucy picks him up in the morning, as always, but when she goes to their usual rendezvous spot before second period, he never shows up. She does not think much of it at the time. The hallways are in an uproar. Banners are hung every few feet, celebrating school spirit, only occasionally vandalized or torn down out of spite. Classes are canceled for graduation rehearsals. Xavier could be anywhere, now that the routines have changed. After third period, Lucy hurries into the courtyard to meet him in back of the Art Wing. But again, he does not appear. She waits for a while, confused. By fifth period she knows something is wrong. She checks her cell phone, but there is no message from him. She goes to his locker and stands there idiotically, as though waiting for him to throw open the metal door and climb out.

At lunchtime, Lucy is alone for the first time in her memory. She is baffled by her strange new freedom. She can sit anywhere she likes. She can eat the contents of her lunch all out of order, without comment—she can throw her food away, opting not to eat at all. She wanders across the grassy lawn, kicking up twigs and leaves. Eventually she climbs halfway up an apple tree and swings her feet in the breeze. The day is unseasonably warm, and students are settled around the grounds in knots, like flocks of migrating birds at rest. Every so often, as Lucy watches, someone will suddenly leap to his feet and begin to do the Bee Dance—flailing his arms and darting away from his invisible assailant. Hidden among the branches, Lucy contemplates what it would be like to join one of these groups. She could do it; she just remembers how. She could plunk down with her bright smile, pushing her hair out of her face, and say, "God, it's hot. Hey, did you understand that part about cloud formation in fourth period?" She does not do any such thing, of course—it would be a kind of betrayal—but still, she *could*.

After eighth period she pauses at the drinking fountain and splashes water on her face. There is still no message from Xavier, though she has been checking her cell phone obsessively, earning herself a reprimand from her English teacher. A group of boys is gathered nearby, and Lucy hesitates, wondering whether she ought to ask if they've seen him. They stand with their heads close together, their jeans slung low around their hips, tossing a ball of tinfoil back and forth. They are discussing the various pranks they might play for graduation—hilarious tricks like going without pants beneath their robes and thereby obtaining their diplomas while wearing boxer briefs, or else taking a hit of acid before the ceremony and hallucinating all the way up to the podium. Lucy rolls her eyes, smirking. Reflexively, she hears Xavier speaking in her mind, his sputtering strictures on their stupidity and inferiority. Then one of the boys lowers his voice, asking whether anyone else heard about that thing in the locker room.

Lucy holds still, her heart beginning to pound. No one seems to know quite what took place, but apparently there was a lot of blood on the floor, a crimson spray across the wall. The boys laugh, deciding that probably someone was murdered. Lucy gasps for breath. In that instant she knows exactly what happened. She has been expecting this moment for years.

The bell rings, and the boys jump and begin to scatter. Gathering her wits, Lucy reaches out and plucks one of them by the sleeve—she knows him by sight, but is not sure of his name.

"Which locker room?" she asks. "I heard you talking."

"What?"

"Which locker room did—"

"Oh. It was the one by the small gym, out in the East Wing." He leans in curiously, his eyebrows raised. "Why? You think Xavier had something to do with it?"

Lucy flushes—she may not know the boy from Adam, but of course he knows who she is dating.

"No, no," she says quickly. "Just curious. It's nothing."

She ditches her last period, slinking quietly through the halls. When classes are in session, the high school changes. The hallways darken perceptively, empty except for the occasional scuffling footstep, a janitor or teacher heading off for a coffee break. Sounds drift, muffled, through the heavy doors. Lucy catches the monotonous drone of a teacher lecturing on free market economy as she slips into one of the stairwells. She will avoid the security guards, if she can—though they are easy enough to deceive; all she has to do is blush shamefacedly and say that she needs to see the school nurse, and they will back away without asking too many questions.

She finds the gym deserted. The wood floor gleams. The windows show a cloudy sky, and dust motes twirl in the uncertain light. Lucy crosses the basketball court, clutching the straps of her backpack. The door to the boys' locker room stands ajar, outlined by a sharp fluorescent glimmer. Lucy can see a stain of red on the floor. Someone evidently began to clean up the mess, but stopped in the middle of the task; a mop stands abandoned against the doorjamb. The blood is still there. A pool beneath the sinks. A smear heading out into the gym. The bristles of the mop caked in it. Lucy stands in the doorway, shaking. She can see how he did it— the razor blade is sitting where he dropped it beside the garbage can. There is a spatter across two of the mirrors. The moldy green towels that the school has reused for years are heaped against the wall, and Lucy can see that they are soiled as well, speckled with dark blotches. She knows that the blood is Xavier's, as surely as though she can smell his own distinctive musk in the crimson puddle on the tile. He might as well have signed his name.

*

She does not sleep at all that night. Her bed is hot, then cold, and the dog is restless as well, clambering around on her calves and trying to cram his furry body in between Lucy and the wall. Eventually she gives up and goes downstairs, wrapped in her blanket. The windows are open, letting in the spring air, a wet wind smelling of freshly-cut grass. Her parents are sound asleep in their bedroom at the back. She does not have to worry about waking her father—his pain medicine knocks him unconscious, sometimes zonking him out during the daytime as well if he sits still for too long—but her mother, if aroused by any small sound, has a nasty habit of marching around for hours, neurotically checking that the oven is off, the toaster unplugged. Lucy does not wish to talk to anyone. Xavier called earlier, just briefly, from the hospital, sounding thoroughly drugged. In a slurred voice he explained that they were keeping him overnight. The gym teacher had found him. He told her he was sorry; he might have been crying. He told her not to try and visit, as she would not be allowed to see him. Only family were allowed in. Lucy promised to come by in the morning and got off the phone as fast as possible.

She knows the routine by now, exactly how it will unfold. She and Xavier have it down to a science. Once he is discharged, she will wait outside the emergency room, in the hollow of the driveway, squinting through the glass doors. She will bring the dog in the back seat, for company and to make Xavier smile. He will show her his wounds. It is her job to wince, and shudder, and shriek with dismay as he explains exactly what the doctors did to him. Xavier will be pale and noble. He will describe some quarrel with his father, some apathetic jibe on the part of his mother. He will explain how he lost control. For the next few weeks, the two of them will be closer than ever. Xavier will need help with unexpected things, ordinary things—tying his shoes, turning a doorknob. Lucy will leap to answer the phone when it rings. She will check on him five or six times a day. She will sing him to sleep, cut up his meat for him, rub his back gently to relieve the tension. For a while, it will be as though she gave birth to him herself.

By three a.m. she has given up any hope of sleep. She suits up, putting on her walking shoes and her jean jacket, muffling Dharma's enthusiastic whining by feeding him a lump of peanut butter to stick his jaws shut. The neighborhood is absolutely still. Most of the houses are dark, each pane a black and shuttered eye; occasionally one upper window burns with a muted glow, a fellow insomniac whiling away the witching hour with a book or a pornographic website. Lucy sniffs the air. The dog seems unusually sober, marching importantly ahead of her as though they are on a mission together, his tail waving in a plumed salute.

Above the treetops, the sky is a great bowl of stars. The moon, as thin as a fingernail clipping, hangs low in the west. Lucy takes the shortest route to the arboretum, walking along the highway. A few trucks lumber past her. Now and then Dharma growls threateningly into a bush or ditch—unusual behavior for him—and Lucy wonders if, because of the strange hour and her own black mood, he feels a burgeoning need to protect her from danger.

At last they reach the woods. Lucy blunders around for a while, unable to locate the trail. In the gloom, everything looks different. Light comes in shifting patches between the trees, so that the underbrush is as shadowy and chaotic as the deep ocean. Lucy skids down an unfamiliar hill, catching her feet in brambles and mud. When she laughs in helpless amusement, the dog pants approvingly. She keeps him on the leash, and he manifests no desire to leave her, though usually by this point he would be bounding around like a rubber ball, mouthing the rope. Together they find the stream. The water rushes like black ink between the boulders—an occasional flash of silver indicates foamy rapids. Lucy settles on a cold, flat stone. Dharma leans against her shoulder, sniffing maniacally and following each new sound with a lift of his ears. As soon as they are done crashing around, the forest returns to business as usual. An owl cries. A fish jumps clear of the water. The trees surge overhead, moving in unison like kelp in a current. Lucy shivers, tugging her coat more securely around her shoulders. The dog lies down, gazing into her eyes.

When the sun rises, they are still there. Something is happening to Lucy. She feels like her mind is trying to clear—as though she has been in a fog for a long while. For the first time, she wonders if Xavier has always known that she does not love him. She has tried to give him the benefit of the doubt; the only way her sacrifice would be worthwhile was if Xavier never knew what she was giving up for him. But perhaps her instincts have been right all along. Perhaps there has been a silent conversation taking place between them: she has told Xavier that she wishes she could leave, and he has answered that he will kill himself if she tries. His ostensible reason for hurting himself has always been something different, of course. But each injury has been a shot across the bows for her. A warning of what might happen if he were ever left alone. She has felt the terrible weight of his life in her hands.

The sun crests the horizon, and the dog rises to his feet, stretching elaborately. The birds begin their riotous chorus. Lucy passes a hand over her eyes. There is an image in her mind of flesh on a table, glistening pinkly in the light. She can name every wound on Xavier's body, each broken finger and bloodied knee. Each one was a piece of himself he threw away, only to claim a piece of Lucy instead. Her fingers. Her knees. More than once, he has nearly disposed of his own life, just to hang onto hers. It is like being devoured slowly; every so often she will turn around, only to find that another part of her has been consumed. Her sense of humor. Her laughing acquaintances. Her capacity for unadulterated happiness. Xavier's hunger for her is unending. Each bite he takes leaves her weaker and dumber, and he has come at last to her vital organs. Of course Lucy has never wanted to sleep with him. In some deep and quiet place, where they are not friends and lovers but combatants engaged in a long and bloody war, she has been fighting for possession of something dear to her—her identity, maybe, or her own soul—and if she gave in at this last hurdle, she would have given in completely. She would have nothing left of her own.

In her first semester at college, Lucy moves around the campus like a ghost. She dresses unobtrusively in secondhand hoodies and jeans. She does not bother to decorate her dorm room beyond a few posters of dogs. Her roommate, she is sure, finds her to be quiet, innocuous, a bit dull—unwilling, for example, to gate-crash one of the keggers at the frat house down the street, unwilling to stay up late discussing the cute T.A. in the Literature 101 class the two of them share. Lucy goes to bed early every night. She does not explore the town beyond the insular campus, wandering, as so many freshmen do, into the theatre district or the shopping malls. The phone rings frequently for her roommate, but Lucy does not get many calls—just her mother, now and again, gently checking in, or her father reminding her fretfully to get the oil changed in that car of hers. Between classes, she spends her time at the library, an immense stone building whose interior is as segmented as a hive, packed with shadowed corners. Lucy sits there by the hour, flipping dreamily through her textbooks beneath the drone of the fluorescent lights.

She feels empty. She finds herself without the words to answer the cheerful burble of her roommate, the calm questions of her professors. She feels like a barely-there person, sketched lightly on the air. When her parents call, Lucy has instructed them not to mention Xavier. They are both baffled by the whole thing, accepting without comprehension her decision to disappear so absolutely from her long-term boyfriend's life: changing her phone number and her e-mail address, asking them not to pass on any messages he might leave with them. Her mother tries, once or twice, to broach the subject in a cozy, all-girls-together sort of way. Lucy responds by hanging up and turning off her cell phone. She has brought nothing of his with her. Her photographs, his letters, their special notebooks, are at home in her childhood bedroom, to be destroyed at some later date. Lucy has not told her new acquaintances about him. She broke down and cried only once, when her roommate, eyeing the posters of dogs above Lucy's bed with some distaste, asked casually if Lucy herself had a pet. To her own horror, Lucy burst into tears, sobbing with such violence that her roommate backed away, stammering apologies. Eventually, she knows, she will talk about it to someone. But for the moment the wound is still too raw.

It was not easy, in the end, to leave him. At first, of course, she couldn't even think of it—Xavier was a broken bird, more dependent on her than ever before. He was unable to attend the last few days of high school. Lucy flew solo at the homecoming dance and class picnic, slices of watermelon and greasy cake on offer. The rumor mill ran rampant, but only a few people dared to approach her directly and ask her just what had happened in that locker room. Xavier did eventually tell her the story: "Some idiot left his razor on the sink. I was in there by myself for some reason; I guess I wanted to pick up my gym clothes. Then I started to think about graduation and everything. How everybody would be leaving. I picked up one of the blades, and before I knew it—" Listening to him, Lucy could not keep from trembling.

His forearms were heavily bandaged for a while, as though in preparation for a martial arts class. When the stitches were removed, Xavier was fitted with splints; even now, if he were to bend his wrists, the cuts could reopen. The summer moved along in a blur of bland, airy weather. All over town, there were celebratory parties. Lucy didn't make her way to any of them—though her imagination did linger on backyards filled with music, an illicit keg in the bushes, hot dogs turning above a bonfire. Xavier would wait for her on his porch each day, gazing down the road for her car. Despite the heat, he wore long sleeves to hide the splints, his body perfuming the day with captured sweat. Both wrists were marked by bright red lines. The doctors had told him he would have scars forever.

One day in July, Lucy drove across town with Dharma, who hung his head out the window, barking at his counterparts on the sidewalk. Xavier met her at his front door, and together they strolled down the hill to the park. He told her how his only fond memories from childhood were in this place, his father pushing him on the tire swing, his mother giving him a few bucks for the ice cream truck. They settled in the grass. The dog rampaged around them, chasing bumblebees. Lucy chatted nonchalantly enough, though she was nervous, her palms sweating, her attention wandering far from whatever Xavier was saying about the latest superhero-themed blockbuster.

She was determined to break up with him at last. Her first, tentative attempts to do so had proved futile. She had tried communicating through hints ("When I go to college, things will be *different*"), but Xavier had proved immune to this brand of subtlety—he only smiled and concurred. Then she began to induce small separations between them, hoping this fledgling space would widen and widen: she spent the evenings cooking with her mother or researching courses online and did not return Xavier's calls until morning. And yet it never worked out as she had planned. He was so eager to see her again, so ardent in his affection, that he perceived any estrangement as a simple inconvenience, rather than an act of will. In desperation, Lucy had texted *I do not love you, it's all over* into her cell phone, and then erased the message, ashamed of her cowardice. She was running out of time. In a few short weeks she would leave for college—fifteen days, to be precise. She was already packing her things, organizing her books and T-shirts, and still she had not found a way to end things with Xavier. If she wasn't careful, she would end up married to him yet, walking down the aisle in a big white dress like an automaton, her mind still churning in vain over her carefully-phrased but never-voiced words of farewell.

And yet she could not do it, there in that idyllic spot, on that mild summer day. Anyone watching them from the street would have seen young love at work. Xavier tipped his head back, closing his eyes in the sunshine. At the edge of the park, the dog bounded after a bunny, dashing through a clump of bushes. The rabbit froze instinctively, and Dharma was fooled, barreling right past it. Xavier was enchanted by the fact that he, as a human being, could see through the guises that animals used to hide from one another.

It was that night that the idea came to her. Fireflies flickered beyond her window as Lucy sat on the bed, packing her sweaters and coats. Dharma panted his swampy breath into her face. The notion came suddenly, blooming with icy precision, full-formed, as though some secret part of her had been working on it for quite a while. Lucy tried to push the thought away, but it returned at once, blotting out everything else. In order for her to leave Xavier—to really leave him, to end the relationship once and for all—she would have to give him something that would sustain him in her absence. Only in this way could she be free of her burden, her acute sense of maternal responsibility. Only in this way could she guarantee that he would be safe. The plan was a vicious one, as bitter and painful as a slap across the face. But that, too, was all to the good. It was necessary that Lucy herself should suffer in the process. She had known that all along. She would need to be punished, and punished severely, for her desertion. That way nobody, not Xavier, or even Lucy herself, could fault her for it afterward. It would have to hurt like hell.

In the morning, she was ready. She took Dharma for such a long walk that her legs grew sore. She let him linger beside each enticing smell; she let him roll in garbage, and afterward she washed him tenderly (which, unlike the rest of his species, he adored, splashing around and trying to bite the stream of water coming out of the faucet). Lucy clipped his toenails. She took a packet of chicken out of the fridge—its presence there had been causing him a certain amount of angst—and served it up for him on a bed of dog food and rice. Her parents were out for the day, visiting friends from her father's hospital support group, and Lucy was glad. She tried to think of what she would say to them later on—that Dharma had run away, that she had left him with friends for the duration of her first few semesters at school, that he had been killed, maybe. It was best that she did not have to face them just yet. In the car, on the way to Xavier's, she touched the dog's crumpled ears, the broken tooth at the front of his jaw, the black patch at the end of his tail.

But there her memory stops—the day burns away into a humming blank. Lucy is aware of what she did and said, standing in the sunshine outside Xavier's house. She knows that she handed over the dog's food bowl and chew toys. She had even printed out a sheet of directions for Dharma's care, just as she would for a pet-sitter, detailing how to brush his fur and cope with his dental hygiene. Perhaps she and Xavier fought. Perhaps she gave in and cried. She doesn't remember; the afternoon is broken into shards, and she has retained only flickers of the moment. Dharma darting after a butterfly. Her own heart pounding determinedly. A gleam of sunlight reflecting from an upper window. She knows that when she gave Xavier the leash, he took it quizzically, and the dog shifted obediently, plopping down beside Xavier's feet, gazing up at Lucy with his eyebrows raised. This simple act caused her to moan a little. She knows that at one point she saw Xavier's expression change, as at last he began to grasp her intention. But for once she was more absorbed in her own pain than his. She knows that she patted Dharma's head, and he looked up at her with his customary expression, hopeful, adoring. There was simply no way to say goodbye to a dog. She knows that, in the end, she drove away.

In autumn the campus grows rainy and dark, the flagstones glimmering with wet. Lucy crosses the quad wrapped up in a scarf and hat. She buys a college sweater. Now and then she lets her roommate drag her out for coffee. She goes to see a few movies in the evenings. She begins to take long walks again, striding past the library, down the hill and into the rose garden, which opens into a quiet wood and a slow, winding river, weighted down with mud.

One day she is seated in her Indian History course, her desk catching the last rays of waning sun through the window. With a jolt, she comes across Dharma's name in the footnotes of her textbook. The classroom fades away, the teacher's voice receding. Turning avidly to the right page, a lump in her throat, Lucy reads for the first time about the origin of her dog's honorific. (She does not think of him, does not let her mind dwell on whether Xavier is letting him sleep in the bed, whether Xavier remembers the way to rub him just so behind his sore left ear. She does not wonder whether Dharma has forgotten her by now, or whether he still waits, languidly in the morning, anxiously in the afternoon, his ears perking up at the whine of a car engine like hers, his golden head turning to follow the smell of her lavender shampoo when it drifts from another woman's hair.) Lucy hoists the book up off the desk. She reads that in the Epics, the great stories of Indian lore, it is written that King Yudhisthira and a party of cohorts climbed the Himalayas. This group braved ice, snow, and the thinning air, but one by one they capitulated and fell away, so that by the time the king reached the home of the gods, all of his companions had succumbed to weakness and deserted him—except for his faithful dog.

Lucy sits up straight, tucking her hair back from her face. Her nose nearly touches the printed page. She reads how the gods welcomed the weary king, asking him to come in and join them. But he refused to enter if it meant abandoning his dog there on the mountaintop. This turned out to be the right choice. The gods allowed the dog in as well, and when the two of them had passed through the gates together, the animal's shape suddenly changed. He transformed before the king's eyes into the god Dharma. Blinking away the tears, Lucy trails her finger down the list of his divine attributes. *The principle of cosmic order. Righteous duty and virtue. One of the fundamental elements that make up the world.*

TWO BROTHERS

Albert Goldbarth

GO NORTH TO WORK ON THE RAILROADS. "Work"—that doesn't come close. Their sweat becomes another skin, as glistening as a frog's. At night they fall into sleep like boulders tipped into a black lake. This goes on for a year. But the money is good, and they each send a monthly tithe of it back home, and every Sunday night they phone their mother, taking their turn in line at the crew boss's office. "Doing good, Mama. Yes. No. How are you? How's Sissy? Yes, Mama. Love."

Roberto is the oldest. Tino is younger by eighteen months. And Tino always had, ever since he was a brat on the stoops, a kind of panther grace and panther musk that dizzied the ladies. He liked to drink. And when he drank he'd have ideas that life was meant to be more than a sledgehammer in a relentless drench of sun.

One Sunday Roberto tells his mother that Tino's throat is sore. The next week, that the foreman's sent Tino to town on important company business. Maybe she even believes it, at first. Maybe she doesn't suspect that Tino's taken up—and taken off—with a high-hemmed lowlife hoochiekoochie flirtygirl, and they've disappeared as completely as two dust motes pirouetted from light into shadow.

Or maybe she does suspect but, out of a motherly courtesy to Roberto's kindly fictions, plays along. "Oh, tell him: before bed, drink tea-and-honey. Oh, my Tino—I'm sure the foreman sees that little glimmer of good in him! Are there any nice girls up there, Roberto?" "Yes, Mama. Tino is seeing a very sweet schoolteacher lady, she works in Cedarville right nearby, I've heard her reciting poems to the children."

Fictions, like anything else, require fuel. Roberto must send his mother two tithes out of his monthly pay. And he must invest continually in the tales of Tino's absence. What next? Tino's a monk and he's taken a vow of silence. Tino's become a poet; he and his lady teacher-friend, they're off on a reading circuit at colleges scattered around the lakes.

The truth is, Tino was often truculently silent, unrevealing of his dreams and his simmering angers, a cipher. He'd stretch out under the blanket on the bunk bed as inert as an iron doorstop, as inscrutable as the carved god of some alien culture. What's troubling you, bro? (No response.) In his absence, Tino becomes more present than ever. In his fictional lives, he's more real.

And from that point on?—you can choose your own story. One—and it's the likeliest one—would be that the compulsion of Tino-X takes over Roberto's interior life completely. Tino in charge of the order's beehives, moving in silence among that apiarian city's gridded rows, the buzzing so eternal that it is this city's silence; Tino overseeing the jars upon jars of honey that, in the rising sun, become the color fire must have when it's asleep and dreaming. Roberto has never one day in his life been religious, but he finds himself kneeling every night and muttering words he thinks might be the words a monk thinks, sum-moned from the quiet, at the foot of the throne of God.

Nor has Roberto ever read a page—of anything. But his brain (and this might not be unlike a hive accreting its honey) fills with poetry, the poetry of Tino-X. He sees himself at a lectern, raging— or would it be simpering over doves and hollyhocks? Or would it be the kind of gassy philosophizing he loosely links with the air over eggy mineral springs? He likes it. He starts to twiddle language around, to play with it—in his mouth, on paper, he plays with it. In the twilight consciousness just before sleep he finds himself saying *The geese are bound for somewhere. / Bound and gaggled.*

But then there's the story in which their mother dies. This news comes in a telegram from Sissy, ten words, that's it. This is the woman who'd wiped Roberto's snotty nose and runny ass and

secretly bought him out of trouble when Delvecchio's thugs—
excuse me, Delvecchio's "policymakers"—came looking for him
with lead pipes over a matter of "pecuniary interests." The woman
who'd saved his browning dried-up flap of foreskin, like a saint's
toe, in a silver filigree box, to give as a keepsake to his bride one
day, a day that's not yet come. His grief is intense, and his anger that
Tino isn't here to share in the . . . Tino! It just now occurs to him:
he won't be faking Tino's salary-tithe any longer, he won't be
fronting for Tino's absence!

And yet this story finds him hooked. He can't give up those
other lives by now. They make him more alive. Roberto is someone
pounding a rail into the earth and keeping the company's trash-
drunk hooligans in line. It isn't much and it sure isn't bait with
which to woo a proper recipient of that foreskin reliquary. But
Tino? Tino is an aviator, gone on record-breaking transatlantic
expeditions. Tino owns a South Seas beach house, where a cloud
of hula-hula girls and coconuts and sailfish is always providing the
weather. Tino is off to deliver serum to a hospital in the frozen
North—huskie sleds and igloos. How can he shut the door on these
extra selves? The locals are gathered gratefully on the front steps of
that hospital, under the radiant sky-bunting of the Northern Lights,
delivering a cheer. *T! I! N! O!* they yell. If Tino ever returned now,
how could Roberto give up this addiction?

And then there's the story where Tino returns, Tino and his
trinkety overeroticized inamorata. Tino the loser, the hard-luck
fool, returns, having "struck it big." It's from "investments," he says;
and then, the next day, "a ranch"; the next, "a dance hall business"—
none of it rings true, although that last might be a sanitized
revisioning of some dirtier truth. He wires money back home to
Mama. Terrific: Tino, who never gave a shit, who couldn't tell you
her birthday, Tino who was nowhere when one of the southtown
Polack brothers knocked up Sissy . . . Tino's the hero now. Roberto's
driving his millionth goddam spike and Tino's the family's savior.
Here, bro: Tino gives him a solid gold pocket watch with an eagle
fob—a beauty! That night, Roberto walks to the middle of the

Cedarville Bridge and flings the watch into the inky black, soliloquizing current.

Perhaps my favorite is the one where Tino never returns—but the woman does. The floozie, the strumpet—she comes back one day, bedraggled, borne into town on the breezes of loss. She doesn't know "where he went." One day she woke up in their room above the dance hall "and he was gone like he'd never been." She's carried a cheap valise—through God knows what adventures on the return trip—with his remaining belongings, to give to Roberto: a laceless pair of lumberman's boots; a solid gold watch with the crystal and both hands missing; an ivory tooth-picker in the shape of a dancer's gartered leg (the sexy spike heel serves as the pick); a fish-gutting knife in an oiled-cardboard sheath; a cardsharp's bowtie. She's weeping. It's all that she has, and she's turning it over to him, the older brother. Does he believe her? He looks: the front of her dress has been ripped by rough manhandling, and she's made a makeshift closure for it out of a fraying pair of lumberman's boot laces.

And in fact it isn't fair to say "the floozie." Whatever of her is in that word, well . . . there are other words Roberto discovers over the next few days. Patient. Tender. Parsimonious with button-thread and bacon fat, but generous with a kind of infectious, unselfconscious laughter. And she reads. To herself, of course, and sometimes to the children up in the Cedarville school, but also at night to him. She reads him poetry in the jitter of the oil lamp, and when the flame is near to its end she slips from her shift into ready sex as easily as a goose slips into water, and then she *is* a kind of poetry. The following spring, Mama and Sissy visit—they like her!—and Mama brings the silver box with the delicate filigree webbing its lid, and everyone has a laugh over that.

And these seem truly endless, in potential—these alternative lives—but dangerous as well, and officially frowned upon. You could get a ticket for exceeding the speed of truth. You could be issued a citation for not complying with actuality, for impersonating a likelihood. Cultural norms suggest prioritizing the people and the objects of the empirical realm—the ski lift and the burglar's mask and the nave and the breast and the hoof and the font and the architect's stencil—and not their ghostly correspondences tapping at our consciousness for admission from out of the realm of conjecture, and into the realm of reality. Ah, yes . . . but who doesn't enjoy a ghost story, or realize that we, too, were conjectural once, and rode here into incarnation on iffy winds of wish and will? Who doesn't feel a twin—Good-Me or Evil-Me, Me-X, Me-Raised-to-a-Higher-Power—sometimes yearning to separate out of the psychic matrix, to declare an independent presence in the world?

In the final story, Tino does return, alone, and with no explanations; he just picks up his hammer and bowl of soggy beans and shaving kit and begins again where he left off. Tino, yes. And yet: not Tino. Tino was left-handed. This one, the new one: right-handed, just like Roberto. And something almost mild and conciliatory guides him now. His silences aren't truculent as much as . . . thoughtful. What happened out there? *Who* happened out there? It's as if, somewhere in the deep of the woods, he entered a wormhole and came out reversed. Everybody notices it, the rail-thumpers, the camp cook, the saloon girls, even the unit boss who's usually above particulars. One day when they're in from a break at work, a woman who's been working the camp all year stares with a kind of wonder at him and says, "You remind me of someone." Tino looks up—not at her, at his brother. He says to Roberto, "All that time I kept thinking of you. I made up stories about you and I became those stories. I turned into you."

PATIENT HISTORY

Baird Harper

THE LAST TIME HER FATHER TRAVELED FOR BUSINESS, Glennis threw a party at the house. A stab at popularity in the final month of high school. A mistake. The carpet got stained and a boy threw up in the potted fern. Worst of all, the football whore Astrid Sallingham had sex with Tad Bucknell on Glennis' bed. This tryst left an invisible stain on the wall which the full moon's light would uncover as a reminder that yet another month had passed without Glennis shedding her own virginity.

She woke to the sound of her father's car backing out of the driveway. He was off to Seoul again, due back at the end of the week for her eighteenth birthday, a day Glennis had marked on her bedroom calendar with a drawing of an anchor.

Her father had promised to bring back a soapstone carving he seemed to believe would dress up a dorm room perfectly. He'd filled out her application to the University of Indianapolis himself, even writing the personal essay—two-hundred words on how having a mother murdered by a serial killer had defined Glennis' character. Or how it had *not* defined her character. She couldn't remember which, only that he'd used the phrase "for all intensive purposes." Her father was a lanky, forgivable man, eternally sunburned, with only three Korean phrases to negotiate the streets of Seoul—*Good morning. I'm honored by your presence. I'd rather not go to another strip club.*

It was Glennis' understanding that Korean men preferred a particular brand of animation in which the girls looked like Catholic-school extraterrestrials, and the men like nude Power

Rangers. When her father left town, she sometimes visited the giant pornography barn along the interstate which had a collection of these videos. And thinking of those hairless shrieking cartoons now, she wondered how it might really be, her first time. And then, invariably, she thought of the man who sold trailers—of his tight stone-washed jeans and his chipped-tooth smile, of the way he grunted getting up from chairs.

Downstairs, their disheveled rescue mutt gazed out the window. Derelict seemed desperate to be gone, but when Glennis opened the sliding glass door, he ranged only a few feet out onto the patio to lie down and mope from there. There wasn't much to do in Indiana in June with a geriatric dog to feed, so Glennis had taken up drinking since last summer, but with an eye toward recovery. She looked forward to becoming benevolently culted by the AA crowd or the born-again Christians, as it would be an opportunity to disavow old lives and maybe even recapture her virginity, assuming it would have gone astray by then.

After a bowl of cereal and a juice glass of Beefeater, she showered and put on her US Navy T-shirt with the blue piping at the collar and sleeve hems. She put Derelict in the Lumina and drove to the King Midas Mall outside Indianapolis. And with the gin warming her cheeks and the dog smiling into the wind, Glennis made brave calculations for both their futures. "We'll be free and unattached," she told the dog. "We'll see the world!" In the mall parking lot she made a sign reading *Free Dog, Just Take*, stapled it to Derelict's collar, and let him out.

"You first, boy!"

The mall was a good place to spend the money her father left her, but more importantly it promised chunks of time passing—long lines at the register, a three-hour movie, a giant sugared pretzel. As she strolled past a store full of reeking candles and psychedelic tapestries, Glennis spotted a lava lamp in the window and decided it should be hers. The icy blue blobs floating in the darker blue liquid would perfectly illuminate the aqua tones of the US Navy poster on her bedroom wall.

"Good for a dorm room," said the stoned register clerk. He wrapped his hands in Grateful Dead T-shirts and lowered the hot glass tube into the styrofoam packaging.

"Can you please hurry up?" she asked. "I ship out next week."

The Navy recruitment kiosk had been moved from its spot by the food court to a new place near the Twin Cinema. Her favorite guy wasn't working. Instead, the one named Petty Officer First Class Fontana stood in the vestibule shuffling brochures.

"Don't need one," she said. "I'm already signing up. Soon as I turn eighteen."

"You know," said Fontana, "you can sign up early with a parent's consent."

"I want to do it myself," Glennis said. "It'll be more official that way." Over the officer's shoulder, the kiosk was being embarrassed by its proximity to the press-on-nail booth. "Why'd they move you to this end of the mall?"

"Vandals." Fontana's stern gaze tracked a stream of shoppers down the escalator. "We kept finding Taco Bell in the cabinets."

Glennis spun away, constructing an image of herself on a ship deck somewhere bright and exotic, a glittering port city on the horizon beneath the steel buttresses of America's long guns.

Across the vestibule, the football whore Astrid Sallingham stepped off the escalator and waved, boutique bags sliding up her arm. Glennis' naval reverie dissolved.

"Is it obvious, Glen?" Astrid turned to show her profile, and Glennis wondered if perhaps there'd been a nose job. "It's my bump," Astrid said, pushing her stomach out. "It's OK to tell people. I'm already telling everybody. People should hear about it from me, right? But otherwise they should just plain hear it."

"What the hell are you talking about, Astrid?"

Fontana pressed closer to their conversation. His stomach whinnied.

"I'm pregnant." Astrid pushed her belly out again. "I'm not sure it was worth it, Glen." She pursed her mouth, opened it at one end, and blew air into her bangs, looking like the exhausted mother of twelve she'd probably someday be. "Just one night of fun, huh. Oh well, in the end it will have been something great, I bet." She looked down at the bulge under her shirt, frowned, then marched off toward the Hoosier Mama.

"Do you believe that?" Glennis asked.

Fontana tracked Astrid until she'd disappeared behind a display of maternity bikinis. "Yep," he finally said, "I believe I'd have done her too."

In the parking lot, Derelict lay in the shade of the Lumina's bumper, wagging his tail at Glennis' approach. Scraps of the *Free Dog* sign hung from his maw. She gave him a good petting and poured the last of her water bottle into his mouth, then got in the car and sped away. In the mirror, Derelict didn't chase. He only reared back and sat down, angling his head curiously at the sound the tires were making.

It felt smart to have left someone behind, a preview of what it might be like to get on that ship for the first time and watch her father grow smaller and smaller on the shore. At this, Astrid came back to mind, time-lapse images of a belly growing bigger and bigger, then the memory of how Glennis' bed had looked after Astrid and Tad Bucknell had been screwing on it, the scrunched white sheets, the stuffed animals piled into a cairn-like sex perch. What had at the time seemed merely gross, now struck Glennis as more cruelly ironic—that her virgin's mattress had facilitated a conception.

When she got home, Glennis called the man who sold trailers and said, "This is it, Rick. This is your chance. I'm saying I'd like to see you."

Rick was a high school friend of her father's whose name came last on the emergency contacts list, a thickset guy with a goatee who endeared himself to people with dirty jokes and embellished compliments. He came through town once in a while to get her father drunk and warn him that he was raising a "stone cold fox."

"Glennis?" Rick said. "Is something wrong?"

"Sort of, but not really *wrong*, no. I was hoping you'd come check on me."

"But everything's OK?" he asked. "Are you sure?"

"I'm just in a place right now," she said. "A rough place. Know what I mean?"

"Sure, Glennis. Well, actually, no. What exactly is the problem? I promised your dad I wouldn't hesitate if you ever needed help, but, well, do you need help?"

"My dog ran away."

"Derelict?" Rick asked. "He ran away?"

"I let him out," she said. "And he just ran."

He didn't speak for a moment. There was a clutter of voices in the background, a cell phone ringing. "It's an hour for me to get there," he finally said. "If you're looking for someone to help look for him, I have a friend who works in animal control up near—"

"He's long gone, I'm afraid." Glennis made a sighing noise she thought might befit a woman in distress. "I could come down there."

"Oh, well yeah. You could do that. Except, I'm still not sure what—"

"I'm in a driving mood anyway," she said. "You're still in Millville?"

Rick smothered the phone and yelled at someone on his end about what time the inspector would have the report ready. "You don't mean tomorrow?" he asked, coming back on the line. "Sweet Hell, Glennis, you wouldn't believe the week I'm having. Everything's gone to shit down here. How about the day after? Yeah. I can clear my morning. I'll buy you a good breakfast and we can set you straight or whatever."

"We should go to that place," she said.

"Which place?"

"That hotel. With the bar and the big glass ashtrays."

"OK, yeah, that one—" He broke off the conversation again, giving more orders. As Glennis understood it, Rick was a big deal in southern Indiana when it came to mobile homes. He designed and managed entire trailer parks, each with an elaborate motif—

an African Safari park with a real Bengal tiger in a cage, a tropical paradise park with a wave pool and year-round palm trees. She'd seen the brochure for the one he'd built down in Millville too, a Hollywood theme called MovieTown set up on the grounds of an old drive-in theater.

"Then tomorrow," Glennis insisted, "for dinner."

"You mean the day after," Rick said. "For breakfast. Didn't we just decide that?"

Glennis drew her new lava lamp out of the box, held the still-warm tube in her hand. "OK, yeah. I can wait until then." She hung up and made herself a drink. There wasn't any tonic left, but the gin went down alright on its own. The afternoon grew sticky as clouds moved in and trapped the day's heat. A weak breeze carried the stink of soy fields. She made dinner and another glass of gin, watched the scrambled porn channel, trying to figure what exactly she was seeing—a wagging tennis shoe, a mustache, a washing machine. When the bottle was empty, she went to her room and plugged in the lava lamp. Lying on her bed, she uncrossed her eyes and stared at the Navy poster. The gleaming prow of a destroyer pushed through the ocean, its radar tackle climbing into the sky. Sleep approached, ushering her toward distant dreamscapes, but then she rolled over to find that the wall stain had reemerged, glassy and blue.

Mobile homes, Glennis had always thought, were for people who hadn't been raised in houses. But now, with the highway carrying her toward the man who sold trailers, certain old notions were coming up for review. She wondered if perhaps Rick lived in one of his own developments, finally deciding that he probably liked trailers enough to sell them, but not enough to live in one himself. That did seem to be the man's style, to dabble without making a commitment. He'd never married, though he'd been engaged several times. And whenever he came through town he'd crash in the guestroom only to pack up in the middle of the night and rush home. "Restless Rick," her father called him. Or "Slick Rick." Or once, when her father thought Glennis was out of earshot, "Two Chick Rick."

In years past, her father's old friend had broadcast a mostly platonic interest in Glennis, an innocuous brand of flirtation she took for generosity. But the previous October, they'd run into each other at a hotel Glennis wandered into while her soccer team's bus got a flat changed in the parking lot. When she spotted Rick in the hotel bar, he invited her to join him on his side of the booth. They talked as she imagined adults did when children weren't around, with the casual swearing and weather-based cynicism. Rick tucked his gin and tonic between his legs and ordered a second one. And every few minutes, he opened up his MovieTown brochure for cover so Glennis could bow to his lap for a sip while he ran his hand into the back of her mesh shorts, murmuring, "I heart the white parts."

Eventually, the big idiotic school bus pulled up in the barroom windows and the moment died. But as Glennis hit the outskirts of Millville some remainder of those aborted passions returned, and she said, "So what if he does live in a trailer."

Millville's town center consisted of a single intersection where a motel, a pharmacy, a tavern, and a Planned Parenthood faced off at a blinking red stoplight. The air smelled burnt, and a wide curtain of smoke divided the southern sky. In the motel parking lot, a tall teary-eyed woman in a basketball jersey moved car-to-car tucking flyers under windshield wipers. When the woman saw Glennis, she lifted her stack of papers and waved for attention.

Glennis hurried into the office, where the clerk offered a pitying smile. "Are you displaced by the fire, ma'am?"

"I'm just visiting," Glennis explained.

The man closed the reservations book. "I'm sorry," he said. "This week I can only give rooms to people displaced by the fire."

"I don't understand."

"It's the owner's policy," he said. "He's very concerned about the com*mun*ity."

Glennis turned and looked out the window. The troubled woman in the basketball jersey had gone back to distributing her fliers. "Is there somewhere else I can go?"

"Not really." The clerk opened the book again, tilting his head to one side and then the other, eyes blinking as if he were taking snapshots. "It's a thoughtful policy, but to tell you the truth I really don't care about those people. I'm almost glad the place burned." With his hand he covered a smile. "I know, I know. I'm just awful."

"What kind of fire was it?" Glennis asked. "Did anyone die?"

The man waved off her questions. "What if we started over from the beginning," he said. "I'll ask you again, and you'll try a different answer." He winked and spun around on his heel. "Hello there, Miss. Are you displaced by the fire?"

"Yes," said Glennis, "I am."

"Awful thing, that fire." He batted his eyes. "I'll get you a room right away."

Her door had a gap in the jamb where the old deadbolt had been kicked in. There were new locks above and below the damage, but when she pressed the door, the entire wall flexed and a crack in the front window grew longer. Inside, the room met lower expectations—a bathroom recently cleaned by a coat of tacky paint, TV controller bolted bedside, yellow sheets full of lint and moth wings. Glennis hid her luggage under the bed, walked across the street to the tavern, ordered a gin and tonic.

"How old are you?" The bartender was a man about her father's age, with tight-cropped hair and a US Army T-shirt tucked forcefully into his jeans.

"That's sweet of you to ask," Glennis said in the voice of an older woman. "How 'bout this shitty heat, eh?"

The bartender made the drink and brought it over on a battered cardboard coaster. "But seriously," he said, setting the glass just out of reach, "I need to see some I.D."

Glennis marched across the street to the pharmacy and bought the largest box of condoms, a variety pack with stallions all over the packaging. "Where's MovieTown?"

The man at the register didn't look up. "Movie *what*?" He left the condoms on the counter, dragging a plastic bag over the box as though trying to catch it from behind.

"The trailer park."

"Oh," he said, nodding as if things were finally making sense, "the trailer park."

The flier pinned to her windshield had a photocopy of a dark terrier lying on a slightly less dark carpet. *Lost Dog*, it read, *Five Years Old, Answers to "Muggins."* But there was no phone number or contact information. She wondered how Derelict was doing on his own, whether he was seeing the world yet.

In the car, she separated one of each color and put them in her purse. The descriptions on some of the wrappings—numbing, ribbed, spermicidal—made promises about the experience Glennis couldn't fully anticipate. She pulled down a hill onto a narrow two-lane, which led her to the drive-in theater-turned-trailer park. But instead of trailers there were only rows and rows of scorched black shells, every single mobile home gutted by fire. At the entrance, a sheet of plywood had been propped up along the curb, spray-painted with the words, *Meeting Tonight — 7pm — Make Yourself Heard!*

The old movie screen rose up at the far end of the lot, its corners coming unpeeled and smoke damage making a smudge up the center. Dozens of metal posts that had once held speakers, stood stunned-looking among the blackened trailer carcasses. Their hulls had split open like torn Coke cans, the ravaged faces of toys and clocks and plates peering out at Glennis as she walked down the lanes between.

Coming around a doublewide, she saw a group of men standing together at the far end of the aisle. They all wore suits except for one man in tight jeans and a hardhat. They pointed here and there, made notes on clipboards, shook their heads, all parties arriving at the consensus that the trailer park had indeed burned down. To keep from being noticed, Glennis ducked into the doublewide. The smell of combustion still lingered heavily. Family possessions had merged with the floor and the ceiling was cratered with the caramelized contents of burst soup cans.

"Glennis?" a voice called. "Is that you?"

She looked out onto the yard where one of the surveyors stood among plastic furniture melted halfway into the lawn. A tangle of charred wind chimes swayed in the foreground. As she stepped outside, her eyes adjusted to the light and Rick's face materialized under the hardhat. He looked taller somehow, his gut paunch had lifted into his shoulders, and his teeth held the sun in a startling way.

"Glennis," he said, "it *is* you. I thought we weren't meeting until tomorrow."

"We aren't." She put a kiss on his cheek, brushed lint off his shoulder. "I've been trying to remember the name of that hotel," she said. "I passed right by it this morning and didn't even look up to see what it's called."

"That's OK, I know generally where—" Rick looked down at his feet, nudging something with his toe until a metal chain rose from the ash. "What're you doing here?"

"I remember you talking about this place and I wanted to see it." She scanned the wreckage. "Do they still show movies on that thing?"

Rick looked up at the screen. "The whole place is burnt down, Glennis."

"Right," she said. "I can see that. I mean, *did* they show movies?"

"What? Maybe. I don't know." He glanced at the group of men in suits.

"These are all *your* men?" Glennis asked. "Very impressive, Richard." She tried to figure if he liked being called Richard. His eyes gave no indication. Dick?

"Look, Glennis." He frowned again at the scorched yard. With his toe he lifted the metal links out of the ash and the full length of a dog chain showed itself, extending to a stake in the center of the yard. "I'm having a hell of a week here, Glennis. Someone drops a cigarette and they blame the landlord." He lowered his voice. "These trailer people, let me tell you, they're just trash." His teeth had been bleached, Glennis thought. And capped. And veneered perhaps. They perched on his gums like Legos.

One of the suits cleared his throat. "Rick, we've got the fire marshal in ten."

"Tomorrow, then," Rick whispered to her. "At that hotel."

Back in town, she parked in front of the pharmacy and walked across the street to the Planned Parenthood. Tall chain-link fences surrounded it. A security guard paced the sidewalk. The building had clearly been a Pancake House in its previous life, and she vaguely remembered eating there as a child, sharing a corner booth with her mother, on their way down to Mammoth Caves.

"I'd like to discuss my options," Glennis told the woman behind the glass. "Is there someone I can just *talk* to?"

Glennis sat down in the waiting room, which was like any other, except you could guess what everyone was suffering with. A freckled girl sat between her mother and grandmother. A blond girl with a man who might've been her father, or perhaps was not her father at all. On the form, Glennis wrote *Astrid Sallingham* at the top, followed by the number and address of a mattress outlet that advertised on TV.

When the nurse called her, she walked down a hallway into a room with two chairs and a small oval table. A poster of a woman cut in half hung on the wall, her organs in different colors like a still-life of odd-shaped fruit.

"So you want to consider your options." The nurse's eyes lifted off the clipboard. Chains dangled off her glasses.

"My name is Astrid," Glennis said. "I'm pregnant by a boy named Tad Bucknell. He has a scholarship to Notre Dame to play linebacker."

"And this is a problem," the nurse asked, "that you're pregnant?"

"Actually," Glennis said, "I'm thinking of having sex for the first time."

The nurse tilted her head, the chains wobbled. "Do you mean for the first time since getting pregnant, or just for the first time?"

"There used to be a corner booth here." Glennis looked at the halved woman on the wall. She thought of Derelict, cast off for the second time in his life. He would not survive on his own. "You should probably know that my mother was stabbed to death by a serial killer. The TV called him 'The Soyfield Killer' because that's where he left his victims."

The nurse eyed the poster, as if curious what Glennis was seeing. "Pardon me."

"There wasn't a box to check for that," Glennis said, gesturing toward the chart on the nurse's lap. "Under patient history. But I thought it might be important."

"It does seem important."

"But really, it's the Navy I'm having doubts about. I'm supposed to join up next week. My dad thinks I'm going to college."

The nurse's chains wobbled again. "I'm afraid I don't understand."

"It's about options." Glennis stood up. "I suppose I'm still weighing mine. Thank you. This has been sort of helpful."

In the waiting room, the blond girl was gone and the man who might've been her father had fallen forward into his hands.

Outside, Glennis moved to the sidewalk and stood in the sun. Across the street, the motel bustled. Women sat on a tailgate watching children play tag in the lot; a maid knocked on doors; a cop took statements from two men on a picnic bench.

In the tavern, she ordered a cheeseburger. "With ice water," she told the new bartender, a slim old man in pleated pants. "No booze, please. I can't be drinking this early in the day." She looked around for the guy in the Army shirt.

The old man rang a bell hanging from the ceiling and shouted, "Happy'r!" and the people who'd been waiting for the prices to drop got up from the tables and moved to the bar with small bills in hand. Glennis ordered a gin and tonic.

The old man cocked his head.

"I changed my mind," she said. "I need a real drink after all."

"And I suppose," the old man said, "that your I.D. was in your trailer."

Her cheeseburger came and she followed it with another gin, and another, and then she took the Lumina for a driving tour of greater Millville—the rusted yards and browbeaten garages, the residents like loiterers on their own porches—until she found again the central intersection, and the refugee motel.

She had to stop the car halfway into her space because a woman was sitting on the concrete beam. As Glennis got out, the woman stood and said, "Sorry 'bout that, hun." She was the tall disturbed person Glennis had seen disseminating lost dog fliers.

"Are you going to the meeting?"

"What meeting?" Glennis asked.

"About MovieTown, hun." The woman hung her hands on the open collar of her basketball jersey. "Don't you wanna hear a bunch of lawyers explain exactly how far we gotta bend over and where they're gonna stick it?"

Glennis followed her around the end of the building into a wide grassy courtyard surrounded on three sides by the motel's brick walls. Dozens of families milled about in front of a panel of Rick's suits. On the end, still wearing his hard hat, Rick stood up and roused the meeting to order by clapping his hands. The adults took seats on the grass while the children ran off to play. Glennis stayed toward the back, hiding behind the woman's teased-out hair.

"First of all," Rick began, "I want you folks to know that I respect you." Someone up front made a comment. Laughter sputtered through the crowd. Rick shushed them with another clap. "I respect you people," he went on, "but I won't be made a scapegoat for your shit-ass lot in life."

The crowd began shouting. The tall woman looked for someone to talk to, eventually finding Glennis. "When my husband hears this he's going to *kill* that man," she said. "He will. I won't even be able to stop him. I won't even *want* to."

The gin-weakened muscles in Glennis' cheeks went slack and she felt a big shameless smile open across her face. She gazed past the woman, at Rick, and she could already hear herself recounting this crazed statement in the morning. She wondered whether they'd get the hotel room before or after breakfast, eventually deciding that Rick seemed like the type of person who'd want to eat first. And what kind of room? A suite probably, with ceiling mirrors and a heart-shaped jacuzzi and a bed that shakes.

One of the suits began to describe a timetable for removing the destroyed trailers and installing new ones as each family made the down payment, but the crowd wasn't hearing it. Order eroded. Rick wandered to the back of the makeshift stage, put his cell phone to his ear. Even from that distance, in the fading light, Glennis could see his conspicuous new teeth as he talked, as he smiled. Glennis wanted to know who he was talking to. Another lawyer perhaps? The fire marshal? But then he smiled again, in just such a way. A girlfriend? A fiancée? No. Just a friend, a guy, an old pal. And then it struck her: Rick must've been talking to her father.

Glennis hurried out through the parking lot, across the street, back into the tavern. People she recognized from the courtyard had filled up the tables. She ordered doubles, made small talk with a man who'd been in the Coast Guard, which was interesting if not at all the same as the Navy. "I want to see *all seven* seas," she explained, but when she looked up, the man had gone to the bathroom, or perhaps he'd gone home, which, she now remembered, was something he'd been trying to do for awhile. The hour became dubious, the clock unreadable. Glennis turned to the bartender and explained that she was only drinking so much because she was thinking of leaving her boyfriend because he looked down on people who lived in trailers. She swore casually and complained about the weather. She described Korean porn and what it was like to be pregnant by an All-State linebacker. How it felt to be defined by a serial killer.

The bartender looked back at her fearfully.

"Yes," she assured him, "I'm afraid too."

"What is it you're afraid of?" he asked.

"I'm afraid my dog's never coming back." Glennis slumped against the bar, letting the room take a spin around her. Poor Derelict. The outside world had probably already caught and destroyed him, left him to rot in some lonely roadside field. "But really, I'm afraid my Navy dreams aren't authentic." These words—hearing herself say them out loud, not in the privileged confines of a doctor's office, but in that busy public space—felt nearly treasonous.

Glennis slid off her stool and tried to walk. She stumbled, caught herself on the pinball machine, then vomited on the glass. She assured the two men who picked her up off the floor that it was only morning sickness. But as they carried her across the street she explained that she hadn't kept the baby after all. Her father couldn't know, she begged, and the Navy wouldn't understand. The two men dumped out her purse on the doormat, a mess of condoms and coins, a crumpled lost dog flier. The men keyed into her motel room and laid her on the bed. They pulled her shoes off and peeled her soaked shirt up over her head and took off her belt, and then they stood in the doorway discussing the possibility of terrible things happening to a girl they knew, until finally they pulled the door shut and their boots scraped away.

The sun rose in the cracked window, and Glennis woke into the nauseous despair that'd been bullying her sleep. Distilled junipers made a vile froth of her stomach. A brittle husk drawn over the brain. Cartoons shrieked from other rooms. Somewhere, a truck beeped in endless reverse. She showered and put on the dress she'd brought.

Outside, the tall woman, still wearing the jersey, sat on the Lumina's bumper smoking a cigarette. "Last night you looked more familiar." She surveyed Glennis carefully. "Which trailer was yours?"

Glennis moved past her. "I'm late for breakfast."

"Well," the woman said, "enjoy the pancakes."

Glennis left the keys hanging in the car door. "What the hell does that mean?"

"Enjoy the pancakes," the woman repeated. "You're going to breakfast."

"How do you know where I'm going?"

The woman ditched the cigarette on the pavement. "I didn't mean anything by it, hun. Just enjoy the pancakes. That's a pretty dress."

Glennis took a breath. She'd brushed three times, but a dry scum still lined her mouth. "I'm sorry for snapping at you," she said. "I'm just sick of this place."

The woman looked up at the big generic *Motel* sign. "We all are, hun."

Glennis let the car's door and roof become crutches under her arms. "Which trailer was yours?"

"Mine was the one with the wind chimes." The woman tried to smile, but her jaw clenched and a frown ran in. "The one," she said, scrambling for another cigarette, "with the little black dog always chained up in the front yard." She found a cigarette, lit it, and inhaled. "I don't think he made it."

Glennis looked up at the curtain of ash still bisecting the sky. "I lost my dog too."

Tears wobbled off the woman's face. The smoke in her mouth condensed and disappeared into her throat. In this moment, the volume on Glennis' hangover dipped and she felt suddenly in danger of crossing over too sincerely into these people's world. But then the smoke poured out of the woman's nose, and she cleared her throat, and said, "Go on now, or you'll miss your date."

Glennis pulled back through town onto the highway, where she hung in the right lane, keeping her speed down, looking for the hotel. Eventually, she came to a place with nice cars out front and a nylon banner over the door advertising a buffet. She hadn't recalled it being a Holiday Inn, and the revolving doors seemed new, but past the check-in desk, it funneled into the same lounge from her memory. The bartender had a different face, but everything else—the booths and wood and mirrors—felt about right. She looked for Rick. "Why shouldn't he be allowed to be a few minutes late?"

The bartender looked up. "Pardon?"

"Gin," said Glennis. "Just gin. In a glass."

She put five dollars on the bar and lifted the drink to her face. The smell promised to trim the rug off her tongue, to make the trip home a little more fluid.

"If a man shows up," she told the bartender, "don't tell him I was ever here. Or, actually, tell him I joined the Navy." As she put the glass down, a shadow fell over her arm and she turned to find Rick, freshly showered, hair still showing the combwork.

"You're drinking?" he said.

She pivoted backwards, into him, rising onto her toes to try to kiss him. He hadn't moved his head down toward her—or he'd moved away, even—and her lips landed on the bony underside of his jaw.

"*Who's* joining the Navy?" he asked loudly, his eyes worrying over the bartender.

"I am," Glennis said. "I'm joining soon, Richard. So this is your only chance."

He patted her shoulder, urging her off the stool.

"They have rooms available," Glennis said.

Rick carried her drink to a booth, not *the* booth, she noticed, but one along the same wall as before. "Glen, are you saying what I think you're saying?"

The condom wrappings came to Glennis' mind, a sharp anxiety about the language of sex cutting through the duller, broader grief of her hangover.

Rick urged her into one side of the booth, then put himself on the opposite seat. "What's this about the Navy?" His voice had turned buoyant and curious. "You know, I was in the Navy. Petty Officer First Class." He made a salute, then sipped a tiny amount of her gin. "You're serious about this?"

"Very serious," she said. "Though I didn't actually ask if they had any rooms, but the sign out front said 'vacancy'—"

"About the Navy, Glen." He took a breath, a big windy sound that old people made when their patience was shortening. "The Navy. Let's talk about the Navy."

"Richard . . . " she said, reaching for him.

He pulled his hands back, hid them under the table. "Look, Glennis, about last fall . . . ." His head tipped forward and he looked up through his eyebrows. "I'd had a lot to drink that day. A *lot*."

Glennis eyed her tumbler. Why hadn't he gotten his own? And the music wasn't right at all. And where were the big glass ashtrays? And Rick's teeth, there they were again, like whitewashed fencing strung to his gums.

"Look Glen, what I mean is I'd love to, well, you know, with you, but it comes down to the fact that I can't pound another sailor. I just can't do it. It isn't right."

"I'm a woman," she said. "They do let us in the Navy now."

He brought his hands back onto the table and clasped them together. "I know that's how it might be these days, but it wasn't my experience. Call it retroactive Naval code, but it shouldn't be yours either. Sailors don't plow sailors. It's the Navy, Glen, not some Army Reserve weekend warrior bullshit. You don't just try it out for kicks. You sign your name on the line and then they drop you into a trench for six months in a nuke sub and make you shine wrinkles off the cruise missiles all day and night. It's hard boring work, Glen, but it's damned worth it when you hear the deck guns laying waste to some godless port town. It's fucking glorious is what it is."

"Are we talking about subs or battleships?"

Rick unclasped his hands, seized her glass, and tipped the whole thing into his mouth. "We're *talking*," he said, alcohol flushing his face, "about the goddamn Navy."

The Navy. The Naval Code. Nuke subs. The goddamn Navy. These words he was saying were hers now—more hers than his even—and they meant something. They described who she was and was becoming. Codes and cruise missiles, sailors and submarines. These were the details of a life still waiting for her, a future coursing through her as she followed Rick out of the bar and across the lobby.

She felt suddenly lighter, as if afloat on her shoe soles, then floating literally, up three floors in the elevator, the buttons lighting up under Rick's touch, then his hands turning the knob on room 402, then his fingers prying up her bra. She laid back into the sheets, silently thinking Navy thoughts, letting him figure it out for her, the force and rhythm of the task. Letting him pull and push and grapple through this exercise, like a man trying to rock a vehicle out of the mud. Forward, then backward, then forward again, until all the false starts of her life-so-far seemed as impermanent as that hotel room, her life up to and including that sweaty grunting moment a thing she could now leave behind.

When Rick finished, she slipped out from under, letting him fall forward, face into hands. She went to the window and looked out over the dirt flats of southern Indiana, the parking lot giving way to an ocean of soy. To the south, the ash still rose from Millville, like an enemy port smoldering in the wake of the destroyers.

The Lumina lifted out of the parking lot and rocked onto the highway. The gathering gin high merged with her hangover into a single all-encompassing impediment elbowing out all thought, leaving Glennis with nothing but the wheel and the wind. Later, home again, as she lay on the couch watching the sun bloody the trees, a memory returned, a memory *of* returning, of watching her mother walk across the dining room of a Pancake House to sit back down in the corner booth. A faint but true recollection like a whisper on the ear. Like a scratch at the sliding glass door. Derelict.

DEAD TURTLE

Rebecca Makkai

MAGGIE ASSUMED IT WAS HER FAULT: that if she'd gotten there a minute earlier, she'd have seen him waggle his stumps, seen him fall eerily still, and she could have knocked on his shell and startled him back to life.

She'd been distracted that morning by Jenna Gupta waiting at the classroom door, by wondering who'd let her into the building. Jenna stood in a puddle of melted snow, hands in the pockets of her puffy purple coat. There went Mr. Gupta, disappearing around the corner.

Jenna waited for Maggie to unlock the room. She said, "I had to get here early so no one would hide my colored pencils."

Every other morning that year, Maggie had put her bag on the desk and looked right away through the glass, past the brown grime and algae the children could never quite scrape off. And if Kirby wasn't swimming around, if he was on the rocks, she'd wait to see his shell rise and fall.

This was 1984. It was her first year of teaching, although she was twenty-eight. She had to remind herself, years later: that she'd been nearly thirty, that she'd worked six years at the newspaper. Because that year, in retrospect, seemed like the first year ever.

Jenna hung her coat and took a pink rhyme sheet from Maggie's desk. She sat silently, her fingers tight on her pencil, her tongue caught in her lips.

It was the first two boys in the classroom at 8:25 who started tapping the glass of the cage. "Kirby's *dead*!" one of them shouted—

later she couldn't remember who it was, though she was sure Michael Curtis had been in the class that year, and he'd have been the type to shout, the type for drama. "He's like this," Michael said, let's say it was Michael, lolling his tongue out and choking himself. Of course the turtle didn't look like that, like a hanged man, but Maggie saw that he was, unambiguously, deceased. He was up on the rocks, his skin dryer and browner than usual, the tilt of his triangular head too extreme for resting.

She wished she'd known all along what a dead turtle looked like. It would have saved her so much worry. She walked toward the tank and pulled the boys gently away. As if she were protecting them from it, even though they didn't mind at all and she was the one who wanted to run from the room.

"He looks peaceful," Jenna said. He didn't. Jenna must have heard the phrase in a movie.

Maggie covered the tank with a white sheet left over from Roman togas. One at a time her students stomped in, snow and slush and blood-rushed cheeks, and one at a time they spotted the covered tank, saw Maggie with her finger to her lips, and slipped quietly into their seats.

It was one of many moments when she looked out at their faces and felt she was inventing her job for the first time. That what she did next had nothing to do with her training or anyone else's, and no bearing on the day's lesson plans, but that it was essential to get right. Gladys Ray, the principal, had given her two pat pieces of advice during staff prep week: "Don't smile till Christmas" was the first, something Maggie had gladly discarded within her first ten minutes in the classroom. The second, meant to be encouraging but really terribly disheartening, was "Your only real job is to keep them alive."

If someone had died on her watch at least it was a reptile, and an ancient one at that. The selfish part of her had hoped he would die over Christmas break, that she'd come back to a note from the janitor and an empty, glistening tank. Kirby was forty-two years old, inherited from Mrs. George when she retired last spring, and not entirely legal. Maggie had sat with Mrs. George in the classroom in early August, and Mrs. George—her hair was so white, her eyes were so blue—had told her to hide the whole tank when anyone official came through. "It's the salmonella," she said. "Soon they won't let you have an animal at all." Maggie wanted to beg Mrs. George to take the turtle with her to Florida, but she also wanted to look competent, wanted this woman to believe there would be some continuity, that Maggie wouldn't just throw out all the outdated wall maps (she would), that she wouldn't discontinue the class traditions—the lost tooth chart, the balloon contest, the buddy patrol (well, she wouldn't yet, but one by one, over the years, till it was her classroom fully, till no one remembered Mrs. George but some of the children's parents, the ones who'd had her themselves). And so she'd looked over at the slimy glass, at the turtle, its shell flaking in a way that reminded her of unhealthy toenails, its yellow-striped head angling slowly around, and promised she'd hide him from the superintendent, promised she'd make the children wear rubber gloves when they changed his water.

That morning, by the time the last ones, the bus-missers, shuffled in with uncombed hair and pink eyes, the boys had already spread the word. She didn't have an announcement to make after all.

One of them—it must have been Calvin Stone, because who else would ask such a thing—raised his hand and said, "Who killed him?"

"Nobody did. He was just very, very old. He was even older than me."

"But you're not old!"

"Thank you."

She realized she had to get Kirby out of the classroom or the day would be lost. The proper thing was probably to call Animal Control, but that might get the school in trouble. She would have sent two children for the janitor—he'd disposed of her snails that fall—but she knew he was out salting the sidewalks, and she couldn't stand the way he looked when she asked him favors, even small ones. Everything seemed to pain him tremendously, to be the final insult in a fifty-year job. She didn't want him in the back of the room sighing and scrubbing as she did Poetry Time.

"We're going to have the funeral now," she said.

And she sent two boys to the janitor after all, though only for a shovel, and she had them all get their coats back on. She asked who wanted to put Kirby in a plastic bag, and chose, from the sea of hands, Jenna Gupta and another girl. Jenna was a child she liked to call on when a proper answer was not required, when the question was "Who can open a window?" or "What shall we tackle first, multiplication or Spanish?" Not because Jenna wasn't bright, but because she could derail a lesson plan faster than anyone. As soon as she had the floor she'd suddenly need to sharpen her pencil fifteen times while everyone waited, or she'd write a swear on her paper and then raise her hand to complain that someone had written a swear on her paper.

Maggie had grown concerned about Jenna in the first weeks of school, when Jenna had stapled through her thumb not once but three separate times, each prompting a nurse visit. And each time Jenna had feigned wide-eyed bewilderment that the stapler had misfired. Maggie remembered something then, from her first aid training: sixty percent of children who poison themselves by accident will do it again on purpose. It had seemed an unbelievable statistic back in June, but now that she was in the classroom she believed it fully, and she locked the stapler in her own desk drawer. By that point, though, Jenna had moved on to swallowing erasers, to hiding her notebooks in other children's desks and claiming they'd stolen them, to piercing her own ears with a paperclip. Maggie had gone to talk to Gladys Ray, who'd cut her off and said, "Oh, you'll think they're all troubled and extraordinary your first year. Everything will come to seem normal, trust me. In five years, you'll have seen it all." But it wasn't true. In a thirty-year career, she wouldn't ever meet a child quite like Jenna again, one so hell-bent on self-destruction, both social and physical.

They all watched as Jenna lifted the turtle with her latex gloves and dropped him into the plastic Walgreens bag the other girl held out. Kirby had gone in upside-down, and Maggie could see the curve of his shell at the bottom of the bag.

They trooped to the far side of the lawn, behind the playground where the kindergartners were already climbing. There was a foot of fluffy snow, but the ground underneath was still soft enough to dig. They took turns with the shovel until they'd hollowed out a cubic foot of grave.

She told Jenna she could put the bag in, and Jenna said, "Plastic pollutes the earth." So did a salmonella-infected turtle, most likely, but Maggie let her shake the bag by its bottom corners till Kirby slid out and landed head down, as if digging the tunnel himself.

They filled the hole, patted the earth and snow with their mittens, and stood in a circle. "Now we can all say something nice about Kirby," Maggie said, which seemed like how the grade school pet funeral ought to proceed, or at least how she remembered them from her own childhood, the buried salamanders, the hamster that might only have been hibernating. "I'll start. Kirby was a yellow-bellied slider. He had an amusing personality, and I will always remember how he watched us eat cupcakes when we had birthdays." She turned to her left.

"Sometimes he didn't smell so good."

"That's true, and let's say *nice* things. Melanie?"

Yes, Melanie Barnes was in the class that same year as Jenna, she was sure, because Melanie was the one whose headgear Jenna had pulled straight out of her mouth in the lunch room, the one whose mother she'd had to call and calm down, even though she hadn't seen it happen, hadn't the slightest clue what had occurred. She remembered trying not to use Jenna's name. "There's a child in our class who's having a difficult year," she'd said.

"Well," Mrs. Barnes had said, "don't we all know who *that* is, and if she doesn't turn out like her mother it'll be the Lord's own miracle."

The phrase stuck in Maggie's head: as if Jenna Gupta were beyond all human intervention.

Her mother, Jenna's mother—that was a story. Or so everyone implied, though Maggie could never be sure what the story was. Unless the story was simply that she'd married an Indian man, which to be sure was unusual in 1984 Minnesota, but not terribly scandalous. Susan Gupta was a slight woman with a voice so soft it was hard not to *insist* she speak up. She was the one who'd been raised in the town, the one who'd attended the school—almost all the students had a parent or two who'd gone there, something that would not be true by the end of Maggie's career—and Maggie assumed the head-shaking, the knowing asides, the whispers that Jenna's transgressions ran somehow parallel to her mother's, had to do with the town's shared memory bank. Susan *Gupta*. Maggie could almost hear quotation marks around the woman's last name, the way the other mothers said it, the way Gladys Ray said it. Susan Cory, they still called her half the time. *You know how Susan Cory was.*

Except that Maggie didn't. But she did have her own information, knowledge she assumed was hers alone. In early October, she'd been at the grocery store, shivering at the end of the dairy case, when she recognized Susan Gupta from Parents' Night. She stepped back with her cart, beyond the corner of the pizza freezer, not wanting the small talk, not wanting to risk an impromptu parent conference. She saw Susan open a carton of eggs and turn each one with her fingertips, checking for cracks. Maggie was mesmerized by the slow, almost sensual way she touched them. Susan looked left and right, but apparently didn't see Maggie. She took one egg and, her faint smile never changing, cracked it on the shelf. Then she let the yolk and white ooze into the Styrofoam capsule that had held the egg. She crumbled the shell in her fist and sprinkled it on top. She did the same with two more eggs, glancing around each time. By now Maggie had retreated fully, was watching only the reflection in the orange juice case at the aisle's end. Susan lifted the whole carton to eye level as if inspecting a work of art, then closed the lid and put it back on the shelf with the other cartons. Maggie might have grabbed it herself if she hadn't seen what she'd seen, if she'd been in too much of a hurry to open the lid. Her groceries would have been ruined, as now someone else's would be. She waited till Susan had rounded the corner, then picked up the carton and carried it level, the whites leaking onto her hands, to the man watering the produce. She said, "I think there's a problem here," and vanished before he could see the misplaced embarrassment on her own face.

Surely that wasn't "the story," the sad story of Susan Gupta. She couldn't just be the town egg breaker. But yes, something was the matter.

Back in the classroom, the children had no focus, wouldn't stop raising their hands to talk about death: dead dogs, dead grandparents, how someone's babysitter died in a car crash, how someone's aunt had a seizure. Michael Curtis said, "Mostly everybody dies by getting shot."

"That's on TV," she said. "That's just on TV."

The only thing she could think to do was turn the talk to animals. And so she told them that chickens caught in a tornado will sometimes end up alive but fully plucked. She told them that when a starfish loses an arm it grows another, which they knew, but that the arm also grows a new starfish, which they didn't know. She told them about sea cucumbers, who eject their organs to distract predators. Then they grow new organs.

She'd always been a collector of animal eccentricities, of historical curiosities and strange facts about food and the chemical elements, and this was part of her motivation in becoming a teacher—she wanted someone to share these things with. Only now she found herself collecting facts and secrets of a different kind, ones she could never tell anyone. There was the single father who broke down crying at the fall conference, telling how his classmates had once opened his bologna sandwich and smeared it in the dirt. There was the mother who openly referred to her husband's affair, right in front of him, right there over the math portfolio. There was the man who couldn't stop shaking, just from stepping back into a classroom. And Susan the egg breaker, of course, Susan the vandal. Maggie didn't want to know any of it.

Melanie had raised her hand. "Miss Petroski?" she said. "Jenna's eating the turtle food."

Jenna held a dark green pellet in her fingers. Even with Maggie looking, even with the whole class now looking, she popped it between her lips. "It's my vitamin," she said. "From home."

When the class was at gym, Maggie went in the lounge and put her forehead on the table. Helen Larson looked up from her crossword and her yogurt. She said, "January's like that. February will be worse."

"My turtle died."

Helen clucked and put her pencil behind her ear. She was five feet tall but could silence a hallway by clearing her throat. "I think he was our senior faculty member! Oh, don't feel bad."

"I don't."

"I have extra newts, if you'd like."

Really Maggie didn't want anything else in the classroom, anything else that might die or give her nightmares. She didn't want to walk in every day praying not to find them desiccated in the corner. The land snails had been a great failure this fall, or rather an unfortunate success. She'd foolishly bought two, and within the month the walls of the tank were covered with babies the size of dot candy. She wasn't supposed to release them, the pet store man had made that clear. Even after she sent every child home with one snail in a jar full of lettuce there were still dozens, and so she'd asked the janitor to dispose of the rest. "Make them an offer they can't refuse," she said. This was back in November, when she thought she had a chance of making him smile, of winning him over. He'd looked her up and down with watery eyes and said, as if it devastated him, "Certainly." And the next morning they were gone, tank and all.

"Well," Helen said now, "that thing was diseased."

Did Maggie, in this moment, ask Helen Larson's advice about Jenna Gupta? Looking back she'd like to imagine she did, that she was thinking of Jenna that day, not just of herself, not just of the turtle cleanup. This might have been the day she asked Helen why a child would want to hurt herself, the day Helen said, "Well, the boys do it all the time. Look at them throwing themselves off the monkey bars. Everything boys do, girls do quieter." Or was that years later, after all? Was it not Jenna they were talking about but some other problematic child—Sophie Brahm or Allie Andersen— from those first few years? They blended together. Not the students, but the years. Early on, her teaching nightmares—every night of August, without fail—were about losing control of her class, and they ended with her standing on her desk and screaming, just as Gladys Ray walked in. But the class was an amorphous mass. As time went on, the dream would select children from over the years: Sophie and Jenna and Martin Hasselton and Laker Jones, young enough to be Jenna's son, and Keith, that boy Keith who'd come for one week and created such havoc she was dealing for the rest of the year with the words he'd taught them. All these children together as if they were contemporaries, the class she'd be sentenced to teach in hell. Some of them, she knew, had turned out wonderfully. Martin Hasselton wound up as the chef at the tapas place, and always came out from the kitchen and told the waiter to give "Miss Petroski" and her friend as much sangria as they wanted, and kissed her cheek and showed her pictures of his daughters on his phone. But in her dreams he was trapped at eight, jumping on chairs and throwing things. Erasers, turtles, life preservers.

Well, she either asked Helen Larson or she didn't. One thing she never did: she never told anyone about Susan Gupta and the eggs. She couldn't say exactly why, except that it had to do with the intimacy of Susan's movements, with the fact she'd thought no one was looking.

After gym they were even noisier. They were giggling about Jenna, about her turtle germs, and someone said that turtle food was made of fish poop, that Jenna had eaten fish poop, that Jenna ate fish poop every day, and this was why the turtle had died—she'd stolen all his food. Jenna didn't react, just glared up through dark lashes. She was a beautiful child. Black hair, smooth olive skin, her eyes improbably green—what might be a dull shade of hazel on any Swedish-Minnesotan child, but startlingly light on a girl named Gupta. Maggie would learn over the years that the pretty ones were almost universally reviled, that Jenna wouldn't have stood much of a chance even if she'd acted normally, even if she hadn't sucked on rubber bands or latched on to other girls and followed them around till their mothers called Gladys Ray.

She refocused the class by telling them about sea squirts: the way the polyps wander the seas till they find a suitable rock, then settle down and become sessile (she wrote the word on the board) and—because they never need to move again—ingest their own brains.

The day was over and Maggie was disconcerted by how empty the classroom felt. Even on weekends when she came in to finish projects, or on the last day of a break when she went in to prep, there had been the crunch of gravel under Kirby's feet, or at least the *potential* for that crunch, and the buzz of his heat lamp. His slitty little eyes, watching her work.

Michael Curtis's mother, at her October conference, had walked into the room and gone straight to the turtle. "*Unbelievable,*" she said. "It's really him." She had been in Mrs. George's class herself, twenty-five years ago. "Honey," she said to her bemused husband, "I think he remembers me. Look at him! Look how he's turning his head!"

Staring at the tank, the way the afternoon sunlight prismed through the glass, Maggie realized that tonight, for the first time in forty years, the classroom would be void of any living thing larger than a bug.

Mr. and Mrs. Gupta had come in for separate conferences in the fall. They'd asked if they could, scheduling was difficult, and Maggie had agreed only because she hoped this meant Mr. Gupta would open up to her in some way about his wife, whose egg-breaking Maggie had witnessed just two weeks earlier. But when he arrived she could see that wasn't going to happen. He wasn't what she'd expected, first of all. A British accent, a long, expensive wool coat, wavy hair tucked behind his ears. From everything the other teachers had said, from what she'd inferred from the parents, she'd imagined Randeep Gupta to be an angry little man, maybe one who controlled his wife or one half-crazy himself. Whatever she pictured, it wasn't this beautiful person who held the handshake a moment too long, who leaned toward her over the table. She showed him Jenna's math, and he looked up and said, "Are these boys old enough to be in love with their teacher yet? Or too old?"

She was flattered for a day or two, until she managed to wonder if this wasn't the "story" after all of Susan Gupta—if Randeep wasn't seducing every woman in town, leaving Susan to avenge herself in the dairy aisle. Or maybe all these women were simply smitten with him, and had decided to hate Susan because each woman thought she stood a chance. (Her favorite animal fact that she'd never be able to share with children: the only species that's been proven monogamous under all circumstances is a tapeworm that lives in the intestines of fish. This is because after mating, the bodies of the male and female fuse together forever.)

Regardless, she hadn't said a word about Susan's mental health. She told him, instead, that other children were "concerned by Jenna's habits." Three years later, she'd have done this all better. She'd have documented everything, and it would have been their fifth conversation, not their first. She'd have insisted on getting Jenna evaluated. She'd have started the conference by asking how Jenna was at home, asking if they had any struggles with her. (Surely they did.) She wouldn't have choked on her words.

Randeep Gupta had smiled and nodded. "She's gifted. I was like that myself, always more interested in the teacher than in the other students."

She'd been flummoxed enough to agree, and soon the conference was over, but Maggie was set to meet with Susan the next day, and she figured this was the better moment, anyway, to bring up the specifics. She would start with the stapler incident, the only one Susan already knew about.

But then Susan had come in looking off-balance. She wore extremely high heels on her tiny feet, and heavy hoop earrings, so that Maggie worried the earrings might literally topple her. But there was something else to it, something more to her fragility than her wardrobe choices. Her eyes were red, and the skin under them looked like it might rip if someone touched it. Susan stared at Jenna's work and made little mewing noises, and asked, in a whisper, if Jenna had any friends. It was the perfect opening, except that it was too terrible a way to start. Because the answer was no, and what could be worse than that? Maggie had said, "There's not much social time in the room. She might try inviting someone over to play." And Susan had nodded noncommittally, and that was it. That was all Maggie had in her.

She'd gone to Gladys Ray again and told her about Jenna tearing pages out of *Where the Sidewalk Ends,* and Gladys had said, "You know they can smell weakness. Like dogs."

Now, in the empty classroom, Maggie wondered what more she might do. But it was nearly February, and there were breaks coming, and then the year would be done. Helen Larson had said that to her: "Once you get through the winter, all you're doing is waiting for it to be someone else's problem." But that didn't sound right. Maybe it was how Helen got through her days, but to Maggie it just made everything worse. The thought that she might hand a child off, unchanged, to the next teacher. It was like playing Hot Potato, just hoping the music didn't stop—hoping the problem didn't become a *problem*—when it was your turn.

Today might be a good day to call the Guptas: "You need to know that Jenna has ingested some turtle food . . ." But they wouldn't be home right now, at four in the afternoon. Jenna was a latchkey kid, which was of course the subject of much scrutiny by the other parents. ("She's completely unattended," Melanie Barnes's mother had said after the headgear incident. "You know he stays at hotels in the Twin Cities three nights a week. While she, while Susan—and meanwhile, that child feeds herself Chef Boyardee out of a can.") Maggie drove by Jenna's house once, having copied the address from her file. A large house, an overgrown lawn, a child's blue bicycle against the porch. What had she been looking for?

Right now there were more pressing matters. The janitor would still be around mopping the floors and emptying garbage, and she went to see if he could move the tank. The longer it sat empty, the more the children would beg for a replacement animal. He wasn't near his closet in the south hallway, but the door was ajar and the light was on, and sometimes he rested in there on a folding chair reading a magazine. She looked. No janitor, but she spotted, on the back shelves, a row of assorted glass jars plus her snail tank from the fall. Stepping closer she saw, sticking to the glass of the tank, the tan undersides of two moist, living snails. There were more down on the dirt, and more on a large carrot in the middle. The glass jars were filled with dime-sized snails. These were the babies, nearly grown and ready to spawn a new generation. So this was the offer they couldn't refuse—the chance to live in the dark with the mop buckets, to gnaw on lunch scraps. She stood gaping. Up above were some of the same spider plants that had been multiplying out of control in Dave Klein's room that fall, only they were limp and almost white now from lack of sun. The slender leaves drooped toward the door, where they must have sensed a constant crack of light. Beside the snails, in what was once a peanut butter jar, a little striped fish swam in frantic circles. Someone else's forgotten aquarium bully, presumed flushed.

She might have felt betrayed, her wishes so flagrantly ignored; or she might have felt mistrusted, she a first-year teacher, he a veteran who knew better; or concerned that the man was deranged; but what she actually felt was horrible guilt. That someone else knew how to keep things alive when she did not. That all along, the creatures she'd tried to murder, the things she'd assumed were dead, were here pulsing away in the heart of the school.

Maggie went back to her room and straightened things. There was the tank, the food bowl still full in the corner. Kirby's heat lamp had turned on, thanks to the timer, and she unplugged it. And here were the empty desks, the papers and books and glue sticks preventing a few from closing all the way. It was like a museum exhibit: *American Classroom, 1984.*

She opened all the desks in the back row and sifted through. It was something Helen Larson had advised her to do whenever she had a moment. "You'd be amazed what you'll find," Helen said. And she always was. Here were fifteen pencil erasers, neatly glued in place, like a little army. A Hershey's Kiss. A cootie catcher. A tightly folded note (*If you couph three times, it meens you want to kiss Blake*). Scratched into the lid of one desk: *Bethany R.* There was no Bethany in the class, and the carving looked old. Had Bethany done it herself, or had someone loved Bethany?

Back at her own desk, idly curious, she flipped through the attendance book. It held two hundred pages, each covering a month, with just a few pages left, and so the records went back fifteen years into Mrs. George's class, back to November of 1969. There were a few notes in Mrs. George's light hand: "Fifth absence this fall!" and "Came to school w/out shoes." There, in 1972, was Bethany Ridgeway. But there was nothing to be learned from Mrs. George's neat, confident checkmarks. One mark a day for a school year, ending in June. And then another set of names, the same handwriting, the same blue pen. As if Mrs. George hadn't even blinked. Twenty children out, twenty children in.

Maggie grabbed her bag and the homework and headed out the front door. Across the yard, on the far side of the chain-link fence, right across from where they'd buried Kirby, stood a child with a purple coat and a blue bicycle. Jenna. When she saw Maggie, she let her bike fall and sped off on foot down the sidewalk. Maggie crossed the yard to see if Jenna had been doing something strange. But it was just her bike lying there, the wheel spinning, and a moment later Jenna came trotting back around the corner, clearly terrified. She slowed her pace and seemed to steel herself before she approached the fence. She said, "Umm, Miss Petroski?"

"Hi, Jenna."

"Michael's probably going to tell you something tomorrow, because he said he might. And it's not true."

"Oh." Maggie wished they weren't staring at each other through chain link. It didn't seem ideal.

"When we were cleaning the tank? Yesterday? Because Michael had the spray, not me. I was supposed to do the water."

"OK, and what happened?"

"The thing is Michael's probably going to say that I poured Windex into Kirby's water bowl."

Maggie studied her face. It was unreadable, as usual.

"Is that what happened?"

"But the thing is that Michael is always mean to me."

"You've mentioned that."

"He said I buy clothes at Kmart."

"Jenna, what about the Windex?"

"Because what happened was he *dared* me to."

"OK." She tried to keep her own expression neutral. "But he didn't *make* you do it."

"And also, I've never told you, and no one's ever told you, but Michael always calls me a spaz, and he stole my shoe in gym."

"Jenna, I appreciate your honesty about pouring the Windex. Kirby was old, but it's important that I know what really happened."

"That's why I got to school early." Jenna looked terribly earnest now although it was hard to be sure. "I told my dad I forgot my math sheets, but really it was because I wanted to tell you. But when I saw Kirby I knew right away he was dead. So I didn't say."

"Well, if that's true, I appreciate it."

"And Miss Petroski?"

"Yes."

"No one would ever tell you this, but sometimes when you aren't listening Michael says you're fat."

"OK. You and I will talk tomorrow, Jenna."

"But if you tell my mom and dad they'll probably send me to another school." She said it like a threat, as if Maggie would think this was the worst thing in the world—a child taken away from her.

"You've been very brave, and I'll keep this a secret between us."

Jenna said, "OK then, well, good." She got on her bike and zigzagged away.

But in the very moment that Maggie promised not to tell, she knew this was exactly what she had to do. It would get Gladys Ray's ear, finally. It would be something to tell a psychologist. It would get Mr. and Mrs. Gupta's attention and perhaps even change things. Maybe he wouldn't stay in the cities as often, maybe they'd hire a babysitter, maybe Susan herself would get some help. Well, probably not—but it was still a start.

It would be a betrayal, certainly. What would that do to a child, confessing as much as she could to a trusted teacher only to have the teacher turn her in? Maggie thought of the sea cucumber, sacrificing its heart, its guts, in order to survive. Only it wasn't her *own* heart she was offering, and that made it so much worse.

But this was the best thing to do. This was the only thing to do. And surely Jenna would grow a new heart.

She walked back into the building, and she walked to the office, and she picked up the rolodex, and she picked up the phone.

It was the story Maggie told her youngest colleagues on occasion, the one she told at her own retirement party, just a bit tipsy, though even then, even thirty years later, she left out the names. Who knew but that Jenna Gupta was someone's cousin, wasn't by now someone's gynecologist or lawyer.

The Guptas moved after another year, but the call worked, or it did eventually, after a meeting that Susan Gupta left in tears, after Jenna ignored Maggie for weeks, her forehead on her desk. They got her to the school counselor, who got her to another counselor. Maggie herself never saw a change, but that wasn't the point. And she was certain Jenna remembered her still, years later, as the teacher who'd ruined her life, the one who'd turned her in. That wasn't the point either, although it was the point of the *story*, as Maggie wound up telling it. She'd say, "The thing is, it doesn't matter if they hate you forever."

*

The other teaching nightmare, distinct from the screaming-on-the-desk one. You walk into your room and see the children and realize you forgot to teach them. There's Melanie Barnes, and you haven't seen her in so long—she's been there all year waiting for you. And Tyler Benchley, and Kiki Short, and Doug Farr, and Michael Curtis, and Eleanor East, and Jenna Gupta. It's the last day of school, and you can only do so much. You try to make one math worksheet that covers everything, and you show them a map of Europe and set up, frantically, a science experiment.

When you awake in your own sweat, you're terribly relieved. That these children are long grown, that you have nothing to worry about, that years and years ago you did all you could.

(Though there must have been more you could do, or why would you have this dream? What did you forget?)

Whenever the first-year teachers came in the break room crying, she'd think of how she'd been that year, how earnest, how strangely selfish. How she must have looked to Gladys Ray, who had no idea if she'd last. How she must have looked to that janitor.

If they sat down, if they seemed to want her to talk, Maggie would glance from her crossword. Just keep them alive, she'd say. Just keep them alive. This job isn't what you think it is.

OUT OF THE MOUTHS OF BABES

Monica McFawn

HE WAS NINE YEARS OLD. He had eczema. He scored very high on all tests that measured verbal ability. Some teachers mistook his brilliance for a smart mouth. Flossing was a point of contention, sometimes. He had a special diet—be sure to follow the special diet. He was different. A different child.

Grace had learned all this about the boy, Andy, in the first few moments of setting foot inside the Henderson household. Much could be made of the order in which the mother listed the boy's traits. He was a young rash, an articulate and bratty rash, a high-maintenance and oh-so-special rash. Grace nodded as if everything the mother was saying was perfectly logical and expected. The boy sat across from her, playing a handheld video game and sucking from a silver juice bladder. He pulled the straw from the juice and used it to scratch his head, then put it back.

"What was that again?"

"I said, keep him off the phone. He doesn't need to be on the phone today."

The mother gathered up her bags, turned to her son, and smiled. Grace would see a usual range of looks from parents during this moment: the clingy ones would blink all misty-eyed; the ragged ones would flash a guilty smile, ashamed at their own relief; the boastful parents would give a kind of wink, imagining all the ways the nanny would soon be dazzled. But when this mother met her boy's eyes, she visibly shrank in her suit as if caught in a compromising moment. The boy looked up from his game and gave his mother a tight smile—the thin courtesy a person gives a beggar who is thanking him too profusely.

The silver car backed out of the driveway, the late afternoon light flashing off its hood. The boy shielded the game screen with his hand and kept on playing. Grace watched him for a moment. He was sandy-haired, with a high rosiness on his cheeks that looked like misapplied blush. His irises, under a frill of tufted lashes, were dappled gray-green like Spanish moss shot through with sun. She considered greeting him, or hunkering down next to him and asking about his game, but thought better of it. She hated the awkward joviality that always marked the first one-on-one discussion with a child, so lately she had skipped it altogether. She had all evening with the boy—the mother would be out late on a catering job—so there was no need to hurry things along.

She began her tour. The mother had shown her around the house—here's the pantry, here's the laundry, be careful about this lock it needs a hard turn, hold down the handle for a second or two to flush—but she always made her own circuit when the parents left. She enjoyed seeing how people arranged their things, found a comfort in the contents of other people's medicine cabinets—those little curios of weakness and disease; she liked noticing the things that had been done for her first-day benefit (toys stuffed under the bed, fanned magazines on the coffee table, fresh soap in the dish) and the things that had gone undone (the rusty sink drains, dirty panties at the top of the laundry pile). She popped her head in the master bath, ran her hands over the couple's bed, then stepped into the boy's room and looked around. The twin bed was neatly made, and books rather than toys filled the shelves. The only concession to whimsy was a stylized bear painted on the wall, its paw in an abstract-expressionist honey pot composed with loose strokes.

The boy was an only child, it appeared. The third bedroom was used as a study, full of dark shelves and dressers. She particularly liked going through drawers. Funny that it was a pleasure, she thought, as she pulled the small brass knocker on the first set of drawers. As a child she had found troubling things: a note from her father to a mistress ("I want to dwell in the minute I first see you"), a bizarre letter that her mother had been long drafting to her own father, the handwriting and mood changing over the course of six pages. When she held these unhappy documents in her hands, the aired secrets seemed to make the silent room buzz, as if she had released a swarm of something. Mostly, though, she found nothing of interest, either in her childhood home or the homes of strangers. The act of opening drawers soothed her in ways she couldn't place. She wasn't looking for scandal or valuables; she just liked looking.

The first drawer in the study was filled with pens and office supplies, the second with tax documents and receipts, the third with framed photographs that had made their way out of rotation. One was of the boy, perhaps three years old, pulling a toy wooden boat through a greasy puddle. He regarded the camera with an aggressive look of inquiry, like a professor about to put a difficult question to an unprepared class. With his free hand he pointed to an appliquéd patchwork turtle on the front of his sweatshirt, as if it were a visual for the coming lecture. She was about to reach for another frame when she heard a man's voice from downstairs. Startled, she shoved the picture back in the drawer and stood up. Was it a delivery man? Had the boy let him in?

As she walked down the stairs, she began to make out what was being said. "Mmmm . . . I see. But what if we have wood termites? You'd just leave and treat them on a second visit?" When she entered the living room, she was surprised to see only the boy: he was on the phone and the voice was coming from him. His back was turned to her and she stopped to listen. "That doesn't work. What if they multiply in between the two visits? Then you'll get more money than if you treated for them the first time through."

The boy, when she listened more closely, didn't sound like a man, exactly. His words began with an eager high chirp and a fuzzy pronunciation, like those of most children, but the ends of his phrases were crisp, even brittle. Within a single sentence he ran through the vocal lifecycle, sounding like both a babbling toddler and an old man with the bass thinned out from his tone. The person on the other end of the line would have a hard time suspecting his age, not in the least because of his apparent penchant for hard bargaining. "No, I need all the vermin taken care of in one go. I have in my hand a coupon from your competitor—Riddex—and it says here that they'll . . ." The boy was getting more and more excited. She could see him bounce on the couch as he read out the coupon in a ringing, triumphant voice. "OK, then. I look forward to getting the manager's call." He hung up the phone and caught sight of her.

"Have a vermin problem?" she asked, seating herself in the loveseat across from him. He looked like any other kid in the face, obstinacy mixed up with vulnerability.

"I don't know if we do. But I want to find the best deal just in case. I like to practice."

"Practice what?"

"Negotiating." He pronounced each syllable of the large word and smiled at the sound of it.

"Did your mother ask you to find a deal on an exterminator?"

"No. But that doesn't matter. It doesn't matter if I talk to salespeople; they're paid to talk." The mention of his mother seemed to put them on bad footing. Grace leaned back in the loveseat and sighed. An easily affronted child—the smarter ones always were. She decided she wouldn't say a thing more. Let him wonder if she was going to tattle on him to his mom. She was thirsty, anyhow. She pulled herself up and wandered into the dining room, soon finding herself in front of a large, gleaming liquor cabinet under a sideboard. There were all kinds of fancy snifters, highball glasses, cut crystal servers and decanters, but she made up her drink—vodka on the rocks—in an orange Tupperware cup. She had lately taken to having her first earlier and earlier, since otherwise she'd spend too much of the evening planning and wondering about the best time to make it. To have the drink in her hand, she thought, was to banish it from her mind. She took a long draw and refilled the cup—to save a return trip—and went back in to check on the boy.

He stared at the phone and she stared at him.

"The manager," the boy finally said. "He was supposed to call right back."

Andy was wearing a shirt with a clutch of tiger cubs screen-printed on the front, and he kept pulling it down as if it were riding up. His mouth was smeared red from a rash or the juice, and his bangs covered one eye. They both looked at the phone for a few moments before Grace spoke up.

"You know, if you want to negotiate on the phone, I've got something better for you than an exterminator."

"What? Are you going to trick me into calling my mom or some special kids' therapy hotline?"

Grace chuckled. She liked how he already knew the games a grownup might play. "No, no. I don't see anything wrong with you talking on the phone. I was impressed with what I overheard. How would you like to make an even tougher call?"

The boy nodded, wide-eyed, as if shocked at being indulged.

"Just give me one second. Let me give you the information you need."

Grace walked to the foyer and dug her cellphone bill out of her purse. With all that was going on, she hadn't had a chance to get those overage charges removed. She hated making such calls and always fell for the representative's tricks and runarounds, buying new products and features and even thanking those perky voices, when she hung up, for screwing her over. Let the boy wander into that maze of automated voices, menu options, on-hold music. He could defend her money from the call-center monster; it would be like one of his little video games. If nothing else, the call would keep him busy for at least an hour or so, leaving her free to call Greg and see what new dirt he'd dug up on Susan.

The foyer adjoined the dining room, so she swung off, refreshed her drink, and reentered the living room from the other side.

"Alright, Andy. Here's my bill. Here's my customer code. The last four digits of my social security number are 7419." She sat down on the couch by him and laid out the documents as if they were a board game. "They're going to ask you for all that. Then they'll ask you how they can help. Here's where you need to be sharp. You're going to ask them to take these charges off." She pointed to a line of numbers. The boy was transfixed and seemed to be holding his breath. He stared at the bill the way most boys his age would stare at pile of Legos, perhaps imagining all the configurations the call might take. Grace noticed his ears were bent down at the tips, as though he had not yet unfolded from the womb. There was no way he would get past the main menu, she thought.

Harmless fun. Still, she explained why the charges weren't fair, and for good measure let him in on some further injustices in her own grownup world. "I have to call a lot of lawyers. They charge me just for talking to them on the phone, and then the phone company charges me, too! Can you believe it?" She laughed.

"Are you in legal trouble?" The boy looked at her. His face was bland and rosy like any little kid's, but his eyes actually reminded her of her lawyer, J. T. Hillman, Esq.—the same sharp look, the pinprick of a pupil that would pop any of your bullshit before it even formed in your head. She'd have to be straight with the boy.

"We'll get to that. Are you ready to call now, or do you need some review time?"

In answer, he dialed. For a while they were both silent. She could hear the hold music muffled by the child's ear. He let out a deep breath and squeezed his eyes shut, but then his face softened and took on a meditative look. He pressed a few buttons with great precision and a bit of flourish, like a pianist. Grace watched him and sipped her drink.

This wasn't nice, what she was doing. He would get frustrated. He might tell his mother. No, he wouldn't do that; she had enough leverage with the exterminator call. They had achieved that equilibrium where she had something on him and he something on her.

"I have a problem with some charges on my bill," he began. His voice rang out with a compelling combo of childish eagerness and unmistakably adult impatience. Grace tensed up. Suddenly, she didn't want to be there to witness the eroding of his innocent confidence. She stood up, wandered into the dining room, and checked her voicemail. Greg had left a message. After he got through baby-talking to her, she heard what he had found out about her sister:

"Baby, I dug through everything. She is as clean as a whistle. A plowed snowdrift—nothing like her sis. Anyway, I stayed up all night and finally found, in the expunged crime record of Henry County, a charge for misdemeanor embezzling. She stole from Girl Scouts. Does that ring a bell?"

Grace shut the phone and topped off her drink. So that's all he found. Her sister Susan, four years her junior, was suing her for about ten grand, money that their mother had not left to Susan, who contended that their mother had not been lucid when she drew up the version of the will that favored Grace, and that Grace had manipulated their mother into excising Susan from the will. This was all true; Grace had done just that. Her mother had thought, in her addled state, that the newly drawn-up will was a petition for freeing the whales from Sea World.

But Grace and Susan had been feuding so long that everything could be framed as a justifiable retaliation. Their bad blood predated everything. Susan stole boyfriends, turned relatives against Grace, tried to get her involuntarily committed. Grace had come back with restraining orders, countersuits, and most recently had hired a private investigator to find dirt. She was disappointed with Greg's find. He was no better an investigator than he was a lover, apparently. Still, the private Catholic girls' school Susan worked at might be troubled by the Girl Scout thing. She stirred her drink and began rehearsing, under her breath, what she might say on Susan's voicemail. "St. Victoria's might be interested to learn that their 2000 Administrator of the Year awardee hasn't always been so upstanding . . ." Ugh. Thin gruel. It would take more than that to rattle Sue.

The boy was—remarkably—still on the phone when Grace returned. He was scribbling on her bill and his expression was that of Renaissance cherub. He beamed and chuckled into the receiver. She could hear a woman's warm voice trilling a laugh. "I'm so glad we had this talk," the boy said, convincingly earnest, chewing on the pen cap. His lacy eyelashes quivered and he rubbed the underside of his nose with his index finger, playing his nostrils like a fiddle. "Bye now." He laid the phone in its cradle so softly it didn't make a click, then pulled up his empty juice box and did a staccato slurp on the straw.

"Well? How'd it go?"

"I got the charges off the bill. And I redid your contract so you now have unlimited minutes and it'll cost less than what you were already paying."

"Really?" Grace figured the boy was lying or simply confused. No way could the boy have done what he'd said.

"Really. And it wasn't even hard. It was boring. Kid stuff." He sneezed into his sleeve. "The representative started talking to me about her life and her kids and junk. Her name's Tracy and she said my call made her day." He squeezed the juice bladder in his fist. "You can call the automated system and check if you don't believe me. It's OK if you don't believe me. Most people don't. I won't be mad."

Grace studied the boy. She wanted him to see that she wasn't just another skeptical, unimaginative adult. She was different.

She felt different, alright. Her cup seemed to have lightened to the point that it was floating off her hand, pulling her arm up with it. Why did she suddenly care what the kid thought?

"I believe you," she began, lurching toward the phone with her cup held above both of them. "But I'm going to check anyhow." She pressed redial and hit the menu buttons while the boy watched like a master observing a fumbling apprentice; he whispered "just hit zero" when she accidentally got to the wrong part of the menu and had to start over to get to her billing statement. A sensual and robotic voice reported in perfect deadpan that the boy had done it. Zero on her balance and forty dollars per month.

"Wow, kid . . . color me impressed." She was now sitting next to him on the couch, the phone between them on the cushion. He had grabbed his video game again and his thumbs twitched on the buttons with what seemed to her a virtuosity. She had been really dreading making that call, and now it was all taken care of, just like that. This small relief was like a shot of clean oxygen in a deep cave. "Andy," she began. "Would you like to make another call?"

"Only if it's tougher."

"It's tougher. I owe some money. A few thousand, in fact. I need you to see if you can get the interest charges off the debt."

"Who do you owe?"

"I owe some money to Firekeeper's Casino. I have a credit card with them. I lost some money playing slots. I think there was something wrong with the machines that day, or something. Usually I can just watch the lights and the fruit and get a payout pretty regularly. I have a system. This one night the same two bananas and a cherry kept coming up. Maybe you could say there was a glitch."

She was lying about the banana and cherry thing, but not about her system. Typically she did get a payout, although she had to admit that her system usually involved simply getting blitzed and pulling from a five-gallon bucket full of tokens at her feet. The servers and staff would all whistle when she came in with the bucket, and the other gamblers—those who were tourists and not locals, so to speak—might turn and look at her like she was something more real, in that context, than they were. The rest of the herd didn't look up. To her credit, the bucket was never actually full. She filled the bottom with several hotel-bar-sized bottles of wine and liquor, covered them with a tin pie plate, then topped it off with tokens. She wasn't about to blow her money on the house's pricey drinks, so all night she would feed the slots and surreptitiously fill up her red plastic cup. She'd watch the fruit and the lights and get to feeling that she was decoding a language every time she pulled the handle. When the payout came, it was like she'd been speaking pidgin to an uncomprehending foreigner and had suddenly achieved fluency. The dings and bells told her she had made herself understood.

"I don't think that would work," the boy said. "And why were you gambling so much? The odds of those machines are, like, really bad."

Grace had to expect some judgment, she figured. She had lost thousands over the years. She had little left for legal fees and nothing left of her mother's inheritance. She wasn't above prostrating herself in front of the boy, if that's what it took to get the job done.

"What can I say? I'm stupid. I mean, you get a payout so you keep playing. Sometimes I don't know when to fold 'em, as they say. But there are people a lot worse off than I am."

"Just because people are worse off doesn't mean you aren't bad." He seemed to consider his own words. "I guess I should say 'no offense.' So, no offense."

"None taken. Hey, we all make mistakes. I'm sure you get in fights with your little friends or steal their crayons sometimes." She sucked down the last of her drink, then picked the now-tiny ice cubes from her cup and pressed them into the dirt of a potted plant on the side table.

"I don't get in fights with friends because there are none to fight. And I don't use crayons. Colored pencils give a lot better control."

Should she latch onto the friend comment and try to find some deeper emotional ground with the boy? Or was it best to just roll on past? The house and the mother told the story: this unusual, cloistered boy no doubt lived a solitary life, too precocious for his peers and too young for any adults to take seriously. She could tell him that she, too, considered herself an outsider, with few allies in the world and even fewer friends. But why draw attention to that? Better to just give him the phone. The call would offer him an escape from his circumscribed life as a boy-genius; that was better than the two of them moaning about loneliness. She ruffled his hair with awkward affection; her hands, wet with ice, got nicely dry in his blond mop.

"I hear you. I'm a colored pencil girl, all the way. Try drawing an eyeball with a crayon! Ready?"

The boy nodded, and again she laid out the relevant information. Grace jumped up from the couch as he began dialing.

She paced around the first floor, hearing snippets of his progress ("Can I speak to a manager?") and debating about whether she needed another drink. She popped the cork from a small bottle of port and escaped her indecision. She returned to the boy and sat across from him; he was in the midst of a monologue:

"You could get into my notes page and erase the earlier records on my account so no one would know what you did. You could also do the opposite and rack up my bill. I think your job would be fun, Jim, for these reasons." The boy's voice, this time, sounded higher and oddly husky, like female smoker trying to babytalk. He spoke quickly and laughed a bit, a charmingly nervous sound that threaded through his words and made everything he said a sweet half-joke "Oh, so it's not fun . . . just in a call center. I guess if I were you I'd want to do something crazy now and again. But I'm already a bad gambler. So I shouldn't propose stuff like that." He paused and pulled the phone away from his ear and held it out at arm's length. This struck Grace as a showboating gesture, as if he were a cyclist weaving through traffic no-handed. The voice on the phone—Jim—let loose a stream of corporate gibberish into open air, but the boy didn't appear to be listening. He pulled the straw from his juice and gnawed on it. In a slow, smooth motion, he wound the phone back to his ear and said a few garbled and urgent words into the mouthpiece.

Another long pause, and then, "No, of course not . . . no more than five or six times, tops . . . As a matter of fact, yes . . . She plays volleyball? The sport of princesses!"

The thread was lost on Grace, but she felt hypnotized by the boy's tone, the widening of his eyes, the small, polished giggles, the cajoling followed by a sudden cold word, which crackled like ice dropped in a hot toddy. Andy was talking on the phone, but she felt his disjointed comments were making an appeal to her personally. For what, she couldn't say, but she was starting to feel different—yes, her head was swimming, but that wasn't different, not really—she felt, watching him, that he was, with his little-boy claw hands, ripping a hole in a heavy scrim that long lay between her and the rest of the world. She was, she felt, surfacing. But she was also getting the bends.

The boy sat Indian-style on the couch cushions, his fluffed-up hair forming a perfect looping curl, like a bent horn, right on the top of his head. In another place and time a boy like him would be trussed up in velvets and dripping gold tassels and paraded through the town on a platform carried high by elders, and as he passed her on the street she would hope simply to catch his eye, or—better yet—to hear him speak. Or maybe she would trek to him, as he sat in the center of a donut of fog high on a precipice. Tell me, oh wise one . . .

She laughed to herself; he was just a kid, whatever that meant. He laid down the phone and said, simply, "Done."

"You did it."

"Yup. Easy-peasy. It's all about what you do and don't say, and I know when to shut up and when to speak. It's like a game."

"You're amazing. Just, wow." The boy had lifted another burden off her as if unhooking a balloon from its bunch to sail away. A giddiness rose up in her and she looked around for something to distract her from a manic laugh. On the side table, she spotted the mother's list. Eczema cream twice nightly. No liquids after nine. Make sure he uses floss and gets the uppers and the lowers . . .

Grace stood up and floated into the bathroom. The cream bore a piece of masking tape marked "Andy." The tube was solid in her hand, fraught; it was one of the boy's things. She returned and presented it to him on her outstretched palms.

"You've got to apply this," she said, and he plucked it from her and squeezed a pearl into his hand. He anointed his inner elbow with what she now recognized as characteristic grace, and she knew the night was back onto appropriate footing: the responsible au pair and the obedient child.

"Is that all you have?" Andy said.

"You have to floss at some point, too."

"I mean, all the calls you have?"

Of course she had more calls! A problem for every call and a call for every problem—she could think of another one right now. But it wasn't the kind of call he could make.

"It's not the kind of call you could make."

"Why not? Does it have to do with your legal stuff?"

"Sort of. And other, personal stuff. It wouldn't be strictly a company call."

"I can make all kinds of calls."

"Well, I'd have to give you more background and you'd really have to listen."

"OK."

She could not really let him make this call, but she saw no harm in laying out, as a form of bedtime story, just what kind of shit she was in. In that spirit she went to the kitchen, where she made up a cup of warm milk and honey for the boy and a milky drink for herself—one of those creamy liqueurs that were normally served hot and topped with whipped cream and sprinkles, though she now just zapped it for thirty seconds in the microwave. She brought the drinks into the living room and turned off all the lights but the one next to them. Then, she began.

She started out telling her story in clear, picture-book sentences, the kind that are one to a page. "There were once two sisters," she said, and in her mind's eye she saw the idyllic accompanying picture—a washed-out pastel of two sisters swinging on a tire swing over a blue ribbon stream. "They were the best of friends," she continued, conjuring another picture—this time of the two of them laughing and giggling as they hid under the clothing racks while their mother yelled in a panic over their heads. Those storybook illustrators weren't good at panic, though. Maybe the girls could be pushing one of those big circle things, like kids from a bygone era. Maybe the story worked better in a different time period.

"Is this a real story?"

"Of course."

"Then why are you telling it like that? Those 'circle things' are called trundle hoops, anyway."

She was on the wrong track here, somehow. The call wasn't about her history with her sister; he didn't need to hear about all that. It was about Greg. Nearly every romantic relationship she'd had in the last five years had come from the situation with her sister. She'd dated lawyers, of course, but also mediators (when they tried that), court staff, even former employees of her sister. Now she was seeing Greg, the private investigator. When she first met him he was attractive because he seemed to have the power to get her free. He was that rope cast down to her in the pit. But soon enough he, like the rest of them, became just another part of the problem, just another part of what she simply referred to in her mind as "Susan." The word no longer conjured up a person, but a constellation of bills to pay, appointments to make, paperwork to fill out, and moves demanding response. Susan was a word for the wild rudder of her life that she had to counteract daily at the helm. Greg was now part of Susan.

She began telling the boy all this, sketching out the feud and the lawsuit and Greg's poor performance as an investigator and how she had gotten involved with him for the "wrong reasons," and that now she wanted to fire him and dump him in the same brisk call. This would be tough, she explained, because fired employees and dumped boyfriends often wanted explanations. She didn't like explaining herself but always felt herself doing it, ad nauseam. Plus, Greg had a funny way of moving his upper lip that reminded her of the lower fringe of a jellyfish, undulating and curling in. He changed the way he walked based on who was watching. When he spoke he sounded intelligent but had a bovine look in his eye that made her doubt the existence of his soul. She wished there were a special kind of radio that would tune in to other people's thoughts, even for just a minute. She'd pay a mint for that. When she was a kid sometimes she thought she could hear Susan's thoughts when the two of them were falling asleep in their bunk beds. The moment was like a crossed-wire connection, and Susan's thoughts were always about the social situation between the fish in their fish tank.

Grace ranged wildly in her talk to the boy. She felt, sometimes, that he was the perfect confidant—mature enough to understand, young enough not to have his insight clogged up with learned falsehoods. At those moments she talked to him like a man. Other times he seemed more like a dog or cat, some questionably sentient being to whom she could spew her thoughts without concern about judgment or even comprehension. She spoke in that vaguely doubting way pet owners confided in their pets, then stopped to giggle at how silly she sounded. Or she sometimes spoke to him like an object, a key stuck in a lock, and in these cases she mumbled to herself about him while looking at him: Stop it. Stop. He's just a little boy, you shouldn't be talking to him this way.

She slumped on the couch. It was dark outside and she stared at the orange bottom of her cup, which caught the lamplight and reflected a small sun on her hand. The cup probably wasn't even microwave safe.

"OK, is that all? Can I call now?"

"You can't. Don't you see? The guy's my employee and boyfriend. It's a call I have to make."

"Why? I could say I'm your new boyfriend. Or new investigator. Or best friend. Or representative. I've been my own father on the phone before and called about the treatment of myself at school. I've said stuff like 'He's a good kid, just weird,' because I know that's how it's said. I can do anything. Plus you don't even like the guy. So it doesn't matter."

Something needed correcting in the boy's logic, she knew, but she didn't feel moved to do it. She looked out the large picture window behind him. The driveway was lit up by small, recessed lights pressed into the shorn lawn. It was raining, and the drive looked, through the distortion, like a bridge twisting in the wind. She remembered seeing an old black-and-white clip of a concrete bridge snapping like a jump rope before throwing off its burden of cars and souls. Something about the image made her take heart: that a solid bridge could get so loopy had good implications, she thought, and the silent, forgotten deaths made her feel she'd dodged a nasty bullet just by being born in a later age. The wind made the rain sluice down the window at all angles. The thin, wet trails all seemed to converge behind the boy's head, making him seem the center of a web—or an incredible deal that all arrows were pointing toward, a pattern of emphasis familiar to her from the neon signage that so often lit up her repetitive nights.

"You're right. Go for it. I'll pay him for his work, but I want out. Get me out."

The boy cracked his knuckles like an old pool shark and made the call. Grace could hear Greg announce his company name in a harangued voice, as if he had been fielding nonstop calls, though Grace knew that was a put-on. She fell back against the couch cushions, kicked her shoes off, and lay down. The throw pillows smelled like potpourri—lilac and geranium, a steamy whiff of green.

The smell transported her to the dank crawlspace in her mind where all her out-of-rotation bitter memories were stored. (The more contemporary ones were on display right behind her eyes.) There, her eyes fell on a bouquet of nettles, dandelions, milkweed, and some spiky yellow flower that grew by the drainage ditches hemming her childhood lawn. She had built the bouquet for her Girl Scout pastime badge, and the flowers she chose were supposed to be both aesthetically pleasing and to call to mind the arrangement of character traits a young scout should exemplify. The other girls had chosen daisies for sweetness, roses for fidelity, petunias for perseverance, and the dull like. Grace's bouquet, she explained, expressed the critical qualities of defensiveness, invasiveness, passivity, and squalor.

The bouquet did not go over well. The troop leader pulled her aside and accused her of undermining the spirit, if not the letter, of Girl Scout Law. The other girls' blank sincerity was thrown up in her face as if she alone had flung open the door to all the forces of ambiguity that would soon enough sully their innocence for good.

When Grace had told Susan about this—at dinner, when their mother and father were arguing and deaf to their talk—little Susan had said a shocking and perfect thing: "She's a cuntbug." Cuntbug. The word had moved Grace profoundly. "Cunt" was a word they shouldn't have heard—lewdly adult. But "bug" commandeered the expression into a realm of childhood whimsy, a place that was far more ecstatically dark than anything a grownup could dream up. She loved her evil little sister then.

One of Grace's arms draped over the couch and grabbed the empty air, searching for her drink or perhaps simply arranging weeds in her stupor dream. She moaned and shifted, then sat bolt upright and cried out, in a voice rent by epiphany: "She embezzled from Girl Scouts!"

The boy put his nibbled straw to his lips in a shushing motion and then said, into the phone, "She's shouting because of how lame that discovery is. It's second-class work."

But her mind was on fire. Susan had stolen from Girl Scouts. Was this not an act of love? Grace's heart was pounding through her body. She leapt up with her orange cup and went to the liquor cabinet for another drink, slopping gin all over the sideboard. She took a clarifying chug. This discovery felt like a communiqué. It sounded absurd, but Grace couldn't help but thinking that Susan had somehow arranged to have her find out about the embezzlement. This was, she felt, an olive branch, presented in the only way possible. Susan could not call her outright, what with all the restraining orders and pending court dates. The only way she could reach out to Grace would be to plant a clue—a loving clue, tied to a memory when they were aligned against something together—somewhere out in the mess for Grace to find.

When she returned to the living room and saw the boy hang up the phone, she already knew that Greg was out of the picture. She felt it in her bones—or, rather, she felt the lead shot of worry in her bones discharge, leaving her as light as a child's balsa plane.

"Greg's gone. I made sure. He wanted me to tell you that you're being shortsighted. I said, sure thing, private eye. He didn't get it. So dumb."

"I've got another—"

"Nah. I think I'm done." He squirmed into the corner of the couch.

"Wait. Just wait." The boy hadn't eaten—the normal dinner hour had long passed. She stepped toward the kitchen as if following a strange choreography—one foot shooting out in a wide side-step, the other in a heel-scraping jazzy thrust. It was the dance of staying upright. When she got to the refrigerator she opened it, clung to the handle, and spied the boy's sober dinner—a gluten-free enchilada and greens—among the fresh veggies, soda water, and cheese wheels. She could not serve such a thing to him. It would be dispiriting.

She thought of a gambler she once saw at the slots, a fat nobody slug who, by dint of his hot streak, became a kind of temporary god. Friends and hangers-on brought him meatloaf in Styrofoam, drinks, crab cakes, pudding . . . it went on and on into the night. If he moved, it was understood, the streak would end. It was also understood that these offerings of cake and meat were really being laid at the feet of Lady Luck, who was at that moment making herself manifest in that bloated husk.

She found a piece of old cherry cheesecake in tinfoil and a can of whipped cream tucked behind a stand of low-fat salad dressings. She snapped off several single-serve Jell-Os from a pack. High in a cabinet, she found a bag of chocolate baking chips. Under the stove, she found a deep roasting pan. She filled it with her finds and topped it off with a few travel bags of potato chips and some Lifesavers she dug out from her purse. She laid the feast at his feet. "Eat," she murmured. "Then we'll talk."

He pulled up the bag of chocolate chips by the corner and studied it. "This isn't my normal dinner," he said, "But that's OK."

She had figured the boy's powers of disentanglement came from an ascetic temperament, a personality naturally averse to the complications that came from any great pleasure, be it food or (one day) gambling or sex or whatever. But he had no trouble digging in. He ripped open the Jell-O pods, topping them with whipped cream. He unwrapped the Lifesavers and placed a chocolate chip in each opening and dunked the potato chips in the cheesecake as if it were a dip. He was both avid and precise, enjoying the treats fully but with an admirable sense of proportion. He didn't shake out the chocolate chip bag when he was finished to conjure a final morsel, but neither did he leave anything behind. (She checked.) God, he was so wise. She watched him from the couch, squirted whipped cream in her mouth, and swallowed it down with a hard sound, like a frightened character in a cartoon. Then she outlined the final call.

The boy listened gravely to her instructions, a golden shred of Jell-O trembling on his lips. He nodded and looked at her in quiet assessment, the way someone will check a dish he is scouring to see if it has come clean or needs another dunk. As the phone rang at the other end of the line, Grace reached out a limp hand in muted protest. She half-wanted him to hang up. But the boy was smiling. She heard Susan's voice, so much like her own, answer with a loud, startled hello, as if she were drunk. No surprise there. Once Grace dated a contractor who built kitchen cabinets for Susan and got to hear all about Susan's habit of changing the plan based on what was in her cup. "She wanted pine when she was drinking a pale ale, walnut when she was having a Guinness, and stainless steel when she was drinking vodka . . ."

The boy began speaking. "I'm calling on Grace's behalf."

And then he tangled with her. Boy, did he. Grace sat on the edge of the couch, knocking back her drink—a fresh one had appeared of its own volition, sensing that things were getting festive. First he soothed her with a string of careful little platitudes, words as smooth as bath beads: "there's no pressure," "you're entitled to your feelings," "darkest before dawn," "easy now." Then, while playing with the webbing between his toes, he rolled out an aggressive opening gambit, a double-jeopardy thingamajig—or was that a catch-22?

"If two people have restraining orders against each other," he lectured into the mouthpiece, "then they can meet without a problem, since they will both be violating the restraining order to the same degree. So to report the violation, in that situation, would be to report yourself." Grace couldn't get within fifty feet of Susan and Susan couldn't get within fifty feet of her, but if they both approached each other, say, in a public place, like at a certain fountain Grace knew with a cherub pissing recycled slurry in perpetuity, then they were safe. Come to think of it, the boy reminded her of that cherub, minus the profane spout; as he talked his eyes were uplifted in blissed-out relief, as if he were letting out a stream of something too long bottled up.

Andy was making short work of Susan. She could see it in the way he grinned and showed his squat baby teeth, like old graves sunk in soil. She could see it in the way he gleefully kicked the couch cushions—a boy revving up a playground swing. He was a prodigy . . . that he was. Grace had given him her worst to deal with, and he waved his hands over it and there it went. A popped bubble. A steamed-out stain.

The couch beneath her chin was chocolate-smeared and a Lifesaver was stuck to the pillow. Lots of cleaning up to do before the mama bear comes home, she thought, and lay down, nestling her drink into the deep-pile, sea-foam carpet. She snapped one eye open to keep it on the boy. An alien sound issued from the phone— her sister's laugh. When had she last heard it? They had been passing each other in the courthouse and Grace had tripped in her heels as she was turning to give Susan a cold look of reptilian indifference, a look ruined when she went down on one knee while J. T. Hillman, Esq., flapped his hands over her like a bird startled off his perch. Susan had laughed then—a sound that bounced off the marble steps and high ceiling, that pinged around in Grace's head exclusively and often. The old laugh and the new played off each other like fancy music with diverging motifs, the sort of music a pair of neighbor sisters, goody-goody brats, used to practice in their backyard on their piccolo and flute while she and Susan tried to hit their instruments with rotten apples from above.

By noon tomorrow the two of them would stand before the gushing cherub. Grace would throw in a penny or two while she waited. Love and embezzlement. Amen and goodnight.

The boy was off the phone now and leaning over her. "Thank you, thank you, thank you," she chanted, lifting her arms as if to pull him in for a pat on the head or a kiss. He was smiling at her but out of reach. His cheeks were flushed and his whole head, even the downy hair, had a heavy-bright look, like hand-colored black-and-white film. A candy knocked around in his mouth.

Her days of nannying had given her a taste for the vividness of children, the potency of those little dominos ready to tip in a snaking line of lifelong complication. But the boy ran it in reverse, as if he had been born foreseeing all the complications and all the ways out. Above her head he made a wide arc with his arms and brought his fingers slowly together, meeting between her eyes at the exact midpoint. "You and Susan will meet like so. Approach at the same pace."

"Wow. Thank you . . . can't believe it . . . that's something else . . ."

Her words faded and she shut her eyes. She was spent. A wrapper crinkled and she smelled fruity, humid breath. The boy pressed two Lifesavers on her closed lids. The couch lurched like an old boat being kicked away from the shore.

He spoke with an easy gallows chatter, a clean perky voice on the dark stream: "My father is a systems analyst and my mother caters parties. I've solved their problems, made all the calls. Even called my mom for my dad and my dad for my mom and patched things up. It was cake. I think I am their last problem, the one they traded for all the others. I've sat at the phone for their benefit and talked to myself, explaining that I shouldn't be this way or know what I know, should just be a regular kid again and not meddle. When I got off, I said, 'Look, see?' and my mom and dad just nodded and looked at each other, like they were afraid. 'I won't fix anything again,' I promised. They are so weird. Is there any more Jell-O?"

She shook her head, careful not to upset the candies.

The boy sat on the armrest with his knees folded up. His face prickled with heat. He picked his nose and stared through the window. Adult lives spread out before him like big sloppy maps their owners could not refold. He leaned over Grace's head and waved bye-bye.

She felt the breeze on her face and was sure they were moving, with the boy at the helm. Better him than me, she thought. She heard a giggle as they took a wild turn. A cool wind traveled into the rings on her eyes and continued on through her. Nothing was on her mind.

In a whisper, the boy practiced for the next day: "I had a great time last night . . . my mother would have called but she is busy . . . no, indisposed. Our needs have changed. We no longer have a need. You'll make a great nanny to some other kid.

"That sounds good. End with that."

THE MAGICIAN

John McNally

IN 1976, THE YEAR WE WERE supposed to be learning the metric system, we fell in love with Katy Muldoon. We were in the sixth grade, and Katy sat at the front of our math class, raising her hand for every question, as though all of the answers to all of the problems were merely floating in front of her eyes.

We loved her when she wore a poncho, which was an exotic thing to wear in Chicago. We loved her when she came to school with her long hair chopped short like the figure skater Dorothy Hamill's. We loved her when she began crying in the middle of class one day for no reason that we could see. We loved the small scar on her forehead, just above the eyebrow, from the time she had fallen off the slide in third grade, and we loved how the scar turned purple after she ran the fifty-yard dash in gym class. We loved her when she smiled at us and when she ignored us. It didn't matter what she wore or did, we loved her regardless.

We were a pitiful lot of boys that year, the year we were supposed to learn the metric system. We rode three-speed bikes and tortured bugs. We learned how to shoot milk through our noses, to peel back our eyelids and make scary faces, and to create obscene noises with our hands and armpits. We had started growing hair in places we hadn't had hair before, and we didn't know what to think of that. We drank Tang and our mother's Tab, and we laughed like hyenas. We were not, by even the most generous definition of the word, cool, but we didn't know that, not then at least.

What we did know was that Stu Bronson *was* cool, cooler than any of us, and far more handsome, with his blue eyes and dark, curly hair. He was in love with Katy Muldoon, too, maybe even more than we were in love with her, and Katy loved that Stu loved her. We saw it in the way she blushed after he whispered to her, in the way she snuck glances at him during test time, and in the way she'd reach up to touch the scar on her forehead when she spoke to him, as though she were feeling it pulse in sync with her racing heart.

"Hey, Stu," we'd say when we caught him alone. "You and Katy . . . ?" We'd let it linger, our eyebrows raised.

Stu would give us a look that asked, *Me and Katy what?* But then he'd shake his head and say, "Nah."

"OK," we'd say. "Because . . . you know . . ." And again we'd let Stu fill in the blanks.

Stu would laugh and wag that pretty head of his that we hated and then walk away. He wasn't fooling us. We knew he was lying, even if we weren't sure ourselves what we were asking, even if Stu didn't know what questions he was answering.

It was the year the girls were all rounded up and ushered to the gymnasium to watch a movie while us boys played air guitar and the nose harp, stopping only when the girls returned, some giggling timidly, others acting grim. They treated us differently than before—not better, not worse, just different—and when we demanded to be taken to the gymnasium to watch the same movie they had watched so that we could see for ourselves, we were told to sit down and be quiet.

Our math class met in one of the three mobile units, a trailer that had its own coat rack and restroom. While we did our conversions from feet to meters, Mr. Bilanski, our teacher, would go into the restroom and smoke a cigarette. As soon as smoke began rolling out of the vent at the top of the wall, we would nudge one another and point at it, then sneak around the room, setting the wall clock five minutes ahead or quickly jotting down answers from the teacher's edition of the textbook.

The last week of October was Career Week, when adults would come during our math period and tell us what they did for a living and describe their jobs. The first guest was Stu's father, who was an insurance salesman. He arrived carrying a briefcase and wearing a rust-colored suit, and we were happy that he wasn't good-looking. Even though we could see only the back of Katy's head, we knew that she was watching Stu's father and wondering why he wasn't handsome, and then realizing that Stu would eventually lose his good looks along with most of his hair. We asked all kinds of questions we normally wouldn't have, like, "What's Stu like at home?" and "How much money do you collect if something terrible happens to Stu?"

Mr. Bilanski, who had been staring down at a ruler, as though mystified by the difference between inches and centimeters, peeked up to give us a look that meant, *Go easy, boys.*

Our own parents, who were roofers and electricians and short-order cooks, didn't come to Career Week. It hadn't crossed our minds to invite them. The other guests were friends of our teachers or people with whom somebody had done business, and they arrived wearing the clothes they wore at work. Marty Roush, a realtor, stepped inside our mobile-unit classroom wearing a gold blazer with a giant gold nameplate pinned to his chest. Bernard Dunn, owner of an auto-repair shop, wore crisp, ironed coveralls with his first name sewn onto an oval patch over his heart. We knew by how clean his clothes were that he made other people do the dirty work, and we couldn't decide whether to envy him or hate him because of that.

On Thursday, when Mr. Bilanski introduced a travel agent named Martha as his wife, we gaped at one another, swiveling in our seats—his *wife?*—until Mr. Bilanski loudly cleared his throat. And we had to admit, she wasn't half bad. She had a nice smile and pretty ankles. We were charmed by the way she walked around the room, occasionally touching the tops of our heads. "How would you like to go to Hawaii?" she asked. And, "Do you know how much a passport costs?" We gave Mr. Bilanski sly looks that said, *Good job, old man!* but he was too busy staring at that damn ruler again.

When we showed up at school on Friday morning, the last day of Career Week, it was dark outside. The sky churned overhead, the wind picking up with such force that several boys' hats flew off. A younger kid whose baseball cap floated onto the grade school's roof started to cry until Katy walked up to him and put her arms around him. The boy buried his head to her belly while we stood on the blacktop, watching a scene take place that we had imagined many times alone at night, except that it was *our* heads pressed against Katy's belly and *our* shoulders she had wrapped her arms around. We didn't know who the crying boy was, but we hated him now. We couldn't help it. We had come to understand that love was a daily sucker-punch, and just when we thought we were over her and she didn't matter to us anymore, we'd see a boy we didn't know pressing his head against her belly and we'd feel pain in the pits of our stomachs and want to go home and pop the heads off our sisters' dolls or flush our Hot Wheels down the toilet or carry all our underwear outside and set the pile on fire while staring morosely into the flames. But more than anything else, we wanted to crawl into bed, curl up, and whisper Katy Muldoon's name, longing for what we couldn't have, until we fell asleep.

But we couldn't go home, and we couldn't crawl into bed, because it was Friday and the day had only begun. We'd been told that today's visitor was a projectionist at the local movie theater, and normally we would have been interested in what he had to say, but since we had already heard so many others talk, we wanted him to come and go as quickly as possible so that we could get back to our normal lives.

When the door opened and we saw our guest, we all took a deep breath. The man had a black mustache and goatee, and he wore black makeup around his eyes, which made them stand out the way a villain's eyes did in the old silent movies we'd seen on TV. He wore a black stovepipe hat and a black shirt with a black cape buttoned around his neck. His pants and shoes were black as well, and he carried a black case.

"Hello, hello, hello!" he said. "I'm zee magician!" He sounded foreign, but we couldn't tell what country he was from. France? Poland? Romania?

Mr. Bilanski dropped his ruler and stood up from his desk. "Uh, I think there's been a mistake," he said.

"No mistake," the magician said. "Just . . . *magic!*" He widened his eyes, and we smiled. We liked this guy.

Mr. Bilanski seemed irritated. He disliked changes in plans, as when Mr. Delgado, our principal, spoke to him over the intercom, ordering him to bring the class to an assembly in the gymnasium. He stared at the magician for a moment. "OK, then," Mr. Bilanski said, sitting. "Come on in."

The magician shut the door behind him, and as he walked to the front of the room, he pulled coins from our ears. When he passed Katy, he pulled from her ear a small white dove. He let the bird go, and it flew to the corner and perched on top of the intercom speaker. Katy gasped, put her hands to her chest, and exclaimed that she had never seen anything so wonderful.

"Monsieurs and Fräuleins," the magician said. He set his black case onto Mr. Bilanski's desk, opened it, and removed a crushed top hat that he popped into shape with his fist. "Might I have a volunteer?" he asked. Our arms shot up, but the magician looked only at Katy. "Aha!" he said. "Only one volunteer in this entire room?" Ignoring the rest of us, he held out his hand to Katy. "Up, up!" he said to her as we groaned and put our arms down. Then he turned to us and said, "My lovely—how do you say?—assistant, yes?"

We glanced over at Stu, who had crossed his arms and was frowning. We were pleased to see him looking even more dejected than we were.

Katy stood at the front of the class, holding the top hat, out of which the magician pulled a stuffed anaconda, a rotary telephone, and a bunny. He set the bunny on the floor, and it hopped across the room. The dove, still perched on the speaker, cooed. Then the magician made a magic wand levitate with one hand while quarters appeared and disappeared from between the fingers of his other hand. As he performed these feats, he asked Katy, "Are there any strings?" to which Katy yelled, "No!" "Is there anything fishy that you can see?" he asked, and Katy, staring beyond us as though in a deep trance, yelled, "No, nothing fishy!" When he was done, the magician stuffed the wand into Katy's ear, making it disappear, and then deposited coin after coin into that dark whorl into which we had all wished one day to whisper, "I love you, Katy Muldoon."

We applauded.

"And for my final trick," the magician said, "I would like for my lovely assistant to step inside this closet." He pointed to the restroom. We started to correct him, but the magician held up one hand to keep us quiet while he opened the door for Katy. She obeyed, waving goodbye to us before ducking inside. The magician shut the door, pulled a wand from his cape, and swished it through the air a few times. Smoke seeped from the vent at the top of the wall, the way it did whenever Mr. Bilanski went in there for a cigarette break.

The magician said, "Is this normal? Zee smoke?"

Our hearts sped up. No, we yelled, it wasn't normal!

The magician's makeup accentuated his wide eyes. "Should I check on my lovely assistant?"

Yes, we yelled, hurry!

When the magician opened the door, he took a step back and said, "She's gone!"

Mr. Bilanski stood from his desk, walked over to the magician, and peered inside. "What the . . . ?"

From where we sat, we couldn't see the restroom. For all we knew, Mr. Bilanski was in on the act, but there was something about both his and the magician's demeanor that made us nervous.

"*Pardonnez moi,*" the magician said, "but I must investigate." He walked into the restroom, shutting the door behind him. As soon as smoke rolled from the vent, we knew for certain it was a trick, and we expected the magician and Katy to appear from another doorway, or maybe we would see both of them watching us with amusement from a window. More smoke filled the room, causing us to cough. A shy girl named Tammy opened two windows. Mr. Bilanski scratched his chin and looked at the restroom door, then cautiously opened it and peered inside.

"It's empty," he said.

Stu joined Mr. Bilanski at the restroom. When Stu stepped inside, we considered shutting the door so that he, too, would turn into smoke, but we didn't. We just sat there waiting for Katy and the magician to return, as we knew they surely would.

Five minutes went by. Then ten. The dove remained perched on the speaker while the bunny hopped from one end of the room to the other.

Mr. Bilanski said, "Where *is* she?" He couldn't begin the math lesson without her, but he couldn't keep waiting for her either. "Something's not right." He pushed the buzzer on the wall to call the principal's office.

Mr. Delgado was a large man with thick black hair who reminded us of Clark Kent. He always called us "mister": "How are you today, Mr. O'Reilly? And what about you, Mr. Haleem?" But today he said, "What is it, Donald? Is there a problem?" as though we weren't even in the room.

Mr. Bilanski told him about the magician. When he described what the man had looked like, we realized that we should never have let him into the classroom in the first place.

After Mr. Bilanski finished talking to Principal Delgado, he said to us, "Wait here. I mean it. Don't leave your desks." Mr. Bilanski hurried outside, leaving the door wide open. The wind, which had been picking up all morning, caused the metal door to bang against the trailer's metal siding. It slammed repeatedly, and someone shouted, "Make sure the bunny doesn't leave!"

We noticed Stu sitting alone, across from Katy's empty seat. He was shivering. We wanted to ask him if he was OK, but we didn't. We had decided that maybe he was, in some remote way, to blame for Katy's disappearance. If Stu hadn't invited his father to Career

Week, there would have been a different lineup of guests and maybe the magician wouldn't have come at all. We worked it out in our heads, making the most illogical sequence of events appear logical, and even though deep down we knew we were wrong, we weren't going to give Stu the benefit of the doubt. We needed to believe it was Stu's fault, because there was no one else in the room to blame except ourselves.

The police spent hours interviewing us at school, asking if we had ever seen the magician before, if we knew something about Katy we hadn't told anyone, and if we were hiding anything important.

As it turned out, no one had ever seen the magician before. No projectionist in the area fit the magician's description. It complicated matters that the magician had probably dyed his hair and eyebrows and that his mustache and goatee were almost certainly fake. The police checked costume shops, interviewed local magicians, and questioned kids at other schools, but no one could say who he was.

Days turned into weeks, weeks into months, and our parents barely mentioned it except to say "That poor girl," whenever Katy's name came up. We, on the other hand, became haunted and obsessed, meeting on the blacktop before school, huddling in the cafeteria during lunch, walking slowly home after the last bell rang, all the while going over what we knew and didn't know.

Mr. Bilanski stopped teaching us the metric system. He had begun feeding the dove and the bunny, showing up early each morning to clean up after them with the janitor's broom and dustpan. Most days he let us sleep or read our copies of *Mad* magazine. On the rare occasion that he actually taught us, he went over basic pre-algebra, things we'd already learned. But one day instead of asking, "What is x?" he tapped his chalk on the board and said, "Who is x?" When he caught his mistake, he rubbed his eyes. "Sorry," he said, and then he pulled his pack of cigarettes from his shirt pocket, shook one out, and lit it in front of us. He hadn't gone back into the restroom since Katy had disappeared—none of us had—but this was the first time he'd smoked in our presence. He sat down, his eyes red and watery, and blew smoke toward the ceiling.

Stu lost weight. His face became gaunt, and he quit combing his hair. There were days he didn't look like he'd bathed. He furiously chewed his fingernails. We probably should have asked him how he was holding up, but we didn't. We were eleven and twelve years old, and we took pleasure in Stu's reversal of fortune even though we mourned the same loss.

When Principal Delgado announced that this year's talent show would be dedicated to Katy, we excitedly dove into our preparations. We were going to do stand-up comedy and gymnastics. We wrote songs and memorized lines from Shakespeare. We gathered in apartments and basements, rehearsing for hours on end, giving each other critiques. "More energy!" we'd say, or, "Not so fast!" or, "Sing like you mean it!" We had a show to put on, and by God it was going to be the best damn show anyone in our town had ever seen. And maybe—who knew?—Katy might appear at the back of the auditorium, applauding us when it was all over.

On the day of the show, two of us stayed home with the stomach flu. Others of us had practiced singing so much that our voices gave out on stage. We saw Katy's parents in the audience, Jim and Helen Muldoon, and they forced smiles and clapped after each act, but during the performances they held hands and whispered to one another. Once, Helen Muldoon leaned her head on Jim's shoulder, and Jim began to weep—or so someone reported to us later.

After we had each failed to achieve the huge heights we were reaching for, Stu Bronson took the stage, and everyone gasped.

Stu was dressed like the magician, with a black hat and cape, a fake mustache and goatee, and black makeup around his eyes. We couldn't believe it! A few girls in the audience began to cry. The Muldoons stood up and left. Mr. P., the gym teacher, moved closer to the stage, looking as though he might climb the steps and do bodily harm to Stu, but then Stu pulled silk scarves from his mouth, one after the other, and Mr. P. stopped to watch. He made an entire deck of cards vanish. We couldn't fathom why he was doing what he was doing, but nobody would interfere. He kept making stuff appear and disappear, some things small, like foam balls, and some large, like an umbrella.

"And now," he yelled from the stage. "For my grand finale, I will bring back Katy Muldoon!"

"That's it," we heard Mr. P. say, but Principal Delgado held up his palm and told the gym teacher to wait a minute. It was as though Principal Delagado thought Stu might actually be able to do it. And we had to admit, we all thought it might happen, the reappearance of Katy Muldoon. If anyone could bring her back, we reasoned, it would be Stu Bronson, the only boy Katy had ever truly loved.

Stu made a big show of drawing shut the black velvet stage curtains behind him. Once the dark backdrop was in place, Stu waved his wand. He chanted what sounded like a made-up spell, and then he opened the curtains. We waited. "Behold!" Stu shouted as he revealed a few feet of brick wall.

We leaned forward and squinted, but Katy was nowhere to be seen. Our hope was crushed.

Principal Delgado climbed the stage and ushered Stu away. Without any closing remarks or an announcement about who had won, the lights came up, and the talent show was over. Even though no one said it aloud, we understood that we would never see Katy again.

The next day at school, we knew what we were going to do. We didn't even have to talk about it.

After the final bell, we walked across the street, stopping just beyond the view of the teachers, and waited until we saw Stu Bronson. He came over to our side of the road and gave us a casual nod, as though we were all good friends. We returned the nod, out of politeness. Then we jumped him. We knocked him down, kicking and punching. Someone grabbed a hank of his hair and pulled. We expected him to scream or beg us to stop, but he lay there in silence. He winced, of course, and put his arms up to block the blows, but he did all this without making a sound, as though he had been expecting our attack, as though his performance at the talent show had been a calculated prelude to what we were doing to him now.

A few teachers stood across the street watching. Normally, teachers came over to break up fights, but today they didn't bother. Mr. Lipinski lit a cigarette and tossed the match into the street before heading to his car.

When it became clear that Stu wasn't going to fight back or cry out for help, we backed off. He remained on the ground, curled up.

"You shouldn't have done that," we said. "What were you thinking?"

Stu said nothing. He was shaking, and his nose was bleeding. The remaining teachers wandered away.

"What happened to her?" Stu finally asked, and we shrugged. "I loved Katy," Stu said, and we told him that we did, too.

When Stu covered both eyes with his fingers and sniveled, we saw that he was really just one of us. We couldn't leave Stu there, so we helped him up and brushed him off. Someone gave him a handkerchief, and then we all walked home together, dropping off one by one, until there was none of us left

We thought about Katy Muldoon every day for many years, and then we thought about her less, until we rarely thought about her at all. We were grown men with wives and children and divorces and secrets we kept to ourselves. We thought we had come so far from the bad manners of childhood and the ill-fitting clothes, from the shyness that overwhelmed us when a girl we liked caught our eye, from the unexpected waves of sadness and anger that we didn't know what to do with. But we were fooling ourselves. The boys were still here, and always would be.

Over the intervening years, whenever we saw a young girl with a short haircut, our hearts would inexplicably speed up, and we would think of Katy Muldoon, even though decades had passed. The magician was never heard from again. It was as though he, too, had vanished from this world, although we knew better. He was out there somewhere.

In our dreams we occasionally see both of them with perfect clarity. We are sitting in an audience, watching Katy climb into a wooden box and crouch down inside. The magician closes the hinged lid and inserts three swords into the cube: one through the side, one through the front, and one through the top. The box is on a table with caster wheels, and he spins the table around for us to see each side, and then he removes the swords. The top panel flips open, and rising up out of the box is Katy Muldoon as she would be today, a forty-eight-year-old woman. She smiles and takes a bow, having performed the greatest illusion we've ever seen, which makes us love her now more than ever, even though she has broken our hearts over and over again and will doubtless break them many more times before the magician concludes his show.

THREE MARRIAGES

Emily Mitchell

1.

SHORTLY AFTER THEY MOVED from their own house in Darien, Connecticut, into a retirement home near Fort Myers, Florida, Lucinda announced that she didn't want to be married anymore to Fred, her husband of fifty-nine years. When she told her children this, they were first horrified and then dismissive. She could not mean it, they said to her and to each other. She could not possibly be serious. They interpreted it as a sign that she was becoming senile, that her mind and judgment, which had until then remained very sharp, were becoming impaired. They took her to get tested for other signs of reduced cognitive functioning, but the doctors they spoke with found Lucinda to be lucid and competent, her memory of recent and distant events remarkably intact for someone of her age, which was eighty-three years old.

"But what about this idea that she's going to leave my father?" her son Harry asked the gerontologist who administered the battery of tests. "If that doesn't count as crazy, I don't know what does."

The doctor looked at him and shrugged.

"I can't comment on whether your mother is making a sensible choice in this matter," he said. "But she is able to talk about her decision with perfect clarity. Being sane is in no way related to being wise."

"But what do you think we should do about it?" her elder daughter Karen asked.

"There isn't anything you can do," the doctor said. "I suggest you take her home."

So they did and for a while they didn't hear anything further about Lucinda's plans to leave her husband. They decided among themselves that her desire must have been a passing fancy, a phase, a strange fit that she has gone through as a result of her recent move.

But it was not. About a month later, with the reluctant help of her younger daughter Cynthia, Lucinda moved her belongings out of the apartment she and Fred shared in the Golden Years Retirement Community and got her own apartment in another, similar community nearby. She petitioned for a legal separation. She spoke to a lawyer about filing for divorce.

Her children were furious with her. One after another they came to see her, her two daughters and one son, and they told her how angry her decision had made them, how selfish they thought she was being. How could she leave her husband now? Their father, they said, was old and not very well. He'd been through treatment for cancer a couple of years before, which no one thought he would survive. But he had survived it and recovered, although he never gained back all the strength he lost during his chemotherapy. Every day during that difficult time, Lucinda had gone with him to the hospital where he would be wheeled down the corridor by the same strong and friendly nurse with long blonde hair and peppermint-pink lipstick to the treatment room. Then Lucinda would wait while he was given the dose of chemicals and afterwards she would accompany him home. And in all that time she never faltered, never expressed impatience with him, was as steady and devoted as it is possible to be. When the doctor reported his tumor gone, she celebrated with the whole family, and since then none of her friends or relatives had detected anything significantly wrong or altered between her and her husband. Why, then, was she leaving him now?

Lucinda did not answer them, at least not in the way they wished to be answered. She merely said that it was what she wanted and she was sorry if it hurt them but she had to do what made her happy with what she had left of her own life. Then she smiled and changed the subject to something trivial and pleasant: the flowers she was planting in her window boxes, the outings she took with her friends to go shopping and to the movies. She seemed content.

For his part, Fred was extremely upset and bewildered by Lucinda's decision to leave; he could offer his children no insight at all into what had happened between him and their mother. After Lucinda moved out, he remained living in the apartment they had shared, surrounded by the belongings they had acquired through their long years together: the many souvenirs from their trips abroad, the photographs of their children, the gifts they'd been given by friends—a hundred daily reminders of his wife's vanished presence. After his initial shock, he settled into a solitary routine; he would breakfast alone, then spend the morning reading the paper. Then he would go down and swim slowly up and down the pool in the recreation center until he was tired. Then he would have dinner with other people from the retirement community, friends, or sometimes one of his kids. He rarely had to dine alone. Occasionally he would run into his wife in a restaurant or at the community center in town where classes and lectures and musical events were held. The first few times this happened, she approached and asked him how he was. But since he either glared silently at her or stood up and walked away without a word, she soon stopped trying to be friendly and ignored him, too. This went on for several months. But one day, when he came back from supper, he found a note that had been slid under the door of his apartment. It said: *Come and meet me by the lake.* It was in Lucinda's handwriting. He read it over, surprised, and decided to follow its directions. There was an ornamental lake on the grounds of the retirement complex and he put on his coat and went down in the elevator and walked over to it. He saw Lucinda waiting on a bench looking out over the smooth surface of the water. She was half-lit by the lamps that stood on posts alongside the footpath, and something about the way she was sitting made him remember how she had looked when they first met: tall and slender with an upright, formal posture and tidy movements and gestures. He came and sat beside her on the bench. Then he could see that her face was not the face of the young woman he remembered; it was lined, the skin delicate and fissured with veins. She turned to look at him.

She said: "I found the letters."

For a moment he couldn't think of what she meant. "What letters?" he asked. She didn't reply. Then it came to him.

When he was a young man, shortly after he got married, he had developed an infatuation for a woman at the insurance office where he worked. There had been letters exchanged, a brief affair conducted in hotel rooms around town, then contrition and a return to his marriage from which he had never strayed again. Shortly after the affair, his former mistress had moved to another state. Lucinda had never even suspected anything as far as he could tell, and he had not felt compelled to confess to her because the affair had never meant very much to him and was not a sign of any deep unhappiness at home so much as an accident of circumstance and immaturity—in other words, a mistake.

But for some reason he had kept the letters. He did not know why, but he had kept them locked in the top drawer of the desk in his study through all his and Lucinda's subsequent years together. And sometimes when they were fighting or when they were at odds with each other, he would go into his study and touch the handle of the drawer where the letters were and this would make him feel stronger, separate from his wife, a person with a secret. He felt the need to do this less and less as they aged, until he almost forgot about the letters altogether. Sometimes he would think of them and say to himself that he really should get rid of them, but he never got around to actually throwing them away; it just never seemed that important. In fact, the letters and the affair they chronicled seemed so insignificant that, when they moved the last time and he sold the desk, he had not felt it necessary to take any special steps to hide them. At their age, what did it matter? It was so long ago that he could not remember the woman's face, only that she'd had dyed red hair and a birthmark down near her collarbone; sometimes he could not even recall her name right away. So he put the letters in a box along with other books and papers; he had not thought of them again until this minute.

"Is that what this is all about?" he asked. "That's ridiculous."

Lucinda shrugged. "I knew that would be what you'd say. I knew the children would say that too. That's why I didn't tell you until everything was arranged for us to separate."

Fred persisted: "But don't you see? It doesn't matter now—it didn't even matter at the time. Why didn't you tell me that was the problem? Are you really that angry at me for something that happened so long ago?" He paused from speaking and an idea came to him: "Are you angry with me because I didn't tell you? Because I kept the secret all this time?" he asked.

"No," Lucinda said. "That isn't it, either. I was unhappy to find that you'd had a love affair, of course. And I was also upset that you kept it secret for so long. But those things I could have forgiven, I think.

"It was when I saw that you had stopped trying to hide the letters from me that I knew you no longer thought that I was a person capable of jealousy. You had stopped thinking about me as a woman and had begun to see me as just an old person who shouldn't feel the same things as other people. If that is true then what is the point of being married?"

"For companionship," Fred said. "To keep us from being alone. Because it's better than nothing."

Lucinda looked at him but didn't answer. Then she stood up and smoothed down her skirt with both her hands. Without speaking another word, she turned away and walked along the lakeside path back toward the apartment building where she now lived and she did not turn around to look at him again.

2.

Karen and David were considered by their friends and families to be as close to a perfect couple as any of them had ever known. Both attractive but not so beautiful that it overwhelmed their other qualities, both clever but not unbalanced by a particular extraordinary talent or passionate calling, they met in college in New England, where they were students at a prestigious private school with a reputation for its programs in foreign languages and literature and for its proximity to wonderful ski resorts which the students often visited when they weren't busy studying. They met in a class on Russian literature in translation.

They dated during their final year as undergraduates and found that they had many things in common. They both liked hiking and tennis; they both had studied French and liked to travel. After they graduated they went together to do a year of social-service work in a school in rural Senegal, then moved to New York, where David began law school and Karen got a job in the editorial department of a women's magazine. With help from their parents they bought an apartment in Manhattan. They married the fall that David took the bar and got his first job working for a big law firm headquartered in midtown.

They lived like this for several years, David working at the law firm and Karen editing articles about interior design and fashion and women who ran nonprofit organizations in various countries in the developing world. They had lots of friends in the city who had gone to the same college as them and whom they often met for drinks or dinner and with whom they went away for long weekends at the beach or up to Vermont to ski. They visited with Karen's parents Lucinda and Fred at their house up in Connecticut often; David's parents, who lived out in Colorado, did not like New York and did not come to visit much. David worked longer hours than he would have liked, and Karen felt from time to time that her job did not provide enough of an intellectual challenge for her. But generally they considered themselves to be very happy. They talked in a noncommittal way about starting a family in a few years' time.

One day, Karen was at home in their apartment by herself. She was looking for a page she'd forgotten to bookmark on the browser of the computer in the second bedroom, which they used as a home office/exercise room when they didn't have guests staying with them. The page she was looking for had the pattern for a sweater she was going to knit for David for his birthday and she couldn't remember the name of the site where she had seen it. She was scrolling through the history file when she noticed an address that made her stop her search. The name in the URL was so strange and unexpected—www.pleasehitme.com—that she clicked on it before she thought about what she was doing. The screen winked and shifted and the site began to load, background first, then rows of images popping into view one after another.

What she saw upset her right away. The page was filled with pictures of men and women, naked or nearly so, displaying various kinds of injuries on their faces and their bodies: black eyes, split and swollen lips, torn skin. Some of their injuries had obviously been inflicted by other human beings—bruises the size and shape of fingers, parallel gouges left by fingernails—while others were just maps of unexplained damage. Some of the men and women wore handcuffs or were tied with rope. But the pictures she found herself looking at most intently showed just expanses of blued and purpled flesh, lacerations and incisions in the smooth sheet of the skin, in which the faces of the subjects were not even visible, only the pale or dark angles of their bodies with their hair and creases, the shapes of the flesh and the bone beneath and the saturated colors of the wounds.

Karen stared in disbelief. She was not naive about the existence of pornography online and she would not have been especially shocked to find a link to a site showing posed and naked women that her husband had been looking at. She would not have been pleased exactly but she would not have been surprised; in fact, she would not have cared about it very much at all. She might have closed the window feeling mild annoyance or disappointment; she might have forgotten it by the time David came home later that evening.

But this was different. This she would not be able to forget, not only because the images were appalling in and of themselves but because there was nothing that she knew about the man she lived with that could help her understand what she was seeing. In all the years she'd known him, David had never shown any propensity for physical violence toward himself or others; the most forceful thing he'd ever done in her presence was to slam a heavy book down on a table once when they were arguing; he'd certainly never raised his hand to her. He did not like grisly films, did not play video games involving gruesome violence or slaughter. He even found piercings and tattoos distasteful because of the association that they had with pain.

Karen sat at the computer with the mutilated bodies and ecstatic-looking faces illuminated in front of her and for several minutes she had no idea what to do. She could not unsee what she had seen. She stood up and walked around the apartment in a circle then decided to go out for a walk to try to clear her head. She shut off the computer and picked up her purse and took the elevator down to the street and walked in a daze in the direction of the park. She was so distracted that she didn't look carefully where she was going and, crossing Amsterdam Avenue, she stepped off the curb and into the path of a taxi that was racing through a yellow light. The driver swerved trying to avoid her, but he did not change course fast enough and the left side of his fender collided with her legs.

She felt the initial impact of the car as something personal, malicious, a giant force that seemed to come out of the air and shove her whole body angrily up and forward. Then she felt the pain of impact as she hit the ground. Her consciousness seemed to splinter and after that she remembered only fragments of what happened, flashbulb instants: the paramedics cutting off her clothes, people shouting, the stretcher she was lying on being loaded into the ambulance, the siren starting up as they began to move. Later she learned that she had broken her jaw and one side of her collarbone when she hit the ground. In the ambulance she lost consciousness altogether.

When she woke up, David was there. He was sitting beside her bed, holding her hand. He saw she was awake and stood up so that she didn't have to move her head to look into his face. He was staring at her with an intense expression of anxiety and tenderness, and for a moment she was flooded with simple relief at seeing him and gratitude that he was there. Then she remembered the events that had led up to her accident, and the bruised and bloodied faces from the screen came into her mind as vividly as though she had seen them only a moment before.

She looked up at her husband, his gentle, rapt expression and her stomach turned. Was he looking at her or at the damage she had suffered? She could picture how she looked right now: her face swollen up and lacerated where she had fallen on the pavement. She closed her eyes and tried to swallow but the muscles in her throat ached when she tried to move them and her mouth was as dry as paper. Her head was throbbing and her jaw ached and her whole body felt like one gigantic bruise. She closed her eyes wanting the world to go away.

"Sweetheart," David was saying somewhere above her. "I'm so sorry." But she knew he did not mean that he was sorry for anything he had done, only that he regretted what had happened. Then he bent to kiss her on the forehead. She saw his face lowering toward her, his eyes sorrowful and his lips pressed together and she tried to tell him not to touch her but found it hurt too much to speak. She made a noise in the back of her throat that sounded to her like the shapeless noise a drowning person might make.

"The doctors said you shouldn't try to speak until your jaw has had time to heal some," David said as he looked at her and bent again to kiss her. She shrank away from him to the far side of the narrow bed but she couldn't move far enough away to avoid him. When he kissed her she felt his lips linger on her skin. She found that her left arm moved pretty well and she raised it even though it hurt and pushed him away. He looked bewildered and she knew he didn't understand. When he tried to kiss her again, she managed to roll over so that she was facing away from him toward the wall.

"What?" she heard him say. "What's wrong?" But of course she couldn't tell him.

Through the weeks of her recovery, whenever he would try to touch her she would pull away. Even when she was well enough to speak and walk around, as her bruises began to heal and turned from red to purple to black to green and yellow, as her cuts began to heal, she still found that each time he came near her she would think of the pictures she had seen and wonder: does he find me more beautiful now than he did when I was well? She would shy away from him, upset and revolted by this possibility. David for his part responded to her coldness with solicitude and careful, gentle attentiveness, which might have been caused by simple pity for her condition but which seemed to Karen to show that in fact he actually cherished her more in her damaged state than he had before and made her avoid his touch more assiduously than ever. Each gesture he made to demonstrate his affection had the effect of putting more distance between them, more strangeness and silence until she could hardly stand his presence anywhere near her; she would flinch when he touched her, she could not look into his face without crying. She felt too upset and ashamed to tell him what she'd seen on the day before her accident. Too much time had passed, she thought, and she'd caused him too much anxiety by her behavior to tell him now what had occurred; it seemed both too small and too vast to have been the seed of their estrangement.

Even a patient husband could endure only so much of this treatment. By the time Karen's face and body were entirely healed they were barely speaking to each other. While she was recovering, he'd moved into the spare room so she'd be more comfortable at night and he remained there, moving more and more of his belongings out of their old room. He worked longer hours and so they didn't have to dine together. Soon this became normal for them, an established routine. They inhabited the same house but moved around each other like flotsam caught in opposing currents. At a certain point it seemed that at any moment one of them would say out loud what they both knew and then they would separate.

But then, sometimes, Karen would come across David unexpectedly in a room where she had not known he would be. She would remember what it had been like between them before. She wondered if that feeling could ever come back and she would imagine it returning as if it had always existed and had only been away on a long journey. Or David would arrive home at night to find Karen fallen asleep with her book still open on her chest and the bedside lamp still on and, coming in to switch it off, he'd notice the dark storm of her hair on the pillow and think how beautiful it was. And so they would each put off for another day saying that they thought that one of them should leave. And another day. And another. And another.

3.

Cynthia met Kris online during her second year of residency after medical school.

She had decided to apply for a residency in surgery, even though this meant a longer training period and even more lengthy hours and greater stress, because she didn't want to settle for one of the specializations that she considered "mommy track" like dermatology or pediatrics; she wanted to attain the highest level of prestige and skill in her field.

When she was accepted, she felt both thrilled and terrified. She moved to Madison after she finished her exams and started her internship at the university hospital there in July.

Of course, she had very little time to socialize or date or to pursue any interests outside work—she'd loved cycling during college and she'd taken several long bicycle trips, including one around the coast of Ireland; she'd played the piano well enough that she'd considered going to a conservatory to study composition and performance; she liked to garden and to cook; but all those things went by the wayside now. She had expected this. She had no time for anything that first year except work and it was thrilling and exhausting. Sometimes she envied the interns who were going into general practice and would be done in a year or two, but other times she pitied them: how could you ever want to leave the intensity of the hospital, a place where you knew the things you did and the decisions you made were of the greatest importance, where you were changing and saving lives every day?

But the body has its own cravings quite apart from the intellect, and sometimes she would feel the absence of a lover in her life as clearly as a hunger pang and then she would wonder if she'd made the right decision. It was not the same for women, she understood; even now, the expectations for a wife were different from those for a husband, and although of course many individual men and women did not conform to traditional roles and found a way to love each other anyway, still when a man she was on a date with learned she was going to be a surgeon or when after a few meetings he found he had to see her only when her work allowed, which was not often, she felt him detach, retrench, withdraw. Sometimes she could tell the exact moment when this happened. Something in the man's posture or in his facial expression changed. The duration of time in which he'd look at her would shorten until at last he didn't look at her at all and then she would get the call or, worse, the email or once even, to her horror, a text message, telling her that he didn't think it was working out between them and he liked her but was sorry, etc.

All the other interns in her track were men and she tried dating a couple of them but they were too much like her: ambitious, focused and competitive.

Then her elderly parents split up, to Cynthia and her siblings' great surprise, during her second year of residency. She had thought that they were happy together or, if not happy, at least content, at least comfortable with each other. Their separation really shook her up; what other model of relationship did she have? Her brother Harry was on his second divorce. Her sister Karen occupied a marriage that seemed great at the beginning but then lost all the air inside it; Karen and her husband David seemed more like ghosts haunting each other than like spouses. Was that the point of all this effort, to end up trapped with someone in a set of small rooms, unable to either leave or truly inhabit your own life?

So Cynthia stopped trying. She focused on her work and when she was working she was happy. There was so much to learn, so much to take in; sometimes she thought she could feel the new pathways of understanding being driven through her brain like roads. She was coming to see the body in ways that she could not have imagined before, to understand how well it could recover from damage and disruption, how adroitly it could compensate when it encountered some unexpected obstacle to the fulfillment of its functions and desires. It seemed to her that this capacity to adapt was its particular gift, its magic. Sometimes she thought she could see through the people around her, through their seemingly inert flesh and into the fizzing, busy miracle of blood and bones and cells remaking and renewing themselves.

She finished her shifts exhausted and most nights or mornings she would come home and crawl into bed and drop into sleep like a stone into a pool of water. But sometimes she was still full of the feverish energy, the adrenaline that had sustained her through the many hours on her feet and then she could not sleep.

On these insomniac nights she poured herself a drink and sat down at her computer and clicked through pages of brightly colored ephemera: news stories about the latest film star to be stopped for reckless driving and ordered into rehab, pictures of children in faraway countries rescued after floods and earthquakes, quizzes that told her which Beatle she would be if she ever had been or ever could be a Beatle. And sometimes she chatted with people whom she'd never met and never thought she would.

In the different chat rooms she would visit, she introduced herself to whoever was already there and described herself a little. She told who she was and what she did, though never exactly where she lived. She talked for a while with the mostly male interlocutors who came her way, and they were variously dull or interesting, intelligent or stupid, charming or crass; she liked each of these qualities or not depending on her mood. Some evenings she was pleased to find herself communicating with someone erudite and cultured about the works of art they both loved and the books they'd read. Other times she was glad when the person typed some blunt obscenity about her breasts or cunt. She replied in kind or closed the window on her screen immediately depending on whether the explicitness turned her on or bored her. Eventually, she started to get sleepy and could go to bed and rest.

This was how she first encountered Kris. The name came up in a chat room for classical music enthusiasts that Cynthia had been to on previous occasions, but she had never seen this user before. *Hello*, she typed. After a moment, the mild reply came: *Hello*.

Who are you? she typed.

My name is Kris, said the screen after a pause. *I live in Norway in a little town north of the capital. Who are you?*

I'm Cynthia. I'm training to be a doctor. I grew up in Connecticut.

There was another delay and then: *Connecticut? I have not been there, but I have been to New York City several times to perform. I used to play the violin in the symphony in Oslo and we went on a number of tours in the United States.*

What do you do now? Cynthia asked.

A few years ago, I left musical performance so that I could develop and run an organic farm. I thought: how hard can that be after learning to play Shostakovich? Serves me right! Farming is so much harder than I could ever have imagined when I started out. It took all my time! Finally, though, it is beginning to turn a profit and I have hired a manager to help me run it so that I can go back to the city almost every weekend. Which is good because I can see my kids more often.

You have children?

Two. A boy and a girl. They live with my ex.

That must be difficult . . .

Well, we are relatively lucky. She's a wonderful parent and we get on well as friends, we just weren't so good at living together in the end. We were too different. Perhaps you know how that can be . . . There was a blank on the screen, the cursor pulsing as it waited. Then Kris typed: *But I'm sorry, I've talked a lot about myself. Please, tell me about you and your work. Being a doctor must be fascinating . . .*

They continued chatting and when Cynthia finally glanced at the clock she had to excuse herself and go to bed because several hours had passed in what felt like much less time. She had been enjoying their conversation so much that she had not noticed. This pleasure was not only because they had so many interests in common, although that seemed to her remarkable enough: Cynthia felt like she was talking to someone who had taken up all the discarded threads of her own life—music, gardening, Kris even liked cycling—and made another life out of them. But there was also an ease between them, a shared sense of humor. When Kris made jokes, which were mostly gently self-mocking, she found herself laughing in spite of her exhaustion. She liked the slight formality of the way Kris wrote, the sign of someone who had learned English as a second language and knew its grammar too well to be a native speaker. Kris seemed to like her too, and before they signed off at last asked if they could meet again the following evening. Cynthia checked her schedule and agreed and they set a time and said goodnight.

Away from the screen, she felt light and graceful as she got ready for bed that night as though someone she could not see was observing her benignly and approvingly.

The next night they met again and the conversation was just as interesting. She wrote about her decision not to pursue music and her work at the hospital. She told Kris things that she had told to no one else: how upset she'd been by her parents' late divorce, how she felt she had to work twice as hard as other people to compensate for being shy and serious and awkward. Again the time flew by. For the next week they chatted every night, even when Cynthia got home very late, and their rapport grew flirtatious. They swapped photographs (she spent some time and effort choosing which one to send) and she was pleased with what she saw: a picture of a blond man with high cheekbones and a prominent nose and slightly craggy brows that she thought looked dignified and that kept his face from being too pretty, which she would not have liked. His skin was creased around the eyes and mouth; he looked in the picture both capable of laughter and capable of great seriousness and concentration. She printed out a small copy of the picture and put it in her wallet in the space with the clear plastic window where other people put pictures of their spouses or their kids. She would take it out and look at it whenever she wanted to feel a little burst of energy and pleasure.

All week she flew around as though the force of gravity had temporarily diminished and she was lighter than she'd been the week before. Her work went particularly well and she was praised by the attending physician, who commended her in front of the other first-year residents. She felt the two things must be connected: her late-night chats with Kris and her good performance at work. She thought she must work up the courage to ask whether a visit would be possible: she could go to Norway or Kris could come to Wisconsin. That night, on screen, she read: *I would like to invite you to come and visit me here. Whenever it is convenient for you, I would love to meet you in person. You can come for as long as you like.*

She typed back: *You read my mind. I was just about to invite you to come and visit me.*

They settled that Cynthia would come to Norway, since she had a short vacation coming up. Kris would come down to Oslo and meet her at the airport. They could spend a couple of days there and then go up to the farm if they wanted to. Kris bought the ticket that night and sent the itinerary to Cynthia. When she opened the message, she felt her heart leap, her pulse quicken. That night she had her first dream about Kris. It was not overtly sexual. They were sitting together on a mountainside, green and bare of trees. Kris reached out and laid both hands on her knee, and this was what she remembered when she woke: how beautiful those hands were, how distinct, with long fingers, strong and elegant, but not unscathed. She woke up with them still before her eyes, imagining what it would be like to be touched by them.

One evening of the following week, Cynthia was having dinner in a Chinese restaurant across the street from the hospital with a couple of the other residents after their shift. When it came time to pay, she opened her wallet to take out her debit card and left it lying unfolded on the table beside her while she looked over the check. The woman sitting beside her, whose name was Sonya, glanced over and said:

"Why do you have a picture of Amund Eilertsen in your wallet?"

"What?" Cynthia said, confused.

"Amund Eilertsen, the actor. That's a picture of him." And she pointed to the photograph behind the plastic window.

Cynthia felt her stomach plummet through the floor. She felt like she could hardly breathe. "Oh," she managed to say. "It's a joke. My sister gave it to me. I used to like him when I was younger and she'd tease me about it and so, you know . . ." She trailed off and smiled in a way she hoped covered the turmoil inside her.

Sonya said: "He was always on TV when we would go to Sweden to visit my grandparents, but hardly anyone in this country has even seen anything he's been in, since he hasn't done many films. What did you see him in?"

"I can't even remember. It was so long ago . . ." The waiter was handing out the receipts and she took hers and absorbed herself in signing it, figuring the tip. She didn't look at Sonya because she thought that if she did, she might start to cry. When the checks were brought back to the table, she said that she was feeling completely exhausted and excused herself to go. She was halfway down the block to her car when she heard someone call her name behind her. She turned around and saw Sonya coming after her holding Cynthia's purse in her hand: she'd departed in such a hurry she had left it on the back of her chair.

When she arrived home it was nearly midnight, the hour when she usually spoke with Kris—or whoever that was, she thought. She understood suddenly, sickeningly, that the words on the screen could have come from anyone; she had no way to know whether the person with whom she had become so quickly and intensely involved even lived in Norway, had been a musician or a farmer or a parent. The shared interests had seemed genuine; Kris had known more than she about music and cultivating plants. The descriptions of journeys by bicycle they'd shared had been so detailed and the pleasure taken in them so similar that they couldn't possibly be entirely made up . . . could they? Also the things they did not share: Kris's manner of talking about being a parent was one of humor and affection, and the frustrations and triumphs of running a small business had seemed true. Last week on a whim she had looked up the brand of organic produce that was supposed to come from Kris's farm and it was real enough, but of course anyone could have looked up that website, used its details. The fact that the farm was real proved nothing.

A pang of sadness and disappointment burst inside her chest. Their affinity had seemed so genuine. But the face of the person she had thought she was falling in love with belonged to someone else entirely, some actor whom she'd never seen.

Why would someone do that, create a whole persona that was not their own? What possible motivation could they have for doing such a thing?

She considered simply vanishing, never again logging into the chat room where they used to meet, blocking any messages that arrived from Kris. But she decided that she couldn't simply leave things unresolved. She poured herself an extra-large glass of bourbon, sat down at the computer, logged into the chat room and waited. When the name Kris appeared on screen she left the initial greeting sitting on the screen unanswered, until the words *Hello? Are you there?* appeared beside it.

I know that photograph isn't you, she typed. Then she sat back away from the keyboard and waited. For a minute nothing happened. Then the words flashed up: *I'm sorry. I don't know what I was thinking. Everything else I told you has been perfectly true.*

How do I know that? Cynthia typed. *How can I believe anything you say?*

Again there was a pause and then: *I understand you must be very angry. I am truly, truly sorry. I thought that if I sent that picture you would continue to talk to me. I did not realize that it would matter until it was too late. I thought that when you came to visit, you would find out then. I thought, somehow, that would be easier.*

Easier for who?

I don't know. Easier to make you understand that the other things I've told you are sincere. I'm sorry.

But why did you send me a fake picture at all? Why not just send a real one?

Would you like me to send you one now?

Yes, Cynthia typed, then hesitated and deleted it. *No,* she wrote instead. *How would I know the one you're sending now is real?*

I see your point, Kris typed after a moment. *Look, I understand I have no right to ask you this, but will you consider please coming to Oslo anyway? I will arrange for a hotel; you do not have to stay with me. I would just like to meet you, once. Then you can go back to the United States and never contact me again if you like. I would understand. Please consider it.*

Cynthia hesitated. Then she typed: *I'll have to think about it.*

Fine, Kris typed, *that is fine. Just let me know. When you are ready to do so.*

I'm going to go now, Cynthia typed. *Goodbye.*

Goodbye, Kris said, and vanished from the screen.

For the next week Cynthia did not contact Kris at all, nor did Kris try to contact her. She felt a growing curiosity about this person whose words she'd found so captivating. She was not so much interested in what Kris had hidden. Obviously, whoever she would meet in Oslo would be different from what she'd imagined—maybe a different gender or a different race, perhaps disabled in some way, perhaps much older or much younger than herself. What interested her more was whether she would feel in his or her presence any of the excitement and intimacy she'd felt so strongly in their writing. Had she experienced some real connection to another person? Or had she just been talking to herself? She wanted to find out.

And yet it seemed completely foolish to travel all that way to meet a stranger who had after all misled her. Should she go or not? Days passed and she still could not make up her mind.

Then a few days before her scheduled trip, her mother called. Since she'd helped Lucinda move into her new apartment, they had seen each other only a few times. Cynthia did not have much time to travel and Lucinda found it difficult at her age to come up to Wisconsin, especially during the long, cold winter months. But Lucinda called her regularly once a week and sometimes, recently, they would talk for a long time as they had not done since Cynthia was a child.

This week, when Lucinda asked how her week had been, Cynthia hesitated. She had planned to say that everything was fine. Instead, she found herself on the verge of tears and then talking all about the person she had met online, the invitation and the photograph. She expected Lucinda, who had been so practical about the end of her own marriage, to say that she must forget about Kris and move on as soon as possible. But after Cynthia has finished speaking, she heard Lucinda take a breath and when she spoke her voice was full of strong emotion.

"I think," she said, "you should go."

"You do?" Cynthia was astonished.

"Yes," Lucinda said. "Kris has not been completely open with you, but keeping a secret can sometimes be a sign of love. I'm not saying that it's right to do, but perhaps it is not the worst thing either. Why not go and find out who this person is?"

The next day Cynthia wrote to Kris and said she'd come to Oslo after all. She thought: whatever happens, at least I'll know. She thought that if she didn't like what she discovered, she could take the train to Stockholm or Copenhagen and spend the weekend exploring there.

As she packed her suitcase for the trip, she felt excitement and nervousness, even though she told herself that there was no reason for her to be anticipating anything.

She slept a little on the flight and then woke up as they were taxiing to the terminal at Gardermoen. She walked slowly with her bag along the corridor to passport control. Kris had promised to meet her on the other side of customs and had described the clothes she should look for at the airport: a blue jacket, black trousers and a gray wool scarf. She cleared immigration and rolled her bag through customs. On the far side, there were people lined up waiting for arriving passengers. She scanned the faces of the crowd, searching for someone at once familiar and totally unknown.

She saw the woman standing over to one side of the concourse. She was leaning on the wall and had one leg crossed over the other.

She was peering into the stream of arriving passengers, but she had not yet seen Cynthia, so Cynthia had a moment to observe her unobserved herself. The woman had high cheekbones and a kindly mouth and fair skin a little burned from working outdoors. Her sandy hair was tied in a long braid down her back and she looked nervous. Cynthia stopped and stared at her and then the woman caught sight of her and stood up straight, her face lit up with hope. Cynthia found herself walking toward her, leaving her suitcase where it stood and holding out both hands to her. The woman reached out her hands, too, and Cynthia saw that they were fine, long-fingered hands, a violinist's hands, strong, freckled and marked by other kinds of work. She recognized them. They were the same hands from her dream. She reached out and took them in her own.

She stood in the fluorescent lighting of the airport concourse holding hands with this stranger while people passed them on either side.

"It's you," she said, and then again: "It's you."

LEVI'S RECESSION

Devin Murphy

Spring:

DURING TRAINING THEY TELL YOU the first thing to do in case of an emergency is go back into the trailer and upright the animals so they don't crush each other. But after the accident the truck was on its side and I'd fallen across the cab and crashed headfirst into the passenger door. When I stood up my feet were where the window had been, my chin was even with the bottom rung of the steering wheel, and the air tasted like aluminum and hog piss. Before stepping into the sleeping compartment I thought the awful sound in the cab was some side-effect of a ruptured eardrum singing out deep in my head. A pile of blankets, pillows, and DVDs were at my feet as I put my ear against the metal wall and listened to the terrible squealing of what had been seventy-five full-grown pigs.

I pulled myself up onto the cab's side panel through the driver's window. Trees lined the fields on either side of me. A menacing blue-gray cloud bank stacked up on the horizon and sharpened in color as it approached. The cab had scraped its way over eighty feet of the road after jackknifing and the line of gouges in the asphalt left by the trailer ended at me.

I'd been driving fast—too fast. My shoulder and head hurt and I was lucky not to have been killed. The thought of dying sent a quick amber glow through me that burned over the crown of my head and flowed link by link down my spine before bursting into a deep blue flame at the center of my chest.

I leapt down off the cab and walked along the truck's undercarriage. It was hard getting the trailer's back gate open, and when it fell loose it hit the street hard and just missed taking off my toes. Five pigs immediately ran past me and started milling around on the side of the road. The individual gates penning the hogs in swung open like a wall of steel mouths. I stepped in and walked the length of the trailer as the pigs' squealing chorus gathered and swelled around me.

None of them were dead. A few were stuck on their sides. Several more had hoofs sticking through the grates, and one that somehow had a leg sticking out a vent the trailer fell and slid on was bleeding from a pulpy stump hanging off its shoulder. I went into that one's pen and did the only thing I could think of to help it. I straddled it, pulled my serrated pocket knife from the worn leather sheaf on my belt, and plunged the point in under its jaw and sliced it across its carotid artery which was tough at first, then gave easy like a padded couch as I tore the blade up and to the side. The animal forced out a prolonged gurgle as it was gashed open and then silently bled out into a crimson puddle.

Maybe I wasn't thinking clearly after that, or maybe it was that amber light inside of me beginning to fade into an overpowering need to do something, but I began herding the rest of the hogs out of the trailer by slapping them on their meaty haunches.

By the time the police showed up all the pigs were wandering around in the field and no one was going to catch any of them. It was shocking how fast they could move, and after a couple of attempts, the police decided they didn't really know what to do with them if they were caught since the trailer was still on its side, so they were let free to graze on the recently thawed cornstalks sticking out of the snow. The hogs ate their way to the line of trees and then wandered off into the woods.

The company man who the police contacted was supportive when I first talked to him from the crash site. He was, "I'm just glad you're OK, Levi" and "You did the best you could, Levi." Then he found out I was five miles from my ex-wife's house, my destination, and about ten off the interstate where I should've been when I lost control on the ice and went on the gloriously terrifying slide.

"There's a problem with my daughter," I said.

"I see," he said quickly.

"It's an emergency," I said, but that didn't mean anything to him, and as soon as we hung up he was on the phone to the company lawyers to see how quickly they could fire me. That's what they did too. "We're going to have to let you go, Levi," he later told me, which was about the worst thing that could've happened. I was making good money that I desperately needed driving the pigs.

I didn't want to go to the hospital, so a tall and ropy state trooper named Terry, who wore a brimmed, gray hat that shadowed his angular face and neatly trimmed mustache drove me from the crash site to my ex-wife's house. Merriam's old farm house is on the high ground outside of Jesup, east of Waterloo. As the trooper drove, my gaze glided over the fields beside the road, white with the last hard snow pushing down the husks of alfalfa and rye. A coolness seeped into me with the rattling of the squad car and gradually, as we turned down one back road after another, clotted into a frozen lump where that wild blue heat had been. I wanted to get to Merriam's as quickly as possible and yet never get there, never find out what news was waiting.

That morning Merriam had called me on the road to tell me our twenty-year-old daughter, Rachel, had been missing for over a week. I sped there and ruined the truck. As the trooper drove, terrible things that could have happened played on a loop in my head. When Rachel was sixteen she got herself an ambulance ride to the hospital in Iowa City where they discovered she'd smashed Xanax in with what must have been a titanic line of cocaine. What she had gotten into before that I really couldn't begin to guess, but since then, she'd moved onto finding darker and stranger ways to cause herself harm. There was a spell where I'd scream like a lunatic at her, and her mother would guilt her up and down and cry in front of her, but none of that worked. I'd look at her skinny, pale legs, her dust-green eyes, and the narrow draw of her face she'd so clearly gotten from me, and my heart would lurch against my ribs because she seemed to be throwing her life away.

A mile before Merriam's house the road turns from pavement to gravel. The ticking of the stones striking the bottom of the car used to be a welcoming sound to me and they snapped my focus to the curve of the driveway leading up to the old farm house. When the trooper pulled up to the house, Merriam was on the porch waiting with my best friend, Mick. She saw the police car and started running toward it. When she saw it was me getting out, her face slackened from an immediate disappointment.

She is slight as a heron, and the crown of her head lines up with my chin. Her pale ivory pallor is covered in shadowy brown freckles that fade into one another and make torn leaf shaped splotches that I've traced with my fingernail. Her red hair changes shades three times on its endless descent over her back and is a fiery burnt umber where the ends finally brush against her hamstrings.

"I thought they'd found her," she said. "Jesus, I don't know what we're going to do?" her voice quivered like she'd had the air forced out of her.

"Is there something you need help with, man," Terry asked.

"We don't want her to get a record," I whispered as she leaned against my chest.

"But what if . . ."

"We're not there yet," I said.

"No. We're OK for now, officer," she said.

"That a girl," I said, getting the first scent of her lavender shampoo that I'd had in a long time. I shut my eyes for a moment and held her with that very real feeling of still loving her creeping up from my fingertips.

When I opened my eyes again Mick was standing next to us.

"We'll find her," he said.

He had on his grease-stained Carhartts with the threadbare holes in the knees of his jeans. He wore a sweat-stained, green John Deer baseball cap with the bill curved tight over the temples like a claw. He pushed his cap off his head and the sharp tip of his widow's peak could have slid down and fit perfectly into the cut of the dust stained, V-neck T-shirt he wore under his thick jacket.

"Where's your truck?" Merriam asked, and all the facts of my life pushed the scent of lavender away. All those problems with our daughter, and the inevitable hurts that got caked on us as we went along poured back. The memory of those dysfunctions seemed to make my skin too tight on my body, and riding the crest of that wave of sorrow was the looming obsidian knowledge that my daughter was missing.

"Where's your truck?" She asked again.

"I'll tell you later," I said. The trooper's car was slowly crunching the gravel behind me as it pulled out of the driveway and the sound made her chest sink further inside of her body.

"Should I call him back and tell him?" she asked.

"We'll find her," Mick said. And he pointed to his truck. "I'll fill you in as we go."

I followed him to the truck, got in, and then I was on the road again, starting our hunt for Rachel.

We drove Mick's '85 Ford till late at night when exhaustion from the last of the morning adrenaline rush faded, and I felt numb for hours until the first birds of the new day were trilling and there was Mick hunched over the wheel still driving. His sweaty aftershave smell filled the cab. His eyes were pinned on the road ahead of him. He had a high forehead and stubby nose, but broad shoulders and the lean torso of a scavenger bird. His large meaty hands rested on the steering wheel and his callused fingers kept tapping in rhythm on the dashboard. He came from Scandinavian stock that adjusted to life on the Great Plains, and he was hardened by humorless, immigrant parents who squashed any dreams he may have ever had of living an alternate life when he was young. He was as much a part of this place as the soil, and he knew every last corner to search.

"We'll find her," Mick said. "She's a bit wild is all. Like her Daddy used to be."

Mick and I had gone to high school together, and though we had never been great friends when we were younger, we seemed to be each other's only friends as we approached middle age.

We spent two days together silently searching for Rachel. If I hadn't been so scared I'd have thought there was nothing prettier than that big curved windshield facing the first of the day's sun and then the last tendrils of pastel leeching from the sky. Between those tricks of sunlight were the endless hash-marks on back roads, rise after rise of rolling prairie beat down by green and yellow harvest combines and chemical trucks with large plastic tanks and long metal booms, and lonely ramshackle barns with wood slats sliced by razors of light and over run with clumps of sagebrush that dotted the horizon.

We stopped for gas and coffee, asked the few people who were in the store if they'd seen anything, then headed south. A rusted brown Ford Taurus turned off a dirt road and Mick waved for it to slow down. When Mick rolled the window down he knocked the lid of his coffee loose and it sloshed down his chest.

"Dammit."

He pulled the cloth away from his skin and let it slap back down a few times.

"You seen a young woman with brown hair and a round face running around here?" he yelled out the window to the car stopped next to us. A leather-faced, old farmhand with a gray walrus mustache shook his head no, nodded goodbye and kept on driving.

Along County Road G there was a small white chapel with a stained glass window framed above the wide wooden doors. The window was blue at the base with a brown robed Jesus walking on water with a yellow light flooding the panes over his head.

"I hope I'm not to the point I need to start praying," I told Mick.

He studied the church and the bright glass as we passed. "Not yet."

We eventually made our way to The Hole, a dive bar in the far northern section of the county. Kelly Gynobly, the bartender, was a large woman who always wore tank top shirts that showed her muscular shoulders and bare neckline below her short black hair.

Kelly also had a red mucus sack held in by a sheen of silver skin instead of right eyeball. The sack sunk beneath the ledge of her eye socket like a large larva egg. Her younger brother hit the eye dead-on with a pellet launched from a slingshot when they were kids and that did something akin to turning the eyeball inside out. The globe swallowed the pellet and held it like a pearl.

"Kelly, darling. We need to find Levi's girl, Rachel," Mick said.

"Haven't seen her in a few nights," Kelly said.

"She's been here though?" I asked.

"She's here all the time," Kelly said, her eye falling away from me.

"She's only twenty," I said.

"No different than when it was our turn at sneaking in here."

I wanted to knock the little stack of tomato juice cans off the bar, pull her toward me, and shake her until she told me where Rachel was.

"Kelly," Mick said. "She's been gone for a week now and we need to find her."

Kelly tugged the white bar rag taut between her hands. "She was in here three nights ago."

"Who was she with?" Mick asked.

"Didn't know the person."

My guts sank when she said that from having listened to police scanners for years while driving, of overhearing chatter about so many small, terrible crimes.

"What'd he look like?" Mick asked.

"Not sure to be honest. Not sure where she went to after leaving either. I'm sorry guys. I wish there was more to tell you."

After leaving The Hole we kept heading north along the river. We drove for several hours on winding back roads that didn't have names. We passed through small towns and stopped into farmers' homes that we knew and asked our questions. It was on a deeply rutted dirt road along the river when we saw a tent through the trees. It was the two-person, winterized, yellow pop tent that Merriam bought for Rachel years earlier. When Rachel was a girl I would set that tent up in our backyard and we'd sleep outside in it on warm summer nights and use flashlights to cast finger shadows on the nylon walls. Mick and I got out of the truck and marched through the woods up to the tent. I unzipped the flap, pulled it back, and my heart started lurching again.

There was my daughter, tangled up in the arms and legs of some skinny little woman who was kissing her collarbone. They shot up immediately and started rocking on their sleeping bags, each hyper as hell.

"Get away," the woman yelled. Her voice pierced the quiet of the woods.

A yeasty, caustic sex smell, something chemical on top of something base and very human floated past me and made my eyes water.

I guess I knew then what was making them so jumpy. Next to their flattened pillow were wads of tinfoil and a light bulb blackened by the purple Bic lighter in the corner of the tent.

"What have you done?" I gasped.

The woman with Rachel was topless and had small breasts with nickel-sized, salmon-colored nipples. A thin chord of blue veins threaded across her forearms and disappeared into her wrists. Her thin auburn hair was disheveled and there were deep circles under her eyes that looked like torn walnut husks. A twitch on her cheek kept pulling up her lip exposing her gum line. She put a hand on my daughter's leg and squeezed her pants in her fist like she was trying to keep me from taking her away.

Rachel gave me this half-crazed look and I knew she'd been smoking meth too. She focused her stare over my shoulder and looked directly at Mick with this strange gravity and swatted the topless woman's hand away from her leg without breaking eye contact with him.

"Did you miss me?" she said to Mick and the last of her words were bitten off by something dark and mean.

Mick's face tightened and his teeth began grinding together so the muscles at the back of his jaw bulged out.

I pulled Rachel out of the tent by her arm. "What have you done?" I said. Her eyes, which turned to me for a moment, jumped quickly back to Mick.

"What the hell are you looking at, Mick?" I yelled. "What's going on?"

There was a history in their stare. I felt it. It started burning up my spine and I wanted to start hammering my fists into all three of them.

Mick looked at me and quietly shook his head and kicked at sprigs of dead grass and snow covered dirt at his feet.

Rachel was trying to wiggle loose but I clamped on tighter and began pulling her to the truck. My fingers wrapped around her upper arm tight enough to leave a bruise. I wanted to leave a bruise.

"What do we do with that one?" Mick said, pointing to the other woman.

"Leave her," I said. "She found her way out here, she'll get back."

Hearing that, the woman stood and stepped out of the tent. Despite the small bags under her eyes and the full heft of her near-nakedness she looked like a child, desperate and vulnerable in this nowhere and alone place.

Rachel kept pulling against my grip which didn't break and then waved the woman over.

"Put some clothes on, at least," Mick said. Something in his voice sounded deeply disgusted.

The woman sat in the flatbed of the truck as we drove back to The Hole. Now I'm glad we didn't leave her there. I think that wouldn't have sat well with me if I left her.

At The Hole, Kelly came outside and walked to our truck before the engine turned off. It was the only time I'd ever seen her in daylight outside of the bar and her bad eye looked like a rotting cherry reflecting a wrinkle of light. She helped the freezing cold woman out of the truck and wrapped her own jacket around her.

"It's OK, Donna," Kelly said.

"You know her?" I asked.

Kelly didn't look back at me but blew a kiss to my daughter and led the woman into the bar. It was one of those touching and tragic things you end up seeing over the course of a full life.

Rachel had little scabs up and down her arms like a severe case of the Chicken Pox that she dug at in the truck between me and Mick as we drove away from The Hole. She homed in on one spot and dug and dug her fingers in until there it was, there was my own blood coming out of this skinny little thing. I longed for that amber light to pulse through me again, but there was only a swamped, thick feeling in my gut before an overpowering wave of affection toward her washed through me—that original softness that came to me when she was born, when it was clear how helpless she was.

By the time the small stones on Merriam's road started smacking the undercarriage of the truck Rachel began coming unglued between us. Her body went slack as a bag of water and she slouched forward with the crown of her head facing her lap. Then she shot up, her spine stiff, and she rocked side to side between us, pressing quickly into my shoulder and then away. Her hairline was beaded with sweat, her eyes jittered around in her head, and there was very little I recognized in this thin, strange creature.

"We're going to fall through the road," she said. Her voice was slow, soft, muffled by layers of spiderwebs at the back of her throat. Then her head rolled against the seat as she arched her rubber spine backward.

Dear God. I used to play I-spy with her in the truck, and now this.

"All the way down," was the last thing she mumbled before Merriam ran out and led her out of the truck and into the house, where my daughter spent the night swinging from paranoid to euphoric, back and forth as if she were on the very edge of life.

That first night after we'd found Rachel was spent talking to doctors, and then on their advice, figuring out how to pay for the rehab clinic in Iowa City. Mick let me stay with him after the loss of my trucking job, and I did for a few days after Merriam and I dropped Rachel off at the clinic. He lived by himself outside of town, along the Wapsipinicon River, which everyone called the Waspie. He started a drywall company after high school and kept the garage attached to this house full of tools, sheetrock, and his flat-hauled, aluminum fan boat and its trailer. Dust from the garage clung to Blutcher, his Newfoundland dog, who licked his dreadlocked ass all day long, lapping his fur up into a nauseating froth that gave him shit breath when he came to put his head on your lap.

"You've got to give this mutt a bath," I said.

"He swims in the river," Mick said.

The dog had a worn down dog bed in the living room of Mick's small house but mostly followed Mick from room to room and lay at his feet.

The dingy dining room had old wood veneer wall paneling and no furniture, but there were half a dozen sawhorses where he'd worked indoors through the winter. The floorboards were caked in drywall dust and the scent of creosote filled the air. A three-tiered tackle box lay open in the corner and the scatter of tools inside gave the room an industrial and profoundly lonely feeling. Carpenter rulers and levels were strewn about as if he had a constant need to do something measured, to weigh an accomplishment to give each day its worth. Blutcher would randomly swat at a screwdriver and gnaw on a splintered corner of a board and I envied the company of his dog who must have helped stem off the terror of total solitude.

After a few days at Mick's, a mounting unease about not working ballooned beneath my ribs, and the way he stared at Rachel in the tent kept moving through my head. Little flashes of her on her back in the bed of his truck on some old dog blanket with the bottom of her feet facing straight up led to my fantasizing about crashing a claw hammer into his head.

"Mick," I said, "I've got something to ask you."

He turned toward me. The knots of muscles at the top of his jaw line tensed and leaned into me like he wanted me to slug him.

"Go ahead."

And I did want to hit him, to unburden myself, but something in the way he offered himself up and the sad surroundings of his undecorated home made me change my mind. It wasn't the right time to know what had happened with him and my daughter as knowing meant losing him too. But I couldn't stay there any longer.

Merriam had an old airstream trailer behind her house. Inside there was a sheath of dust on the window ledges and book spines but it was comfortable. Beyond the trailer on her property was a dense thicket of pine trees where her grandfather planted a Christmas tree farm with the notion of selling them over the holidays. That was before he ran off with another woman, leaving the trees sixty years ago to become a perfectly ordered forest.

"I don't want to be in your hair anymore so I'll move into the trailer behind Merriam's house," I said, and something in his face slackened and released. We were quiet then, pinned to each other by the sharp corners of what needed to be said. I didn't know what he was thinking then but fear for my daughter and worry about losing my job and not having money for her rehab were compounding within me while Blucher kept his glorious yellow eyes that reflected firelight on me.

Summer:

At the start of June the rivers in Northeast Iowa flooded. The Wapsie River rose so high over its banks the corn fields three miles on both sides turned into small lakes. Rows of corn stalks rose out of the dark waters and soy bean fields were covered outright. Islands of elm trees with old ranch-style farmhouses floated across the horizon. In town the water filled the basements and root cellars and pushed away the cinder blocks propping up old cars so the vehicles slumped into the rising murk.

The grass that stood so straight and swayed easily with the slightest breeze was flat to the ground, and when the water level dropped, it angled toward the receding flood waters as if each blade reached after it, thirsty for more. Whole fields and forests swirled into a mesmerizing mud pits and prowling swampland.

When people came out to see the damage, it was with slack, silent faces. They lifted up waterlogged clothing and shook it out one or two times as if that would dry it off. Then they dropped everything they picked up back into the slop at their feet once they realized it couldn't be salvaged.

Within days of the water receding, the front lawns were piled with soggy carpets and drywall torn off the struts with the tips of glittering nails sticking out in every direction. Each home had a pile in front of it that started as a few rotten boards, then grew into a pulpy mass made from the contents of the home.

Everyone in town had flood insurance, and those on the outside of town that most likely didn't seemed too embarrassed to say anything either way. People either took comfort in the fact that things could be repaired eventually or sank knowing that this was going to leave its watermark on the rest of their lives.

The liquor store Merriam worked at was ruined. The bottles with the warped labels and the soaked boxes got counted as destroyed and a check from some large insurance company would eventually come for the purposes of restocking the store. But the bottle seals weren't compromised, so Kevin, the shop's owner, let Mick and I take what we wanted home with us. We took seven full loads of Mick's Ford and pulled the air boat from his garage and loaded the empty space with the cases. When that was full we moved onto Merriam's basement, which was up on the town's bluff and still dry, and filled it wall to wall with flood damaged liquor— enough that we could start drinking until our skin turned a different color. When the room was full, boxes rose up in stacks that only left a narrow walkway to move through and the room smelled musty from the wet cardboard.

Once we'd done that, Mick hired me on to start clearing out some of the nicer homes in the surrounding towns. Those people were paying cash to have the most immediate work done before the insurance checks came in. We worked around the clock for almost a month, mostly cutting loose the soggy drywall and lumber where it was going to cause mold damage. I ended up sleeping at Mick's again so we could roll out of bed to get right to work. When we came home Blucher would tear out in a fury to chase after the truck and bite at his reflection in the hubcaps and get washed in the dust and gravel kicked up by the tires.

"At least he knows how ugly he is," Mick said, as he parked next to the fan boat.

After the official insurance claims were filed, tradesmen paid by some big insurance company came from Chicago, Des Moines, Omaha, and anywhere else they could be contracted to make the drive, and work for us dried up.

After more than a month of being in rehab we were finally allowed to see Rachel. Merriam and I got in a fight on the start of our drive to Iowa City and we drove the rest of the way with our own silent accusations and angers brewing between us. Those little fights had sapped me. That was probably why I liked being alone on the road all of those years. Being *married* to my wife was enough for me; it quelled the manic need to fill my heart that consumed most of my youth. Being with the woman drained me of something that felt essential. That was probably my deepest confession and at the heart of why my marriage failed. It may well lay at the heart of why my daughter was seemingly seeking her own self-destruction.

At the clinic Rachel was led into a visiting room where the two of us were. She wore pajamas and her hair was long and greasy like she hadn't washed it in weeks. She stood on the other end of the room from us and didn't say a word, didn't move, and it was a horrifying moment where none of us knew what to do. Then she stepped forward with her shoulders and arms still slack at her side and walked into her mother's chest to be hugged. She buried her head in the nape of Merriam's neck and didn't look at me. And maybe it was because she didn't look at me that pierced me with another of those little grappling hooks, those fine strings that Rachel had flung at my heart to suspend herself by. I felt the weight of her hanging at the center of my life, a spectacular marionette attached by millions of glowing strings like a cascading harp. She swayed back and forth, a pendulum pushing aside who I had been until she consumed everything else that ever mattered to me.

"I want to go home," she said.

Merriam and I had spent our negative energy on that drive to Rachel, and after we brought her home it was easier being with her. Probably because we both felt the pull to linger around the house and watch over our girl. We got in the habit at night of sitting on her porch together and looking out at the dark wall of swaying Christmas trees. It was nice sitting with her and it helped me forget about the weight of panic that made me feel small in a way I feared I couldn't recover from.

When it was clear Mick and I weren't going to get any more local work, and the liquor store was closed until it could be renovated, we decided to tap into our new liquor supply. We brought a lunch cooler of ice outside to fill our cups with. Merriam drank vanilla flavored vodka, and I drank a fifteen-year-old scotch that had the labels soaked off. The glue beaded up on the bottle and I scraped what was left of it off with my thumbnail. Some nights Mick would come over and Rachel would even sit out with us, brooding as she sipped on a fruity iced tea and only spoke in choppy, regurgitated therapy speak.

"I'm feeling pretty down tonight." She even worked in a bit of melodrama, saying things like, "I need to work on my self-worth."

What I really wanted was for her to come out and tell me what she needed, so I listened silently, asking her to keep talking when her words trailed off so she might unburden all her secrets we had yet to discover. But she was still jumpy as the meth had changed the chemistry of her brain. She shifted herky-jerky-like, as if her bones were trying to wiggle out of her dry, flushed skin. I drank my scotch, letting the peat flavor swell on the back of my tongue and watched her, equally happy she was safe and home and furious with the monster of her own wasted promise.

*

On a night Mick didn't come over and Rachel didn't get out of bed, Merriam suggested we drive my truck across the field to the river. We brought drinks and a blanket. When we got there we slowly got drunk while sitting on the hood of my truck. Then she leaned in and started kissing me. That led us to going at it in my truck, wildly tearing at each other, as it had been so long since we'd even touched. Flashes of her body filled the dark—a rounded curve of her bare calf muscle, her breast falling away from her rib cage beneath swaths of her wild orange hair. She had long pubic hair, something she had always trimmed down when we were married. I grabbed it between my fingers and pulled softly till it was taught and then give it a yank to push her over the edge. It was like we were strangers, and this didn't come with all the weight of our previous lives— divorce, misspent time, things ruined, people hurt—which all flooded back so damn quick and stayed for so long that it took until then for us to be capable of being near each other. Momentarily pretending we had no such past felt like it was saving us.

She lay belly down on the flatbed of the truck. Her hair draped over the exposed knobs of her spine and fanned out to cover the nape of her pink back. I put my palms on each of her butt cheeks and rubbed in concentric circles until she clenched up, began to laugh and rolled over and pulled me next to her so we were laying stomach to stomach and looking into each other's faces.

After a while, perhaps so we wouldn't have to talk, she said she wanted to fire my gun. I turned the headlights on and we stood in front of the truck to shoot. My first shot popped off and the long echo of the single chamber deer rifle thrummed over us. When it was her turn to fire I stepped back to see the smooth lines of her naked body as she aimed my rifle into the woods. Her skin glowed in the headlights. She fired. The recall kicked hard and the rifle fell from her hands. When she turned toward me there was a one-inch crescent moon gash on her forehead from the gun's scope snapping back. The mark welled up and blood flowed over her eyes and down both sides of her nose before dripping onto her bare chest.

She fell to her hands and knees and threw her hair over her head so the tips fell to the ground and little droplets of blood sealed the long strands together. I reached for something from our pile of clothes to clot the blood with and came away with my sock which I pressed against her head until the bleeding stopped. Then I used the other sock to clean her off but only managed to smear blood across her body.

After bandaging the cut on her head properly back at the house, she went to bed. I went to the stoop of the trailer to try to sober up and think about what to do and tried to convince myself it was OK to be idle for a while, but the idea even made me uneasy. Then I thought about everywhere I'd been while driving trucks to calm myself down.

If I traced my driving career, I'd probably dig the pen into a large circle around Interstate 80 through the Midwest and scratch it in until the paper tore and there was a big hole in the map of the country—like those years had indeed fallen through the road. Interrupted by rest stops, Country Inn Suites, and Cracker Barrels, those years measured in miles passed in the dark, moving hogs and cows around the middle of the country, stopping in those nowhere railroad towns out west in Nebraska: Red Cloud, Oxbow, and even near Kearny during the Sand Hill Crane migrations, when millions of birds bottlenecked over that twenty mile stretch of Interstate 80 and filled the sky. At the big truck stops, I power-hosed out the animal shit and scrubbed the floors and walls. I did stretches on the truck, leaning against the cab and doing dips from the foot ladder and pull-ups hanging off the trailer with my legs kicked under it. There was very little spectacular about the whole thing, but I missed seeing strangers lugging U-Hauls and going about the business of changing their lives, and I missed the perpetual motion of having somewhere to be, having some task that needed doing.

I wasn't going to get another job driving a rig anytime soon, so I looked for work as a technician working on the giant windmills springing up all over, but would have had to go back to school at the community college to get certified. So most of that first part of summer I floundered, playing house cop to my daughter and making sure she didn't sneak off anywhere else. I'd look in on her every night, and it was comforting to see her there, but something heavy descended on me staying in one spot, and I made a habit of sitting on the deck of my trailer and staring out in the woods at night. That's how I discovered the shadow that stalked our property in the dark.

First, there was a flicker of dark black off in the distance that my eyes shot to. Then the shadow moved again, growing slightly as it got closer. When it moved a third time it became clear it was the swing of arms and the distinct gate of a grown man. I was about to ease over and grab my rifle from the truck when the green brim of a baseball cap caught a sliver of moonlight in the field. Mick moved from tree to tree and then stopped to look at our house. He must not have seen me as he eventually walked out the woods and started taking long, slow steps to the back of the house where Rachel's bedroom window was. In the open, the full outline of his body took shape, thick shoulders, and the beginning of a padded mid section, slightly bowed, long legs, and the curved brim of the green cap.

Mick kept walking closer and closer in those slow, methodical steps. Part of me wanted to see how close he'd dare get but when the premonition he'd actually peer through the glass hit me, I made a throat clearing sound. He froze in mid-stride and his silhouette lingered at this odd angle like an ugly sculpture. Then he turned back and with the same slow steps began his retreat to the woods.

After that night I often caught a glimpse of my only friend secretly lurking behind tree trunks in the shadows. It was a habit I had no idea how long had been going on for. I tried to convince myself he was watching over my family, warding off whatever unlucky spirit had crashed into our house, but I knew he was just part of the messy rut our lives were stuck in.

I had a hundred chances to confront Mick about what he was doing at my daughter's window but every time I thought of doing something, a deep sadness filled me that kept me from saying a word. Before I knew it, it was late summer, and we spending time together silently working on his air boat, checking the hull and aluminum prow for dents or cracks that needed to be pounded out, welded or patched. We took off the fan cover and wiped the caked layer of smashed bugs off each blade, then we checked the motor, ratcheting the gears tighter and flushing out the silt and shards of olive grass. When it was ready, we trucked it on Mick's trailer and backed it into the water so we could explore the river for the night.

On the Wapsie's widest and longest straightaway, still deep from the floods, Mick opened up the throttle on his fan boat. The motor vibrated up the chair through my legs and the fan felt like it was going to suck me backward if I didn't hold on.

He lit a Colman camping lantern and the fiery mesh bag burned an orange ring that rose up toward the fixture where it exploded into painful white light that softly whistled the rest of the night until the propane ran out. We bolted it onto the bow and the light gave us ten feet of visibility as we glided downstream like some amped up waterfowl over the vile murk of the river which was probably no different than the middle of our hearts.

The skeleton of a rusted old car was sunk into the riverbank. The chassis was packed into the mud but the petrified engine block was exposed. It was now one rust-fused heap of steel. Flecks of rust chipped from the body drifted down river, glittering orange and fine as sand. In the slime-rimmed shallows near the car, bullfrogs groaned to each other as they ate up the bug larva floating in the stagnant eddies. Downriver there was a sandbank with white egrets roosting for the night. When we fired the engine up and started blowing toward them they shook their bodies loose and lifted off the water and spread out against the manic scatter of stars. Smaller birds darted across the water for insects. An owl fluttered past like a ripple in the dark. Night hunters were about the business of looking and always looking for something and that longing felt natural to me too, like maybe I was wired to search for the missing part of myself.

Mick had the spotlight swiveling back and forth from side to side of the river, which glowed like pooled mercury. That's how we caught the yellow eyes of deer lapping at the water, frozen, surprised at how quickly we rounded the corner and came upon them. There were little water varmints swimming along the banks too—muskrats, weasels, and river otters. Often, we saw the outline of full-grown, farm-fed hogs lumbering through the untended brush. At the speeds we were going we saw a flash of them, the arch of a dark shadow where the heft of their bodies stood out against the night.

The current leaned up against and parted on large rocks that I steered wide of without slowing down. When the boat's port side dipped into the river on the turn the lantern revealed the submerged rock, but it was too late. The contact pitched me from the steel umbilical of the throttle and I flew directly ahead of the bow and damn near got run over by the boat. Mick got launched twenty feet through the air and crashed into the thick mud on the lip of the river. I was floating in an eddy with my life jacket propping my head up when he stood to look for me.

"You OK?"

"I'm not sure."

He had a mouth full of what looked like algae-slicked mud that he fished out of his with a hooked finger.

"It tastes like there's a party in my mouth and everyone there is throwing up," he said.

Floating on my back, that feeling of being so truly alive with amber light welled up inside of me again. I shut my eyes and prayed for that feeling to buoy some essential part my life.

The boat capsized with the top of the fan lodged in the sand and anchoring it to the bottom of the river. But I drifted like this wild place had stripped away the inessential clutter of my life and brought me closer to my true heart.

I took my lifejacket off and dove to unclasp a rope coiled under the bench. Mick tied one end of the rope to the far side of the boat and wrapped the other around a tree to make a pulley. We heaved on the rope until the upturned fan cover was leading into the mud and used that as a lever to pull the boat back over. Once we tied it to shore we saw the sharp rind of twisted steel scraped back leaving a large hole. The engine was leaking a rainbow sheen into the water.

It was almost a ten-mile walk back up river that night and we didn't get back to the truck until four a.m. By the time Mick dropped me off at the trailer behind Merriam's, the sun was starting to come up. I went inside, stripped off my wet clothes, and dove into my cot without showering. Burrs were tangled in my hair. There was a pleasant ache in my legs from walking so far and a soft burn on my grimy arms from stinging nettles that slapped against my skin.

The full sunlight coming into the trailer made everything hot and sticky when I woke. It felt like I was some sort of outlaw, far from any place I'd been before, running from something. But not thirty yards away was my old life that paralleled my life now.

We hiked back to the boat the next night and pounded out and sealed the haul, greased the bearings and joints, blew out the air filters, and replaced the fan belt by stretching and wrestling a new belt on with two crowbars. We wiped off the fan blades so the river muck wouldn't fling itself loose and spray us. When we had it ready to work our way back to the truck, I nudged the gears until they caught, and we were off again. And we went fast—faster than we had, as if some pure imbecilic beauty had taken over and we were begging to crash again.

Mick white-knuckle gripped the bench on both sides of his lap but kept quiet about our speed as if he owed me something—some epic apology that could not be laid down in words. I'd already played out his crime in my mind but it was clear by the look in his eyes when we found Rachel in that tent that she had hurt him, and who was I to heap onto that. That grudge would have to be one of those things to let go of if I were to hold onto anything. So we left that unsaid, but somehow agreed upon going so fast it felt like we were passing into some other world and immune to our own, seeking the moment of crash and launch, at least the possibility of it to pitch us into forgiveness.

*

Fall:

The money ran out before the last round of bills for Rachel's rehab came in and if we didn't pay the bills we couldn't get the prescriptions for the medication she needed. Mick already gave me a loan for the second round of payments, and there was no asking again as work had been slow for him too.

"We could cut the Christmas tree forest. Loggers will pay good money to have at it," I said to Merriam, but she gave me that disgusted, you're-less-than-a-man look that boiled a wild urge to start swinging that axe handle myself or to drag her back to the truck by the river with me. But those feelings were too deep to call up and that left me feeling futile, with the only trace of our one night together on the raised ridge of skin beneath her brow.

"Find something else," she said, ending our conversation there.

Then Mick got a big drywall job subcontracting at a nuclear plant in Nebraska. He could pay me for a few days of work so I drove out there and we split a room at the Motel 6. At night we ate in the local diner where most of the plant's single workers ate. They had signs up that said *We'll get to the future on the back of Nuclear,* and a couple for and a few against Yucca Mountain in Nevada, which was the proposed site to store the waste from all the nuclear facilities in the country. Neither of us knew much about what was going on there. What I could figure was that there were spent rods that in my imagination would be glowing green, that were cooled in underwater ponds on site at the facility. The proposal wanted to haul that waste onto trucks and drive west to Yucca Mountain. So instead of hundreds of little radioactive dumps there would be one spectacular tragedy against the environment.

One night I called Merriam from the motel.

"How's Rachel?"

"She's not changing." There was an awkward silence between us then. "How's it going out there?"

"Fine."

"You making any money?"

"Not a lot."

"Can you work more?"

"Can we please sell off the trees? Let someone cut them?" I asked again, but her silence screamed her disappointed and I hated her all over again for that.

In the surrounding towns there were little signs staked in the yards trying to condemn nuclear energy because of fear that some of that contaminated cooling water would get into the watershed and taint the Ogallala Aquifer. But those few signs were in the middle of nowhere, very infrequent, and riddled with buckshot holes.

Driving back to Iowa a day earlier than I expected after my portion of the job was done I imagined the world we were creating—one where my meth-head daughter will sooth her scars with radioactive water that seeped up into the river. She'll drift in the current beneath the shadow of the giant wind farms and wait for a glimpse at feral pigs her father filled the woods with. Then I prayed she'd find forgiveness for my inadequacies as she floated toward the true shape of her life.

It was dark when my headlights finally lit up the base of Merriam's hill at the border of her property. The taillights of her Dodge pulled out and started down the back side of the ridge heading toward town. I followed her so we could meet in town and eat together at the 24-hour Egg and I Diner. But then she pulled off the road to town and veered west to the county line. I turned too and drove behind her in the same sort of trance long drives always put me in. When the homes started getting more and more frequent she took several turns into a neighborhood development and parked in front of one of the houses. I pulled alongside the curb a few houses down and from a block away saw the halo of her overhead light jump up as she opened the door and her long left leg swung out of the cab. As she slammed the door shut her hair fell loose across her whole back. A lean man with a long stride, orangutan arms, and neatly parted black hair walked out of the front door and wrapped himself around her and placed his chin on her head before leaning down and kissing her.

A quick fantasy about slamming the accelerator, hopping the curb, and running them down overcame me as they turned shoulder to shoulder and glided into the house.

That night slowly deepened around the truck in front of that stranger's yard. My mind was wandering and I suppose it needed to land somewhere. Days went by without a single thought of the river, but at that moment the scent and color of it swooped down on me like a dark heron. In the truck the river pulled to me. It was slowly moving through all of Iowa, measuring the wide swath of darkness and I wanted to be on it—beneath the eyes of resting birds in the trees and the open sky. Along the banks was the silent wall of trees yellow with swatches of fall, full of vermillion and burning ochre. Everything but the shores and the dark waters drifted away until Merriam came outside alone several hours later. She bounced across the yard, jumped up into her Dodge and quickly did a U-turn so she was heading back toward me. As she got closer I switched my cab light on. The shadow of her head angled toward me and her brake lights tapped red for a long moment and then off as she sped up and drove away.

After staying there for several hours, unsure of what to do, the sun came up. In the full light of morning I drove to Jessup to find Bill Harrison and lied to him about having the right to sign the lumber on Merriam's land away and filled out the papers like they were another divorce document. After the papers were signed, I drove aimlessly on the backroads until I was almost out of gas. Then I went back to the trailer and lay down in bed and began sleeping in short fits. Each time I nodded off I dreamed I were a snake being carried over the treetops in twin talons beneath the bony wing of a giant black bird.

With no work for a spell after that, all that time was spent silently prowling the grounds around my trailer and the house. Watching Merriam kiss that stranger made me heartsick, useless and weak, and that drained most of the anger out of me. We didn't talk about it, as saying anything would have meant sharing the feeling of utter hopelessness, which I couldn't do, as I wanted so badly to be strong to help Rachel, whose body and mind were doing horrible things to her and kept her sleeping day and night. I couldn't bear saddling her with any more troubles. She was in her slug period. She slept fifteen hours a day. When she was awake she barely ate, and she dragged herself to the front porch where she sat with that thousand-yard stare fixed on the giant Christmas trees. I wanted her to go to community college, then on to Iowa State University. I wanted to save her life, to drop it back into her lap like some glowing rod that could spark something inside of her.

Over that next week, Merriam and I let quick glances fall over each other and then looked away. When it was time to take Rachel back to Iowa City for a checkup and therapy session, I didn't go along. The lumber company was scheduled to start cutting the forest later that morning. When she returned she'd see how deeply she'd hurt me. But the part of me that hurt the most, the vindictive side that made the call to Bill, shrunk up when the men with trucks and machinery actually showed up.

They had two large excavators fitted with serrated pinchers for forestry work, and a giant Volvo feller-buncher that cut and caught the trees in one motion, laying them down for the excavators to sheer branches and load into the trucks. Several dozen men showed up wearing embroidered jackets that said *Harrison Lumber, Making Every Tree Count,* and they worked quickly, sheering off a layer of the forest from north to south, pushing back the line of trees before turning back and cutting more. Most of the day the forest roared with saws and trucks, which made me deeply regret my decision by the time Merriam and Rachel got back.

Their Dodge had to swing wide in the driveway to escape a departing truck laden with logs. Merriam got out and walked right up to me. "This is a crime against your family," she said, and she and Rachel scurried away into the house.

The noise of chainsaws on the property was everywhere. I shut my eyes and listened to the Christmas trees, bound for cutting sixty years ago, finally being eaten away. Harrison would make every tree count and so would I. The money from the trees could send Rachel to the community college for an associate's degree. She could do well there—she could get aid to go on. It was at least a chance, and a chance was worth their combined scorn.

Later in the day I walked to the back of the house and saw them sitting next to each other looking out the window. They were sharing a thick comforter. Rachel had her head on Merriam's shoulder and it was clear why Mick would want to sneak up to the glass and see these women. When I turned back to the collapsing woods I expected to see him running away, chased off from the shelter of his natural longings.

Several days after the trees were felled I took Rachel to the river to tell her about going to college at the start of the next term. It was secluded beneath the colorful parachutes of fall Cottonwood and Willow trees, and that made me long for the lost Christmas trees.

"Your mother thought you might want to talk to me," I lied, wanting Merriam's stamp of approval to make my daughter open up to me, but she didn't say a word.

"You know I love you," I said, needing her to believe those words.

The sound of the water calmed me enough to try again for some connection.

"It's OK with me whatever you are."

"And what am I, Dad? I thought I was your daughter."

"I just mean. You were with that woman." Her eyes were burrowing into mine. "And the drugs. But whatever all this is about, you're my daughter and I'll do anything for you."

"Now you're here for me, huh. Isn't that convenient," she said. She began walking away from me, then stopped next to the thick trunk of a Cottonwood tree. I could see her shoulders rising and falling with each breath. Then she turned back. "I always wondered what would happen if you lost your truck, if you'd be around more or if you'd still be an emotionally removed, absentee father."

She'd never used those words before. They had come from her rehab, some therapist, but the words clearly shaped her feelings and found their mark on me. Then she turned again and worked her way through the trees back toward the house. I wanted to call out to her but I didn't know what to do or how to fix anything.

After a prolonged quiet I kicked off my shoes, peeled off my shirt and waded out to the icy depths of the river. The cold water against my skin was the closest thing to the electric joy of life that Rachel must have felt filling her body with petrochemicals. Out past the sand ants and the Jesus Bugs flittering on the surface, I let the current sweep my feet out from under me and slowly carry me downstream. I latched onto a rock with my hands and dangled like a perch facing upstream and let my body levitate in the current, my pale white feet fluttering behind me. Rachel got hung up on similar rocks or some fierce barbs in that awkward place between childhood and what came after that. She stalled out and couldn't cross over, and as much time as I'd spent the first few years trying to figure out what went wrong, it felt like too much to consider under the water. Underwater was a steady thrumming whoosh. There was no room for anything other than wanting the next wild gasp of air waiting above the surface. Near the rocks the sound churned and whorled and seeped into my ears and coated my brain with a constant roar that swallowed all the little breaths and massive screams I began letting out beneath the Wapsie.

Winter:

In late October, I finally got a job as a tow truck driver and began tooling around town waiting for a break down or fender bender. In town the slow swirling gray chimney smoke crested the rooftops, curled through the branches, and drifted off in high columns on the wind. In the little borrow pit ponds the silhouettes of geese floated on the surface, their necks bent back and tucked tight on their bodies. At night I drank flood liquor in my trailer. Though when the first big storms hit on Interstate 80 and cars couldn't stay on the road, I started running the truck without sleeping, only stopping to get warm. Between Des Moines and Iowa City hundreds of cars slipped out of the rut of exposed road and the snow pack pulled them into the median or spun them off to the side where there was no getting out.

We got this Arctic blast that plunged down from Canada in late December that zipped every door up with ice and frosted the eastern part of the state at night. It got so cold in the trailer one night, Merriam let me come inside the house for the evening.

Mick came over too and we built a fire. Mick and Merriam were drinking the flood liquor. I had to go out later that night with the tow truck to work the interstate so didn't drink. I didn't trust myself to drink around them then. After unhinging my jaw and swallowing so much disappointment I was sure if I drank, all that would slip out and I'd say or do something terrible. But as the night crept on, Mick and Merriam got deeper into a bottle of vanilla flavored vodka and I could see Merriam's mood begin to darken.

"Got to keep warm," Mick said, tossing a shot back.

"It's so cold because this one cut all the trees and there's nothing to block the wind," Merriam said. There was that familiar sharp barb to her voice that knifed under my skin and touched a raw nerve at my core.

Hadn't I driven trucks for years for them? Hadn't I been trying to find work for them?

"I wanted to see who was out there in the woods," I said.

Mick's eyes hardened on me.

"You're an incompetent, is more like it," Merriam said.

Her words sucked the air out of the room and instantly I hated her for following through on her desires with someone else. I hated Mick for whatever desires he'd chased that led him to my daughter's window. I hated my daughter for inhaling chemical smoke that ate away at her brain, even if it was my fault in some way, even if I was a terrible father that crushed some weight-bearing part of her.

"And you're a slut," I said to Merriam.

"You have no right to call me anything. I don't owe you anything at all. We don't have to care about each other's feelings anymore. That's what a divorce does. It frees us from each other."

"You guys sure look free of each other," Rachel said.

"Rachel. Just sit there and shut up."

"Hey, Levi, watch what you're saying," Mick said.

"What does any of this have to do with you?"

"I'm just saying, you're being rough."

"That's my business then. This is my family, you pervert. You're lucky I haven't shot you in the backyard yet."

"What the hell are you talking about?" Merriam asked.

"Why don't you ask him," I said, pointing to Mick, who put his shot glass down and stood up uneasily like he wanted to walk to the door.

"What the hell is wrong with you, Levi?" Merriam said, and something twitched deep inside of me. After months of trying to hold everyone together, I'd finally sucked down too much of the hurt that had slammed down on me. It was time to shed the life we'd had. My wife and I were finally done. My daughter's life was perched on a fine blade between recovery and regression. Mick was a lost soul. I was locked in the struggle to fend off deep depression that would flatten me if I didn't do something. Mick must have seen all of that flaming across my face.

"Calm down, buddy," he said.

"Don't buddy me. How can you buddy me when you've been with my daughter?"

"What?" Merriam managed to breathe out.

Mick put up his hands and his eyes darted to Rachel.

"What is he talking about, Mick?" she said and turned to Rachel. "What happened? *Tell me!*"

Rachel's face turned sheet white and no more words were needed for Merriam to see what her silence really meant.

"Oh my God," Merriam gasped. "Get out of my house," she yelled, and I didn't know who she was talking to. "You touched my baby, you bastard. And you, you knew about this?" She wound up and threw her glass at Mick who ducked as it shattered against the stone hearth. Then she stepped forward and kicked me so hard in the shin I fell backward and toppled over the wooden rocking chair.

"You bitch."

"Mom. Stop it. He didn't molest me or anything."

"What the hell happened, Mick?"

"She came on to me," he whispered, his secret truth floating across the room.

"I felt sorry for you," Rachel snapped.

Then Mick's eyes narrowed and those knots of muscle at his jaw line tensed. "I hate you, you dyke," he yelled, like everything in him needed to explode.

"Don't you say that," Merriam said.

"You're a sad old asshole," Rachel spit back.

"You touched my daughter. You've been coming to my home after doing that?" She turned to me. "You let him come to my home after that." She was trying to line up where to put all her rage. "What the hell is wrong with you, Rachel?"

"Maybe I've got daddy issues," she said, a nasty smirk spreading across her face.

"Do you not care who you hurt?" I asked and then saw my words scrape through her ribs.

If nothing else I had sparked off a purging of our deepest wounds. I'd given them a voice which was something they had never had before. Then Merriam was walking around the room yelling, "*Shut up. Shut up. All of you shut up.*"

The burning logs snapped in the fireplace and for a stupefying moment Merriam stood rigid. Then her body seemed to lose its stiffness, her anger turned liquid, and those unseen maladies drained from her into the floor.

They all began to grow distant then, as if everyone in the room was being pulled away.

Mick walked to the box of liquor bottles near the door, pulled out one in each hand and walked out of the house. His lean frame filled the succession of window panes on the side of the house as he trudged toward the clear cut field without bothering to hide his familiarity with his path through the vanished woods. The three of us in the house remained there in silence. Rachel let herself fall backward onto the couch. She wrapped the thick blanket over her shoulders. Her face was flushed a deep, deep red. It was a good sign, like at least she were feeling something again. I felt the sudden urge to run my hands over her arms, start at her shoulders and rub down to her wrists, over the little pocks and skin discolorations where the scabs had been.

We sat in silence until Merriam cried herself to sleep on the easy chair and Rachel nodded off into a restless sleep soon after. Then I stoked the fire and got dressed in a gray zip-up sweatshirt and green Carhartt jacket. I stuffed a knit cap down over my ears, put on my big neon green reflective highway jacket, and went back outside, knowing someone had to make some money for our broken family.

The county roads led me south to Interstate 80 along the train tracks. It was so cold the train company sent out people to ignite the switches on the tracks to keep them from freezing, and off in the blustery distance were parallel lines of fire, arching flames glowing above the dark fields. It was past midnight when I pulled into the state troopers' office to see which side of the road they wanted me to clear. One of the troopers told me to head west and pick up the first vehicle stuck in the snow and keep going from there.

The first car was a sedan with a thick layer of snow on the roof about ten yards off the road. It had that little pink strip of tape blowing around on the antenna that said the police had already been there. I pulled alongside that one but noticed yellow flasher lights winking on and off ahead of me and drove to take a look. The fresh tracks getting snowed over led to a minivan that had slid off the shoulder. From the angle of the tracks it was lucky not to have flipped. There were footprints in the snow where whoever was inside pushed their way out and paced back and forth until going back to the van. A man wearing a big fuzzy hat with a wool snowball dangling off the top rolled down the van window and started waving his arms and started yelling.

"I have kids in here," he said.

I helped him, his wife, and two little boys bundled in fancy puff jackets climb up to my truck where they squeezed in and watched me hook a chain to their front axle. The electric wench pulled their van out of the snow enough to use the boom to mount the car onto the wheel lift. The van had Illinois plates with a Chicago Land Rover dealer trim on them. The icy beams of headlights from other cars were still whishing past too fast for the weather which was good because I was getting paid per vehicle towed.

The father kept shaking his knee up and down. "I wasn't going that fast," he said to his wife. "I wasn't." His voice sounded deeply disappointed in something. Himself I guess, his inability to get his family through the storm.

"It happens," I said. He looked at me like I was some hill-jack, and he was probably right. I didn't blame him for thinking of me as stuck in secluded irrelevance, rank and file with the other nothings out here in the middle of the country. He led some other life and none of this was part of it. They were on their way to or from somewhere so much different than this.

Look around you, I should have said. Cars were scattered everywhere. These small wrecks were part of getting on the road.

"I wasn't going that fast. It's just, look at this, look at it," he said, sort of disgusted with the snow blowing sideways over the fields. Something in his tone made me think that he was probably one of those men who think the Midwest is flat, in the same way for a long time I felt my life was flat, but that isn't the case. The rails blaze through the night, the fields bubble and dip, there are subtle bluffs where the soft gold and purple light of the evening lies down on the frozen corn fields, tracing the contours of everything until it reaches the river that cuts through the heart of this whole place and swells over the steep banks. I wished I could tell him this was as much a part of his life as what he had planned for and saw coming with polished promises from such a great distance, but he wasn't ready to hear that from me, and I wasn't sure I could have found the words yet.

"Look at this," he said, holding his gaze in his lap as I carried him and his family of strangers safely away.

A BOOK OF MARTYRS

Joyce Carol Oates

YES. I WANT THIS.

He asked if she was sure. She said it again, Yes.

The vow was unspoken between them: once started on their drive into a more northerly part of the state, once embarked upon this journey, they could not turn back.

It was a drive of approximately three-and-a-half hours on the interstate highway if there were no delays: road construction, accidents, state police checkpoints.

There was a police checkpoint just outside Madison. Triple rows of cars moved slowly, reluctantly, like ice congealing, to form a single lane. Her heart beat hard in dread. They will turn us back. They know.

Stiffly—politely—the Wisconsin state police officers asked the driver to show them his license and vehicle registration. In the passenger's seat she sat very still. She expected the officers to ask for her ID but they did not.

She dared to ask who they were looking for. It is protocol. Police officers don't answer such questions from civilians. Police officers are the ones to ask questions. She felt a crude blush rise into her face; she'd made a fool of herself.

She was behaving as guilty people do.

In any case she was of marginal interest: Caucasian female, hair dark blonde, early twenties, weight approximately 110. So they would size her up, impersonally. They were looking for someone else.

And the man beside her, at the wheel of the car: at first glance maybe her father, second glance maybe her husband. Yet the driver and his passenger didn't seem married, wouldn't have seemed— to practiced police-officer scrutiny—to belong in any discernible way together.

The driver was a rawboned Midwestern type, you would think. Tall, slope-shouldered, sawdust-colored hair worn long, receding from a high forehead. White shirt, khakis. Genial, cooperative. Eyes lifting to the police officers' suspicious eyes, to signal to them, Hey—I'm a good citizen. Average guy. Nothing to hide.

Conover was of an age somewhere beyond the older of the police officers, which would put him in his early forties, very likely. He had an easy authority to which, in other circumstances, the officers might have deferred. The faculty parking sticker on his rear window, issued by the University of Wisconsin—Madison, would have alerted the police officers to his possible, probable identity: one of those hip university professors determined not to resemble a professor.

"I hope it isn't anything serious, whatever has happened. Whoever you're looking for." Conover paused, smiling. His words were innocently inane, like the murmured afterthought—"Officers."

They took away the driver's license and the auto registration to run the data through a computer in their vehicle. In the car, Conover and his companion whispered together like abashed children.

Behind Conover's steel-colored Toyota a line of vehicles was forming, traffic brought to a halt. No one made an attempt to turn around at the barricade and flee.

Without explanation the police officers returned, handed back Conover's driver's license and vehicle registration, and asked to examine the glove compartment, the rear of the car, the trunk. Now a little stiffly Conover said, "Of course. Officers."

She knew: her lover was a longtime member of the ACLU. By temperament, training, and principle he was an adversary of what he'd call the police state. He distrusted and disliked police officers.

Yet, without being asked a second time, Conover pulled the lever on the floor to unlock the trunk.

"Maybe they're looking for drugs."

"Maybe somebody has kidnapped somebody."

"And put them in the trunk?"

"Maybe the victim is dead. The trunk is the logical place."

Conover spoke lightly, much of his speech meant to evoke amusement. But he wasn't so relaxed as he was pretending, she knew. He had not scheduled enough time for them to make the drive to Eau Claire without feeling rushed; he'd been coolly pragmatic, planning the drive. Neither had wanted to make the appointment in Madison, or anywhere near Madison.

Now, a police checkpoint was slowing them down.

Conover was rubbing his jaw. He'd shaved that morning hastily; there was a swath of silvery stubble on the underside of his jaw. He'd been six minutes late picking her up at her residence, so she'd been awaiting him anxiously and had run out to him eagerly, oblivious of who, in fact, might be observing.

The state police were taking their time examining the trunk. Drewe had the idea that they were picking up bits of desiccated leaves to smell them—as if the leaf fragments were evidence of a controlled substance. She felt an impulse to laugh, this was so ridiculous.

"Maybe they will arrest us. They will stop us."

"Don't be silly, Drewe. Just don't talk that way."

"Conspiracy to commit murder. That's a crime."

"You're not being funny."

"I'm not. In fact."

They sat in silence. Conover was staring through the windshield, unseeing. He'd scratched at his jaw and started a little just-perceptible bleeding. She was perspiring inside her loose clothes.

Now you've gone too far. Good!

Her demon-self chided her, teased and tormented her through much of her waking days. And in the night, the demon concocted her dreams in a swirl of fever.

It was nothing new. He—it—had sprung into a powerful and malevolent independent life by the time she'd been eleven years old, when it was beginning to be said of her half in admiration and half in disapproval, *That girl is too smart for her own damned good.*

Her parents were religious Protestants. Not extreme, but definitely believers. Her father was a superintendent of public works in Glens Falls, New York. Her mother had been a kindergarten teacher for twenty years. They were not unintelligent people, yet their repeated criticism of their only daughter who'd gone to college and then to a distinguished Midwestern university on full-tuition scholarships was something on the order of *Pride goeth before a fall.*

She was feeling nauseated now.

In recent weeks these purely physical spasms came upon her, in rebuke of her public poise and self-control.

Conover had been drawn to her cool demeanor, he'd said, the elegance of her public manner. That she was a sexually attractive young woman as well, in the most conventional of ways, was not a disadvantage.

Conover nudged her. Was she all right? Mutely she nodded, Yes.

It had been suggested that Drewe eat a light meal two or three hours before the procedure. But this wasn't practical for they were on the road early. An early breakfast would have turned her stomach. And she'd had virtually nothing to eat the previous night, so maybe the nausea was only hunger. Voracious and insatiable hunger. And a dull headache, and the sweating-beneath-the-clothes which were deliberately plain, ordinary clothes—none of her eye-catching consignment-shop costumes—a pale blue, long-sleeved shirt said to be mosquitoproof, which Conover had bought her for one of their hiking trips, and dark blue corduroy pants with deep pockets. On her feet, sandals. For there would be no hiking today.

On the third finger of her left hand was a silver, star-shaped ring, which Conover had brought back from an academic conference in Delhi. He had not (probably) meant for Drewe to wear the ring on the third finger of her left hand, she supposed. But Conover was too gentlemanly to object.

It was helpful, yet a kind of petulant rebuke, the way the police officers shut the Toyota trunk with a thud. Disappointed that they'd found nothing—no evidence of criminal activity.

"OK, mister."

The younger of the two police officers waved Conover on. Both were stony-faced. Conover waved at them in return as he moved his vehicle forward, a kind of salute, playful, not at all mocking, in its way sincere. "Thank you, officers. I hope you find whatever—whoever—you're looking for."

There would seem to have been nothing funny in this remark yet they laughed together, in the vast relief of coconspirators who have not been caught.

It was seven weeks, two days now.

She'd counted, assiduously. Like a fanatic nun saying her rosary, she'd counted again and again the days since her last period.

There was something so vulgar about this! She resented her situation, the banality of her biological destiny.

She had not told Conover. Not immediately. To keep such a secret from your lover is to feel a thrill of unspeakable power. For always there is the possibility, He doesn't have to know.

He can be spared.

Or—His life can be altered, irrevocably.

When she told Conover, his expression could only have been described as melting.

He did not say, My God how has this happened, we were so careful.

He did not say, This can't be an accident, Drewe. You are not the sort of woman to have accidents.

He said, Oh honey. How long have you known?

Meaning, How long have you been alone, knowing?

She'd made two appointments with a gynecologist in Madison. She'd had an array of tests, blood work, Pap smear, mammogram. She'd been very quiet during the initial examination. The gynecologist had said several times, Excuse me? Are you all right? Drewe had alarmed the young Asian woman by staggering lightheaded when she slipped down from the examination table in her paper gown, but quickly she'd laughed and assured the doctor that she was fine.

"Just a little surprised. And I guess—scared." But laughing. Wiping at her eyes, and laughing.

The procedure at the Eau Claire clinic was scheduled for 11:30 a.m. Arrival no later than 11 a.m.

It would be a surgical procedure and not a medical procedure, now that the pregnancy was seven weeks. The medical procedure had appealed to Drewe initially, for it involved merely pill-taking, but her gynecologist had dissuaded her. Too much can go wrong. You don't know how long you will be bleeding and where you might be. The more protracted the discharge, the more opportunity for an acute psychological reaction. Drewe had felt sick, a sudden indraft of terror, at these matter-of-fact words.

She was not a minor. She was twenty-six. Except feeling much younger now. Helpless.

Your decision, Conover had said. Of course. No. Not my decision alone. Our decision. It's your body. It's your life. You will decide. Gently, yet with a chilling sort of equanimity, Conover spoke these words. And so she knew: Conover was the one to decide.

So she'd made the arrangements. She'd chosen WomanSpace in Eau Claire out of several possibilities. Driving three-and-a-half hours to the clinic would be a strain on them both, a kind of punishment for Conover as well as her, yet worse would be the strain after the procedure.

She could not imagine. The return home. What intimacy between them, then! It was the terrible intimacy she most craved with the man. Not with any man had she had a true, vital intimacy, that had entered her deeply, into the most profound and secret depths of her soul. In fact she had not known many men in her young life. Conover, who'd impregnated her despite their calculated plans and wishes, would be that man.

And so, it was arranged. They had only to execute their plans. Probable arrival back in Madison in the early evening.

"Stay with me tonight, OK?"

"If you want me."

"Don't be ridiculous! I always want you." She wanted to believe this. She smiled, so badly wanting to believe.

Though the great land-grant university at Madison was very large (45,600 enrolled students, a campus of more than nine hundred acres), the Madison community was somehow small. You saw the same people often. You recognized faces, knew names, even of people you didn't personally know.

Both Conover and Drewe would have been mortified to have been seen together and recognized at the Planned Parenthood clinic in Madison, which was so prominent in the university community.

To the Eau Claire WomanSpace clinic she was bringing a hardcover volume of Milton: *Paradise Lost*. There was desperation in clinging to this hefty volume, which she'd first read as an undergraduate of nineteen. She'd been ravished by the austere, sublime poetry of Milton, a reprimand to the doggerel of her demon-self.

Of man's first disobedience, and the fruit
Of that forbidden tree, whose mortal taste
Brought death into the world, and all our woe . . .

Conover asked what the book was?—and Drewe told him.

Conover said he'd read only just a little of Milton, as an undergraduate. "Read me something now, darling. Convince me that poetry matters."

Drewe thumbed through the familiar, much-annotated pages. In her most level voice she read to Conover the passage in which Lucifer, the fallen archangel, says, *Better to reign in hell than serve in heaven*. To which Conover grunted in approval. She read the longer, surpassingly beautiful passage in which Eve sees her own reflection for the first time in a pond, in Eden:

I thither went
With unexperienced thought, and laid me down
On the green bank, to look into the clear

Smooth lake, that to me seemed another sky.
As I bent down to look, just opposite
A shape within the watery gleam appeared
Bending to look on me: I started back,
It started back, but pleased I soon returned,
Pleased it returned as soon with answering looks
Of sympathy and love; there I had fixed
Mine eyes till now, and pined with vain desire.

When she'd finished, Conover remained silent for a while, then said, as if there might be an answer to his question, "This myth of 'paradise'—it's always lost. Ever wonder why?" They were approaching Eau Claire: thirty-six miles to go.

But it was 10:20 a.m., they would not be late.

"Oh, God. Look."

As they approached the WomanSpace Clinic on Hector Street they saw them: the demonstrators.

Pro-life picketers. Milling together on the sidewalk in front of the clinic and in the street. Some were carrying signs. Drewe's contact at the clinic had cautioned her, There might be demonstrators. Try to ignore them. Walk quickly. Don't engage them. They are forbidden by law to touch or impede you in any way.

Stunned and dismayed, Drewe stepped out of the car. Quickly Conover came around to her as the demonstrators sighted her.

Like piranha, they seemed to Drewe. Horrible, in their rush at her.

There might have been thirty of them, there might have been more. Drewe had a confused impression of surprisingly young faces, young men as well as women, even teenagers. At once she felt sick with guilt.

Unlike her friends and acquaintances in Madison, these strangers in Eau Claire knew her secret.

Immediately they knew, and they did not sympathize. They would not forgive.

"Goddamn! This is unfortunate." Conover took hold of Drewe's arm, urging her forward.

The pro-life demonstrators' voices lifted, pleading. Yet sharp. Excited, aroused. They were happy to see her. And they were of all ages—young, middle-aged, elderly. Though she'd been instructed not to look at them, Drewe could not stop herself; she could not stop from making eye contact with some; they were on all sides, blocking her way as they'd been forbidden to do, forcing Conover to shove against them, cursing them; there came a Catholic priest of about Conover's age, with something of Conover's furrowed forehead and earnest genial manner, dressed in black, with a tight white collar; like a raven, the man seemed to Drewe, a predatory pecking bird intent upon her.

Hello! God loves you!

Listen to us! Give us five minutes of your time—before it's too late!

Your baby wants to live—like you.

Your baby prays to you—LET ME LIVE! You have that choice.

There came a WomanSpace escort, a lanky young man in a dark lavender sweatshirt and jeans, to take hold of Drewe's other arm. Just come with me please, just come forward, don't hang back, you will be fine. Just to the front door, they can't follow us inside.

Yet the demonstrators clustered about them, defiant, terrifying in their fanatical certainty.

Look here, girl! You had better know, it's murder you will be committing.

And God knows, God will punish. You'd better believe.

The woman blocking Drewe's way was in her forties perhaps, bulgy-eyed, with a strong-boned fattish face, shiny synthetic russet-red hair that must have been a wig. There was something gleeful and demented about her. She was holding a rosary aloft, practically in Drewe's face, praying loudly, Hail Mary Mother of God pray for us sinners now and at the hour of our death Amen. In her other hand the woman held a picket sign—a ghastly magnified photograph of what appeared to be a mangled baby, or embryo, lying amid trash. Drewe had been warned not to look at these photographs—(digitally modified, not "real")—yet this ghastly photograph she saw clearly.

You could see that the woman was thrilled to be in combat, she'd been awaiting this moment to spring at Drewe. She was jeering, disgusted, but thrilled, fixing Drewe with a look of derisive intimacy.

She knows me. She knows my heart.

They were almost at the front door of the clinic, which was being held open by another WomanSpace assistant. Yet the woman followed beside Drewe, taunting her. Drewe wrenched her arm out of Conover's grip to push at the woman—"Leave me alone! You have no right! You're sick."

The woman, surprised at Drewe's reaction, took a moment to recover—then shoved Drewe back. She was strong, a small dense mountain of a woman, with a flushed and triumphant face.

Murderer! Baby murderer! Strike the sinner down dead!

Oh!—the woman had hurt her. A shut fist, against Drewe's upper chest.

Conover and the lanky escort hurried Drewe away, up the steps and into the clinic, where the demonstrators could not follow. With what relief, Drewe saw that the door was shut against them.

She wasn't crying. She would not give the woman that satisfaction, to know that she'd hurt her.

Not crying but tears trickled down her hot cheeks.

Not crying but she could not stop trembling. Pro-life. Their certitude terrified her.

The surgical abortions were running late.

There'd been complications that morning at WomanSpace. Many more demonstrators than usual, a busload of particularly combative League of Life Catholics from Milwaukee. The Eau Claire PD had been called earlier that morning, a summons had been issued.

Conover complained to the staff: why wasn't there another way into the clinic?

He was told that no matter what entrance was used the demonstrators would flock around it. Other strategies had been tried and had not worked out satisfactorily.

"The civil rights of your clients are being violated. That's an aggressive mob out there, and could be dangerous."

It was not a secret: abortion providers were at risk for their lives. Abortion doctors had been killed by snipers, Planned Parenthood offices had been firebombed.

Incensed, Conover sat beside Drewe, in a vinyl chair nearly too small for him. By degrees, he quieted. He'd brought work with him for the long wait and would take solace in that.

Drewe sat in a haze of such startled thought, she could not coherently assess what had happened.

A woman, a stranger, had assaulted her? Yet more astonishing—Drewe has assaulted the woman?

And all this had happened so swiftly. A terrible intimacy, in such close quarters.

"They seemed to know me. They recognized me."

"Don't be ridiculous. They don't know you."

"They know why I am here."

"I should hope so. They aren't total idiots."

They aren't idiots at all. They are true believers.

Drewe had to fill out more forms though her gynecologist had faxed a half dozen documents to the clinic. The receptionist, a harried-looking woman with a strained smile, took her name, checked her ID, asked her another time about allergies, asthma, any recent surgery, silicon implants—next of kin.

Next of kin: what were they expecting?

Conover said she could leave it blank probably.

In a hurt voice she said, Shouldn't she give them his name?

"Sure. I'll be right here, in any case."

It didn't seem like a convincing answer. Yet Drewe could not put down her mother's name, her father's name . . . No one in her family must know.

Not that Drewe was ashamed—though, in fact, yes Drewe was ashamed—but rather, Drewe resented others knowing about her most personal, private life.

Even knowledge of Conover, who wasn't divorced quite yet, had to be kept from Drewe's family, who would have judged her harshly, and pityingly.

A married man. Of course he says he's "separated."

Too smart for her own good. Headstrong, never listened to anyone else. Pride goeth before a fall.

She returned to her chair to sit and wait. She wanted to ask Conover, Had she really hit that awful woman, when she'd thrust that rosary in her face?

Drewe was a natural storyteller. But to whom could she tell this story?

The waiting room was ordinary, nondescript as a dentist's waiting room, except for the pamphlets, brochures, and magazines on display, all on feminist themes, abortion procedures, federal and state laws; yet, perversely, for WomanSpace was a Planned Parenthood clinic as well as an abortion provider, there was a wall rack entirely filled with pregnancy/birth/infant information. Drewe wondered at the incongruity and the irony.

Slatted blinds had been pulled shut over the windows at the front of the waiting room. Yet outside you could hear raised voices that seemed never to subside.

Drewe could have wept with vexation: She'd left *Paradise Lost* in Conover's car, after all. And there was no way to retrieve it.

Drewe then told Conover, in a discreetly lowered voice, for she did not want to annoy or distract or further upset others in the room, who were very likely waiting for consultations or procedures like her own, of how, when she'd first been taken to a dentist, by her mother, at the age of four, she'd become panicked in the waiting room, and in the dentist's chair she'd become hysterical. Her mother and the dentist had tried to calm her with NO^2—"laughing gas"—but this, too, had frightened her. In disgust the dentist had told Drewe's mother, Don't tell a child "this won't hurt" when it will hurt.

She was speaking in her quick bright nervous way.

"Not now, honey," Conover said, touching Drewe's arm. "Just be calm now. Maybe later." Had she been talking too excitedly? At first she had no idea what Conover meant: Later? Of course she knew:

later, after. It was not really surgery, only just a procedure. Vacuum suction through an instrument called a cannula, and she would be sedated; though conscious, thus not running the risk of an anesthetic.

She'd read all about it of course. It was her way to know as much as she could of whatever subject might be approached intellectually, coolly. She'd memorized much of what she'd read.

And now, as if in one of the pamphlets she'd read, came the vision of that heavyset woman—the jeering face, accusing eyes.

Baby murderer. You.

Drewe glanced about the waiting room. Was she being watched?—was she somehow special, singled-out, more guilty than the others?

In the waiting room there were two or three women of Drewe's approximate age. But she seemed to know, they were not university students. And a girl of perhaps seventeen, soft-bodied, in a paralysis of fear; her mother close beside her, gripping her limp hand. The scoldings, disgust, had ended. Now there was only a mother's sympathy and anxiety.

Drewe would not have told her mother about this surgical procedure. Not ever. She would not tell her mother about becoming, by accident, pregnant.

When they'd entered the waiting room, there had been no men. Conover had been the sole man. Since then, another had entered, with a thin, ashen-faced, heavily made-up woman; both of them grim, not speaking to the other.

Drewe wondered if men, in such situations, glanced at one another, to establish some sort of—bond? Or whether, and this was more likely, they assiduously avoided eye contact.

Conover appeared oblivious to the other male in the waiting room. Yet, Drewe guessed, Conover was well aware of his presence.

Drewe guessed too that Conover had been disconcerted by the pro-life demonstrators. Conover was accustomed to demonstrating, not being demonstrated against. He had been involved in the Occupy Wall Street events in Madison. He'd organized a teach-in at the university. His politics were "leftist"—"activist"; he had a history of participating in marches and protests, particularly when he'd been younger. (On a protest march on State Street, on the eve of the American invasion of Iraq in 2002, Conover had been injured by a riot policeman's club, dislocating his right knee. Since then, he walked with a perceptible limp and sometimes winced with pain when he believed no one was watching.) His father had been a high-profile labor attorney arguing federal cases.

It was against Conover's political principles to "cross" any picket line—but this was a different situation, surely.

Conover was a distinguished man in those circles—an academic, an intellectual. Outside those circles, few would have known his name. He was an historian whose books on pre-Civil War America, particularly on Abolitionism, had won him tenure, visiting professorships, prizes. Yet he was also a man whom confinement made restless, anxious. He sweated easily. In the waiting room he crossed his legs, uncrossed his legs. He shifted in the vinyl chair that was almost too small for him. In bed, his legs frequently cramped: with a little cry of annoyed pain he scrambled from bed to stand on the afflicted leg, to ease the muscle. Sometimes his toes cramped too, like claws.

Don't be scared, he'd said several times. I will be with you.

He was reading an article on his Kindle—a piece submitted to a historical journal for which he was an advisory editor. Drewe, who had no reading material of her own, tried reading with him, but could not concentrate.

At last the receptionist called Drewe's name—but it was not her name, as Conover told her, startled; he tugged at her wrist, pulling her back. Still, Drewe rose from the vinyl chair, seeming to think that her name had been called. "Drewe, that isn't your name," Conover said again, and Drewe stammered, "Oh, but I thought—maybe—there had been a misunderstanding." She had no idea what she was trying to say.

Another woman will murder her baby, then. It's a strange dream, but it isn't my dream.

Was it true, the baby wanted to live?

But she wasn't carrying a baby. Only a cluster of congealed cells.

She might explain to Conover. Try to explain.

And calmly he would say, You've changed your mind, then. This is for the good, I think.

Is it? For the good? Oh—I love you. She was saying Yes!—I mean no . . . I don't know.

Conover hadn't heard. He continued reading, taking notes as he squinted at the shining screen.

Another woman had come forward to be escorted into the rear of the clinic. Someone in the waiting room was crying softly. Drewe did not want to glance around for fear that in this bizarre waking dream she would discover that the afflicted person was herself.

In fact, it was the young girl with her mother. Very young, pale, wan, and scared. Probably not seventeen, nor even sixteen. It was difficult to imagine such a child having sex—having sex inflicted upon her was more likely.

Maybe she'd been raped. That was an ugly possibility.

With a pang of envy Drewe saw how the mother continued to hold her daughter's hand. The two whispered and wept together. And how, when the daughter's name was called, both the daughter and the mother rose to their feet.

Drewe's eyes locked with the daughter's: warm-brown, liquidy, terrified. She looked quickly away.

"Drewe?"

Conover was watching her. His face was strained, the tiny shaving nick on the underside of his jaw was bleeding again, thinly.

"You're sure, are you? About this?"

He is trying to be generous, Drewe thought. It was an effort in him, he was trying very hard. Like a man who has coins in his closed fist he wants to offer—to fling onto a table—to demonstrate his generosity, even the flamboyance of his generosity, which will be to his disadvantage; but his hand is shaky, the coins fall to the floor.

She reassured him, her lover. The woman was the one to reassure the man, he had made a proper decision.

She heard herself say, another time: "Yes."

*

Strike the sinner down dead.

Baby wants to live. Baby prays—LET ME LIVE!

By the time her name was called, sometime after 12:30 p.m., Drewe was exhausted. She had not slept more than two or three hours the previous night and her head felt now as if she'd been awake for a day and a night in succession.

Something was happening in front of the clinic: some sort of disturbance. The demonstrators had interfered with one of the clinic's patients, there'd been a scuffle with one of the WomanSpace escorts, the Eau Claire police had been called another time.

There were shouts, a siren. Drewe was trembling with indignation. The fanatics had no right.

She'd used the women's lavatory at least three times. And each time she'd scarcely been able to urinate, a tiny slow hot trickle into the toilet bowl, she'd been desperate to check: was it blood?

It was not blood. It was hardly urine.

The abortion-clock was ticking now, defiantly in her face. She saw how all of her life had been leading to this time.

The lifetime of the cell-cluster inside her would be no more than seven weeks, three days. Conception, suction, death. From the perspective of millennia, there was virtually no difference between her own (brief) life of twenty-six years and the (briefer) life of the baby-to-be.

Sick. You are sick. You!

But her name had been called, at last. Numbly she had no choice but to rise to her feet and be led by a nurse into the interior of WomanSpace.

Conover leaned over to squeeze her hand, a final time. Drewe's fingers were limp, unresponsive.

The woman was speaking to her. Explaining to her. Calling her "Drewe"—a familiarity that made her uncomfortable. Conover had been left behind—that was a relief.

A man might participate in his lover's natural-childbirth delivery, but a man would not participate in any woman's surgical abortion.

He would not be a witness! He would never know.

Drewe was naked and shivering inside the flimsy paper gown. Her lips were icy-cold. Her skin felt chafed as if she'd been rubbing it with sandpaper.

She'd been allowed to keep on her sandals. A middle-aged woman doctor with pulled-back hair and a hard-chiseled face had entered the room. Her manner was forthright, with an air of forced and just slightly overbearing calm. She spoke in a voice too loud for the room as if there was some doubt that the trembling patient would hear and comprehend what she was saying.

Dr. _____—Drewe heard the name clearly, yet forgot it in the next instant.

Dr. _____ was asking how she felt? How do you think I feel?

Mutely and meekly Drewe nodded. As one deprived of language, making a feeble gesture to suggest, Good! Really good.

Dr. _____ was telling her it was required by law that she have a sonogram before the procedure.

A new law, recently passed by the Wisconsin state legislature.

A sonogram, so that Drewe could look at the cluster of cells— the "fetus" in her womb, at seven weeks. And she must answer a fixed sequence of questions.

Do you understand. Are you fully cognizant of. Have you been coerced in any way.

You are certain, you have not been coerced? Drewe was astonished. She'd been through all this—these questions—not a sonogram: she had not had a sonogram—but all this talk. She wanted to press her hands to her ears and run out of the room.

Dr. _____ was explaining that there are different sorts of coercion. Drewe would have to declare whether anyone had exerted pressure on her in any way, contrary to her own and best interests.

Drewe stammered—she'd already answered these many times.

Yes. But this was a new law. They were required to ask more than once.

She shut her eyes. No no no no no. No one had coerced her.

"Are you feeling all right, Drewe? Did you have anything to eat this morning?"

Eat! She'd forgotten entirely about eating. She could not imagine ever eating again.

"Let us know if you feel nauseated. Immediately, let us know."

The nurse was administering a sonogram. Drewe lay on her side on the examination table, staring at an illuminated dark screen, an X-ray showing a tiny ectoplasmic shape, ever shifting, fading. She recalled fraudulent photographs of spirits, ghosts, "ectoplasms," at the turn of the previous century. But this wasn't fraudulent. She could see her own pulse, the fierce beat of her blood.

Baby wants to live. Just like you.

The baby's father did not want the baby. He had not said so, but she knew. Of course, she knew.

Conover loved her—but did not love her enough.

He had his own children, of course. His children who were already born. Grown to adulthood, or nearly. They were safely in the world, their very existence no longer precarious and dependent upon anybody's whim. A daughter, a son, seemingly on cordial, but not intimate terms with Conover.

The separated wife had been deeply wounded. The divorce, if there was a divorce, would be bitter and debilitating. Drewe had come belatedly to Conover's life.

The doctor with the pulled-back hair was regarding Drewe with surprise. Were Drewe's eyes welling with tears? Where was Drewe's old resolve, the one that had caused her family to say, It's like she isn't even one of us, sometimes. Like she doesn't even know us.

The doctor was asking Drewe if she was having second thoughts? She didn't need to make a final decision of such importance today.

Yes. She was saying, insisting.

Yes. That was why she'd come—wasn't it? She was not going to go away without . . .

Her voice trailed off, uncertainly.

The patient was given sedatives. Some time was required before the sedatives began to take effect. She saw a tiny pinprick of light, the baby-to-be, fading, about to be extinguished.

They helped her lie on her back, on the table. Her feet in the stirrups.

So open, exposed! The most secret part of her, opened to the chilly air.

She was feeling panic in spite of the pills. But much of this she would forget, afterward. As her uterus was sucked empty, so her brain would be emptied of memory. A machine thrummed close by, loudly.

She saw now the sequence of actions that had begun in early morning and was now irreversible: running from her residence hall to the curb, to climb into the steel-colored Toyota beside her lover; kissing him on the lips as an act of subtle aggression and buckling herself in the seatbelt, her hard, curved little belly that had not yet begun to show, as her small hard breasts had not yet begun to alter, or not much. Almost gaily—brazenly—she'd begun that sequence of actions, that had led to this: naked, on her back, knees spread. And the tiny pin-prick of light all but extinguished.

She would be awake through the entire procedure, it was explained to her. Not fully awake, but in the way of someone seeing a movie without sound, at a little distance.

When the mask was fitted to her lower face she felt an impulse to push it away, panicked. She'd forgotten the mask's purpose—the laughing gas to control the pain.

There was a natural lock on the mechanism, Drewe was told. So that she could not inhale too much at one time. So that she wouldn't lose consciousness.

The procedure would take no more than minutes.

So fast! Yet so very slowly Drewe felt herself drifting off to sea, her eyes heavy-lidded, the sickly-smell in her nostrils and mouth so strong that, as she breathed, she felt an instinct to gag.

The cervix was being dilated. She did not think, My cervix!

A straw-like instrument was being inserted into her body. Up tight between her thighs. The machine began to hum, louder. A sucking noise, and a sucking sensation. Quick-darting cramps wracked her lower abdomen. These were claws like the claws of sea-creatures, digging into her. She began to count, One two three four ... but lost her concentration, for the suction-noise was so loud, close beside her head, and the cramps so quick, biting and sharp, and the laughing gas was filling her brain like helium into a balloon; she was in danger of floating above the table to which (she realized now) she was strapped, as her knees were strapped and splayed.

The cramping came now in long, almost languorous ripples. A kind of sensuous cruelty, as if a lover were hurting her, with crude fingers, fingernails, deep inside her body.

She'd begun to cry. Or was she laughing.

Please no. I don't want this. It was a mistake. Let me up, this was a mistake.

God help me ...

She fumbled with the paper that clung to her sweaty thighs. Into a waste basket it went, crumpled. Then, her clothes—into which she bound herself with badly shaking fingers. She was herself again. Only herself.

Though the cramping continued. And she was bleeding, into a sparkling-white cotton-gauze sanitary napkin.

For a while she lay dazed, comatose. She had no idea how much time had passed. The procedure itself had been less than eight minutes, she'd been told. On her left wrist was a watch, but it was too much effort for her to look at it.

The silver-star ring on her left hand felt loose. Or her fingers were sweaty. There was the danger that it would slip off.

Then, she was being rudely awakened. She was being led out of the recovery room. She was leaning on the nurse's arm. Sweat oozed in tiny beads at her hairline. She was being told she should make an appointment to see her gynecologist in Madison in two weeks. And she was not to "resume relations" for at least two weeks. Did she need contraception?

She laughed. Contraception!

She'd always used contraception. She'd been terrified of any intimate encounter that was not contraconception. Yet, the contraception she and Conover had been using had failed.

Conover was waiting for her. Conover looking tired, and the lines in his face deeper.

Conover took her hand. Conover stooped to kiss her sweaty forehead. Conover said in a lowered voice in her ear what sounded like, My good girl! I love you.

This was so un-Conover. Drewe pushed a little away from him, laughing.

"'Good girl.' Sounds like a dog."

There was a commotion in front of the clinic as another woman tried to enter, forced to run the gauntlet. But as the two of them hurried to Conover's car, the demonstrators paid little heed to them—they focused instead upon the frightened-looking new arrival, a dark-skinned woman in her mid-thirties, in the company of an older woman. The lanky-limbed escort had come to the assistance of the woman, aggressively.

Drewe looked for the woman who'd dared to strike Drewe with her fist—but she couldn't see her.

Look straight ahead, Conover was saying. We're almost there.

His arm around her waist. She was stumbling, feeling weak and lightheaded—the cramping in her belly was like quick-darting electric currents. She'd understood that Conover had been shocked to see her, when she'd reappeared in the doorway of the waiting room, hanging onto the nurse's arm, not seeming to see him in front of her. She'd been smiling and blinking in the dazed way of one who has been traumatized without knowing it.

Get in! Take care . . .

Conover helped her into the passenger's seat. Behind them, swarming after the new arrival, the demonstrators were loud, excited. Conover had locked Drewe's door for her. She was staring out the window—looking for someone—she wasn't sure who . . .

Conover was shaken, but quickly recovered. Near the entrance to I-94 South, he stopped at a deli where he bought sandwiches and bottled water for Drewe and for himself, and a six-pack of cold beer for the long drive home.

Try to eat, he told her. Then maybe try to sleep.

Drewe couldn't eat much of her sandwich. Conover ate his and the remainder of hers. He drank most of the Evian water, thirstily. And, in furtive illegal swallows, at least two of the beers.

Though he'd urged her to sleep, Conover couldn't resist talking as he drove. He was too edgy to drive in silence, or even to listen to a CD. He laughed, talked, told stories he'd told her already, but not at such length and with such detail.

These were stories from history, not personal stories. Judging by the way in which he told them, he'd told them before, to other audiences. Abraham Lincoln caricatured in pro-Confederacy newspapers as a Negro, or a black ape—"The hatred of Obama is nothing new in US politics." Draft Riots in New York City—notable Wall Street "Panics"—the defeat of the Bank of the United States by wily "Old Hickory"—Andrew Jackson. Conover did not specialize in personal stories.

Drewe realized that she didn't know her lover's children's names. Possibly he'd mentioned them, but not frequently. Drewe knew the former wife's name but little of the woman. She had not asked, out of tact as well as shyness. Or maybe it had been disdain, for a family she had hoped to supplant.

They arrived back in Madison by nighttime. Drewe said, I think I want to be alone. Just drop me off, thank you.

Her lips were parched. Her eyes ached as if she'd been staring into a hot sun.

Conover said, "Don't be ridiculous! You're staying with me."

"I don't think so. I think I'd better be alone."

"I thought we'd planned this. Tonight."

"I don't think so."

"Drewe, look—I'm here."

He took her hand. Both hands. She was feeling very weak, there was little strength in her hands. She had leaked away, like liquid down a drain.

She did not say, You are here, but not-here. Better that you are not-here in a way that I can see.

He relented and drove her home. Seeing that she was adamant, and just very possibly on the brink of hysteria.

Parked at the curb in front of her residence hall, Conover talked to her earnestly. Lights on all six floors of the building were on. It was an aged stone building of some distinction. A women's graduate residence in which Drewe had lived, in a single room sparse as a nun's cell, for two-and-a-half years.

Conover lived in a large but somewhat shabby Victorian house, a mile away in a neighborhood called Faculty Heights. Drewe had visited this house, and often stayed overnight, but had never lived there, and understood now that she never would.

The relief in his face! She'd seen.

The dread in his face. That she would weaken, that she would plead with him to love her as she loved him.

Or worse yet, as women do, plead with him that she could love enough for two.

She was bleeding into the sanitary napkin. He said, "I'm not going to leave you. Come on."

She said, "No. Thank you."

She said, "I need to be alone. For now." She opened the car door. She saw her hand on the door, and the door opening, and she saw herself leaving the steel-colored Toyota and walking away. It was the edge of a precipice: the fall was steep and might be fatal. Yet she saw herself walking away.

Conover hurried after her, to the door of the residence hall. Drewe said, sharply, "It's all right. Please—I need to be alone."

"You don't need to be alone, that's—that isn't true. I'm not going to leave you alone."

She turned away. She left him. In secret bleeding into the already-soaked napkin, she walked away, not to the stairs but to the elevator for she was too weak and too demoralized for the stairs and would wait for the sluggishly moving elevator instead. At the opened door—through which several young women passed, into the foyer, glancing curiously at Drewe and at Conover—he called after her, he would not be leaving but waiting for her in his car.

From her room on the fourth floor, she saw his car at the curb, and his figure inside, dimly. When vehicles passed in the street their headlights lit upon him, a stoic and stubborn figure in the parked vehicle. He'd turned on the ignition to listen to the radio, probably. He would finish the six-pack of beer.

Cautiously like one composed of a brittle breakable substance—very thin glass, or plastic—she lay down on her bed. Her skin was burning, she was very tired. The cramping was not so bad, dulled now by Vicodin. Her life would be a painkiller life: she would be aware of pain but would not feel it, exactly, as her own.

She was bleeding, thinly now. She'd changed the sanitary napkin and replaced it with a fresh sparkling-white one, for the WomanSpace nurse had thoughtfully provided her with half a dozen in a plastic bag.

There was no serious danger of bleeding to death, yet the word *exsanguination* sounded in her head like a struck gong.

Forty minutes later, when she struggled to her feet, the Toyota was still at the curb.

He'd been trying to call her on her cell phone, she discovered. She'd turned the phone off at Eau Claire and had not turned it on again.

She slept again, fitfully. Sometime after midnight, parched-mouthed and eyes aching, as if she had not slept at all, she staggered to her feet and to the window. And the car was gone.

THE GAP YEAR

Lori Ostlund

1.

IT WAS LATE, WELL AFTER MIDNIGHT Beth supposed, and she was trying to sleep but Matthew was in the kitchen folding origami, the steady whisper of the paper giving itself over to form all she could think about as she lay there in the middle of the night in their empty house—in the middle of their half-over and suddenly empty lives. It was how Beth thought of their lives now, now that Darrin was gone and she could no longer say whether *half over* was such a bad thing. When Darrin was young, Matthew had also stayed up late making origami, flitting from shape to shape, a turtle followed by a crocodile, a cat, a fish. These he hid inside their son's favorite cereal and in the meat drawer of the refrigerator because Darrin had a soft spot for cold cuts, both he and Beth enjoying the pleasure of watching Darrin discover a swan snuggled with an elephant, there atop his bologna.

Matthew did not mix animals, not anymore, for the whole point was to give himself, his hands, over to repetition. These creatures were not made in anticipation of a son's delight; they had no purpose, no future either. For even as Matthew created them, his hands were already anticipating their destruction, finishing the final fold, then delivering them onto the pile that would become their funeral pyre. This was their morning routine now (and hadn't Beth always liked routine?): Matthew sweeping the pile into a paper bag, taking it to the back patio to be burned, lighting it. He left the sliding door open, and the smell of burning paper wafted in, becoming their new morning smell, the smell (like coffee or bacon) that told Beth to face the day.

2.

They met at a gay bar on the west side of Albuquerque, both of them straight, and later Beth wondered whether Matthew came up to her that night simply because in a gay bar, straight people could pick each other out the way that gay people were said to be able to find one another in every other crowd. In fact, she had never asked him why he approached her that night, perhaps because she never quite got over needing to believe that he saw her there with her friends—the Sapphists, he later called them—and thought, *Now that looks like an interesting person.*

She was wearing glasses with owlish frames that did not flatter her face, for that was her goal back then—to be seen as the sort of woman who conspired against her own beauty. Matthew approached her as she stood at the bar trying to get the bartender's attention. "Excuse me," he said. "Are you near or far?"

He'd meant her eyesight, but she just stared at him, wondering about his scar, a simple white line that emerged from his left eyebrow and continued upward.

"To what? From what?" she said at last, and he pointed at her glasses and said, "Your vision, Four Eyes," in a teasing, playground voice. "Are you near- or far*sighted*? I'm twenty-twenty, but that too can be a burden." He sighed, as though struck by the ways that his life had been made more difficult by perfect vision. She was just starting graduate school in linguistics, and she thought about how the Japanese and Chinese looked at a character and arrived at the same meaning yet articulated it with completely different sounds. She recognized all of the sounds this man was making yet had no idea what he was trying to tell her.

"May I buy you a drink?" he asked, and he ordered her some sweet, green concoction involving Midori and pineapple juice. "It's awful, isn't it?" he said gleefully after she'd taken a sip. She nodded because it was. "But very tropical, don't you think?" She nodded again. "When I graduate next year I plan to travel to lots of tropical places, so I'm getting myself in the mood." He paused. "Maybe we'll go together," he said. The pause was what kept her from walking away right then, what assured her that he was not just some smooth talker who went around making preposterous suggestions to straight women in gay bars.

They stood in a corner away from the dance floor and talked. They were the same age, twenty-three, though she was starting a doctoral program while he was still struggling to finish his undergraduate degree in English, struggling because he was tired of having his reading dictated to him by a syllabus. "I'm tone-deaf," he announced then, as though listing reasons that she should consider getting to know him. "And I was portly as a child."

She asked about his scar. He reached up and stroked it with his finger, and she noticed his hands. She had not known that one could find hands attractive. "It's a rather boring tale," he said, though over time she learned that this was how he prefaced all of his favorite stories about himself. He went on to describe a pair of glasses that he had invented as a child—two plastic magnifying lenses held together with pipe cleaners and tape—which he'd worn while riding his bicycle one afternoon: down a hill and straight into a tree. But right up until the crash, it was a glorious feeling, everything rushing toward him, so close he should be able to touch it though he knew better. He understood how magnifying glasses worked.

"Then how did you hit the tree?" she asked.

"Well," he said. "I suppose that even our intellect fails us sometimes."

Around midnight, Lance, Matthew's best friend, approached them, dripping sweat from the dance floor. "This is Lance," Matthew said. "He's a rice queen."

"What's a rice queen?" she asked.

"It means he likes Asian guys," Matthew said. "It's a bit of a problem here in New Mexico."

He and Lance laughed, the two of them collapsing with their

arms around each other. Beth did not believe love happened in a flash, love at first sight and all that. Rather, she imagined it working something like a frequent-buyer card, ten punches and you were in love, and as she watched the two of them cackling like a pair of spinster sisters, she looked at Matthew and thought, This is the first punch.

3.

Matthew had grown up in Los Alamos, New Mexico. When he mentioned this to strangers, they assumed that his father had worked for the national labs. His father had been a mailman. "Really?" these strangers always said, as though they could not imagine anything as unlikely as scientists receiving mail. Once, halfway through a shift, his father went to the post office to drop off several bags of mail and found the entire place shut down, men in white hazmat uniforms combing through the sorting area. "They told him to take the rest of the day off—no explanation—and I told him he should not go back to work until there was an explanation. I was twelve at the time, and he chuckled and said that the mail needs to go out, that when I was older I would understand about such things."

Matthew told Beth this story to sum up the sort of man that his father was. It was early in their relationship, and she noted how he sounded—at once proud and exasperated—which told her something about the sort of man that Matthew was. In the picture he showed her, his parents looked more like grandparents; it was his high school graduation and they stood flanking him, looking proud but slightly baffled by the occasion. His mother was sixty-two in the photo, his father sixty-eight. They had come to parenthood late.

A few weeks into his first semester of college, his parents' neighbor phoned to tell him that his parents had driven the wrong way down the exit ramp of the interstate and into oncoming traffic. They were both dead. His father took that ramp every day for thirty-six years, so the mistake made no sense, but the doctor said—dismissively, Matthew felt—that these things happened when one got old. People became disoriented. Perhaps his father had had a stroke.

Matthew dropped out of college for the semester and took a job counting inventory. This was how he met Lance. They both lived downtown and began driving to work together in the wee hours, which was when inventory was generally counted. Early on, they were sent to Victoria's Secret, where the two of them counted every bit of lingerie in the store. Afterward they went to Milton's Diner for breakfast, and Lance looked down at his breakfast burrito and said that he was tired and bored after a night of counting women's underwear. This was his way of revealing that he was gay. They each ordered a second burrito, and Matthew told Lance about his parents. It had been two months since the accident, but Lance was the first person to whom he had spoken of it. Lance had saved him in those first months after his parents died, Matthew told Beth. They were like brothers.

4.

Matthew had learned to fold origami in preparation for their first trip abroad, their first trip together. Traveling would involve lots of waiting, he said, and it was always good to have some trick up your sleeve. He packed stacks of folding paper, from which he produced an endless menagerie, each cat and rooster snatched up by one of the children who pressed in shyly against them to watch him fold.

Once, on a bus in Guatemala, when he had no paper, he took a dollar bill from his wallet and transformed it into a fish while the little girl across the aisle looked on. He pretended not to notice her interest, but when he was finished he swam the fish across the aisle and dropped it into her hands. Above them on the roof rode two boys no older than twelve, makeshift soldiers with rifles taller than they were. Beth had watched them climb on. They were all she could think about. She was twenty-four, not yet a mother, so she imagined only fleetingly the sorrow that the boys' mothers must feel at seeing their sons already schooled in death. Mainly she considered them from her own perspective, the fear that she felt in this foreign land, knowing that right above her were two guns, their triggers guarded by fingers not yet skilled at shaving. As she watched Matthew fold, she wondered whether he did so to distract himself from the boys and their guns or whether he was like the girl, focused solely on the beauty of the fish taking shape before them.

5.

It was a Saturday afternoon, Darrin's junior year, and they were pestering him about taking the SAT. Finally he came out with it. "I want to travel," he said. "I want to do a gap year." He showed them the website for the program he had in mind: a ten-month trip around the world, working in the rain forest in one country, teaching English in another—while they stayed behind, paying a hefty sum for him to do so, to fly around the world dabbling in local economies. There would be adults, three teachers who would lead seminars, arrange details, and make themselves available by e-mail to anxious parents.

Beth had never even heard of a gap year, but she didn't like the sound of it, the way that it made Darrin's future seem removed from them, made Darrin seem that way also. "I just need a year away from school, a year that doesn't matter so much," he said, and they kept quiet. But later, as she and Matthew lay in bed together, she said, "'A year that doesn't matter.' How is that even possible?" Matthew laughed gently because he understood that she was afraid.

6.

They—not Lance—were the ones who ended up in Asia, the last leg of a one-year trip through a host of hot countries. Matthew had graduated, finally, but Beth quit her program halfway through. Actually, she took a year off, but when she got out in the world and saw what was there, she could not go back. She had grown up in a small town in Wisconsin, and she understood only then that she had been about to exchange one small town for another, academia.

They had been together a year when they started their trip, but their relationship had never really entered the public realm, the realm of parties and shared errand-running, so Beth did not truly know who Matthew was out in the world. She learned on that trip that he talked to everyone. Using Thai or Spanish gleaned from guidebooks and taxi drivers, he conversed tirelessly about the weather and food, about where they were going and where they were from and whether they had children. Beth considered these questions either tedious or nobody's business, often both, but Matthew did not see it that way. He was happy to tell people how much he loved rice, to say, over and over, that they were from New Mexico—"*New* Mexico. It's in the United States"—to explain that they had no children, *yet*. Matthew was at ease, in his body and in the world. Beth was not, but on the trip she learned to mime and gesture and even laugh at herself a bit.

One afternoon in Belize, four elderly Garifuna women lounging on a porch called to them as they passed in the street. Three of the women were large, but the fourth was as thin as a broom handle, and she sat slightly apart from the others, as though her thinness were something that they did not want to catch. The women were eating homemade fruit popsicles, and Matthew immediately began flirting with the women, asking which of them might offer him a lick. He pounded his chest, and the women laughed and told Beth that she had a handsome devil on her hands, waggling their fingers at her in warning.

"You two better come in and eat something," said one of the fat women, and the four rose like a chorus about to sing.

The women gave them rice and the leg of a stringy hen, with watermelon popsicles for dessert. Later, they asked Beth and Matthew how young people danced these days up in their country, and Matthew pulled Beth up to demonstrate. The women clapped and sang, creating a rhythm that Beth willed her body to follow, and for a moment it seemed to, but the rhythm changed suddenly and her body went in the wrong direction. One of the women leaned forward and slapped Beth's buttocks hard, while the others roared with laughter and shook their hands in front of their faces as though they had chili in their eyes. Matthew laughed also, a laugh that said, *Buck up, Four Eyes. This is life. Isn't it great?* It was the laugh of a man who was in love with her, who saw in her stiffness and reticence something exotic.

7.

Mornings had always been their time as a couple, both before Darrin came along and after, for even as a baby, he had had no interest in mornings. Sometimes she and Matthew leg wrestled— she got to use both legs—or Matthew brought her coffee in bed and the two of them sat propped against the pillows, talking quietly, wanting this time together, alone. What they had wanted, that is, was not to wake their son, and she wondered now how they could ever have done such a thing, plotted to have even one precious second less with him. But they had. They had reclined together in this same bed, giggling and covering each other's mouths, saying, "Shhh, you'll wake him."

Other days Matthew woke up feeling loud. "I feel loud today," he would say, loudly of course, and he would stand on the bed and sing one of the Bible camp songs from her childhood—"Shadrach, Meshach, Abednego, lived in Judah a long time ago. They had funny names, and they lived far away"—songs that she had taught him in the early days of their relationship when she was first learning to let go and be silly around another human being. Or he would lie on his back with his arms and legs straight up in the air like a dead cockroach and belt out old Carpenters' tunes. "I'm on the top of the world," he sang as though he really meant it, for that was the thing about Matthew: he was never sheepish about acknowledging his happiness, did not believe that happiness should be discussed only in terms that were ironic or self-deprecating. Eventually Darrin would come running in, begging to be flown around atop Matthew's extended legs while Beth watched and laughed and tried hard not to picture their son slipping from her husband's feet, tumbling through the air, his head crashing against a bedpost.

Now, she and Matthew got out of bed each morning, still exhausted, and said standard morning things—"How'd you sleep?" and nonsense like that. They rose and dressed and went into the dining room, where the night's origami awaited them, sometimes a hundred cranes or giraffes, piled up on the table: a heap of wings, a heap of necks.

8.

The first month, Darrin e-mailed them almost daily, sending pictures of all the things he knew would interest them: his sleeping quarters and meals, his work and the other students, the people and buildings that made up his days. He ended his messages with easy declarations of his love for them because that was the way the world was set up now—easy access to communication, easy declarations of love—and Beth was grateful for both. He rarely wrote more than a few sentences, but she could hear his voice in these quick updates filled with enthusiastic adjectives, for he was like Matthew in this way also, never embarrassed by his ease with superlatives, by the way that he declared her spaghetti *the absolute best* and her *the most wonderful mother in the world* for making it.

At some point—it was the second stop on the itinerary, collecting plants in Belize for medical research—the girl began appearing in his photos. She was plump with wildly curly hair and a careful smile. Because it was his way, Matthew e-mailed Darrin, asking about her, and Darrin wrote back days later, saying only that her name was Peru.

"Peru? Were her parents hippies?" Matthew wrote, and Darrin replied, again after what seemed a deliberate delay, "Missionaries."

This, his one-word response without explication, troubled them. Was she religious, they wondered, and if she was, what did that mean for their son? Would he return speaking a language that they did not understand, his conversation laced with earnest euphemisms like *witness* and *abundance*? After years of worrying— with Beth imagining all the ways that they could lose him and Matthew steadfastly refusing to imagine any—was this what it came down to, that their son could simply grow up to be a man they did not recognize?

"Well, please be sure to have safe sex," Matthew wrote next.

"No need to worry," came back their son's reply, an ambiguous response that they also discussed far into the night: did it mean that he was not having sex, or that he was but the sex was safe? Or was it simply his way of telling them to stop worrying, of declaring his adulthood?

9.

On the plane from Thailand, they each made a list: on the left, cities that seemed appealing, and on the right, cities that did not. They were heading home, but they had not yet determined where home would be. Somewhere over what Beth thought was the Sea of Japan, they decided on Minneapolis. Beth worried that they were making the choice based on the overwhelming memory of heat, a year's worth, but Matthew said so what if they were. Weren't most choices made as reactions to something else? They were in love, but traveling had taught them that they were also well matched: they knew how the other responded to crisis and boredom; they could live together in a very small space yet not grow distant. The trip had left them broke but had also taught them that they did not need much, and so they rented a tiny apartment in Saint Paul, which was cheaper than Minneapolis.

They were in a new city, both of them working at their first real jobs, Matthew as a high school English teacher and Beth as a newspaper caption writer. It was a job that she both liked and did well, for she had the ability to look at a photograph, feel at once the narrative sweep of it, and sum it up in a few precise words. Each night, they lay in bed talking, just as they had through ten-hour bus rides and bouts of stomach ailments. Matthew dissected his day, celebrating his students' successes one minute and then bemoaning their lack of curiosity the next. Mainly Beth listened, preferring to talk about her day when it had gone well, keeping the small frustrations, which were a part of any job, a part of life, to herself. She distrusted how emotions sounded when put into words, the way that words could reduce the experience to something unrecognizable. It was like reading descriptions of wine, she decided, for when she uncorked the bottle and took a sip, she never thought, "Ah, yes, quite right, *nutty* and *corpulent* and *jammy*."

10.

Matthew wanted to meet her family now that they were only three hours away. Beth felt that relationships worked best when families were not involved. Early in their relationship, she had told him the story of her father and his brother, wanting Matthew to know that she trusted him. The story had made him keen to meet her father. He was like many fathers, she said, quiet and largely absent. He worked as an accountant, in an office containing a desk and a coffeepot. What she remembered most from her rare visits to his office were the stacks of cashew canisters along one wall—empties on the left and full on the right, like debit and credit columns—and the way that her father bent over his ledgers, nibbling one nut at a time, brushing salt from a page before turning it.

Each evening he came home at six and the family sat down to dinner, a silent affair because their father wanted them to focus on chewing and swallowing and, especially, on not choking, goals from which talking and frivolity would surely distract. Then he returned to his office, where he stayed until midnight, balancing the books of farmers and beauticians and storekeepers, all of whom trusted her father to keep them safe from financial ruin.

One night when Beth had just turned seventeen, after she had done something stupid and teenager-like—taken the family car out on a muddy road and gotten stuck so that she missed her curfew by four whole hours—her mother came into her room, where Beth was sulking over her father's overreaction, which had involved a six-month grounding. Her mother sat on the edge of the bed and took one of Beth's feet in her hands, holding it awkwardly because they were not a demonstrative family. "Well," said her mother, "it's time you learned about Thomas."

Thomas was her father's younger brother. Until that night, Beth had not even known that her father had a brother. "When your father was a boy, just eight years old," her mother began, "he and Thomas were sent out in the front yard to play one Sunday afternoon. Thomas was four, so it was your father's job to keep him occupied for an hour or two while your grandparents read. At first they made a pile of leaves, planning to jump in it, but it was a windy day and the leaves kept blowing away, so they decided to play hide-and-seek."

Her mother had paused here, but then went on to describe how, as her father crouched behind a shrub, watching Thomas turn in slow circles in the yard as he tried to spy him, a brown car pulled up to the curb and a man got out. "He looked kind," Beth's father later told the police, words that had brought his mother to her knees on their kitchen floor.

The man stood for a moment on the sidewalk on the other side of the low fence that enclosed their yard, Beth's hidden father watching. It was this image—these layers of voyeurism—that haunted Beth: her father looking at the man, who was looking at Thomas, Thomas who was looking for her father. "Say," the man called to Thomas. "Are you the little boy who lives here, the one who likes marshmallows so much?" The man extended his arm and opened his fist: a marshmallow rested in his palm like a tiny pillow.

Thomas turned and stared at the man, then made another half turn, surveying the yard, torn between hide-and-seek and marshmallows. "Yes," he said to the man, and the man opened the front gate, walked in, and picked him up. Beth's father stood up from behind the shrub; the man stared at him for a moment, stared the way a magician might stare at a thing that he had not meant to conjure. Thomas's pant leg was hiked up to his knee, his calf plump and white, the man's hand wrapped around it like that of a butcher assessing a particularly meaty shank. The man smiled as he took his hand briefly from Thomas's calf to wave good-bye to Beth's father.

Beth's father understood that everyone considered him old enough to have been suspicious of the man, so it was not until years later that he confessed to Beth's mother: he stepped forward not to stop the man from taking his brother but to say, "I like marshmallows, too."

Her mother made her promise never to tell anyone about Thomas, especially not her siblings. The only person she had ever told was Matthew. When he finally did meet her parents, her father was just as she had reported, and Matthew was disappointed to find a man whose words and demeanor did not reflect a childhood of unspoken guilt and grief.

Instead, her father engaged Matthew in "men's talk," offering detailed descriptions of the way that mechanisms worked, which was precisely the sort of thing Matthew hated. "Say, I bet you haven't seen one of these," her father said, showing him the front door lock that he had installed when Beth was young. The lock resembled a rotary phone, on which she and her siblings had dialed their way into the house. While their friends had all coveted the lock, Beth and her siblings had regarded it as a reproach, proof that their father did not trust them to keep track of keys. At the time, their mother claimed that he had installed it because he could not bear the thought of them locked out, waiting in the yard. Only later did Beth understand that her mother was right.

Each time she dialed the lock with her brother and sister standing impatiently behind her, she wanted to tell them about Thomas. But she never did, and she thought that this—maintaining a secret of such magnitude—explained the distance between her and them. Lately she had found herself wanting to call them, but she saw in this impulse something selfish: she would be offering her father's secret in order to obtain an audience for her own sorrow. In truth, she had no idea what she wanted from anyone now, except to be left alone.

11.

When they had been in Saint Paul a year, Beth learned that she was pregnant, and they began hurtling down the slippery slope of adulthood. The wedding happened quickly, during their lunch breaks, but it took them months to find the right house. They visited a Victorian owned by an elderly couple, the Enquists, who had lived in it for forty-two years but were moving to North Platte, Nebraska, to be near their son, who owned a bar there. When they explained this, they wrinkled their noses as though something smelled bad—owning a bar, North Platte, being near their son. In truth, it was probably everything—the combined facts of leaving their home—that caused their noses to wrinkle, but Beth and Matthew did not want to think about the old couple's unhappiness since it was necessary to their own happiness. They knew that this was the house for them.

That night they were both too excited to sleep, so they lay curled up in bed together, attempting to inventory the house from memory, its closets and windows and electrical outlets. Finally Beth dozed off, awakening with a start when Matthew jumped onto the bed next to her, waving a piece of paper—an offer letter filled with embarrassingly intimate expressions of their love for the house and their desire to *make* love in the house. He had used words such as "enamored" and "smitten," had described the appliances as "sexy," the molding as "bewitching." In closing, he had written, "We beseech you to accept our offer."

She remembered even now, especially now, how she had stared at Matthew, who looked strange in the predawn light, unfamiliar, how she had thought, not entirely at ease with the fact, This man is my husband.

Though she wanted to say, "These are old people. This is Minnesota. Don't you *want* the house?" she said simply, "It's a lovely letter, Matthew." He smiled and bounced on his knees on the bed. "I'll take care of it," she said, implying that she would deliver the letter, but at work that morning, in between captions, she rewrote it, stripping it down to the basics of money and time frames and expectations.

The baby that she was carrying inside of her, a boy whom they were planning to name Malcolm, never saw the inside of this house that they had purchased for him, never hung his clothes in the closets that they had lain in bed tallying up, never got scolded for forgetting to do so. When Beth was six-months pregnant, she stepped on a patch of ice on the sidewalk outside their new house and went down hard, trying to break her fall with her right arm. She was in the emergency room having her arm set when the bleeding began.

A year went by, a year during which they did not talk about children or pregnancies or the treachery of ice, but the following winter they broached the topic of having a child, *another* child, their conversations tentative, circling the subject, until one night Matthew took her hand and said, "Listen, I've been thinking that we should adopt. It's selfish to think we need to re-create ourselves." Beth felt the same way, but there was a part of her—a small part, but a part—that believed that what Matthew was really saying was that he did not trust her to deliver a child safely into the world.

About Darrin's origins they knew very little, except that he was Canadian. They went up to Winnipeg on a Tuesday, signed all sorts of forms, and drove home with him that evening, in the course of one day crossing borders and becoming parents. It was winter again, and Beth drove while Matthew sat in the back with Darrin, singing to him and reporting everything, every clenched hand and grimace, every aspect of their son's face, so that by the time they got back to Saint Paul, they both knew him as intimately as if his features were their own.

12.

She left her job because she wanted to have those first few years with him, wanted to watch him sleep and feed him sweet potatoes and pears that she chose from the bins at the produce stand and pureed in the blender, combing through the pap with a fork to find the chunks that he might choke on. She had imagined that she would go back to work when he was two, three at the latest, but by then she had come to realize what a minefield the world was—cords dangling tantalizingly within reach, furniture corners like Sirens, wooing the most tender parts of him as he ran drunkenly through the house—and she couldn't leave.

Sometimes, when fear overwhelmed her, she tried to pull back, to take a mental snapshot of the scene unfolding in front of her and produce a pithy line of text for it, and sometimes this even worked, and she could see the events for what they were—small, happy moments. *Boy, six, learns to ride bicycle without gouging out eye. Birthday boy blows out candles without igniting hair. Tuba player, fourteen, marches in parade without collapsing under the weight of instrument.* She understood that an uneventful day was, in fact, the sum of the many moments that could have veered toward tragedy— but did not.

When she prepared potatoes for dinner, pricking them with a fork, she sent Darrin off to his room. She didn't want him getting ideas about forks. And when he was allowed to watch, she made a point of screaming "Ow!" each time she sank the fork into the potato. "He's going to think you're torturing it," Matthew said as he stood in the kitchen one evening, drinking wine and watching this ritual. "Is that what you want?"

"It's better than him stabbing himself with a fork," she said, as though they had been presented with these two options for their son—sadism toward potatoes or masochism—and made to choose.

Their son spent hours stacking dominoes into neat piles, piles that he toppled explosively but with a giggle, enjoying the fickle sense of power that this stirred in him. Beth liked the dominoes also, not just their ability to enthrall her son but the sound that they made in doing so, the steady clicking like the beating of his heart. On the evening of his third birthday, as she closed the oven door on another set of wounded potatoes, she became aware of the house's stillness and walked fast—running would only frighten him—down the hallway to Darrin's room, where she found his dominoes stacked in orderly towers, but no Darrin. Him she found on the bathroom counter, kneeling in front of the open medicine cabinet, an empty bottle of shoe polish in his hands, the white polish that she had used to keep his baby shoes in order.

"Milk," he said, smiling at her sweetly, white parentheses framing his mouth.

In the emergency room, after he had been made to vomit and the doctor assured them that he was fine, Darrin giggled while Matthew rubbed his belly like a magic lamp. Beth could not laugh, not even when Matthew said, "Look, Darrin. Mommy's still wearing her apron." Instead, she drew her coat around her as though it had been pointed out that she was naked.

"Don't you ever get worried?" she asked Matthew later, when the three of them were back home and she and Matthew were in bed, lying on the mattress that remembered the shapes of their bodies so perfectly that she thought maybe she had been silly to be that frightened.

"That's your job," he said, moving against her in the dark.

But later, after they had made love and fallen asleep, Matthew awakened her to say, "We guard him in our different ways, you know. You keep him safe by visualizing every bad thing that could happen to him, as though—I don't know—you think that you can control it somehow, contain it to your mind. But I can't bear that, can't bear living with those images, so my job is to pretend that those things are so impossible that the thought of them never even enters my mind."

He began to sob, and she held him, thinking about the tenderness with which he had rubbed their son's belly. "I know," she said, for she did know. She understood that fear, like love, took many forms, that it did not have to manifest itself in just one way to be any less real, and Matthew lay beside her sobbing as though he were confessing an infidelity and not that he, too, loved their son so much that he could hardly bear it.

13.

His e-mails became less frequent, less effusive, and they did not know whether this was because he had a girlfriend who commanded his focus, or because he did not trust them to understand the details of his new life. In fact, they would never know. One morning when he had been gone six months, as they were drinking coffee and Matthew was singing in his loud, off-key voice, the phone rang. "This is Peru," whispered the voice on the other end.

"Peru?" said Beth.

"I'm one of your son's teachers. On the trip?"

"His teacher?" Beth said. "I don't understand."

"Oh my God," said the woman, for Beth thought of her that way now—as a woman. "I can't do this." She began to sob.

"Hello?" said Beth, but the sobbing grew distant.

"What is it?" Matthew asked, standing up from the table and coming over to her. Beth shook her head.

A man came on the line then, another teacher, who identified himself as Rob. This man Rob explained to her that their son was dead, electrocuted in the swimming pool of their hotel in Chiang Mai just a few hours earlier. "The students were finished giving English lessons for the day, and Darrin and a few of the other guys were in the pool having a beer." He paused. "An electrical box fell into the water."

Rob waited for her to speak. She wanted to ask, "Why were eighteen-year-olds drinking beer?" and, "Why was there an electrical box above the pool?" and, most of all, "Why was my son sleeping with one of his teachers?" But in the end she said only, "And the other boys?"

"They're OK. Darrin was closest to the box," said this stranger, Rob. "Listen, if it's any comfort, the doctor said that he died instantly."

It was not a comfort. How could there be comfort in the word "instantly," in any word that meant her son had lived even one second less on this earth?

Matthew took the telephone then. She was vaguely aware of him discussing details, two men taking care of business, but then he said, "No, I'm coming for him," and everything about Matthew— his voice, his body, his heart—seemed to break into pieces right in front of her.

He told her that he could go to Thailand alone, but she would not hear of it: they had picked up their son together at the beginning of his life, and she would not consider doing any less at the end. She explained this as she wiped off the counters and washed out their cups, but when she turned, looking for the dish towel, she saw that Matthew was sitting at the table wearing it over his head like a small tent into which he had disappeared to be alone with his grief.

14.

They did not tell anyone that they were going, except for the cat sitter, to whom they said only that there was an emergency in Thailand. Beth knew that she should call her parents, but she remembered the way that the conversation about Thomas had ended all those years ago. "Did they ever find him?" Beth had asked, meaning did they find a body, for she understood that nobody had ever seen Thomas alive again. "No," her mother had said. "And let me tell you, for a parent, not knowing has got to be the worst thing." Beth knew now that her mother had been wrong, that there was something far worse than not knowing—and that was knowing that her son lay unequivocally dead in a hospital somewhere in Thailand.

Later, after they had booked a flight, they went into the bedroom and began to pack, their suitcases lying open at the foot of the bed like two giant clams. They had not spoken of their individual conversations with Rob, had not compared notes in order to create a complete account of their son's death. They had not talked of anything but the logistics of getting to Thailand, of getting their son home.

"Why was he drinking?" she asked Matthew, hurling the question at his back as he filled his own suitcase, and then, "I want this woman arrested. I want her to pay." Beth lay down on the bed, placing her feet inside her own half-packed suitcase, and began to cry.

Matthew sat beside her, holding his hand to her cheek. "We need to take comfort in knowing that his last days, his last minutes even, were happy ones," he said. He sounded like a minister or a therapist, someone schooled in the art of discussing other people's pain, and she wanted to tell him so, wanted to say, "You see?" for she had been right all these years and now he was proving it, proving how inadequate words were.

15.

The final punch in Beth's falling-in-love card had come in Thailand, at the end of their hot-countries tour. They flew from Jakarta to Malaysia, spending an afternoon in Kuala Lumpur before getting on the night train. In Thailand they bought tickets for a ferry that would shuttle them out to an island whose name Beth could no longer recall; the ticket sellers had considered demand but not supply in offering the tickets, and when the ferry began to load, it was clear that there were not enough seats. "Next ferry tomorrow," called out one of the young ferry workers, blocking the gangplank. He gestured at the flat, empty roof of the boat to indicate that it was available.

"Let's go," Matthew said. Already, disappointed travelers had begun to jump from the dock down onto it.

"Absolutely not," she said. "Have you not heard of something called 'weight capacity'?"

Matthew bent as though to kiss her but instead bit her nose, hard. "Ow!" she said, and he laughed and tossed their backpacks onto the roof of the ferry, leaping down after them and turning to offer his hand. Nearly since they met, Matthew had been declaring his love, to which she always replied, "Good Lord" or "Heavens," intentionally prim responses that made both of them laugh and bought her time, but when she jumped onto the roof of the ferry, they both knew she was nearly there.

The last punch happened two days later on a snorkeling trip with thirteen other tourists. She remembered the other passengers well: a young British woman who vomited uncontrollably and several French boys who laughed at her until Matthew explained to them that they were not helping matters, sounding so reasonable that the boys had stopped immediately. There were Germans and a family from Brazil, about whom she had wondered why they would come this far to be in another hot, wet place. Three Thai boys ran the boat, one driving and the other two tending to the passengers' needs, bringing the vomiting woman a pail, picking the Brazilian children up and pretending that they were going to toss them overboard. They said nothing to Beth, though they made small talk with Matthew, asking whether he liked to fish and how much his watch had cost. The driver multitasked as he drove, eating and turning to joke with the other two, even pulling his T-shirt off over his head—all without slowing down. He struck her as the sort of young man who would only become more reckless when presented with fear, particularly a woman's, so she said nothing, her face set to suggest calm, though Matthew, who knew better, rested his hand on her knee.

It took them nearly two hours to reach the cove. They were supposed to spend the day there, but around one, the young Thai men began to round everyone up, pointing at the ocean, which had become a roiling gray, and at the dark clouds suspended over it. They departed hastily, a forgotten snorkeling mask bobbing near the shore behind them. That morning, everyone had conversed happily in English, but the storm made them nationalistic, each group reverting to its own language, needing the comfort of the familiar.

The waves grew higher and the passengers quieter, except when they hit a particularly big wave. Then, everyone flew into the air and came down hard, sometimes atop one another or on the floor of the boat, making a collective "umph" of surprise and fear. Beth noticed that the two Thai stewards were pointing at a distant object bobbing on the waves. As they got nearer she could see that it was a boat, a boat filled with the same configuration of Thai boys and tourists, except this boat was not moving forward, bucking the waves. Instead it rose and fell listlessly, its engine still, while the people on board screamed and waved their arms. On Beth's boat the two stewards huddled around the driver, who had been so cocky speeding across the water just hours earlier. Now he looked tired and young. They were arguing, and the driver finally wrenched the wheel, turning their boat toward the stranded one.

"We can't take everyone," called out one of the Germans, a woman who had refused to stop smoking even though her lit cigarettes pocked the arms and legs of her companions each time the boat hit a wave, "or we will all die." She said it in English, the *w*'s becoming dramatic *v*'s, and then she took a long drag on her cigarette and glared.

Nobody spoke, and then Matthew said, "Look, there's room." He wiggled closer to Beth, and the others did the same. The driver maneuvered their boat parallel to the stranded one, and a steward from that boat, a young man—they were all so young—with an owl tattoo on his left bicep, instructed the men to link hands across the water. "Why don't we tie them?" asked one of the French boys, and the steward explained that they needed to be able to break free quickly when a big wave came or the two boats might be slammed together and destroyed. Only then did the passengers on the stranded boat seem to realize what was expected: that they were to perch on the edge of their boat as it lurched beneath them and then leap across the gap to safety. A few cried, but one by one they did it, collapsing into the arms of those on the other side. It was a slow process. Every few minutes, someone called out, "Wait!" or "Quickly!" and the men dropped hands and let the boats surge apart.

On the floor of the other boat sat a woman flanked by two young children, a baby in her lap. She was dressed as though for a job interview, and atop her bosom a large cross bounced. She screamed at her husband in what sounded like Swedish, and though Beth did not know Swedish, she knew what the woman was saying. When the husband grew tired of pleading with her, he picked up the oldest child and carried him over to the side, where he stood for a moment, lips moving, before leaning out over the churning water with his son and letting him go into the hands of the French boys on the other side.

He did the same with the second child, but when he reached for the baby, the mother would not let go. "No, we will die here together," she screamed, in English this time because she wished to include everyone in her fear. After her husband had pried the baby loose, she sat with her head in her hands, refusing to look as her husband leaned out for the third time, offering the baby, their baby, into the outstretched arms of the French boys. As he let go, a giant wave flung the boats apart, the clasped hands slipping from one another like sand.

Later, the father, sobbing, would say that he had heard King Solomon whispering in his ear, "Let go of your son." As he told this story, the baby rested in his arms, mother and siblings on either side, a family reunited. Beth sat beside Matthew, who looked sheepish yet pleased by the rounds of applause in his honor, for in that half second after the baby had been released, Matthew's hand shot into the gap and caught it by its chubby leg. Even as the boat bucked mightily, he held on, held on as though nothing but life were possible.

16.

Lying in their bed listening to Matthew fold origami night after night, Beth does not cry. Crying happens during the day, when every sight and sound reminds her of Darrin: the hole in the wall from an arrow that he had not meant to release; the creak of the refrigerator door; the tubes of toothpaste in a brand that only Darrin liked, sitting in a drawer unused, useless. Today, she goes into his room and vacuums for the first time since he left a year and a half ago. When she is finished, she panics and rips the vacuum bag open on the floor outside his room, sifts through the compressed pile of dirt and dust, looking for something—a hair, a thread from a favorite shirt, a sliver of dead skin, a fingernail chewed off and spit onto the carpet, the lint from between his toes. Some piece of him.

She falls asleep there on the floor, curled up around the vacuum bag as though it were Gertrude, their cat. When she awakens she does not open her eyes right away, but she knows time has passed, can tell that the sun has shifted and is about to disappear. She knows also that someone is sitting beside her. Matthew. She can feel the weight of his hand on her calf. They have not touched like this since before the phone call from Thailand, touched in a way that is not about passion, though there has been none of that either, or practicality, passing the salt and emptying the dishwasher, but that is simply about the intimacy of every day. Then, as though Matthew senses that she is awake, his hand is gone.

"You think I drove him away," she says softly. "That I worried too much." Her eyes are still closed. She hears him breathing and finally the slight intake that means he is about to answer.

"No," he says. He sounds tired, all those nights of sitting up, folding origami. "I don't think that." He pauses, sighs. "The truth is that I don't think at all. I teach, and I grade papers, and I smile at the other teachers to let them know that it's OK when I catch them laughing. I stop and put gas in the car on the way home from school every Friday."

In her pocket are the pieces of Darrin that she picked out of the vacuum cleaner bag—a curly black hair that could only be his and some dried mud he'd dragged in from an all-night graduation party. She knows that if she opens her eyes, she will see Matthew rubbing his scar as he does when he is thinking, the scar that she had asked him about all those years ago in the gay bar the night they met, when he told her about the bliss of riding his bicycle down the road wearing magnifying-glass spectacles, the world so close, so deceptive. "Have you spoken to Lance?" she asks because she cannot think of that night without Lance.

"I talked to him last week," he says. She thinks about the last year, how she knows nothing of what his days have entailed— lunches eaten, books read, people talked to.

"How is he?"

"Lance is Lance," he says. "He's still in Albuquerque, still waiting for the perfect Asian man to come along, still counting inventory, if you can believe it. He sends his love."

She never understood Lance, with his degree in political science, counting cans at Albertsons. She recalls all the times that she and Matthew, smug in their own success, analyzed his situation, saying things like, "How's he going to meet someone when he spends his life aspiring to nothing more than counting inventory?"

"Poor Lance," she says, and she means it, but then it occurs to her that she no longer has the right to feel sorry for Lance, Lance who wants more than anything to meet someone, to settle down and just be together.

"He's pretty amazing, though," Matthew says. "He can walk into a 7-Eleven, look around, and predict within $200 how much merchandise they have on hand."

"I guess that's why he stays," Beth says.

"What do you mean?" Matthew says.

"To have that kind of certainty," she says. Her eyes are still closed.

"Or that kind of fear," Matthew adds and then falls silent.

The day of the funeral, Matthew's hands rested atop their son's coffin, side by side, as though the coffin were a piano that he would soon begin to play. His hands were what had first attracted her all those years ago, the unchewed nails and the veins rising up across the backs. They had seemed at once sexy and capable. She remembers how they came from nowhere that day at sea, grabbing the baby from the gap, and how she had mistaken this as a sign of how their lives would always be.

She begins to sob, quietly at first, but then more loudly, and she waits for Matthew to say something, to try for the right words. "He was the absolute best," she says finally. "The A1 most amazing son in the world." Matthew laughs, and the sound startles her here in their silent house. She feels his hand on her ankle, tentative but holding on. She does not know whether it is pulling her down or up toward the surface, but she opens her eyes and does not move away.

A PURPOSEFUL VIOLENCE

Noley Reid

TWILIGHT ON KORESSEL STREET was shrouded in a sulfuric haze of other families' fountains, Roman candles, glow worms, and bangers held tree-level by clouds that refused to move beyond the Ohio River. It was Fourth of July, 1951, and Noemi had told the boys "No bottle rockets," so they pouted and whispered in the living room inside a fort of couch cushions. They had swiped a box of matches and Jack lit one and passed his palm over it. Leo lit his own only to blow it out and light another again and again. Leo was older by ten months, but Jack was in charge. In the kitchen, T.E. watched Noemi work at the stove. Peas and potatoes in the Revere, meatloaf in the oven. He was a lineman, so she had wanted electric burners, saying he'd be able to fix them if they ever faltered. She walked barefoot in the house, always had, and the *shoosh* of her tan nylons across the linoleum was at once a reminder of her body and her rules.

"Back me up on this, please, T.E.," she said, stacking four plates next to the stove. "You never know where they'll come down, and they shoot so fast up into the sky."

The timer dinged then Ludlow, Ohio, went dark.

"Tonight?" came her voice, but he had already shut off the gas line and was heading up the stairs.

He had no clothes other than uniform tans, so he needed only his lineman's belt and pole strap. Noemi had him keep these under the bed. She appeared in the doorway, hands pressed behind her back, elbows like a bird on a nest. "Be careful," she told him.

That was fine.

He fit the belt high to his waist, tight so the bulk of the flashlight and snips, rubber-insulated gloves and spools would stay up.

"I'll do sparklers with them," she said.

"Do the snakes."

"They make such a mess. Will you hose it down tomorrow if we do?"

He touched her waist, kissed her, and smiled. "Yes, dear."

"Don't joke like that. You know I don't like it."

"Yes, I'll hose down the driveway if you do the snakes," he told her.

"You're always joking like that." She was working her way to something but he was content to leave it in the house with her.

He went outside to wait for the truck, stood down by the sickly redbud tree that deer ate half the trunk of years ago. Truth was, he loved blackouts. In all that darkness, the trick was to find something live.

He had loved linework ever since he trained in the Army. He tested into gunnery but couldn't keep his equilibrium at altitude, so he'd gone on to electrical. Suspended midair from a helicopter's bonding platform, current buzzed every inch of him in the hot suit. He used a thirty-foot hot stick on the EHV lines that towered over the training classrooms. He hadn't been in a hot suit since he served in Tunisia, but sometimes while tying off a mule tape that bundled neutral and primary lines with others, he could feel a dull prickling of current through the rubber over his hands.

Now Will Newsome and he drove out to the river, where the boys' school sat on the other side of an old stand of serviceberry, bog birch, sweetgum, and spruce. The county had put in electric poles alongside the tree line to plan for new tract houses in a year or two, so anytime there was an outage, T.E. and Will covered that area looking for hanging limbs or downed trees creating a short circuit. They each took a direction and walked the line.

Pops of silvery light sputtered in the distance. Rockets whistled through the air and he wished they were the boys'. Ludlow didn't have its own Fourth of July parade or fireworks, so most of the families had driven up to Zanesville just over an hour away. T.E. shined his light up onto the wire, following its drape from pole to pole. Branches, he couldn't tell what kind they were by the light of his flashlight, were still as statues beneath and above the lines. The trees were supposed to be gone, and that they weren't meant he and Will would be out here working more and more and Noemi would be wishing she'd stuck with the gas range.

Slowly he walked south, deciphering the branches that posed potential trouble to the lines. He saw nothing. Another spray lit behind him and he could tell this was a pin oak tree. The pole came up only a third of its height. A shame to lose that one, but the homeowners would plant more trees: willows and elms that they would keep out of the wires.

The air off the river was thick. Stale air he was surprised could compete with the growing sulfur cloud. Here, the leaves beneath his boots were soft, winter's fall but gone to mold. He thought about each silken leaf, the way it must tear with his step. Tearing along the veins. Another burst in the sky lit the ground and he realized that was where he was looking, though he still trained the flashlight up on the power line. To the east, a gold constellation streamed from the sky, lighting up enough ground to see he was now behind the boys' school. The leaves shone wet with rot. The dimming flash of western tree trunks seemed people receding from sight.

Low sky absorbed the cloud of smoke. Bottle rockets shrieked in the night. He thought of the boys and then Noemi with sparklers, pictured her writing her name with his in the sky. Without cause at all, T.E. moved his light down to the earth. There was something there. Ahead of him. It was the body of an animal, something dead and undisturbed. Big like a dog or a deer. His light was meant to travel a tenth of a mile, was too bright. So even standing over the thing in the leaves, he wasn't sure.

He switched off the light, but the sky lit green and so was the little girl's face: sick green skin bruised and bloodied, her mouth a silent ocean of scream and dirt.

*

"What if we wear Dad's goggles," Jack said. "Then we can't lose an eye." He pressed his fingertip into one of the half-thawed peas Noemi had served thirty minutes after the lights went out. Not only didn't it squash but he lifted his finger and it stayed there, stuck to his skin for a moment.

"He only has one pair," said Noemi.

Leo got a pea to stick, too, one per finger. He held up his hand, appeared to conduct a symphony before shaking them off like mud from a dog.

"You'll pick those up and wash the floor before bed," she told him.

"He started it," said Leo.

"Then you'll *both* sit there till you're finished." Noemi took the candlestick from the table so they could no longer see just how much frost remained on their supper. She set it aside on the buffet then went in the kitchen to watch the sky, hear its distant crackling. T.E. stood outside the screen door. She could see his head and it was funny.

"I didn't hear the truck," she said. Through the door now, she saw him. He was naked. Not boots or belt. Nothing. "My land. What are you doing—come in!" She tried to push open the door but it knocked in to him. "Tandy," she said.

He did not move.

Noemi reached an arm through to help guide him around the swing of the door just to get him inside.

She stood before him in the middle of the kitchen but it didn't occur to her to touch him. This looked like a game. She could not touch him. When she looked, he was like a stubborn boy before a bath, hands at his sides, feet still. Her voice was tight and high. "You'll scare the boys," but they were away at the table until she would relent and dismiss them for bed.

He moved forward, went straight to his knees. Leo's and Jack's voices hushed. At first she stood over T.E. She did not know what to say or do. This sweaty, hairy man she'd loved enough for twelve years. His shoulders were wet, the muscles of his chest bright under the fluorescent. This man who swam the winter Ohio to save a favorite photograph of her. No matter that she'd thrown the picture in on purpose; no matter her tantrums. Now he kneeled before her and so, chewing at half of her lower lip, she held him. A naked man. And the stench of his body was sweet like fire.

"Tandy," she said, and finally he looked up.

"There were all the firecrackers," he said. "Behind the school. I looked down and there was something."

He kissed her lips and she could feel a spark there, a bit of that lightning.

"I thought it was a dog."

His skin was not cold. She kept expecting it to grow cold. She touched his shoulder, his thigh, his cheek. No raised flesh, no chill. His cheeks were red like a burn failing to heal.

The boys weren't talking in the dining room. There was a naked man and maybe they could sense it. What a strange night this was.

"A dog?" she asked.

"A girl," he said. "A little baby. And she was dead."

It wasn't until two policemen came to the door later in the evening that he spoke again. Noemi went to get him clothing. She'd gotten Jack and Leo to bed finally and stood at their door wanting a do over because maybe if she'd let them have the bottle rockets, T.E. would have kept his eyes on the electrical lines, and Leo wouldn't be too afraid to cry. She took down trousers and a blue oxford, undershorts and socks.

One of the officers said, "It would sure help if you had seen anyone around the area."

"Why are their peas on the floor?" said T.E.

They sat at the dining room table. T.E. left the pile of fresh clothing in front of him, picked at the peas on the boys' forgotten plates. "She wasn't covered."

"Did you touch anything?" said the other. "Uncover her?"

"No," said T.E. He stopped eating. "Nothing."

"Right," said the first to Noemi. "We have to ask." And they left.

*

Once T.E. had told Noemi, he was sorry. He couldn't explain it, this sense that he'd been supposed to find the girl. Something like fate cleaning up the shit done by others, not that he could do anything that night or now, but he could think about that dead baby and respect her.

He stopped sleeping. He'd lie next to Noemi listening to how deep her breathing could go. How far in she could take herself away. He couldn't fault her for that. He didn't want to.

He stopped working. Went on a sort of disability from the union. Two stray albino cats appeared and he fed them. Tuna straight from his fingers because he liked the wet of their noses and the way they shook the hunks of meat to the backs of their throats. He went for walks. Long and longer walks. Through the neighborhood. Skirted the town, then past Crestview Trailer Park where the homes could blow away and a person could disappear completely leaving no trace. Then on past the rows and rows of new tract houses, Ludlow's own Levittown. One evening, when the boys were pirates in the tub and Leo refused to make his brother walk the plank, Noemi said, "T.E., you've made him go soft and the world will crush him." T.E. walked until Jefferson Memorial and dusk, and he was not surprised to arrive there.

He had not seen these woods in natural light since long before the Fourth of July. The ground dipped lower beyond the electric poles. Down he moved, down closer to the trees. He no longer watched the wire slung pole to pole. His eyes were in the leaves, the mounds and flat spaces.

Nearer and nearer until he saw there was a woman there at the edge of the trees. He stood back in the cool of this woodland watching her, listening to every breath as shallow as his. The woman wore an overcoat—in July heat she held it shut around her middle. Her hair was shoulder-length, black, a loop of bangs curled under like Noemi wore hers but this woman was not pretty like his wife. Disproportionately wide through the hips, her legs thick to her shoes, graceless in her movement. And when she turned and he saw her face, it was permanently and rawly ugly in a way he could not imagine as only recent. A pair of cardinals alit high in the woods, some color to this early evening's shade. The woman knelt down in the moss phlox at the base of one tree, one spruce where it looked as though a bleating doe had lain down to birth or to die. But that wasn't the tree. Not that one.

T.E. stepped forward into the light of clearing that was the spot. He knew who this woman was. There had been photographs: of the house the girl had been taken from, of the parents. He had no right to the girl or any grief going on here but he could not leave.

"You," said Kay when his feet came near enough the leaves.

He followed her onto the school's property, behind the playground and field where he knew Jack knew how to catch a football and run as fast as blood could push air through his lungs.

When they reached her black Nash, she sat inside it, filling the space of the cabin in a way Noemi never would let herself. Kay looked right at him and was not afraid. She drove. He didn't take his eyes from her as she made the turn away from the school. Past the trailers, past the streets of town and the lanes of Ludlow-proper where he lived, out beyond and up to Route 83. She pulled in to Ludlow Auto Lodge. She waited, stood at the first room's door while he paid $7.00 in the office for a key. Wrapped in her coat and her arms, fireflies lit and went out around her, she even shivered.

They lay on their backs atop the coverlet, arms at their sides and hips touching. He didn't kiss her. They didn't embrace. They still had their shoes on. They closed their eyes and neither one of them undressed—not even her coat—or made effort to push aside clothing, but it happened and when they were through fucking and lay again flatly beside each other, he heard her voice for just the second time. "What did she look like?" it said.

Eyes still closed, he could feel her rearrange the skirt of her dark blue dress. Her stockings were strangely woolen; they had chafed the crooks of his arms. He felt the burn there now, the sting of his sweat overtop panic. "Sleepy," he said. "Sleeping."

The mattress gave around him for she was sitting up and her heels touched the floorboards with a tap just like Noemi's whenever she slipped into them at the front door. Kay left the room, left the parking lot, who knows where she went, he didn't.

The next evening Noemi sent the boys up to their bedroom to bring T.E. down for supper.

"Daddy," said Jack and Leo, storming in on him where he sat at the end of the bed. There was a clothlike brown leaf next to T.E. but the boys didn't see it and when Leo jumped up to drive his favorite milk cart horse along the comb grooves of his father's Brylcreemed head, T.E. grabbed hold of both his upper arms and threw his son hard to the floor.

"What's wrong with you?" he said, standing himself. He had spent hours smoothing a crease from the veins of the leaf and now it showed again.

Leo nursed a knee scuffed by the floor, then ran his horse in place atop the pink scrape. He kept his eyes there, on the horse's hooves running the white line of skin rolled back from the curve of his knee.

T.E. handed the leaf to Jack to see what would happen. The mean was crawling all throughout him now. Yes, it was purposeful what he did, and when Leo's face worked hard to hold still, to not give sorrow its place, T.E. felt different. "You neither, Jack," he said and took the leaf away. "Go on down," he told them. "Go tell her I don't want a thing."

That evening, Kay's gray woolen stockings were oversewn with lumps of thread where a run might have started. Before shutting his eyes, T.E. saw these patches like scabs around her knees and ankles and all he could see behind his eyelids was the baby's blood and bruising.

Again, neither one of them took hold of the other, neither one seemed to manipulate clothing or flesh but, eyes shut, their bodies somehow came together in a fold of seeing and not seeing. "What did she look like?" Kay asked again, once they came apart. "Did you listen for breathing? Did you touch her? What color were her eyes—they can change depending."

"The leaves were last year's, from winter. They were what I was stepping on. I couldn't hear them—that's how soft they were." He placed his leaf upon her belly, death covering up where the life began. "They were in her hand. There were leaves in her hand. Just one hand."

Grief racked her body and he meant only to hold her then, but instead they fucked and when they were through with this new, purposeful violence, their breathing slowed and they finally slept.

It was days more before she asked him what the other hand held.

Days and nights more until the sheets cascaded to the floor and the bed's casters scuffed the boards beneath. "Her own mouth," he whispered then. "Full of dirt."

No one in Ludlow, Ohio, believed Tandy "T.E." Parsten was anything more than the poor sap who stumbled upon the body— not the cops, not the grocers or the little old ladies, not even the kids at school, but the *Courier*'s articles—"Mother of Baby Dinah Takes Comfort Where She Can" and "Affair to Shed New Light on Murder of Baby Dinah?"—months after, surely made them resent their sympathy. It was pure insinuation, nothing built on any of the reckless facts neither of them attempted to hide.

Noemi never told T.E. to move out. And they never spent a single whole night in any other bed. He seemed even to believe she understood. But a lump in his throat grew and it was cancer. After his surgery, Noemi sat in the waiting room. Kay came. She sat next to Noemi. She'd never seen T.E.'s wife, of course, but the paper had run the same sad photograph of Kay with Dinah blowing out last year's candles; Noemi certainly knew who she was, this frowsy sack of a woman.

"I'm sorry for your loss," Noemi said, looking right in to her eyes, as black as her hair.

Kay's lips parted as if she would speak but nothing came out, not even air. She tucked the ends of her scarf inside the lapels of her coat. September was trapped inside the hospital walls, and Noemi fanned herself with a *Family Circle*.

Noemi placed the magazine atop her lap, conscious of the pleats of her dress, conscious of the precision in the way her knees touched together. "You have a choice here," she whispered, studying the pointed triangle her skirt made in sitting. "One of us is going to take him home and nurse him. The other is going to leave and that will be the end of it. I have two boys by Tandy, but I suppose that's not what really matters." She touched Kay's hand. It looked like Leo's, with the ragged cuticles and chewed nails. "Tell me, please, do you love him?"

Kay was quiet. They watched the end of the hallway where doctors converged on the nurses' station. Two orderlies wheeled a gurney by their room, then left it and the patient atop, to speak with one of the nurses. It was hard to tell if the patient was alive or dead. He did not move. The sheet was up to his nose.

"I'm always so cold," said Kay. "Just always so cold." And she left.

Doctors performed a radical neck dissection on T.E., snaked and shimmied the lymph nodes right on out with forceps and a scalpel—that was how Jack thought of what his mother told him. She only talked to Jack. "Leo, well, he's so sensitive," she'd say. So now the boys' father was coming home like none of the other business happened at all. He would surely come walking through that door, scoop both of the boys over his shoulders, and holler at their mother that he never wanted to go out walking again. And maybe that could work just fine, since the *Courier* had finally stopped writing about the dead girl.

This morning, there was a tray with cereal bowls and a pitcher of milk on the floor by the bunk beds. Jack woke up to the clinking of Leo's spoon. They hadn't seen their mother at home—she'd leave early and be gone until late. Even when they vowed they'd stake out the window, they never made it. All week long she had been telling Jack what was going to happen, that Daddy's cancer was still bad in his throat and mouth, that no one knew why, but he'd be just fine. Jack carried that.

Leo didn't carry anything anymore, left his milk cart carriage horses lying around the house. Jack had stepped on one last night getting into bed and his heel still ached. He turned up his foot now and, sure enough, there was the pink welt. He nursed it, rubbed the pad of his heel. He called up to the top bunk, "She said he might die." It wasn't true, that she had said so, but Jack said it nonetheless.

Leo's face appeared over the side of the bed, a rug hung out to beat.

Jack slid a finger lengthwise down his throat and watched as his brother's Adam's apple moved down, up, down. So now Jack scaled his throat lengthwise and made like he was peeling back the sides, like curtains. He practically reached his entire hand inside his neck and felt around, started pinching bits of skin between his fingers. Leo went vomitous-pale. Jack's hand became what he sometimes dreamed, the doctors taking pieces of their father like souvenir shelling at Euclid Beach. He yanked at *Leo's* neck.

"Stop it!" Leo said, swatting at the fingers. "What *is* that?"

"Forceps," he said, letting go. "Tongs."

Leo shuddered. Spittle shook off his lips down onto Jack's quilt.

"Eee-ooo!" said Jack. And Leo, his face, still stricken, disappeared. "He won't," said Jack. There were ladder steps hooked over top the cheap maple frame. Jack kicked them to get his brother's attention. "He would have already."

Leo's curls made him look like a dog sometimes, the way they matted and snarled. That's what Jack saw when his brother looked at him wishing, wishing Jack wouldn't always try to push him off a ledge. But that was a big green monster under the bed and when the lights came on or early autumn sun filled the windows she wasn't there to draw curtains over, who could blame an eleven-year-old for feeling normal. Even so, Jack suspected there was a time before now and a time beyond now and they were entirely different places.

There they sat waiting on Leo's bunk. Jack rubbed his heel until it turned white. Leo poked a finger into the indentations from a horse ear. "Jesus, quit it!" said Jack. Leo laughed through his nose in and out like he wasn't himself. They settled in to the quiet, waited there until they heard the front door. Leo slipped his hand inside Jack's. They went extra slowly down the stairs.

Their mother looked taller through the spine, her arms longer and bowed out like a swallow flying. She stepped out of her pumps, click-clack, then gathered Jack and Leo to her sides. There was a stranger coming.

"Please don't stare," she told them. "Don't you break your Daddy's heart."

The boys nodded.

"There's one thing more," she said, whispering. She bent down, tugged a curl that hung down loose above her ear, and brushed it twice across her jaw line. Up she stood. "You should know, they took his whole tongue."

She spun back around to him so all they could see through the front door was the swing of her dress. "Let me, T.E.," and she reached for his elbow. She tried to help him in because something about lymph nodes made you weak when they were gone. Jack took one of his father's hands too, said, "Hello." Leo was right next to his brother, and they all looked at this sickly man to see what would he say.

Their father's entire face was twisted. Like if you took hold of the center of someone's face, the nose Jack supposed, and just started twisting all their skin: lips and cheeks clear out to the ears—one of his was practically sitting on his cheekbone now. Gauze encased the front and sides of his neck, and at their base an inch of putty-colored tube hung down. Alongside the bandage, his skin was gouged, pink and slick in jagged paths.

"Jack," said their mother. "You take these." So now Jack had a collection of paperwork and a crossword puzzle in his hand, her purse too, which he set down fast. She walked their father on down the hall to the living room and his couch and Leo and Jack followed to say it was them made it up for him.

Jack said, "Here," and handed him the papers and puzzle.

"Go on now. Daddy's tired," said their mother and she shut the door.

She stayed inside. Jack and Leo waited there in the hallway for her to come out. They wanted to know everything. They needed to be sure this was fine. That going in for cancer and coming out clean, that that meant everything else was healed, too. Just like he'd been a cable splicer with the 141st Signal Corps but come back whole.

Leo slipped to the floor and sat there. "You owe me a nickel."

"Huh?"

"Fair and square. You owe me a nickel."

"He came back," said Jack, disagreeing.

"Not all of him."

Jack stared at Leo. A kid in his class drowned and died at a birthday party. Jack and Leo had been eating orange sherbet. The boy's mother started crying on him and he coughed up all the water. After that, Leo pooped his pants the next time their mother served sherbet at home.

"Just go away, please," Jack said. He kicked at his brother's legs until Leo left.

Within the living room, Noemi positioned T.E.'s things on the coffee table—he was Tandy only when things were good and she was certain he wouldn't mind hearing his real name in her mouth.

"We'll start fresh," she said. She lifted his feet and stacked two pillows beneath them. She smoothed the sheet the boys had merely draped across the back of the couch, tucked its hem down behind the cushions. "I understand you," she said and meant to say more.

T.E. had been looking out the window since coming in the room. He hated this room. But he was weak, couldn't lift his left arm higher than his hips and his right not higher than his waist. Of course he had to live downstairs. Now dark was coming across the yard: the laurel and boxwoods, the berried hollies outside, all were in shadow. A lip of sunset held the clouds like blankets to a chin, but the sky would be thick any moment and the little china doll lamp's reflection would make it all disappear. He was glad for that. She would go away soon, too. There were the boys to think of.

"Just . . . ," she began, "don't ever talk."

She took away the pencil and folded newspaper Jack had carried. It was his puzzle but he didn't protest. He began to ease himself down to the couch, which was lower than the hospital bed. Noemi cupped his elbow and took on his weight to help him slowly down.

"We have you back now," she said. "Keep the rest to yourself." She dropped the paper and pencil into the wastebasket.

Now, Noemi stood in her kitchen all these months later wondering how she had got to here: fluffing his pillow, mopping the drool tangled at the edge of this grotesquery's mouth where it pooled and crusted. The discharge nurse had warned against letting it collect, said Vaseline would keep it from rashing in the night, but it must be tended to in the day. Daily, Noemi collected stray homework pencils and pens the boys forgot and snapped them in half for fear of her husband finding a way to speak.

He wasn't even going to die now.

As she filled fresh water in the white Corning bowl she had always mixed frosting in, and folded clean cloths—one dry, one in the water—she considered what she always considered, fantasies she would never commit: dirty rags, urine-filled water from those awful cats he made hang around the house, a dirty Kotex rinsed clean and pressed to his lips in the dark.

She called to the boys, "Take this to Daddy." She held out the dry cloth to Leo but he walked away, went back upstairs without a word.

The other boy came forward. "I'll do it," he said.

Jack pushed open the door to the living room. There sat T.E., lengthwise on the sofa, Ohioan Family Sweepstakes booklets across his lap. He tapped at the page of stamps Noemi had brought for him today.

There was nothing else now. And never would be.

A layer of fuzz encased his thinking, made dull and soft the pain in his neck and mouth. Noemi concocted gray puddings he ate with a special plunger spoon that shoved the food down his throat. The drains oozed putrid stink. But his tongue, his tongue moved through the vowels of each word they said around him. Until they stopped talking, which they always did, and then his phantom tongue slipped through numbers and alphabet cycles. If it ever stopped moving—when he lay in the dark on this couch at night listening to the boys whispering and Noemi's footsteps coming halfway down the stairs—then he felt its absence and what the absence of his tongue felt like was the same as gauze stuffed to capacity, was a gulp of water when he needed air, was a mouth full of screaming.

He gave himself—what there was left of him—over to this life. There was no alternative. In his hands, he held the sweepstakes booklet. It may as well be a winner, there was no meaning left anywhere in the world. He had to get all the blue stamps on the blue page, yellows on the yellow, like that. Jack held the bowl for him. That was one good thing, what change in Jack there'd been.

"Take it, Daddy." Jack gave him the fresh bowl and picked up the one on the carpeting. Barely a wisp of reflection in that one, he'd sucked the cloth dry. "Put it in your mouth." He looked away, out the window to nothing in particular.

His father took the dry cloth and held it to the side of his face, blotted the spit. Then he squeezed out enough water not to drip on the sweepstakes letter and envelope. He unfolded the cloth, tucked a corner between the edges of his mouth. Sometimes Jack wasn't sure where the pieces of his father's face would be when he looked; they seemed to move and never be where he expected them. The twist of his cheeks and nose and chin collapsed his lips inward so that they were nearly gone. Jack felt a duty to check because his father was sort of like having a puppy now. The lips were still there and Jack felt better, good enough to fill the booklet with stamps.

His father pointed at the blue, yellow, green stamps on the page, then at the empty pages in the sweepstakes booklet. He gave the page to Jack who began folding at the perforations.

Jack's mother came in. "You mustn't keep too much in your mouth at once," she nagged. "You know that, Tandy."

It could pool and sitting upright without a tongue, he'd have no way of swallowing it down. She'd warned Jack to keep watch of their father. She took the cloth's edge from his cauliflowered mouth, set it back in the bowl. "Every few minutes," she said, "or if you feel you're going to cough."

Just saying the word made a gagging terror creep up T.E.'s throat. He bit what lips he had left and shut his eyes until the cough passed. A sudden coolness on his chin reminded him to wipe the drying cloth there.

Jack held up the booklet and all the stamps were pasted in. Every page full. T.E. checked the letter again: *Simply purchase enough of the following products to fill the pages of this book. Every booklet is a winner. That's right, every booklet!* It was something.

Jack turned eleven that December and Leo tried to give him his milk cart horses. When February came, Leo turned twelve and enough time had passed that his mother made a sugar-dusted cake. She hid a fancy Wham-O slingshot beneath his father's couch's cushions. "Go find it," she said but Leo only stood in front of the couch blinking.

His father patted the cloth over his mouth, the skin of his hand so thin it looked like it had been cooked. Leo wanted to help his father, or crush him.

"Fine," said his mother, reaching behind the cushions and giving him the slingshot.

Leo never set it down. He stayed out of the house as much as he could, aiming mostly at basement windows already cracked by bigger neighborhood boys. Kids at school had forgotten their father, the girl, her mother, and the real man who took the baby. Leo hadn't. March came. His father began leaving the living room door open. April. He reclined on the patio chaise-longue, his bowl and cloths in his lap. May. The cats came back around, flicking their pointed white tails. Once Leo stood behind his father in the kitchen, startled to stillness at seeing him up and about, and watched as T.E. ransacked the drawers and, finding nothing, finally pressed his thumbnail to the paper to write what Leo later saw was TUNA.

On the last day of school in June, the boys came home to an empty house—his mother had taken a job at the town library after wages and IBEW Local 683 short-term disability ran out. They pushed through the front door and it was as though neither one of them had been aware it was summer again. That day, heat and sun made the world yellow. The cats nosed out of the bushes next door. Leo picked up a rock and aimed but it didn't hit either one. They walked Korressel to Lynch, Lynch to Prescott, Prescott to Dade. There was T.E., head on knees, sitting winded at the edge of somebody's yard.

"Dad," Jack called out and ran to him. Leo hung back.

T.E. looked up. He pointed to his chest, pointed to the road. His knot of a mouth nibbled at a gray cloth. He set it back down in the frosting bowl made luminous in afternoon sun. His breathing had calmed by now but he still didn't move. He seemed to be waiting for them to leave. Leo picked up a dusty piece of gravel broken away from the edge of the street. He fit it to the band of his slingshot and pulled the rubber taut.

"Jack," he said. "Watch this." And he aimed at a street-parked, brand new Buick LeSabre's hubcap and let go. The rock skidded beneath the car, and before picking up another, Leo turned back to look at his father, to be sure he was right: he could do anything.

T.E. swatted the air. He swatted and swatted, pointed to them and then the direction home. Go on, he wanted to scream. His chin dripped and the spit stung where he'd nicked himself trying to shave the deepest twist of skin beneath his lips. He held the dry cloth to his jaw. It was damp and sour smelling now because he'd been at this walk so long. The boys just stared at him. Jack's hands shrugged in his pockets. Leo had the look of a child wearing a grown man's shoes.

"*Unnnnhhh,*" came out of T.E., the monstrous sound he never believed was his own. It didn't sound like a deaf person or a moron—what it sounded like were these impersonated by someone fully normal.

He waved both of his arms now and Jack and Leo both took off running. Adrenaline lifted and carried his body. He walked and walked, dabbed the cloth to his chin, looked away when cars passed to save them the horror.

*

The damage that had been cut through T.E.'s neck held his head nearly in place. His eyes strained to follow the black wire strung pole to pole. He used to drive this road in his bucket truck. Its electric lines often failed. Something about the narrowing of Dade Avenue out far enough to where the asphalt changed to red dirt and rock. The newer lines always needed something. He and Will would have had to open and close switches, replace fuses, locate the source of the current's sag. He walked the stand of scrub pines that edged the yards.

Babies were always crying and there were always babies—though none cried now—but when he stood square at the gravel drive of a small, moss-stained clapboard house, he was certain he'd long ago worked in her yard along with the dark of night and only candles within the houses. He was certain he had heard the girl, the baby, crying long before that night.

He arched his spine backward to look at the sky. No sycamores, no poplar trees here, no spruces either. June sun beat the shingles so black they looked soft, molten. A car passed by and somewhere beyond a backyard, a screen door tapped shut in its frame three times. He knocked at the door.

Kay appeared, looking around his body to the other yards more than at him. She took his wrist, then the bowl and drying cloth, which he'd held with both hands.

You still wear sweaters, he wanted to say.

"I cannot help you." But she was drawing him in to the house.

She pushed aside a cheap empty dish meant maybe for candy, set down the bowl on the hall table, turned back to him and studied his face. She had never seen him like this. T.E. dabbed the drying cloth to his chin to catch the drool and cover the worst.

It's like a mouth full of dirt, he needed to say, like I have a mouthful of dirt.

"Please don't show me that again," she said.

It didn't matter that this was a mistake, a colossal mistake now; he was doing it. His head floated above them from the effort of his walk and her words. He seemed to watch his free hand pull her body to his, his free hand unzip his trousers, his free hand lift the heavy folds of her winter skirt and penetrate the shadows beneath the hang of her abdomen. Against the hall table, his bowl sloshing the inch of water that remained, Kay's eyes were shut.

Open them, please. Please open your eyes, he could not say.

So he pushed her, fell with her to the floor, one claw-foot of the table catching her button earring and tearing it free. He never knew her ears were pierced. He'd never seen that. Her ear bled and his prick went soft but he kept thrusting at her, until all it was was pelvic bone to pelvic bone and the abrasions of force.

She did not stop him. She did not try. She only cried, and that was a voice he knew, too: sorrow turned rage turned back to desperate grief. How many times had he been sick thinking about how long she'd lain there wanting to breathe right.

He'd walked in the house three minutes prior and now what he hoped was that their brief and last noise would bring someone. A neighbor, an aunt. The husband with a gun to shoot him, shoot him please. Another child with all her teeth unbroken.

But evening fell around them with moon and owls hooting. Kay still lay partially beneath him, though free enough she could move if she tried. T.E.'s penis hung out of his pants, no longer wet from Kay's body, just cold and obscene.

He sent his mind back up to the ceiling, to the sky now. Told it to travel Dade to Prescott, Prescott to Lynch, Lynch to Koressel. To leave the frosting bowl and Noemi's rags here. To slip back inside the house, his house, that kitchen. Let the drool pour from the twist of his face, let Leo turn bad with it, let Jack be the one soft now as dough. Let Noemi follow him upstairs and let him tell every single second of this past year to her through the pressing of his unclean skin to hers. Filth would be his words, the soil and leaf mold would be his tongue. And she, Noemi, would learn every word of its scream.

IN THE BAG

Christine Sneed

WHEN RAIN STARTED TO FALL, they were arguing, something they did often and inconclusively. Home was still two blocks away, and it had been Wes's idea to walk instead of drive to the burger place because his car needed gas but he hadn't felt like stopping for it. Wes was Wendy's older brother by twenty months, and he'd recently returned from a junior year abroad in Madrid, during which time she'd been living with their parents and commuting to a college ten miles away. Wes's university was in Madison, three hours north, where he had an academic scholarship that covered his tuition. Along with a second address, he'd acquired muscles and more self-confidence in college, and a different, giddy girl always seemed to be calling whenever he came home to mooch off of their parents (laundry, food, money, undeserved praise) for a weekend.

On four out of fourteen nights since his return from Spain, Wendy heard him sneaking in a girl through his bedroom window after their parents went to bed. He knew that Wendy knew too—her room was next to his on the first floor, their parents' on the second, and he'd threatened to tell them about the pot she kept in the decoy book (*Great Expectations*) on her bookshelf if she so much as hinted to them what he was doing with Sasha Phelps in his room until four or five in the morning.

When rain started to fall on their bare heads, Wendy was telling him that she didn't like being blackmailed, but he started to run toward home before abruptly stopping half a block later, she nearly bumping into him hard from behind.

"What's your problem?" she cried, the sudden sprint on a full stomach making her feel queasy.

He didn't answer. She bumped his shoulder as she stepped around him, seeing immediately why he'd stopped. Someone had dumped a green canvas bag onto the sidewalk, the kind taken to the beach or sometimes used as a book bag. Wes bent down to pick it up, pushing what looked like a small notebook and a pack of bubblegum back inside.

"Let me see," said Wendy, reaching for the bag.

Wes sidestepped her. "There's stuff in here that shouldn't get wet," he said, zipping it shut. "You can look when we get home."

"Is there a wallet in it? We should see if we can find an address."

"There's no wallet. I already thought of that, Wendell Wiener," he said, using his old nickname for her, one he'd shared with his cutest friends. He started jogging home again, something she had trouble believing wasn't making him sick. At lunch he'd eaten a huge serving of very greasy fries, ones he loved and ate so often whenever he was home that Wendy wondered if he was bulimic because he never seemed to gain an ounce. If she ate as few as four fries, the next day she felt bloated and only ate carrots and celery until she felt thin again. She envied her brother his metabolism, his out-of-state college and scholarship, his height, his popularity, his sex life, his apparent imperviousness to self-doubt, his year in Spain, his flat stomach, his ability to sleep late without guilt, his good grades, his bank account which somehow had $4,321 in it when, a few days earlier, she sneaked a look at his bank statement. She had no idea where he'd gotten so much money, unless their parents had given it to him, but she doubted this because their mother always made a point of saying that she and their father treated Wes and her equally. Even though this was a bald-faced lie, they weren't known for handing out large sums of money. Her brother, she assumed, had to be a drug dealer or a thief.

At home, he pretended to hand her the green bag but then snatched it back, raising the rain-spotted sack high over her head. She made leaping grabs for it, unable to stop herself, her brother laughing maniacally.

"I found it," Wes said. "Why do I have to let you look at it?"

"Let me see what's in the fucking bag," she yelled.

He kept holding it over her head, but after two more leaps, she stopped and went into her room, slamming the door behind her. No one, not even their mother, had the same ability to summon the angry, jealous child she'd often been while she and Wes were growing up. She could hear him on the other side of her door, dumping the bag's contents on the table in the next room, laughing as he called for her and told her to stop sulking. "I'll let you play with her lipstick if you come back out," he called. "I'll let you use her hairbrush and chew her gum."

"Fuck you," she said, but not loud enough for him to hear. She wished that he were still in Spain. She also wished that she'd taken the trip to Honduras with her spring quarter liberation theology class to build houses for the poor for a month. She could have had an adventure too if she'd really wanted one, but as the deadline for the trip registration approached, she watched it come and go, relieved when she no longer had to decide what to do.

She wasn't afraid of taking risks, not really, but she was unmotivated. And despite what Wes thought, she wasn't a virgin either, but it felt as if she might still be one. Her brother seemed destined to walk the earth as one of the sexually (and frequently) satisfied, but her own carnal experiences had so far been very limited and disappointing, nothing like the rapturous, lace-festooned interludes her two closest friends bragged about having with their boyfriends on many, many occasions. Wendy had had sex twice, both times with the same boy on the night of their senior prom, a fact that embarrassed as well as depressed her—this springtime dance having long been, to her mind, little more than an excuse for her classmates to rent hotel rooms meant for one couple, but into which they would squeeze four or five, where most of them would then drink themselves sick and have unsatisfying sexual encounters with dates they didn't care about, often within plain view of the other drunken couples.

Even now, after a whole year of college and its many opportunities for meeting men, she hadn't been able to find a boyfriend, let alone a second person she wanted to have sex with who also wanted to have sex with her, but her brother could appear at home after a year away and within five minutes arrange for a pretty girl to drive over to the house in the middle of the night and climb through his bedroom window until he forced her to slink back to her own house before dawn, where her parents were possibly listening for her return with fury and serious misgivings about her future prospects for self-respect and a long-term, monogamous relationship.

Why wasn't Wes the one going to the girl? Wendy wanted to know. Why was everything handed to him as if he were a fucking Saudi sheik? And where had he gotten all of that money? She had $285.76 in her bank account, a hundred dollars more than the previous month, but compared to what Wes was drawing from, her checking account was like a twelve-year-old's piggy bank, stuffed with old tooth-fairy and birthday money.

She was lying on her bed with a pillow half-covering her face when Wes knocked. "Hey," he said. "You've got to see this." His tone was conspiratorial, but she suspected that this was a ploy to lure her out for another round of pogo-sticking for the bag.

"No," she said, the pillow muffling her reply. She did want to know what he had found but continued to lie motionless on her bed.

"Wendell," he said. "Open up." He was directly outside her door now and began a frenzied knocking that he didn't stop until she got up and let him in.

She glared at him. "What do you want?"

He smiled, showing her the small gap between his front teeth. Her friends all had crushes on him, and with a painful, almost bodily distress, she understood why. He was the sort of boy who would never have looked twice at her if she hadn't been his sister, the sort whose beauty frightened her—his clear, suntanned skin, his full lips and green eyes and impressive muscles and sense of humor and seeming ability to have a good time anywhere, at a moment's notice. And now he spoke Spanish well too. He had seen parts of the world she hadn't seen and might never have the chance to. He, it seemed, had really lived.

And what did she have to show for herself? Zits, bloating, PMS, uncomfortable and hasty sex with Mike Plaski that didn't even lead to any more of the same, a pregnancy scare (completely paranoid and ridiculous, as it turned out), a solid B/B- average from ninth grade to the present, a depressing job as a cashier at CVS, eczema around her nose, a mild stammer when called on to speak publicly, size ten feet, an egg allergy, slightly bowed legs, and a hand-me-down VW that had backfired once in the high school parking lot, an event that she had not been allowed to forget for two solid years. She did have pretty, long blondish hair, decent tits, a cute, contagious laugh, and rent-free living (though she had to wash all of the dishes and dirty laundry the house generated, which was quite a lot for three people and now with Wes at home, it was almost absurd how much clothes-related filth and culinary disorder the four of them produced). She also had a crush on someone she had met in her composition and rhetoric class, a guy from Skokie, four miles from where she lived, named Elliot Wittke, who seemed to like her too though after three weeks, he had not yet tried to get her out of her clothes, and she was very tired of settling for awkward make-out sessions in his car, often parked in or near her parents' driveway. Just what kind of infernal bargain did a passably good-looking nineteen-year-old girl have to strike to get some sex?

"This chick wrote letters," said Wes, almost reverent. "They're totally crazy. I think we might need to send them to the guy she wrote them to." He waved three small pink envelopes in front of her face before handing them to her. She looked at the front of each one, seeing that they had all been addressed to the same recipient, Mr. Mitchell Coverly, his street address in a Wisconsin town neatly printed below his name. There was no return address on any of the envelopes and when Wendy unfolded the first letter and looked at the signature at the bottom of the second page, the letter-writer had only signed off with a cursive *B*, nothing else.

"Read them," said Wes, his eyes gleaming with what looked to her like prurient excitement.

"I will if you'd shut up," she said.

He went over to her bed and sat down. She glanced at him, feeling uneasy about him acting so casually in the place where she had both her most ungenerous and most pornographic thoughts. Once in a while she caught him looking at her breasts too, but she had a feeling that this was only a habit. Most guys she knew couldn't seem to keep their eyes on a girl's face for more than a few seconds before they checked out what was on offer below her neck.

B's handwriting was painstakingly neat, almost childlike in its uniform letters.

Saturday, June 11
Dear Mitch,
I thought you might have called me back by now, especially after my last message, but it's pretty clear that you're not going to. So, here's a letter, one that your new girlfriend might intercept if she's living with you now, which I bet she is. I hope she opens it and sees what an asshole you are if she hasn't already figured it out.

Last week, I was still pregnant. This week I'm not. It could only have been yours because you're the only guy I've been with in two years. I never lied about that. But you'll probably be happy to know that I had an abortion.

Here, Wendy looked up at Wes who was giving her a maniacal smile. "I told you it's some crazy shit," he said.

"I feel bad for her."

"Maybe it's all fake," he said, but he didn't sound convinced.

She shook her head. "It could be, but I bet it isn't."

Please call me as soon as you get this letter. I'm not going to try to make you pay for it or anything, I just really want to talk to you. I thought you would want to know about all of this. I would if I were you.
Yours, B

Wendy opened the other two letters and saw that one had been written before June 11, the other a few days after.

Sunday, June 5
Dear Mitch,

I really need to talk to you. I knew about a month ago that I was pregnant, but I could only tell your voicemail when I found out because I think you were up in Canada already and your cell was always off. When you came down from the mountain or got out of the woods, whatever it is you were doing, you probably just hit delete as soon as you heard my voice, not even bothering to listen to my messages.

I don't know if I want to keep it or not, but it would really help me to talk to you. I won't make you marry me or anything like that, but if I did have her (or him), I'd be willing to share custody and you could be in her (or his) life as much as you wanted (or as little).

Carla says I should have an abortion because it's too hard to raise a child on my own, and I did make an appointment. It's two days from now. Sage says I should have the baby but give her (or him) up for adoption. I know that you'd want me to get rid of it. I had a dream last night that you were here at my house (you were wearing a White Sox hat, which was weird because I know you like the Brewers) and you said that you didn't want a baby with me. I woke up feeling like shit.
—B

"Damn, that's harsh." Wendy's throat threatened to close over. She cleared it forcefully, not wanting Wes to hear a catch in her voice.

"Yeah, it is."

"I hope you're using condoms," she said, not meeting his eyes.

He snorted. "Of course I am. I'm not an idiot."

Wendy looked over at him for a second. "Even if they say they're on the pill, use a condom. You never know."

A tremor of unease passed over his suntanned face. "Yeah, of course. You don't have to tell me."

She had never before spoken so frankly with him about his sex life, at least not in this way—as if they were adults, sensibly discussing the possibilities and problems they might encounter. Maybe he had even gotten a girl pregnant, and she had decided to have an abortion, or maybe he had a friend who had. If she and Wes had had a different kind of relationship, she would have asked him. As it was, with their teenage years filled with so much aggressive teasing, they did not ask each other those kinds of questions, or if they did, they rarely ever answered them, responding instead with "Why should I tell you?" or "Fuck off, retard."

The third letter had as much bad news as the other two:

Tuesday, June 14
Dear Mitch,

I don't think I should have gone through with it. I can't sleep now and I can't stop thinking about what it was like to be in that room with that suction hose thing and really bright lights. Even if my parents would probably have disowned me if they'd found out I was pregnant (it doesn't matter that I've been out of high school for three years now—it's still wrong, in their eyes, to have sex before marriage, let alone get knocked up by someone who lives in another state and always made you pay for the gas when he was coming down to see you), I feel like I should have kept the baby. Carla says I should see a therapist because a lot of women need to after they go through with it and that's what they told me at the clinic too but what could I say to a shrink besides that I regret it? And what would the shrink say besides, "Well, you have to stop living in the past. That day isn't coming back." I guess I'm doing that anyway (living in the past) by writing these letters to you, ones I don't even have the guts to send. But maybe I will find the guts before too long.

I miss you, even if you were a complete prick to me sometimes. Sorry if that seems mean, but you were. I was so nuts about you. I would have done anything to be with you.

—B

"She must live around here," Wendy said quietly. "I think we should put up signs in the neighborhood saying that we found a green purse. Maybe she'll see one and call us."

Wes looked skeptical. "We'll just get a bunch of nutcases or con artists calling us if we do that."

"How else are we supposed to find her?"

He was cracking the knuckles in his right hand, something Wendy hated, but she did it too when she was anxious. "We could call that Mitch guy," he said.

"What?" she said, alarmed. "No, no way. I really doubt that he'd even care, and it's also pretty obvious that B. has mixed feelings about telling him she had an abortion."

"We wouldn't have to tell him about the letters. We could just say that we found the bag and his address was in it and we wondered if he knew where the owner lived."

"I don't think we should get him involved."

"It's my decision," said Wes. "Technically, I'm the one who found the bag."

She exhaled angrily. "Fine," she said, tossing the letters at him. "Do whatever you want. You can get out of my room now too."

He smiled at her but didn't move from the bed. "I'm not saying that I'm going to call him. It's just an idea."

"I want to look through the bag and see if there's anything you missed that might help us find her."

"All right, Wendell. Go ahead and look. It's in the living room, but you're not going to find anything."

It took her about five seconds to see that he was right. There was nothing in the bag but a travel-size package of Kleenex, a small cosmetic case, a pack of grape Bubble Yum, a hairbrush, a few stray pens from the now-defunct LaSalle Bank, and a red, child-sized memo pad, the kind Wendy had carried in grade school, into which she had dutifully copied her homework assignments. Inside the notebook were a number of sentences, written and rewritten, from the letters that she and Wes had just read. The bag had probably been stolen from B, and the thief had removed her wallet and cell phone before dumping it unceremoniously on the sidewalk.

"I'm going to try to get a hold of Mr. Mitchell Coverly," said Wes. "Just to see what happens."

"Wait until I get back from work before you call him if you find a number," she said. In fifteen minutes, she was supposed to start her shift at the CVS store a mile away, the same store she had worked in since her junior year of high school. She wished that she had the nerve to call in sick, but she had already called in twice in the past month. If she kept it up, Bob, the day manager, might have to fire her, even if he was a nice enough person, and she had babysat for his two children a few times, ones his wife had left him with the previous year after she fell for a blackjack dealer in Las Vegas, a man she met while she and Bob were on vacation, celebrating their ten-year wedding anniversary.

"I'm going to Google him," said Wes. "I bet he's a deadbeat. Maybe he even has a prison record."

"You can find that out on Google?"

He laughed. "Of course. You can find out whatever you want. What century have you been living in?"

"You need to get out of my room now," she said. "I have to change for work."

"I'd go with your little black dress and spike heels," he said, finally getting up from the bed. "You'll make killer tips."

"Ha ha, you're not funny," she said, shutting the door behind him.

"What?" he said through the closed door. "Don't they give you tips at CVS?"

At work, ringing up the purchases of the exhausted mothers who came in to buy milk and cigarettes and king-size candy bars, and the garrulous vagrants who used handfuls of nickels and dimes to buy one-liter bottles of cheap beer while telling her the jokes they had just heard (*Why was the blonde staring at the orange juice container? Because it said "Concentrate"*), she wondered why she cared so much about what happened to B. As Wes had briefly wondered, it might all have been an elaborate ruse, a way of getting attention from strangers; maybe it was even performance art, B. doing a whole series of green bag drop-offs in various neighborhoods around Chicago and its suburbs, waiting to see to what lengths people would go to find her or Mitchell Coverly.

But Wendy felt almost certain, as Wes also seemed to, that B's was real distress, and twice she checked her cell phone to see if her brother had sent a text to tell her what he had found online about Mitchell Coverly. There was no message either time, and when she called him during her break a little before five, the call went directly to voicemail, which meant that his phone was off or else he was on the other line. The latter was much more likely because as far as she knew, he never turned his phone off. She hoped he wasn't on the line calling Mitch without her there to listen.

When her shift finally ended at eight p.m., she knew there was a good chance that Wes had gone out for the night, but to her surprise, his car was still in the driveway. Their mother's car was in the garage but their father's was missing, and she remembered then that her mother had told her before leaving for work that they had tickets to a play in the city and would not be home until late. Would she make sure to wash the tablecloth in the dining room and throw in the napkins too? It had been at least a month since she had washed them, and, wrinkling her nose, her mother had added, "They're so grungy. I can't believe that one of us didn't notice this sooner."

This meant that her mother couldn't believe that Wendy hadn't noticed the grungy linens sooner, not herself or Mr. Rudolph, who rarely noticed anything inside the house because his attention was focused so strenuously outward—on the hospital where he was a radiologist and on the house's exterior—the gutters that needed cleaning and the grass that needed to be mowed so often, which, thankfully, Wendy did not have to do. Her parents hired landscapers for that, even in the summer when Wes was home, because after he left for college, he had tacitly been absolved, it seemed, of all household chores, into perpetuity.

Her brother was in the living room when she walked into the house, watching a show with three big-breasted women in pink-and-white bikinis who were giggling and jumping up and down on a trampoline, their breasts bouncing in a way that looked very painful.

"Nice show," she said.

"I knew you'd think so too," he said, not turning to look at her. "Spike TV rocks."

"Yeah, that's what every thirteen-year-old boy says."

"Really? Wow, then I'm in good company."

"What did you find out about Mitch?" she said. "Why didn't you call me back?"

"You were at work," he said, his eyes still on the girls. He was slouched low on the sofa, one hand, its nails in need of clipping, resting on his thigh; his other hand dangled over the sofa's armrest. The room smelled a little like cigarettes, but she had never known Wes to smoke. She wondered if it was a habit he had imported from Spain, along with the Spanish lace he had given their mother and the chocolates he had bought for her and their father.

"So? You could have left me a message."

"I knew you'd be home later."

"God, you're such a jerk."

He had finally turned around and was gazing at her now, his expression mild. "You should figure out how to control your temper. Few things are so important that you need to get pissed off about them."

She stared at him, incredulous. "Since when did you become Dr. Phil's apostle?"

He ignored this. "Our friend Mitchell Coverly works for a company like Outward Bound. It's called Northern Horizons or something like that. He's on Facebook too. I sent him a friend request and he already accepted it."

"He did? He doesn't know you."

"So? Not like that matters to most people. I looked at his pictures and some of his wall posts. What a loser. He's wearing this yellow bandana in most of the pictures, and he's got on tube socks that are pulled up to his knees in two or three of them too. It didn't look like he meant it as a joke either."

"Did you find a phone number for him?"

"Yep."

She sat down on the other end of the sofa and tried not to look at the TV. The giggling was reaching a fever pitch now, an announcer saying, *Guys, it doesn't get any better than this. Believe you me.* "You didn't call him, did you?" she said.

He hesitated, baring his teeth in a sinister smile. "Maybe I did."

"I hope you're kidding."

"He's got a new girlfriend. B. was right."

"You talked to him?"

"No, it's on Facebook. She's posted a million stupid little notes on his wall and it says that he's in a relationship with her."

"What's her name?"

"I don't know. Lisa something."

"How old is he?"

He sighed, impatient. "Why don't you go look? His page is open on my laptop."

"You didn't really call him, did you?"

"Yes I did, but he hung up on me when I asked if he knew a girl whose name started with B."

She stared at him. "No way. What an asshole."

He nodded. "For all we know, she was stalking him."

"I doubt it."

"I do too," he said, switching the channel to the Cartoon Network where two dogs in berets were sword-fighting. "Enough with the hos in bikinis for now."

"Wes, don't say things like that."

"Why shouldn't I? They're probably getting paid a ton to be on that show. They're celebrating their inner hos. That's what one of them actually said. They just want to be famous like all the other hos, and if they have to bounce around in bikinis in front of a huge audience of drunk frat boys to get there, they're going to do it."

There were so many things wrong with what he had just said, things that with his allegedly high IQ he had to know were wrong, things that Wendy had learned about the previous fall in her women's studies class, called The F Word: Feminism Today, but she didn't feel like arguing with him about this depressingly omnipresent misogyny, not right then. For one, he would win because he would either outyell her or else, maddeningly, outmaneuver her argument.

Mitchell Coverly's Facebook page was as Wes had said—his girlfriend, Lisa Bittford, had papered his wall with dopey little notes about how great it was to do a *Mad Men* marathon with him and how cute he was when he said the word "nuclear," just like George W. Bush said it. She knew he was a Democrat but she could forgive him for that ;). Hee hee!

God, they're both such *tools*, Wendy thought. Poor B. How would she ever recover from the abortion if she didn't at least get to talk to Mitch and tell him exactly where to stick it? And to see herself replaced by an idiot-loser like Lisa Bittford! It was almost too much to bear.

"Give me his number," said Wendy. "I'm going to call him."

Wes regarded her. "I thought you wanted to leave him out of this."

"I've changed my mind," she said, heart pounding itself bloody in the center of her slightly overweight body (seven pounds, which was not the end of the world, but she wanted to weigh 125, not 132). She clicked over to Mitchell's Facebook profile and found his phone number, two numbers, in fact—one a landline, probably, the other his cell. She didn't need Wes after all. "You and he have birthdays that are only two days apart," she said, this coincidence for some reason strengthening her resolve.

"So? What are you trying to say?"

"Nothing."

"Are you saying that he and I are alike because we share the same astrological sign?"

"No, I'm not saying that," she said huffily. "I'm just noticing a detail I thought you might find interesting."

But his assumption was right. For such a self-absorbed jerk, his perceptiveness often made her pause.

She went into her room and dialed Mitchell Coverly's number, the landline, she guessed. Dialing his cell phone seemed too brazen. She promptly realized her mistake, however: a girl with a raspy voice answered and Wendy hung up, heart pounding in her ears. A few seconds later, her own phone rang. The girl was calling her back, charging at her through the phone lines like an enraged bull.

"What?" said Wendy, her own surliness delighting her. She

wondered for a second if she should think about becoming a bounty hunter or a cop instead of wasting her time on communications courses with the vague hope of someday earning a living in radio or television.

"Who is this? Is that you, Betsy?" the girl rasped. "Stop fucking call here, or I'm going to go down there and beat your ass."

"Who's Betsy?" said Wendy.

"Fuck off." The girl hung up.

"I know B's name now," Wendy called to her brother down the hall. "It's Betsy."

"Alert the media," he said.

She went back into the living room and glared at him. "You don't care about her or the letters anymore?"

"I didn't say that, but I was thinking that your first impulse is probably the right one. We should back off. Your pal Betsy can write her asshole ex more letters that she won't send to him. Or maybe she will. Whatever she does, it's pretty obvious that Mitch and his new girlfriend don't want to hear from her or anyone who might be calling for her." He paused, changing the channel again, this time to *The Price Is Right*, one of Wendy's favorite shows. "Don't you have other things to worry about? What about that guy Herbert? Isn't he enough to keep you occupied when you're not making your tips at CVS?"

"His name is Elliot," she said. "Fuck off."

"I will," said Wes, laughing a little. "Just give me a few more hours and I will fuck right off."

"Why don't you have a job?" she snapped. "How did you get so much money? Are you dealing pot?"

He stared at her, nonplussed. "What are you talking about?"

"I saw your bank statement when I was getting the dirty clothes from your room the other day. How did you get four thousand dollars?"

He blinked. "What are you doing snooping in my room?"

"The bank statement was lying on the floor next to your shorts. I wasn't trying to look at it. It was just there."

He snorted. "Whatever. It's my scholarship money. I didn't have to pay tuition to study in Spain, so UW cut me a check for what I would have gotten if I'd stayed here for the year. It's what I lived on when I was in Madrid."

"Yeah, right," she said, feeling cheated.

"I'm not lying, Wendy. But think whatever you want."

She had really hoped that he was doing something wrong, tarnishing his stupid, golden-boy image. And why hadn't he given any portion of his free thousands to her? Or rather, why hadn't their parents made him give some of this money to her? Why should she have to work at a shitty job all summer and all during the school year and do housework that never stopped and pay for her own books and car maintenance and insurance when all her parents had to pay for was her tuition? They had plenty of money but were such tightwads! Her father was a doctor and her mother sold commercial real estate but they were still too fucking cheap to hire someone to do their laundry and clean the house, which meant that Wendy had to toil away like an indentured servant and also sell cigarettes and malt liquor to homeless guys all day, ones who reeked of B.O. and onions and leered at her tits while her brother got to sit around in his apartment in Madison watching idiotic shows on cable with his roommates and drinking beer and having sex with trampy girls 24/7.

Her life sucked.

(*What's a Jewish American princess's favorite wine? I want to go to Miami.*)

But then she remembered poor B., someone whose life actually did suck.

Provoked by the thought of this wretched girl's problems, she dialed Mitchell Coverly's cell phone. Her call went straight to voicemail, but she didn't leave a message. She tried him again three more times before she went to bed. His phone rang the second time, but no one picked up, and the other two times her calls again went directly to voicemail. Not long after her last attempt, she heard Sasha arrive at her brother's bedroom window, her soft knock followed by muffled laughter as Wes hoisted her up. Wendy buried her face in her pillow and screamed, but it didn't make her feel any better. Elliot was such a schmuck, such a boring kisser and tentative groper, so lame with his choices for their dates too—a movie, a round of mini-golf, a movie again followed by gyros at a cheap place that she never went to because it gave her indigestion. He hadn't even thought to take her downtown to the Hard Rock Café or to the Rock-and-Roll McDonald's on Clark Street, which the two boys she had dated in high school had at least taken her to once or twice. She had to find a way to meet a more interesting guy who wanted to have sex with her, ideally several times a week, and in his own apartment that she might eventually be invited to move into. She had grown up hearing from all corners that boys were sex maniacs and should be approached with caution, as if one were approaching an amorous stallion, but so far her experiences had made her think that the opposite was true.

A thump—Wes's bed frame hitting the wall—made her scream again, this time the pillow not fully absorbing it. The rustling sounds in the next room stopped for a few seconds before resuming.

She got up from the bed, dressed hastily in her running clothes, gathered her purse and phone, and went out to her car. Her parents had returned an hour earlier but she had been sequestered in her room, trying to read a book and intermittently playing online Scrabble, and did not go out to greet to them. They had knocked on her door and Wes's and said goodnight, both she and her brother answering without opening their doors, something they had only been allowed to get away with since starting college.

All of the lights in the house were out, except for the low-wattage one over the stove, the kitchen looking like the scene of recent domestic unrest. Wendy had not put hers or Wes's dinner dishes into the dishwasher and he appeared to have come out later and made himself a bowl of cereal—both the Cheerios box and his dirty bowl sat on the countertop, a few loose Os strewn beside it. What a goddamn slob, she thought, a sense of injustice, her most faithful companion, making her stomach contract with bitterness.

She had B's letters with her but had already memorized Mitchell Coverly's address, and from the two times she had been up to the Wisconsin State Fair during high school, she knew where West Allis was. Her iPhone, purchased the previous winter on credit, helped her find the exact location of his house within an hour and a half of her flight from her horny brother and oblivious parents. The house was a brick duplex and no lights were on over the front doors or in any of the windows. She pulled up in front and looked at B's letters in the glow from the streetlamps. It was 1:45 in the morning on a Wednesday night in mid-June, and she had driven across the state line to confront a stranger whom her sixth sense told her was a jackass, one whom the mysterious B was well rid of, even if B didn't quite believe this to be true. There was also the chance that B had concocted the entire abortion scenario simply to get attention, and that she had been bothering Mitchell and his new girlfriend for months, whittling their tolerance for her bad behavior down to zero.

Wendy had no proof of anything, and certainly no good reason or the authority to insinuate herself into this stranger's dramatic mess, whatever its true dimensions were. Looking at the dark façade of Mitchell Coverly's house, Wendy felt the deadening heft of her vanity and loneliness and desire for romantic upheaval. Her brother would never have done what she had done, would never have fled across state lines at midnight, headlong toward the uncertain burden of someone else's problems. He lived his own life in the rooms and cities where he had found a way to belong; he did what he could to find pleasure and joy there too, and did not, as far as Wendy knew, look upon anyone else's good fortune as a cruel and personal shortchange. The other day he had even said to her, "When are you going to get over yourself and stop thinking that everything that happens has something to do with you?"

She knew that he was right. So very little had anything at all to do with her or with anyone else. It was hard to accept this fact, but her brother appeared to be able to. Her brother was almost admirable if she could manage for a minute to see him in this light, if she could forgive him for everything that he seemed to have that she did not.

THE LOST CAVES OF ST. LOUIS

Anne Valente

You were two, always—twinned in heart and lung, bone and soft baby belly, two halves of the same whole as your mother always told you. She'd rest your heads upon her lap and tell you, *here—you both began here.* Two worlds split from a single cell, your world and then hers, and then a world that became both yours and hers.

A world of paper fortunes. The game of Monopoly. A tire swinging from an oak tree. Your yard in summer beneath a sweltering Midwestern sun and a sprinkler, your bare toes splashing mud puddles, your skin beaded with water. Blanket forts and flashlights. Ice cream floats, the taste of artificial grape. Counting to ten, hide and seek, your sister burrowing into the smallest spaces of the house. And the game of cat's cradle, the slimness of her fingers sliding through yarn—cat's cradle is what you remember most, the loops and the boxes, the way the string bound tight across her wrists.

You are in fifth grade. You are learning the solar system in science class, and in art, how to paint a silhouette. In social studies, Mr. Kottleman begins the year-long unit on Missouri, a local history you must learn before you take on every other state. Mr. Kottleman is balding, his wisped hair graying at the temples. A sheen of sweat glares from the receding line of his hair as he begins with the most local of histories, the history of St. Louis. When he says the word, *St. Louis*, he wipes the back of his hand across his forehead. It is a word you hold close as kin, the only city you've ever known. Its landscape is a map of your heart, every weeping willow and shaded oak, every degree of the heat index, every percentage of swelled humidity. You think you know everything about your birthplace until Mr. Kottleman introduces his first lesson, a local history you've never heard: a series of caves latticing the underbelly of St. Louis, the lost caves of this city.

There is a complex network of natural caves beneath our town, he says. Beneath every street, every apartment building, every monument.

He tells you that no other city in the world contains such an intricate system beneath it. He tells you the caves existed long before the city grew above ground. His face reddens as he discusses the early use of the caves, natural cooling and storage for St. Louis's beer industry. He coughs and looks out over the class. He moves on from beer to the Underground Railroad, how the caves were rumored to serve moving populations, and as he speaks you look down at your feet, sneakers resting against the carpet underneath your desk. You wonder what lies beneath them, whether the caves stretch far enough below the city to pool into the suburbs and unfurl beneath Brookdale Elementary. You imagine a gaping hole underneath you, underneath every single one of you. As Mr. Kottleman speaks you wonder how solid a foundation is, how solid it ever could have been with the caves snaking beneath you while you slept and while you walked to school, caves that had always been there without your knowledge, caves that cast the surface in a false certainty while they waited silent and dark underground.

Lauren Doherty is having a sleepover. The invitation is in your mailbox when you arrive home from school, a birthday party and back-to-school gathering, an event that your mother gently says would be good for you to attend when you show her the invitation over chicken breasts and canned peas.

You have not been to any parties since the summer. The invitation is addressed only to you. You turn the envelope in your hands after your parents go to sleep, after the lights of the house have gone out and you lay in bed, restless. You climb to the window.

Your name looks naked on the envelope without hers. Your name is trapped in the throats of every teacher in your school, every teacher accustomed to calling both of your names from the classroom roster, every teacher still stunned by what the summer stole away.

Her bedroom door is closed. Nothing has been removed; your parents still hold out hope. You look out the window and watch the first of fall's leaves swirl to the ground and settle inside a lone circle of light pooling from a streetlamp.

In art class, Mrs. Barnes sketches your silhouette. She places you on a stool against the chalkboard and tapes white paper behind you, then she shines an enormous light upon you, one large enough to cast your shape in shadow. The class waits their turn as Mrs. Barnes approaches the white paper and drags a pencil along the outline of your face. She is so close that you breathe her in, the scent of stale perfume and apples and faint perspiration, her arms raised over you to draw.

You take the finished silhouette back to your desk. You begin to shade in your face. Your nose was always more blunt but your mouth and chin are the same shape as hers. You pull your pencil across the stenciled lips and feel your breath catch in the core of your throat.

In science, Mrs. Jones dims the lights and shows the class a videotape on the Milky Way, the Earth's galaxy. She explains dwarf stars and red giants as they flash across the screen, then a simulated image of a black hole appears and she squints into the darkened classroom. She explains that black holes are centers of gravity so strong that nothing escapes. She explains that event horizons are the edges of black holes, the point where nothing that goes can return.

You know black holes. You know how deceptive Midwestern sun can be. You know that even with a bright disc burning high overhead, scalding the surface of your skin, the summer closed in upon itself and grew darker than night. You know a truth beyond swimming pools, beyond hopscotch and sno-cones. You know that so much light creates shadows, what hides in sweltering shade.

You know that your sister rode her bike around your neighborhood as the June sun sank to dusk. You know that she never came home. You know that police searched for days that became weeks, then weeks that have become months. You know that only her bike was found in the grass alongside one Keds shoe and a severed piece of rope.

You have the same pair of shoes, hidden now in your closet, the gift you both received for your tenth birthday. You've never again worn the shoes but the rope is what you fixate upon, a rope with no connection to your family or your neighborhood. A rope with no clues, no saliva, no skin and no blood. A rope you imagine binding tightly around your sister's hands and feet on nights when you can't sleep, though you can imagine nothing and no one beyond this.

Mrs. Jones narrates the video's slideshow of constellations. You look up and April Wexner is watching you. April is new this year, a girl you've only spoken to in class groups, a girl with hair dyed Kool-Aid red. She sits next to you, slumped in her seat. Her eyes take you in. You look away but not before you spot small cuts on her arms, cuts as faint as stars, cuts that she hides with the sleeves of her sweatshirt when she sees that you have noticed.

Your father sits in his armchair most nights, reading the newspaper and old issues of *National Geographic*. He keeps a cellar full of issues dating back to the early 1930s, a collection that he once enlisted the two of you to flesh out, telling you to keep your eyes peeled at garage and estate sales. He once set you both on his lap when you were small enough and showed you photos of Asian elephants and space probes and lost civilizations, your heads resting against his chest, so close you heard the thrum of his heart. He built the tire swing in the backyard and set up the sprinkler every summer, and there are blueprints for a treehouse in the garage, you know. You found them in August when you were searching for a flashlight to keep in your room at night, a small light to destroy the dark. They were hidden in a bin, blueprints that looked dusty and unfinished, and you ran your hands over your father's block script before settling the pages back and closing the lid.

Your mother has grown nervous while your father drifts away. Your mother gave you a personal alarm, mace spray, a fake ring of keys to throw, all hidden inside your backpack. Your father works late and barely looks at you. After dinner, your father reads and your mother sits on the couch watching television. The sound fills the living room and seeps into the empty cracks of the house, the cabinets and crawl spaces your sister always found during hide and seek. Your father doesn't look up when a laugh track reverberates through the room. You inch from the couch into his lap, too big, and nestle against his chest like you both used to do.

You tell him about the caves, what Mr. Kottleman told you. You ask why he never told you about them, if he knew they existed.

He pulls his reading glasses from his face. His eyes look tired.

I think I heard about them once, he says. He pinches the bridge of his nose. Then he slides you from his lap to the ground and moves down the hallway to their bedroom, closing the door behind him.

Mr. Kottleman moves on to the 1904 World's Fair, the next phase of St. Louis history. He discusses the remnants of the fair, the Palace of Fine Art that became the city's art museum, the enormous flight cage that became the aviary of the St. Louis Zoo. He begins to discuss the foods that the fair introduced and your gaze drifts to the window. You know the flight cage well, where a spoonbill once snapped at your sister's legs. Your parents had whisked you both to the children's zoo, where you could pet guinea pigs and rabbits, leaving the aviary behind though the spoonbill's hue still burned in your memory, bright pink.

You approach Mr. Kottleman after class, when everyone else has gone to lunch. He sits at his desk cleaning overhead slides and you stand patiently until he notices you.

I want to know more about the caves, you say. Tell me more about the caves.

There is something sympathetic in his gaze, a faint yet unmistakable flicker. He hesitates, watching you the same way every other teacher has been watching you, then he opens a drawer and slides a book across the surface of his desk, *The Lost Caves of St. Louis*. The book jacket is worn, the edges tattered. You can borrow it, he says, so long as you bring it back. Then he pulls a paper lunch bag from his desk and sends you off to the cafeteria, the book gripped firmly in your hands.

You hide it at the bottom of your backpack through the day and through the entirety of dinner. Though the book isn't a secret, you feel the need to hide it. Your mother asks how your day was and you tell her your silhouette is nearly finished. You don't mention the book or the fact that the closer the silhouette comes to complete, the more it looks like your sister's face and not yours.

After you close your bedroom door, after you hear your parents watch television for a while longer then close their own door, you pull the book from your backpack and curl into the window. Your hands smooth the pages. The book smells of mildew, of some other time. You turn the pages and learn that the major breweries of St. Louis were built deliberately above caves, that the Lemp Brewery and Anheuser-Busch each had their own natural cellar. You learn that the caves were used as storage for arms and ammunition during the Civil War. You learn that the caves were turned briefly into a tourist attraction and you think of Meramec Caverns, where your parents took you and your sister last year, where you pocketed fool's gold and found the ghost of Jesse James.

You learn the coordinates of entrances to the caves, street intersections sprinkled throughout the city that concealed their mouths. You learn that the entrances were eventually filled with rubble and sealed. You also learn that the caves still exist, that they are navigable by those who know them. You put the book down and watch the street beyond your window, the stilled silence, what lies beneath it.

*

After the police came, after your parents and neighbors searched the streets for your sister, after nothing was found and the alert went out, an investigator took a sample of your blood. She took you away from your parents at the police station into a special room filled with sterile needles and glass jars. She slid a needle into your arm and you watched the vial fill. She told you to look away. She told you that your blood would help them, that your blood was the same as her blood, that your DNA would diverge as you grew but for now, as her twin, was a near match.

She measured your height and your weight. She noted the color of your eyes, the shade of your hair. But when you offered her your hands, anything to find her, the investigator shook her head and her eyes slide away from your gaze.

Your fingerprints are different, she said. They're the only thing that separates you from your sister.

You hold her words close, even still, a talisman when you imagine your sister. You imagine her elsewhere, some elsewhere without any definition but this: that if the complicated patterns of your fingertips are the only piece that breaks her from you then she must be close, so close, a candle in the dark.

On the playground during recess, you sit on a swing alone when Lauren Doherty approaches you. You look up and the September sun radiates behind her, casting her blonde hair in a halo of honeyed light.

She asks if you are coming to her party, a response you still haven't sent. The invitation is pinned beneath a magnet to the center of your fridge, an invitation you see every morning when you pull the milk from the refrigerator door. Your mother handed you the RSVP card and told you to take it to the mailbox, the *yes* checked, but you've kept it beneath your pillow, wearing the edges down with tips of your fingers when you can't sleep.

You squint up at Lauren, a friend to both of you but always closer to your sister. You tell her you will be there. You tell her you can't wait. When she smiles and runs back to the foursquare box where other girls are waiting, Michelle Cohen waves to you from the grid, motions for you to join them. You shake your head and move away from the swings, the rubber burning your thighs, suddenly blistering beneath sun. You climb into the tube slide where the light is muted, a pink glow that surrounds you in plastic heat.

After school, you stand in line waiting for your yellow bus to arrive. You live close enough that you have always walked home, but your mother has made arrangements for you to ride the bus since the new school year began. Your backpack is heavy upon your shoulders. You pull the book from your bag and begin to read more. You learn that explorers have found bones in the caves, bones belonging to rare and extinct animals that were never native to this land. You close your eyes and imagine large bears, strange platypuses, creatures you'd never dream living among the squirrels and rabbits of St. Louis. You turn the page and find photos of human remains as well. You learn that the caves were a hideout, that settlers and outlaws sought refuge and never reemerged. You learn that for years the caves emitted strange sounds long after anyone could have lived within them, human sounds of crying and soft speaking, echoes beyond the natural resonance of an underground world.

A breeze lifts from the trees and billows across the sweat of your skin. Despite the heat and the straining sun, your arms ripple with gooseflesh. You close the book and April Wexner is standing before you, watching you stand in the wind.

She asks what you're reading and your cheeks flush with the sun's heat. You slide the book into your backpack and rip the zipper closed. But her face remains open. Her face is a blank page. You shrug your shoulders and mumble *nothing* just as your bus pulls up. As the brakes hiss to a stop, April asks if you want to come over.

You know you should board the bus. Your mother will expect you. But April is a planet on the school sidewalk, emitting a gravity that pulls you into her small orbit. You nod and she smiles, her mouth pale next to her fire-red hair. You hoist your backpack to climb onto her bus but she leads you away on foot, toward your own neighborhood, a short walk that takes you only three streets away from your own house.

April takes the shortcut through the churchyard across the street from Brookdale Elementary, a path your sister always avoided, her skin blistering to red welts every time her legs brushed past poison ivy. You were never allergic, but once, you covered your legs in calamine lotion too to know what she felt, to let the pink encrust your skin.

April leads you to the front door of her house, a small ranch with a carport. She guides you to the kitchen, pours you a glass of lemonade. No one is home. She watches as you drink and for a moment you wish you hadn't come, the silence between you pushing against your ribs and robbing the air from the room.

Want to see something? she asks. When you nod, she leads you through a sliding glass door to her backyard. She walks down a steep hill to the edge of the yard where a stretch of woods begins, a dense patch that fills the center of your neighborhood.

She points to a spot on the ground where the grass hasn't grown.

We buried my turtle there last month, she says. He died after we moved.

You ask what happened, though you don't want to know. You want to kneel down instead. You want to run your hands across the earth.

April tells you old age, words that spread a wash of relief. You feel her watching you as she speaks, and when you meet her gaze she asks again what you were reading.

You tell her about the caves. You tell her Mr. Kottleman loaned you the book after the discussion in class. April nods. She looks away from the ground. Then she begins to walk into the woods, her steps so deliberate that you follow her.

You push the honeysuckle aside, the tangles of milkweed and bramble that slide against your face as you follow her deeper into the woods. Your shoes sink into the soft mulch, a forest floor of decomposed leaves under a lack of sun. April leads you further down the hill, deeper into the brush, until she arrives at a ravine and stops.

She looks back at you. There is a cave down there, she says. A husk of a helicopter seed clings to her hair. You focus on the bright red of her strands, how they seem to swallow the husk, and you know then that she already knew what you were reading before she asked you here.

I found it this summer, she says. I come down here when I want to be alone.

Your eyes slip to her wrists, covered even in this heat by her long sleeves. You ask *why* before you can stop yourself, before you realize there are so many reasons why she might want to be alone. But her face is calm, as if there is nothing you can't ask. She tells you something happened to her last year. She tells you this is why her family moved here.

You stand next to her. You hear her breathe in the heat. You know there are things beyond naming, things past the realm of words to speak them. Things that prevent you from asking.

I know about your sister, she says.

You look up and her eyes flame through you.

They were searching for her when we moved here, she says.

You think of the police, the signs your parents posted, the neighbors fanning out through the trees and the woods. You think of what everyone must know, what you thought was your own private ache.

It's OK, April says. You can talk about it with me.

But you don't want to talk. Your feet move. They approach the ravine and slide down through moss and dirt until they catch on the lip of the cave, a cave you never knew existed. A small cave, not the deep cavern you imagined but big enough for you to stand, a cave hidden inside a neighborhood you've always known. You stop before its gaping mouth and hear the soft rhythm of your heart in your chest.

Go ahead, April says. You can go inside.

But you don't want to go inside. You don't want to move. You only want to scream your voice into the darkness, a voice no could tell apart from hers. You want to call into the cave and hear her voice bounce back to you. *Hello, hello, hello.*

When you walk home from April's house, the sun beginning to sink behind the trees, a police car sits in your driveway and for a moment you are sure she's been found. But your mother runs from the house, her face tear-stained and tight, and she grabs you and screams *where were you* and you know then that the officer standing behind her with his arms crossed against his chest was called for you and not for her.

At dinner, your mother barely looks up from her pork steak and creamed corn. Your father's eyes move between you and your mother before he says quietly, *don't do that again.* He focuses on his plate, as if what he's said is law. You tell them nothing of the cave, only that you made a new friend, that this is where you were. You tell them she lives down the street and your mother's eyes fill on a forced smile, then she blinks and disappears into the kitchen, clearing the table of your finished plates.

After your parents go to bed, you lay in your bedroom watching the ceiling fan above you. The blades rest immobile, the daytime sun burned away to a cool night. You know summer is fading. You think only of the caves. You think of a mouth just streets away, what network stretches below the ground from the city to your neighborhood. You think of every hiding place beyond outlaws and settlers, an entire elsewhere of coordinates the police never considered. You think of the turtleshell buried in April's backyard, a secret suspended inside the ground, a bone displaced from some other land to the shelter of this earth.

Mr. Kottleman discusses St. Louis during wartime, the expansion of the suburbs through the 1950s. You already know of this era from post-World War stories in *National Geographic*, the photos of new televisions and shopping malls that your father showed both of you in the magazine's glossy pages. As Mr. Kottleman speaks you think of the caves silent beneath the ground as strip malls and drive-in theaters built slowly above them. You think of the entrances to the caves, sealed as post-war industry grew, forgotten beneath a booming city but always intact.

When the class adjourns for lunch, you approach Mr. Kottleman's desk and hand him back the book. Already finished, he asks. You nod. You hesitate before leaning in close, before telling him that you think you found a new entrance to the caves.

Mr. Kottleman leans away. His face darkens and he tells you that there are many caves throughout St. Louis, many just a few feet deep, that the one you found is not necessarily connected. Then he looks at you. His eyes study yours. For a moment he seems to hesitate, to make some judgment you can't read in the lines of his face. Then he tells you there's always a chance that the cave you found is connected, words that seem to knife him to say, stabs that register as a wince.

In science, Mrs. Jones discusses the planets of the solar system beginning with the furthest, the remote and tiny Pluto. She tells the room that its classification as a planet is routinely debated. She pulls down an overhead diagram of elliptical orbits and explains that Pluto's path is erratic, that due to its small size the force of the entire solar system will gradually disrupt its orbit.

Pluto is in constant danger of collision or scattering, Mrs. Jones tells the class. As she speaks you imagine a small planet slowly drifting away, into a dark and unknown universe. You glance at April and she is watching you. She passes you a note when Mrs. Jones isn't looking, lined paper you unfold to read her brief scrawl, *Are you going to Lauren's party?* You don't know how April has already made friends, the school year too new. But you look up and nod, and April smiles at you as Mrs. Jones moves on to Neptune.

After school you board the bus, a route that takes you past April's house and the woods where the ravine waits. You squint into the trees behind every house, the woods barely visible from the street. You imagine the walls of the cave and look down at your hands, the lines on your fingertips as thin as thread.

On the night of Lauren's party, you wait in your bedroom with your sleeping bag while your parents finish clearing the table and washing dishes. The backyard oak tree is visible from your window, strong branches that would have held a treehouse. The empty tire swing sways. The leaves are beginning to turn, their edges light brown and crisp. The setting sun backlights through the green center of every leaf, casting the backyard that once held your sister's laugh in a quiet, muted glow.

When your parents drop you off at the party, both kiss your head and watch until Lauren's mother answers. There are already nine girls populating the basement, April among them, and Lauren announces that you are the last to arrive and the festivities can begin. You unfurl your sleeping bag beside April's, take a can of Coke from a table, accept a piece of marble cake. Lauren's mother snaps pictures while Lauren unwraps her gifts, bracelets and board games and a small box of earrings from you. Then Lauren's mother puts on a movie and disappears upstairs, and you each take turns putting on your pajamas in the bathroom before settling into the pillows and sleeping bags on the carpet. You expect to only watch a movie, the same as every other sleepover you and your sister ever attended. But halfway through Lauren sits up, listening for her parents' footsteps that have stopped, and turns down the volume of the movie and tells the room it's time for Truth or Dare.

You know this game. You've played it only once, last summer with your sister in her bedroom, a game that ended in divulging favorite colors and favorite foods, hers cheese pizza, which you already knew. Lauren's voice is different. It carries an edge, a hard tack. Your friends gather into a circle on the carpet and Lauren begins by asking Mindy Jackson the question everyone will end up answering, *Mindy, truth or dare?*

Mindy shrugs. She says truth. Lauren thinks a moment then asks, what boy in our grade would you most like to kiss? Mindy reddens, though everyone knows the answer. Everyone knows Mindy's crush is Albert Doolittle, a crush she's never admitted aloud because everyone makes fun of his name. She closes her eyes and whispers the word, *Albert*, and the basement erupts in shrieks.

The game rolls. Mindy asks Delilah Hanson if she's ever masturbated. Delilah dares Michelle Cohen to prank call Justin Nunez. When Justin's mother answers the phone, Michelle hangs up and explodes into giggles, then she turns to Sherry Alman and dares her to streak across the room in only underwear.

You wait silently in the circle, a pressure building in your chest. You wait for someone to speak your name. But when April's name is called and not yours, you look up and she catches your eye before choosing truth.

Lauren smiles, her turn to ask. She doesn't hesitate. She knows what she wants to say. You watch her face and know when she speaks that she's held this question all along, a question she knew before the night began: *why did you move here?*

April doesn't flinch. She says her father was relocated, but Lauren smirks. That's not what I heard, she says. What's the real reason, she asks, for those scars on your wrists that you're doing a bad job of hiding?

Your stomach weakens. You feel like someone has punched you. You will April not to speak, to never let you know what happened to her, to spirit you both away from this room.

But her mouth opens. My uncle raped me, she says. Her eyes bear down into Lauren. The room falls silent.

During my cousin's birthday party, April says. While everyone was inside. He took me down to the woods. He said we were looking for sticks for s'mores.

Your blood throbs in your ears. Lauren draws back, a question she never should have asked, and Michelle Cohen reaches across the circle, touches April's shoulder. You think of the cave, of April inside, alone at last at the edge of the woods. You think of severed rope, your sister's bound hands. Your vision clouds, black dots moving in from all sides. April looks at you, a question you know she will ask you to move this game onward, away from herself, and your stomach rumbles and you excuse yourself to the bathroom where you hold your hair back above the toilet but nothing comes, nothing but still water and the faint smell of urine and the mirror image of your sister's face, blinking back.

When you emerge from the bathroom, the game has stopped. The circle has disbanded, the lights have dimmed. You climb into your sleeping bag and pull the zipper tight. April peers back at you, her bright hair poking from the sleeping bag beside yours. Her eyes are wide but you close yours, to shut out the room, to make this world disappear.

Your mother tucks you in on Sunday night, something she once did for you both every night, a ritual you've noticed she has resumed since she called the police when you didn't come home. She pulls the comforter to your chin and sits on the edge of your bed, watching you in the soft shade of your bedside light.

You want to tell her about the cave. You want to tell her about April, what happened to her. But the words falter on your tongue and you blurt instead, is she ever coming back?

Your mother stiffens. She looks at you then looks away.

Oh, honey, she says. They don't know. They just don't know.

You want to ask why, why no one knows. You want to ask about the severed rope, the one piece your parents have never acknowledged.

Your mother looks at you and the line of her jaw hardens.

There are bad people in this world, she says. She looks like she wants to say more and you know for the first time in her voice that there are things she knows that you don't know. She holds your gaze for a moment then leans in and kisses your forehead. She squeezes your hand and turns off the light. She tells you that what you need is sleep.

You watch the ceiling come into focus through the dark. You know there are bad people. You know what April told the room. You also know where she goes to get away. You think of every turn at hide and seek when you never found your sister, the times you played when it took her hours to emerge if you fought, if you said something that hurt her badly enough. You think of the landscape of this city, a map you thought you and your sister knew better than the cartography of your own skin, and how even still there are secrets inside the earth, places the worst of men can never find.

Your silhouette is finished. You tried to draw yourself. In the end, you only drew her. You slide it into your backpack, a portrait you will never show your parents. You take the bus home from school.

When you get off at your stop, you intend to go home until you remember your mother isn't there. There is a PTA meeting this afternoon, one your mother said she would attend before she made you promise to come directly home and lock the door. You hesitate on the sidewalk. You know you have an hour. You turn before you can think and you move away from your house, down the sidewalk toward April's street.

April opens her front door before you knock, as if she's been watching out the window, as if she knew to expect you. Her arms are bare for once in short sleeves, her cuts forming the rungs of a scabbed ladder up her forearm. She notices you looking. She doesn't pull away. You step into her house and she closes the door behind you.

I need to see the cave, you say. She nods and leads you into the backyard, your backpack still clinging to your shoulders.

You follow April down the embankment, through the woods to the ravine. Branches thrash against her arms but she moves ahead without slowing, the scars a beacon leading you further. April stops at the edge of the ravine and nods her head forward, that you should go, that the cave is yours alone.

You stand next to her. Her hair catches the slanting sun.

I'm sorry about what happened, you whisper.

I would have asked your favorite animal, she says, if you would have chosen truth.

You close your eyes. The forest encircles both of you. You take a step and your feet move down the ravine. You move through moss and dead leaves and the tangling away of receding brush until you are standing at the mouth of the cave, a yawning cavity that could swallow you. You look behind you, but you can't see April. You know she is still standing there, somewhere in the woods, but here, you are alone.

You step into the cave. You inhale its wet scent, a damp that blankets your skin. You imagine your sister, every small space she ever sought in your house. You pull the silhouette from your backpack. You kneel and set it on the ground. *Come out, come out,* you whisper and a breeze picks up from the forest floor, blowing leaves through the opening of the cave. The breeze is cool, the first that breaks the summer's heat, the first sign that autumn is settling in. The breeze whistles through the cave and it sounds like a sigh, like someone crying. You move in close. You press your palms to the cave wall. The silhouette flutters in the wind and the breeze whips against your ear. The breeze is navigable. The breeze is a voice. The breeze is every sound that the city has lost.

LESSONS

Laura van den Berg

1.

THERE ARE FOUR OF THEM.

Dana, Jackie, Pinky, and Cora are cousins. Pinky is also Dana's little brother. They call themselves the Gorillas because all gangs need a name—see Hole-in-the-Wall Gang, Stopwatch Gang, Winter Hill Gang—and also because they wear gorilla masks during their hold-ups. They are criminals, but they still have rules: no hostages, small scores, never stay in one town for more than a week. It's late summer and they're roving through the Midwest, from motel to motel, making just enough to keep going. Dana watches the impossibly flat landscapes of Lafayette and Oneida pass through the car window and wonders how they all ended up here. Why didn't they go to school and get regular jobs and get married and live in houses? The short answer: they are a group of people committed to making life as hard as possible.

Cora says they need to think bigger. No more knocking over delis and drugstores and dinky banks. They need to do a real heist. There are millions to be made, if they could just grow some balls. Jackie has simpler desires. She wants a boyfriend and a set of acrylic nails. Pinky is thirteen and wants to build a robot. Dana is more about what she doesn't want, as in: she doesn't want anyone to go to jail or die.

In L.A., a gang of female bank robbers have been making headlines. They wear Snow White masks and carry semi-automatics. Witnesses have reported them doing tricks with their guns during heists. They're rumored to be retired Romanian acrobats. Naturally the press loves them. They've been nicknamed the Go-Go Girls.

"Why aren't we ever on TV?" Cora complains one night. They're in a motel in Galesburg. They have plans for the Farmers & Mechanics Bank on Main Street. Dana lies on one of the musty twin beds; her cousins are curled up on the other. Cora is green-eyed and lean with cropped auburn hair, like Mia Farrow in *Rosemary's Baby*. Jackie is shaped like a lemon drop. Her dark, wide-set eyes remind Dana of a well-meaning cow. Pinky is working on his robot in the bathroom. He's been collecting materials from gas station and motel dumpsters: pins, wires, batteries, little black wheels. Earlier Dana stood in the doorway and watched him screw two metal panels together. He sat cross-legged on the floor, his lips puckered with concentration. The overhead light flickered and buzzed. The spaces between the shower tiles were dark. She'd never seen him work so hard on anything before.

"Those are the kind of people who end up in shootouts with the police," Dana tells Cora. The Go-Go Girls have just stolen two million in diamonds from a bank in Beverly Hills. Dana picks up the remote and changes the channel to a cooking show. A woman is finishing a dessert with a blowtorch. Dana closes her eyes and listens to Pinky rattle around in the bathroom. Did they want a shootout with the police? She considers the Dalton Gang and John Dillinger. Is that what they want, to bleed to death on the street? The room is hot. The smell of burning rubber wafts through the bathroom door. No, she decides. No it is not.

There is a river in Elijah, Missouri, that always appears in her dreams. They all grew up in Elijah. In this river they learned to float. Dana would stare up at the clouds and imagine they were spaceships or trains. In this river they would dive and search the bottom for smooth, flat stones. In real life it's a slender, slow-moving river, but in her dreams it's as wide as the Mississippi and silver, as though it's made of melted-down coins. From the shore she sees a raft with no one on it. She wants to get on the raft, but doesn't know how.

That night she wakes sweaty and breathless. She sits up. Pinky is next to her, asleep on top of the covers. He's rangy and sharp-elbowed. His arms are folded under his head. His mouth is pink and sticky from chewing Red Hots. She touches his pale hair—tow-headed, her father used to say—and feels heat rising from his scalp. Outside she hears rain falling. She lies back down. She tells herself to go to sleep. She tells herself to stop dreaming.

In the morning, they case the Farmers & Mechanics Bank. They drive around the block twice in their Impala and then park at the pizza place across the street. To their left is a small roundabout with a patch of green and two withered trees in the center. It's called Central Park, which makes Dana think of the real Central Park in New York City, a place she will probably never see. A truck rattles past. The exhaust pops and Dana twitches in her seat. Cora is driving. Dana is sitting next to her. Jackie and Pinky are in the back and of course her brother is trying to wind two wires together. Dana imagines that when the Go-Go Girls case their new targets, it's all high tech, with thermal imaging binoculars and fancy cameras. They just have their eyes.

They watch people come and go from the bank. They consider the flow of traffic on the street. They send Pinky in to pretend he's filling out a deposit slip. In Central Park, an American flag snaps in the breeze. A church bell calls out the hour. The bank is unassuming, just a brick building with tinted windows. When Pinky returns to the car, he gives a report on the interior layout, the number of tellers, and the points of exit and entry. According to him, there are only two tellers and they're both fat and slow. Dana watches a young woman emerge from the bank; a white envelope is tucked under her arm and she's holding a little boy by the hand. It startles Dana to think that the course of your life could depend on when you decide to cash a check or buy a roll of quarters.

"This one is going to be a breeze," she says.

"Where's the fun in easy?" Cora replies. She turns on the radio and surfs until she finds the news. Tornados are in the forecast. Last night one of the Go-Go Girls was spotted at a nightclub in Malibu. There was a big chase with the police. Naturally she escaped.

"A nightclub!" Cora slaps the steering wheel. "She was probably sitting in some guy's lap. She was probably drinking champagne."

"Champagne gives me a headache," Jackie says from the back.

"That's because you've never had the good stuff," Cora tells her.

"How would you know what the good stuff is?" Jackie replies.

At the motel, they clean their guns. Except for Pinky, who locks himself in the bathroom. They can hear him banging around in there. It sounds like he's acquired a hammer and a drill. Dana doesn't know where he could have gotten those things.

"He really wants to finish that robot before we leave town," she says.

"What if someone has to pee? Or take a shower?" Cora asks. "What then?"

"Your brother is so weird," Jackie says.

Their guns are old Smith & Wesson revolvers. They wipe them down with the white face towels they found in the motel room. Afterward they take out their gorilla masks and line them up on a bed. Black synthetic fur surrounds the rubber faces. The mouths are open, showing off plump pink tongues and fangs. They put the masks on. They pick up their guns and point them at each other. They aren't loaded, so they pull the triggers and listen to the hollow click. *Bang*, Dana whispers into the sweet-smelling rubber. She can see a bullet flying from the chamber and pinging her right in the forehead. She can see it burrowing into her brain. When people get shot in the movies, they flail and scream and stagger. Sometimes they even pretend to be dead and then come back to life. But that's not what it would be like at all, Dana thinks. She imagines it's just like turning out a light.

2.

In Elijah, they lived on a farm. The property held two gray houses, a chicken coop, and a dilapidated barn. The metal skeletons of cars rusted in the front yard. The barn was filled with dust and moldy straw. On the edge of the property, a small cross made from sticks had been pushed into the ground. It was a grave, but Dana never knew who it belonged to.

The mothers—hers and Pinky's, Cora and Jackie's—were both the same: long-faced women scrubbed free of dissent and desire. Dana never heard either of them make a joke or sing. One of her earliest prayers was asking God to not let her end up like them. Cora and Jackie's father was gone. Years ago he had driven away in the middle of the night. Dana remembered him being like lightning cracking in the sky, quick and mean. Her own father was stern but quiet, the kind who didn't need to raise his voice to incite fear. Once, during a homeschooling lesson, she learned ninety-five percent of the ocean was unexplored and thought her father must be like that, too: filled with dark, unseen caverns. Sometimes she longed for a father that popped and exploded like Cora and Jackie's had. At least then you knew what they were capable of.

Little was actually farmed on the farm. Her father didn't believe in working for pay. That was the government's system, he said. They were sovereign citizens. They ate homemade bread, snap beans that grew on vines, peppers, collards, and venison; they drank water that came from a well. They had chickens and a milk cow and a white goat. By the time the girls were seven, they knew how to handle a gun. They could hit the center of a bulls-eye. They could shatter the clay pigeons Dana's father tossed into the air. Every Sunday they had target practice because that was God's day and He would want them to be prepared. Cora always had great aim. Pinky never liked the shooting. He got his nickname from the way he flushed whenever he fired. He didn't like the weight of a gun in his hands. He didn't like the noise. He knew better than to say these things in front of his father, of course, but he told Dana when they were alone. She would lick her index finger and wipe dirt from his face and tell him that he would get used to it in time.

Once, when Dana was thirteen and Pinky was eight, their father took them turkey hunting. They were instructed to climb a tree and stay put until he called. From the branches of a chestnut oak, they watched him crouch in the tall grass and lure the turkey with a whistle. The bird moved slowly through the woods. Fall leaves crunched under its scaly gray feet. When it appeared, its tail feathers were spread into a beautiful rust-colored fan. Dana thought he looked big and regal, and for the first time the gap between what she knew and what the animal knew seemed cruel. It only took one bullet for the turkey to fall, heavy and silent as a sack of grain. Pinky put his hands over his eyes. Dana rubbed his back. When their father called, she hesitated. She pretended they were invisible in the tree. He kept calling, but his voice never sparked with anger. It wasn't patience, though. Dana understood that it was something else. When they finally went to him, he rolled the turkey over and showed where the bullet had gone in. He made them kneel beside the bird and touch the hole. It was gummy and warm. He told them fear of death was their greatest human weakness. He pulled a brown feather, the end tipped with white, from the turkey's tail and stuck it in Dana's hair.

The winter the girls turned eighteen, everything changed. A notice came in the mail. No one had paid taxes on the farm in decades and now the government was saying they owned the land. Her father tore up the first notice because he didn't believe in taxes, but they kept coming. Dana saw the envelopes stamped with *URGENT* that he brought home from the P.O. Soon they had just sixty days to pay. That was when their training became serious. They had target practice daily. They had drills where they would run along the perimeter of the property, rifles in hand. Even Pinky had to come. He always lagged behind the girls. Dana worried about him slipping on the ice and shooting himself in the foot. They would go out bundled in parkas and leather gloves and hunting caps, their breath making white ghosts in the air. After the first hour her arms would burn from the weight of the gun, but she would keep going. They were given a pair of binoculars and told to look out for strangers. Every night their father waited up in the kitchen for something to happen, for someone to come. Every night they recited a prayer that was meant for the eve of battle: *His days are as a shadow that passeth away/touch the mountains, and they shall smoke/Cast forth lightning, and scatter them.* During a snowstorm, Dana said she didn't see how anyone from the government could find them in this weather, and her father pointed out that snowfall could give the enemy perfect cover. That night, he asked her to wait up with him. He kept opening the front door and looking outside. Snow gusted into the house and padded the hallway with white. Flecks of ice got stuck in his dark eyebrows and hair. He showed her a pamphlet newspaper called *The Embassy of Heaven*, which had a Bible quote on the cover: "Do not suppose that I have come to bring peace to the earth." He said he had been writing to the newspaper and asking for help.

"Help with what?" They were sitting at the kitchen table. A rifle lay across his lap. Last week he'd torn out the landline and now a bundle of red and green wires dangled from the kitchen wall. They had a radio that got two stations, local news and gospel music; in the background she could hear the drone of an organ. She kept telling herself that the tax notices and her father's new habits would all pass eventually, like a hunting season.

"With the soul of this land," he told her. "With the soul of this family."

They'd turned the generator off for the night and the kitchen was cold. Dana had wrapped herself in a wool blanket. The room was lit by an oil lamp. In the half-dark, she could see how much her father's face had changed. The crescents under his eyes had hollowed out; his pupils looked darker, his cheekbones and chin sharper. His skin carried the sheen of a light sweat, even though it was freezing outside. The surface was falling away. She was finally seeing what lay beneath.

No one from the bank or the government ever came to Elijah. The snow kept falling. The river stayed frozen. By February the notices had stopped appearing in the mail. It seemed they had been forgotten. Still things did not go back to the way they were before. Dana's father thought it was a trick. He started working on a secret project in the barn. His face kept changing. At night she could hear her parents arguing and sometimes Dana would find her mother crying as she collected eggs from the chicken coop or squeezed milk from the cow. Both the mothers seemed exhausted by the vigilance they'd been required to keep. They lost the energy for homeschooling. When they gave the children their schoolbooks and sent them away, Dana's father didn't notice.

Of course the children weren't really children anymore. There was only so much time they could spend shooting skeet and patrolling the property and flipping through musty textbooks. The idle time sparked a curiosity they had never felt before; it was as though they had each swallowed an ember and now it sat simmering in their stomachs. One afternoon Cora had this idea to wait on the road for a car to pass. They had some sense of what the outside world was like. They had accompanied Dana's father on trips to the farm store and the P.O. in West Plains. Once a month they went with the mothers to Fairfield's Discount Grocery, just a few miles down the road in Caulfield. Every fall they drove to visit Dana's grandparents, who had a computer and a TV, in Arkansas. But they had never done anything on their own, just the four of them.

After an hour of waiting, a truck rolled by and they hitched a ride to Miller's One Stop in Tecumseh. They wandered the dusty gas station aisles. Under the glare of florescent lights, Dana stared at the rows of cokes and the freezer full of ice cream sandwiches. Before they hitched a ride back, Cora pocketed a tube of chapstick and a plastic comb. At home, they mashed the chapstick into Pinky's hair and then combed it so it stood upright.

On another outing, they discovered that, five miles beyond the gas station, there was a town with a movie theater and a liquor store. The theater had an old-fashioned marquee and two screens. One of the films was always R-rated. The girls started talking the liquor store owner into selling them cigarettes; Pinky was the lookout. They would smoke behind the store and then toss the butts into a field. Once they let Pinky smoke. He coughed and dropped the cigarette and Cora flicked his ear. They were always back well before dark. Their parents didn't seem to know they'd been gone, or catch the strange smells they brought home. The farm was over two hundred acres and Dana figured they thought their children were out on the land, like they'd always been. But their children were learning quickly. They were learning the outside world and the pleasures it held weren't so bad. They were learning that they had never really believed in God; they had only ever believed in fear.

After they stole a map of American highways from the gas station, they spent hours sitting on the floor of Pinky and Dana's room, tracing the lines out to California and Oregon and Florida.

"Here." Cora lay on her side and pointed at San Louis. She had been eating sugar cubes from a cardboard box and her fingertip glistened. "That's where we should go."

Jackie was interested in traveling south, to New Orleans or Fort Lauderdale, but Cora said those places were too hot. Dana was intrigued by the small patchwork of northern states. They had studied geography during homeschooling, but now they were looking at the map in an entirely new light, as being full of places they might one day go.

"Too cold," Cora said when Dana touched the hook of land extending out of Massachusetts.

"Do you promise to take me with you?" Pinky asked. He didn't look his age, thirteen. He could have passed for ten or eleven. He reminded Dana of a rabbit; he had the same nervous nature and quick-beating heart. He never requested any particular place. He just wanted to make sure he wasn't left behind.

"We'll see." Cora ran her finger along the edge of California.

"Of course we'll take you," Dana said. He wasn't cut out for life in Elijah. It was too rugged, with the target practice and the long winters and the dead animals. She didn't yet know that he would be even more ill-prepared for the life she and her cousins would choose.

One night, in the early spring, they packed a single suitcase, hitched a ride to West Plains, and kept going. That was six months ago. Their parents never came looking for them, or if they did, they must not have looked very hard. Maybe they thought their children had fallen in with the government or the devil and were beyond hope. Or maybe they just didn't know how to search.

At first Dana thought leaving Elijah meant getting away from how things were on the farm, but now she thinks the past is like the hand of God, or what she imagines the hand of God would be like if God were real: it can turn you in directions you don't want to be turned in. They are still in a battle with the laws of the land. The laws that say they shouldn't steal or point guns at people. And she feels the same resistance to these laws that her father must have felt toward paying taxes. Why not do these things? she found herself thinking. Who is going to stop us?

Their first robbery was at a feed and grain store. They wanted money to buy a used car. It was so simple. They had stolen a shotgun from the bed of a truck they'd hitched in. All they had to do was walk inside. Dana told the teenage boy behind the counter to empty his register because that was a line she'd heard in one of those R-rated movies. She called him a cocksucker, too, since criminals seemed to say that all the time and she wanted him to know that she was to be taken seriously.

The boy gave them everything he had. Feed and grain stores aren't used to being robbed.

3.

The night before they hit the bank, Pinky tests his robot in the parking lot. Dana is the only one interested enough to watch. The floodlights are on; tiny bugs hover around the glow. The robot is covered in a pillowcase. It stands on the black asphalt like a ghost. Dana is smoking one of Jackie's cigarettes. She doesn't smoke much anymore, but it's the night before a job and that always makes her nervous. Once the thing is started, there's no sense in worrying because it's done, it's over. You can't rewind. But being on the edge, that's the hardest part. It's like standing in front of a burning building and knowing that it won't be long before you have to walk inside.

She sits on the ground and watches her brother peel away the pillowcase. The robot looks like a kid's science project. It has a round silver head and black buttons for eyes, an economy-sized tomato soup can for a body, and large plastic suction cups for feet. It doesn't have any arms. Dana realizes that, for some reason, whenever she thinks of a robot, the first thing that comes into her mind are its arms.

"What do you think?" Pinky says.

"Nice work." Dana flicks the cigarette into the lot.

He tweaks some wires and the robot starts lurching in Dana's direction. It squeaks and sighs. A suction cup slips forward. It's working! She can't believe it. She stands up and begins to applaud. She feels proud of her brother for building something. For finding a way to escape his circumstances.

The robot takes one full step before toppling to the ground. The eyes pop off and slide under a car. The head gets dented. Pinky rights it and adjusts the wires, but he can't bring it back to life. Dana stops clapping. She sits down on the sidewalk.

He carries the robot over to her. "Do you want to hold it?"

"Sure." She holds it away from herself. It's surprisingly light.

"On TV people build robots that can talk." Pinky licks his lips.

"It probably takes a lot of practice," she says.

An old woman with flame-red hair shuffles past and disappears into a motel room. Above them Dana hears slamming doors.

"I don't want to leave," Pinky says. "I want to stay here and keep practicing."

"You want to stay in Galesburg?"

Pinky tells her that whenever they leave a place, he worries they won't make it to the next town. He worries the car will break down and no one will give them a ride and they'll starve to death or get heatstroke or something equally horrible. He's breathless. His eyes are glassy. She pictures his rabbit heart pulsing under his ribs. Probably leaving him in Galesburg would be the best thing for him, though she knows she could never do such a thing. She was the one who took him away from the farm and now she has to live with the consequences.

She gives the robot back to him. She doesn't tell him that if they die, it won't be from starving to death in their car. Instead she says everything is going to be fine, just like she used to in Elijah. No one is going to die. Soon he'll have all the time in the world to build a new robot.

"Does this one have a name?" she asks.

"Donald." He squeezes the robot's metal stomach and asks Dana what she thought their father was building in the barn.

Dana shrugs. She's never given much thought to what he was doing. She just remembers looking out her window and seeing him trudge into the mouth of the barn at dawn and not emerging until after dark. His skin would be caked in dust, straw caught in his hair. But mainly she had been preoccupied with figuring out how to live her own life, with how to spend her time. Dana wonders if her father is still working on his project in the barn, whatever it was. She imagines going back to Elijah one day and finding him a shrunken old man and feels an ache shoot through her chest.

"I snuck in there once and watched him." Pinky describes pliers and cords and strips of metal. He talks about smelling smoke and seeing tiny silver sparks. "I think he was building a robot. I think that's what he wanted to do."

Dana looks at her brother and feels woozy. She never should have taken him along. It was a game at first, but now it's something much more serious and he is becoming an attachment she doesn't need.

"You know what they say in the movies?" she asks him.

"What?"

"They say you have to be cool." She can see a man in a ponytail delivering the line, but can't remember which movie it's from.

"OK." He's staring at the ground. She can tell she's not getting through.

"Say it to me."

He keeps hugging the robot. In his arms it looks like a heap of trash. It's only recently occurred to Dana that some people might call what she did—taking her brother away from their parents—kidnapping.

"Be cool," he tells her without looking up.

"You got it," she says.

4.

Dana was questioned by the police only once. It didn't have anything to do with the Gorillas. Rather she was a witness to a hit-and-run. This was two months ago in Jefferson City. She had just walked out of a bank the Gorillas were casing and was waiting to cross the street. A car ran a red light and struck a girl on a bicycle. The girl was dead by the time the ambulance came. Dana could remember the twisted handlebars and the crushed bell. She could remember the peculiar angle of the girl's torso and her open eyes. Her lips were parted. Her teeth were straight and white. She was still wearing her helmet. She looked like a life-sized doll someone had left in the street. Pedestrians gathered. The police were called. Dana tried to slip away, but someone identified her as a witness and she was taken down to the station. She got to ride up front with the officer. She wondered what Cora or Jackie would think if they saw her, if they would think she had turned on them.

At the station, the officer brought her a cup of coffee. He was handsome, with his broad shoulders and gelled hair. So this is the lair of the enemy, Dana thought as they settled into an interrogation room. She held the warm Styrofoam cup with both hands. If only this officer knew what she had done, what she was going to do, she would not be answering questions over coffee. There would be handcuffs and threats. She figured that one day he would see her face on the news and feel like a dolt.

He asked her the usual questions: what she'd seen, if the light had been red, if she'd gotten a look at the driver, if she remembered the license plate. She answered honestly. She hadn't seen anything but the collision itself, hadn't taken in anything but the shock of the crash. She didn't mention that she hadn't been paying closer attention because she'd been busy imprinting the interior of the bank onto her brain.

"Do you need someone to identify the body?" Dana asked. She surprised herself with the question.

"You knew her?" The office frowned. He pulled in his chin and a little roll of fat appeared.

He had mentioned the girl was a college student. Dana muttered something about being classmates and seeing her around campus. She didn't know what had come over her. She had never seen a dead body before and up until then, that was A-OK. But she had been gripped by an urge she could not recognize or understand, only follow.

"Her parents are coming in from Chicago," the officer said. "We could save them the grief."

Dana sighed. Didn't he know there was no saving anyone any grief?

They took an elevator down to the morgue and passed through a cool, shadowed hallway. They stopped in front of a dark window. Dana could hear music coming through the glass. It was faint. A Michael Jackson song. For a moment, she imagined the medical examiner moonwalking around the autopsy room. The officer asked if she was ready. She nodded. A light came on.

The girl was lying on a coroner's table. She was naked, which alarmed Dana. It didn't seem right for her to be uncovered; someone had been careless. Her breasts were small and her knees seemed too big for her body. Her eyes were closed. Her hair looked wet and sleek. The blood had been cleaned away. Dana wondered where her bicycle helmet was. She couldn't believe this was the same girl she'd seen sprawled out on the street. It looked like her body had been replaced by a fake. How could these parents from Chicago identify their daughter with any kind of certainty? Maybe that was what happened when you died, Dana thought. Your real body went once place and a replica was provided for the rituals. And if that were true, where did the real bodies go? Someplace nice? Probably not.

"So is it her?" the officer said.

"What?" Dana turned from the window.

"Is she your classmate? Do you know her name?"

"It's not her," Dana said.

"What do you mean it's not her?" The officer frowned again. He was getting less attractive by the minute.

"I made a mistake," she said.

"Who makes that kind of mistake?" For the first time she noticed the gun holstered to his hip.

Dana wasn't afraid to just tell the officer the truth. After all she hadn't broken any laws, that he knew of.

"Look, I wanted to see a body. I wanted to know what it would be like." She thought of that turkey in Elijah strolling through the woods one minute and still the next.

The officer said she could show herself out.

5.

At first everything goes perfectly at the Farmers & Mechanics Bank. They are all in their gorilla masks. Cora is pointing her gun at the tellers. Dana is aiming hers at the handful of customers who had the misfortune of being in the bank. They are crossed-legged on the floor; they have been ordered to sit on their hands, like elementary schoolers who can't stop hitting each other. Dana tries to ignore the little girl with braided hair. Pinky is guarding the door. Jackie, the getaway driver, is idling around the corner. Dana watches one teller load bricks of money into a bag. He has red hair and a moustache. The other teller is a woman. She's used so much hairspray, her hair doesn't budge when she whips her head left then right. Her lips are slick with pink, her lashes clumped with mascara. There's no sign of the fat, sluggish tellers Pinky described, but it looks like these two will do just fine.

It's the woman who fucks everything up. They see her hand slide under the counter and know she's going for the alarm. Cora shouts at her—*hands in the air*—but the woman doesn't listen. Pinky is pacing by the door and pawing his rubber face. Dana takes small, quick breaths behind her gorilla mask. *Be cool*, she whispers, but it sounds artificial and weak. Stronger words are needed. She just doesn't know what they are.

The gunshot stops everyone. The mustached teller stops putting money in the bag. Pinky stops pacing. The customers stop squirming. The female teller is clutching her left eye. Blood seeps between her fingers. Cora's gun is still raised. It takes Dana more time than it should to understand that one of the Gorillas has just shot a bank teller in the face.

Her hands are numb. She concentrates on not dropping her gun. She opens her mouth, but nothing comes out. She thinks she's going to suffocate behind the mask.

"Give us our money." Now Cora is aiming at the other teller. His shirtsleeves are drenched in sweat. He goes back to heaving cash into the bag.

A woman in cowboy boots raises her hand. Her mouth is open, but she's not saying anything. She's pointing at something by the door. Dana turns and there's Pinky, slumped against the wall. He's kneading his gorilla mask in his hands. The customers and the tellers and the security cameras are all taking in his face. They are memorizing it. They are branding it onto their brains like Dana did with the interior of that bank in Jackson City.

"He is in such deep shit." Cora is waving her gun. She swivels toward Dana. "Can't you do something?"

But Dana can't. If she were a Go-Go Girl, then maybe she could, but she is just herself. The female teller is hunched over the counter and whimpering. She sounds like the wild dog Dana's father once had to shoot in Elijah. He kept coming onto their property, frothy and snarling, but once he had a bullet in him, he was docile as a lamb. Blood is still squirting through her fingers, as though her hand is a dam that's about to give. She's blinded at best. In the distance, Dana hears a siren. She looks at Cora and her cousin nods. They run for the exit. She pauses only to yank Pinky up by his shirt collar. He drops his gorilla mask on the sidewalk, but right then it doesn't matter. All that matters is diving into the waiting Impala. Of course Jackie wants to know what happened and where's the money and why isn't Pinky wearing his mask. Cora tells her to shut up and drive. They blast out of Galesburg. It's nearly dusk. The sun looks like it's setting the sky on fire.

They drive through the night. Pinky is up front, next to Jackie. Dana and Cora are in the back. The window is cracked and Jackie is chain-smoking. They are heading to a little town called Wapello. They think it will be a good place to lay low, but soon Pinky's face will be all over the news and there will be no laying low from that.

"He can't stay with us anymore," Cora hisses in the backseat.

Dana just shakes her head. He could get plastic surgery, she thinks. A crazy idea. She gazes at her brother's profile. They are on a dark, straight highway. A little slicing, a little rearranging. She thinks of how handsome he could be.

On the radio, they hear that one of the Go-Go Girls has been shot in the stomach. She fell behind during a get away. The officer who shot her said that he meant to hit her shoulder. Turns out that she wasn't an acrobat or Romanian. Just a girl from Minnesota.

"This is the problem with being famous," Dana announces to the car. "It makes everyone want to kill you."

No one says anything. Not even Cora. Dana leans her head against the window. As they're passing signs for Kirkwood, she thinks of the girl at the morgue and her parents in Chicago. She wonders if the cop ever tells her story, about the woman who conned him into checking out a dead body. If anyone ever tells her story.

Tornados are still in the forecast. A few times Dana thinks she sees a big black funnel moving toward them in the night. She thinks she hears that locomotive sound and feels the ground shake. She imagines being swept away. But there is nothing coming for them. Not yet. There is only this highway and this car and this darkness. She leans forward and squeezes her brother's elbow. He doesn't move, doesn't look at her. The remaining Gorilla masks are piled in his lap. He knows he's in a world of trouble.

They stop for gas and Dana makes Jackie hand her the car keys. When she says she wants to be sure no one gets left behind, Cora gives her a look. Pinky needs to use the bathroom. Dana stands outside and jingles the keys. She can see her parents hearing about Pinky on the radio. She can see them turning up the volume and leaning in close. Maybe they are being kept company by a robot made of soup cans and chicken wire, or maybe they are alone.

Through the bathroom door, she hears the toilet flush. Her brother takes his time washing his hands.

When they're all back in the car, Cora passes her a note written on a paper napkin. *We are leaving him at the next fucking gas station!* it says in jagged black letters. Dana crumples the note and drops it on the floor. She slumps back and something crunches under her sneaker. She peers between her knees. It's the robot. Pinky got one of the eyes glued back on. If she tilts her head the right away, the metal gleams and she can tell herself it's their treasure, their loot. She thinks about rescuing the robot from the floor and giving it to her brother. She thinks about doing him that kindness. Instead she nudges the robot under the driver's seat and then feels sad about it. Poor Donald. She has to remind herself that robots don't have feelings. All these little choices that push her closer to something she's not sure she wants.

They pass a billboard with the slogan: WANT A BETTER WORLD? It's too dark for Dana to see what's being advertised, but she guesses it's something religious. Of course she wants a better world. Who wouldn't want that? A world where everyone was like Pinky, pure and soft and full of dreams. Or she could just do things differently when it came to those small choices. She could give her brother the robot. She could throw her gun in a river. These could be her lessons. It's right there for her, that better world. She barely has to go looking.

Dana knows this, just as she knows that this is not the day she will find it.

LONG BRIGHT LINE

Josh Weil

THROUGH THE WINDOW CLARA COULD SEE the men: dark still hats huddled together. The only thing moving was their pipesmoke. It curled in lamplit clouds. Then—a whoop!—the clouds blew, the huddle burst, the hats were flying.

Out in the street the gaslights seemed to feel her father's cheer; on her mother's face she watched them gutter.

"Look at him." The woman's grip was strong as any man's. "How happy!" But the fingers were bonier, worn to hooks. "Look," she commanded, "and tell me where he sets his heart." Then the grip became a shove. Her mother's *fetch your father*, and *that damn club.*

The Society for Aeronautical Enthusiasm. Sometimes when she was sad or scared or simply felt the inexplicable weight of herself, she would intone the strange words like an incantation: *Aeronautical enthusiasm, aeronautical enthusiasm, aeronautical . . .* She said it now . . . *enthusiasm . . .* starting up the station steps . . . *aeronautical . . .* shoe-clacking through the empty lobby . . . *enthusiasm . . .* to the shut door . . . *aeronautical enthusiasm.* She knocked.

Inside it was all smoke and suitbacks, elbows at her headlevel, her father bending down, face flush as drunk, but eyes clear, grin pure, whoop a straight shot of glee. He scooped her up.

"Fifty-nine seconds!"

How long had it been since her father had held her like that?

"Eight hundred and fifty feet!"

Lifted her so high? With each hoist and drop she felt her years shake off, seven, six, five, her brother's age, Larry in the corner watching, *this is what it's like to be him.*

Before her face: a piece of paper, some smiling stranger lifting and lowering it for her to read. At the top, the station master's name. At the bottom, that of the man her father called *their father*: Bishop M. Wright.

"The Flyer!" Her father raised her high again. Near the ceiling the air made her eyes water. "The Flyer!" He lifted her into the pipe smoke clouds.

But she wasn't, wouldn't be. The balloon ride he'd won—best guess at time and distance of the first flight—was a prize he unwrapped on the cold walk home: how they would scale the sunset, skim beneath the stars, a Christmas present more miracle than gift. Just not for her. *Why?* The basket size, the limits on weight. *Besides*, he said, *ascending so high would surely swell that head of yours.* He tugged her braid. *No doubt big as the balloon itself.* Laughed. While around them little Larry ran in circles, whooping.

On Christmas Eve all she wanted was to stay up late enough to watch them float by above. But if she did, her mother told her, putting her heavy shoulders into the rolling pin, how could Saint Nick bring her her gifts? She spoke in sentences choppy with work: What did Clara think they were doing up there, her father, her brother, in that balloon? Airborne beside the sleigh, pointing out good children's houses, steering the reindeer toward the right roofs. Why else would they have had to do it on Christmas Eve? The last word pressed out by a hard push. Why else leave their women alone this one night a year she liked to share a little brandy with her husband, squeeze beside him on the chair, sing carols, hear *that sweetness in your father's voice*, let her own loose just a little . . .

"But what about Larry? *He* won't be asleep."

Her mother set the pin down, crouched: her face suddenly level with her daughter's, her eyes strangely soft, her brow smooth as the dough she'd rolled, her hand ice cold on Clara's cheek. From her forearm flour fell like snow. "You know," she said, "they won't see anything. Going up at night. Sweetie, out there it'll just be cold and dark and not one damn thing to see."

There was the whole world. Edge to edge. Lit by the stark stare of a full Yule Moon. And out in the white-bright yard, at the verge of the snow-glowing fields, a seven-year-old girl illumined, looking up. Behind her: the sleeping house. Above: the starry sky. In it: nothing moving. She watched until her eyes stung. No teardrop silhouette slipped across the luminescent globe. Would the men up there have lit a lantern? Would she see its wink? The stars had fled the moon for the rest of the sky, piled so thick upon each other she had no hope of picking out the one she wanted . . . But there! Could it move so fast? Careen across like that? Disappear in a blink before . . . And she was running, running in the direction the light had shot, running for the place on the horizon where she was sure she'd seen it come to earth.

Sometime in the night her father found her. She woke to his hands unclamping her huddled curl, hauling her up. In his arms she shook so much the stars seemed to rattle. The moon was down. His stumbling, his breath: he was drunk.

"Did you see us?" His quaking grin. "We went right over."

"No you didn't."

"Yes!" His teeth a pale tremulous strip. "Your brother waved! I showed the house to Saint Nick. His sleigh landed right there!"

"No it didn't."

"You missed it? All that commotion? The hooves on the roof? Us caroling while we circled above? You truly missed it, truly?"

Had she? His breath fluttered against her face, or her face shuddered beneath it. *Had she?* Inside they waited for her: the presents, lurking beneath the tree, irrefutable.

Papa, what did it look like?

Oh, magnificent! The white balloon, the light of the moon, the stars so close!

No, Papa, what did it look like down here?

Oh, so vast, so small, so strange to think we all live out our lives down there!

No, Papa.

The world! Astounding!

What did I look like? Papa, what was it like to look down and see me?

Like this, next Christmas Eve, had he been ballooning again: a small girl sneaking out after supper, out past the last light of the candle-lit windows, beyond the haybarn, the silo, the snow-blown fields, away from the dwindling singing, the laughter—mother, father, brother, home—his eight-year-old daughter disappeared in the blackness beneath the sky. And then: a spark. A golden bloom. Like this, Clara: a little fiery face looking up out of all the darkness of the fields, your little face flickering with the light of the oil lamp you brought, your breath a sunset's clouds, your eyes two glittering stars.

Aeronautical enthusiasm, aeronautical enthusiasm . . .

All the winter of '05 she chanted it, silently, to herself, a spell to melt the snow, a wish for the rush of spring, and had he looked for her that March, that April, May, on the days when she skipped school, shirked chores, left her brother to play their wellhouse echo game alone, her mother on her knees wringing out the wash, had he looked her father would have found her here: in the Scotchbroom behind the splitrail fence that bordered the cattle paddock they called Huffman Prairie, here, on her belly, behind a scrim of reeds, watching him.

Watching him watch them. Two men in tweed coats and flat caps obsessed with some giant machine. Day after day, they worked on it, trained it like a horse, except—when one at last would mount it, and the other, joined by a helper, would give it a mighty running push—it flew. Its muslin wings stock still, its engine roaring like a mudstuck truck, its driver clinging to the controls, and yet it flew surely as any bird. A bird aloft with a man on its back. Its shadow swept the stampeding cows, the whooping men. Her father too. (*Tell me where he sets his heart*). He seemed to shiver in his clothes. *Here*, Clara thought. Rose on tiptoe, raised a hand to his eyes. *Here*.

Sometimes he would join the others running down the field after the roaring bird. Sometimes he would help push it off the earth. If they were far away, she might not manage to tell him from the rest. She might imagine it was him up there guiding that flying machine. How she wanted to ask him! What did it feel like? *What would it*: that wind in *her* hair; that sudden lift below *her* belly? But all June she lay flat on the ground, behind the weeds, keeping quiet.

Until, one day in mid July, she screamed. How he heard her over the crash, she didn't know. But when she peeled her palms from her eyes, there was the wreckage slammed against the ground, and two far figures running: one toward the crumpled machine, the other toward her.

"No, no, no, no," her father said, and, "can't" and "daughter" and "not how the world works. Don't you ever think of anyone but yourself? How could you make her do your work, your mother worry, poor sick woman!"

She was? How had Clara not noticed it till now? She would have crouched beside the bed and shut her eyes and said the incantation, but learning what the words meant had leeched the magic from them. *Enthusiasm*: merely eagerness. *Aeronautical*: only relevant to things that lifted off the earth, took to the air, soared for the heavens.

This was the last thing her mother said to her, one word: *selfish*, or *selfless*. She wasn't sure. She only knew her mother had turned in bed, clutched her daughter's face, held her gaze, said the word with such vehemence Clara flinched at the flecks of spit. Her mother's fingers gripped her skull, eyes bore into hers. But did she mean herself or Clara? Was it an apology or reprimand? Warning or wish?

She was at Huffman Prairie the day her mother died. September, windless. No figures in the field, no Flyer for them to push. She walked out there alone. At the end of the narrow track, a launching dollies lay overturned. Behind it, in the wet green grass, the bleached board looked white as bone. She lay down on it, aligned her spine with the rail. Stared up at the sky. Spread her arms.

That evening, returning to her father's stricken silence, her brother's sobs, a home whose walls had become more thin, she would wonder if it was something you could see: the soul ascending. If that day she had simply been watching the wrong place in the firmament.

Fall had come by the time her father brought her back to the field. He told her it was her mother's dying wish.

"To see The Flyer?" she asked.

"For you to see it," he said.

Huffman's was crowded. Farmers and friends, the entire Society, even the old man her father called *their father*, come out to watch the flight. That day, the machine made it above the windbreak and kept on, became a hawk, a kite, a sparrow, a spec, was gone. But she could hear the sound somewhere, coming back around, circling her, homing in.

Her father seemed to have forgotten how to steer. She would hear his footscuffs wandering the house, floor to floor, gliding room to room, his tail rudder busted, blown by winds only he could feel. Her brother: a brooding boy, so serious—seven years old and up first to fry the bacon, last in from the barns—so careful cleaning the plow horse's hooves, so watchful over the hung tobacco for the slightest sign of rot. He spent his eighth birthday on the back of a cart, alone in the cold, forking fresh hay to the shivering Jerseys, worry frozen on his face.

While Clara spent her tenth in her room writing a letter to a woman she'd never met: *Dear Mrs. Miller, Can you please describe your ride in the dirigible? How long before you will go up again? And would you consider taking along a girl? I'm still quite small, and very light . . . .* By the time she was a teen the walls around her were plastered with clippings, posters, photographs: Lieutenant Lahm alighting from his balloon in the field at Flyingdales Moor, the Wright brothers on the racetrack at Le Mans, the note she got back from Hart O. Berg (*You never know . . . I'll ask Orville . . . Maybe one day you'll pilot your own!*), the first woman ever lifted off the earth inside an aeroplane signing her name with an O bold as a daredevil's loop. And the daredevils themselves! Glenn Curtiss of that lush mustache, sly-eyed Arch Hoxsey with his wry smile. Her first pack of cigarettes she purchased solely for the Ralph Johnstone card inside: goggles raised, chin-strap sharpening his jaw, that slight swerve she so loved in the cock of an eyebrow above his steady gaze. At school, the girls talked of which boys they'd like to date. She smoked her Meccas, kept quiet. The boys discussed their options for careers, mocked her when she mentioned Raymonde de Laroche. (*Her license!* she shouted; *That's France!* they jeered). *Why do you even bother?* her few friends asked, when, already fourteen, she fought for a seat in the science class, *You know this is your last year, anyway.*

Still, the day her father sat her down it was a shock. She had tried her best to bring him back, curled beside him on the couch reading aloud the news (Blériot across the English Channel! Latham breaks a thousand meters!), hoping to rekindle the heart her mother had heard in his whoop that long ago first flight. Hadn't she brought him into her room to show him each poster she put up—the Los Angeles expo, the Grande Faime D'Aviation de la Champagne? Hadn't they gazed together at the mademoiselle in her windblown dress waving at the silhouetted planes, daydreamed of standing beneath a sky aswirl with aviators thick as bees? All spring she'd tutored boys in science class, saved just enough: two tickets to the aero meet in Indianapolis that June!

But here was her father shaking his head. "You're a woman now," he told her.

Her brother, across the table: "We need you here."

"And what," she demanded, "if I go anyway?" To Indianapolis that June, or back to school that fall, or away forever.

"This isn't New York," her brother said.

"This is your home," her father told her.

"Sis," Larry reached over, touched her arm, "can't you see this is your job?"

In the last year, he had become taller than her.

"There isn't any union," he said. "You can't go on strike."

And, on his lip, she thought she could see a hint of hairs.

When summer came she stole away to Asbury Park. Walked to the train station, bought a seat east, saw the ocean for the first time, the boardwalk, the beach, slept on sand, discovered the effect her shoulders had on men, her smile, snapped up a ride, attained a ticket, was there on the field when Brookins crashed into the crowd, when Prince plummeted 6,000 feet, held her breath with everyone else, praying for his parachute to open (*open! open!*), felt the spectators' communal shudder, would sometimes feel it again, back home, alone in the kitchen cracking the back of a bird, or serving a spatchcocked half to her brother, or sewing a split in her father's yellowed longjohns, or stepping off the train onto the platform of her small Ohio town the day that she returned. But for one August night, at the edge of the Atlantic, looking up, she had been struck by a sudden sureness that it would be all right. The moon. The Milky Way. The Stardust Twins swooping through. That was what the papers called them after that first night flight, Johnstone and Hoxsey circling each other in the lunar glow, their pale-winged biplanes soaring smooth as owls. And her, beneath them, swept by the peace of certainty. Neck stretched back, face flat to the sky, she knew it: she was not meant to be up there; she was meant to be down here, here like a cairn seen from above, a landmark, her.

Let Bessica Raiche climb behind the controls that October.

Let Harriet Quimby claim her license from the Aero Club.

Here is Clara Purdy, standing far out in her father's field, surrounded by electric lamps. All these months she has collected them, repaired ones given her for free, purchased others with earnings made from sewing piecemeal, stolen the rest from her own home. Here is the cord she's spliced, snaking away to the windmill her brother installed just this past September. It is November now, cold and clear and night. She stands in the high grass, waiting for wind. Behind her the turbine is still, the generator asleep. Above, the sky is breathtaking. What is the chance someone flies over tonight? What does it matter? For the first time she understands what she felt in August: it doesn't. The wind will gust, the turbine will whir, the charge will shoot through the cord, the lamps will all light up, and she will know how it would look from high above—the concentric circles, bright bulbs swirling inward to her here at the center—and that will be enough. The dry grassheads stir against her shins. The filaments await the spark. Here it comes.

After the fire, they lived in a fourth floor flat in Dayton, the three of them cramped close, her father and brother away all day in the old bicycle building, assembling engines for the new Model B. The intricacy of understanding, the advanced industry: the Wrights wouldn't hire her. Instead, she spent her sixty hour weeks on the National Cash Register line, setting small round buttons—red number five, red number five, red number five—in their place on the machine. At home, her father ate whatever she cooked in his usual silence. Her brother, chewing, wouldn't even look her way, ever unforgiving of conflagration she had caused. That spring, when flames consumed a shirtwaist factory in New York, he slid the *Daily News* across to her (*a hundred and a half dead*, jabbing his finger at the newsprint, *most of them women*) . . . Beside it, her eyes took in a different headline: in India, a Sommer biplane had delivered the first air mail. *What*, she thought, flushed with excitement, *would come next?* Her father, reading aloud one night, his voice aghast: a ship, an iceberg . . . He couldn't stand it, handed her the paper. She drew in breath. Was it true? Quimby had piloted across the Channel? Alone, a woman! *Eight thousand suffragists*, her brother announced, slapping the paper, shaking his head, *marching on the capital like a bunch of Albanians trying to overthrow the Turks.*

Nearly a thousand days went by before the flood of 1913 gave her a whole week off. Alone with herself for the first time in years, she climbed the stairs to the roof, thunked down a satchel bulged with buttons. Every shift she'd swiped one round red number five and now, crouched high above streets deep with water, she lay them out with a typersetter's care. Above, surveying aeroplanes circled. She wrote them notes in big red letters: COME CLOSER! LOWER A ROPE!

In Austria-Hungary an airship floated, testing photographic tools. An army aviator tried out his loop-de-loops. Biplane, dirigible: ball of fire erupting in the summer sky. A few days later Archduke Ferdinand took a bullet to the throat. A few weeks after that, all of Europe was at war. In a few years, her brother too.

Mid-September, 1918: two thousand planes aswarm over Saint-Mihiel, blasting thick as scattershot across the sky. It was the biggest air battle the world had ever seen, and the next night, while her new husband finalized what that afternoon had wrought, Clara stared up past the strange shoulders (later, she couldn't recall if he'd removed his undershirt, if he'd still worn his glasses), at the ceiling of waterstain clouds and watched the dogfight in her mind: a welkin of dark specs swirling, the opposite of stars. If Abner Lowell noticed (later she would know of course he had) he said nothing (of course he wouldn't), just as the few guests—his family, his friends—had looked at her drained face and silently assumed it must be grief (her fallen brother, her heart-felled dad). A few whispered she must have married out of desperation (her new husband's bony chest, his paltry school teacher's wage), but they were wrong. Clara had married the man for his location.

"Near Toledo," he'd told her, shelling a hot peanut, slipping it into her palm. "A little town you wouldn't know."

She'd chewed, flashed him a look of *try me.*

"Maumee," he'd said.

"On the Maumee River?"

Laughing, he'd coughed out, "You!" It was what he would later say was their first date. "You've got to be a bargeman's daughter!"

Smiling, she'd swallowed, held out her empty hand.

"A little land," she told him, a few months later, after they'd moved up north. "A little place of our own out in the country."

"But Dear"—he called her *Dear* and *Sweets* and *Mrs. Lowell*—
"We have a house already. Right here, right around the corner from
the school."

"Abner," she said, "I grew up on a farm."

"But why so far?"

"I want our children—"

"Why pick a place near precisely nothing?"

It was true: the plot she'd found sat equally far from even the
tiniest of towns. Grand Rapids, Whitehouse, Waterville. It wasn't
even on the routes between them. But it was beneath the one she
wanted, right below the one up there.

Mornings, she made him hot cornmeal muffins, liver and onions
the way he loved, helped carry his schoolbooks out to the car, stood
in the dirt drive waving. She kept the bills in order, the mousetraps
empty, the dust down, herself up, a wife he'd want to come home
to, a home he'd be happy to find her in. Except he wouldn't.

Afternoons, after everything else was done, she'd change into
her coveralls, head for the tractor shed. Alone in all the horse-
worked county, the Allis-Chalmers had cost her every cent of life
savings her father had left, and every day before dusk she would
crank its engine over, hitch its thresher on, rumble out into her
field. Or, as Abner called it, her canvass. The tractor he called her
Big Bad Brush. In the summer, she painted with it, mowed her
pictures into high grass. In the fall, she ploughed pen-lines, the
overturned topsoil dark as ink. Winter found her bundled in the
aviator's coat and hat her husband gave her, long leather earflaps
whipping in the wind while she made her etchings on the earth,
her shovel a chisel, snow peeling away like curls of wood. She
planted daffodils. Dug up the bulbs each fall, stitched them back
into the dirt like needlework, watched her embroidery bloom sunbright each spring.

From the sky, the airmail pilots watched it too. Twice a day they
flew the route, eastward in morning, westward late afternoon.
Perched atop the Allis-Chalmers, or kneeling in the new-turned dirt,

or simply standing still in a swirl of snow, she would listen to the hum, scan the sky, smile up, wait for the dip of a wing, the tiny stick arm flung back and forth in a far-off wave. She would watch them dwindle away to Cleveland, morning awhirl in their propeller blades, watch them disappear towards Chicago, sunset on their struts.

And home from his day at the Maumee Secondary School, hunched over the kitchen table doing his preparatory work, her husband would catch a flutter in the corner of his eye, look out the window: his wife in that distant field of daffodils, her breeze-swept hair all auburn fire in the late light, her cap lifted into the last of the sun, waving, waving. She always left his supper warming in the oven. He always let it warm till she was done, would come clomping in, shuck her boots, sit down to eat beside him. Sometimes, he'd go out to her. In winter storms if visibility was bad the pilots, searching for landmarks along the route, might fly so low their wheels seemed close enough to grab, the silver belly suddenly there tearing through the all-white sky, the aviator's face a flash of goggles, the airplane roaring by. He'd stand behind her, arms around her, feel the gust, the rush, the thrumming of the engine in the air.

"What's it this time?" Abner would ask.

She'd tell him: President Roosevelt on his first flight, Von Richthofen shot down over the Somme, the new airmail stamp. "See there's the biplane, there's the '24', over there the 'cents'."

And Abner would gaze at the indecipherable arcs in the grass, the random squiggles in the snow, the mystifying daffodils, and fill his face with what he hoped conveyed belief in her, faith that from above it would all be clear. Until she began digging portraiture in dirt. Eddie Rickenbacker. Bert Acosta. Jack Knight. Airmail pilots that might *right then* fly over on the Chicago-Cleveland route. "Do you think," Abner said, his voice very level, his eyes somewhere off in the field, "that they might . . . I mean, that they really . . . That they could actually really recognize themselves?"

She meant to nod, but instead found herself starting to shake inside his arms. Against her back, his chest shook too. Their laughter filled the field.

Once, after a fight (Him: weren't kids the entire reason they'd moved out there? Her: that's just the way people without meaning in their lives try to make some. Him: and didn't she want that, too? Her: what did he think she did all afternoon?) she'd asked him, "Why did you marry me?" Because, he said, he loved her. "What does that mean?" He'd told her then he'd never seen someone so consumed by what most moved them, never been that close to such a burning need, wanted to assuage it or be burned up in it, to feel even a little of it in the warmth of what he felt for her.

Abner was the one who brought her books—Klee, Kandinsky, Mondrian—who suggested they drive four hours to Cleveland just to see a room bedeviled by Kazimir Malevich's strange bars and slabs. She didn't understand what stirred behind it, no more than she understood what stirred in her. But dragging the thresher in wild swaths, plowing scattered squares of earth, planting bulbs in shapes that seemed to suggest themselves, she was sure of this: it was a style that far better fit her tools. A tool itself that let her grasp at last at what she had begun to conceive of as a gift. A gift Abner had wrapped for her. The way he wrapped himself around her the night the postal service flew its first transcontinental flight.

That night in February of '21 the snow spilled down as if to douse their fire. They had lit it in the middle of her field, at dusk, no telling when—or if—the plane would hurtle overhead. All day she'd waited for news, pulled open the Ford's door to retrieve the evening paper from her husband's outstretched hand: the last heard from the airmail pilot, he was headed straight into a storm above Cheyenne. Cheyenne to North Platte to Omaha to Iowa City to Chicago to right overhead: at night the only thing to guide him would be a few post office workers' flares, nothing to mark the path between but what bonfires a few farmers might keep alight. Abner helped her haul out the half-rotted boards, pour on the gasoline. They brought blankets, a bottle of bootleg, sat close to the fire. All around her: Abner's enfolding coat, his enveloping arms, the warmth of his breath on her cheek, of his cheek against her ear, of him waiting all the long night with her. Sometime after midnight, they lay down together between the blankets. Sometime before dawn, he fell asleep. Sometime after first light she woke her husband, straddling him with her heat, tenting him with her body, the bottom blanket rough on her knees, the top blanket blocking his view of the sky, her own eyes focused only on his face. "I hear it," he said. "Darling, I hear it." She shook her head, rocked on his hips, kissed him quiet.

So why did she still daydream pilots down? That they would see her wave, circle round, land in her field, take her up. In a De Havilland with a scooped out second seat? Or curled on her knees in the bin behind the engine, the mail hatch sprung? A gloved hand on her cheek (she could smell the leather), the twist of her neck as she turned to see (she could feel her whipping hair) his goggled eyes, his chapped lips, her first kiss at five hundred feet, six, seven, a thousand . . . Why, when she first heard of the postal service beacons—fifty foot towers erected all across the country, a trail of landlocked lighthouses flashing their specific signal (me, me, me) to pilots plying a sea of stars—did she feel betrayed? They built one five miles away. At night she could see its blinking flare (here, here, here). Why when all those women (only one aviatrix shy of a hundred) came together in Curtiss Field to make their mark in the history of flight did Clara turn with even more determination to her own canvass?

Now, she worked at night. She spent all the allowance Abner gave her on a single headlight for her Big Bad Brush, ate her suppers sitting on the tractor's seat, stayed out past the last window gone dark in her house. What sent her to the shed to sharpen thresher blades at the news of Earhart's first Atlantic flight? What about word of the woman's solo crossing kept Clara up till dawn mapping out her next work of art? Each one, each season, outdid the last, pushed her abilities to new feats of skill, scaled the atmosphere of her imagination. She clipped grass by hand, cut staggered banks in sweeping slopes, accomplished tricks of shading by varying stalk heights. She incorporated color in the spring, in winter watered carefully considered ditches to show the sky fleeting paintings made of glinting ice.

And when, one summer morning in '37, the kitchen radio reported that the Queen of the Air had gone down over the ocean, was feared drowned, she found she couldn't breathe. She stood up from the table. It was a schoolday. The house was empty. The news announcer's voice seemed to cinch her throat. And, even before she heard the airplane's purring approach, she was fleeing into the field. Maybe it was her frantic waving, maybe the desperation in her shout: this time the pilot swung around, returned, roared down to her.

A Boeing Monomail, army drab, no room to sit anywhere but in his lap. The leather of his jumpsuit creaked. He had to reach between her legs to take hold of the controls. The noise was deafening, the treeline rushing. The earth dropped.

There was her world: the house, the empty driveway, the field where she did her work. The flesh on the back of her neck urged her *look at the sky*, the giddy slide of her stomach told her *you're flying*. But she couldn't take her eyes off the small, and smaller, square of landscape that was her canvas below.

At her cheek, the aviator was saying something. His chapped lips brushed her ear. For a second, she pulled her stare away, glanced at him: his goggles were so smeared with engine grease she couldn't see his eyes, just the rawness of his sunburned nose, the wetness of his grin.

"Take me back," she said.

"Down?" he shouted.

She shook her head. "Back around, back over, I want to see it again."

It was the first time that she ever had. Till then, it had all existed solely in her mind. There, *there*, if she concentrated hard enough she could forget the feeling of his hand creeping across her chest, if she fought the wind in her eyes and focused hard enough, she could imagine that there was nothing around her but air, that she was up there, flying, looking down, alone.

Maybe it was the depression. Early on she'd offered to plow her canvass under, grow vegetables instead, but Abner insisted No: even when parents lost their jobs, students still needed teachers. Though when, that autumn after her first flight, Lucas County consolidated its schools and proved him wrong, her homebound husband spent his days gazing at her field, his nights commenting on her progress, his energy in coming up with ways that he could help—*Observe you from the roof, shout when you're about to lose the line. I know: a business in balloon rides! Listen, I'll write a letter to* Life Magazine, *to* Art News, *get you noticed!*—his whole self seeming to clutch at her work as if it could become in some way his. Maybe it was the fact that all his attempts to garner her attention finally did. Late in '41 rumors began to go around: her flowers sprouted in secret patterns, her tractor furrowed code, Mrs. Lowell was planting messages for Japs. That winter, at Abner's urging, she undertook a radical revision of her aesthetic. He brought home images of far eastern art, read her haikus. And in the fresh snow of the new year's first storm, helped her shovel a field full of brushstrokes:

見えるかな
野原の上の
流雲

There it was, black shovel lines in white, giant characters carved beneath the January Sky. Two days later an army corporal showed up at their door, watched them while, with the Big Bad Brush, Clara plowed their work away. Afterward, Abner admitted it was probably time to stop. He looked so sad, sitting there in his coat, his pants wet to the knees, his head hanging forward, his hands hiding his face. His fingers were all knuckles and loose skin. He was going bald. How had her husband become a man of fifty? How had she become a wife of forty-five?

And maybe it was simply that: so much time together, so many years gone by.

At first, she didn't think of the separation as something that might last. Just a few months away from each other, Abner working at his new job in Bowling Green, her in Toledo, working thirty miles from him, doing her part to keep the country stocked in B-17s, apart only until the war was over, maybe a year at most. But it was four. Four years living in her own room in a single-sex boarding house, four years in which she found she liked working alongside other women, liked earning enough on her own, liked the feeling of finishing the nose cone of a behemoth bomber, assembling the canopy of something that would one day soar over Hamburg, Dresden, Mainz. She was the oldest woman working at Libbey-Owens Ford. Gran Gunner the others called her, smoking cigarettes, snapping gum. On their lunch breaks they laughed about messages for airmen slipped into secret cracks, read aloud *The Blade*'s dispatches from the fronts, passed around pamphlets by the old BCFA, debated its new milquetoast moniker—Planned Parenthood—and whether General Spaatz was right to bomb Jerry's oil before his rails, and if it made sense to join a dying WTUL, shared home-canned pickles, packs of cigarettes, wondered what they would do after all this was done.

On Fridays, after work, she would wonder the same. Abner would pull into the Libbey-Owens lot, take her back to a home that, all weekend, they would pretend still felt like theirs. The wall calendar Allis-Chalmers always sent her, now swapped for one his students made. The sink corner that had once held her hand cream, now crowded by his shaving mug. He'd move it over, turn the month. Sometimes by Sunday they could almost feel like them again. Though more and more she worked the weekend shifts—overtime, extra pay, Saturday night out with the girls—Sunday coming every other week, then once a month, then not. On the phone, Abner would speak things he'd never said before—how much he'd wanted children; how he used to lose himself in his guitar; all he'd given up for her, would, still wanted to—as if the distance between them made him brave. But it was just distance. Close was this: the cigarette smoke of the women she worked with, their laughter around card tables at night, her own eyes caught in the curved reflection of a bomber's canopy, looking back. Sometimes the smile she saw saddened her. Sometimes, wiping a rag at the glass, she tried to see her husband instead. Sometimes she simply stared through herself until she saw the driveway, the house, some new shape coming up in the field.

Weeds, scrub willows, the driveway buried somewhere beneath the grass. She stood in the sun, seedheads scratching at her stockings, looking at the house. He'd written her—moved out, a simple flat nearer the school he worked at now, she could stay in the house, or sell it, *it's up to you*, he'd transferred the deed to her. But not the car. She'd walked the last two miles. Such flat land: the whole way she'd watched the house grow near, the road to town slip out of sight, its treeline dwindling to distant shakings, far-off Toledo disappearing from her life. The air grew thin. Her stomach dropped. Her juddering heart: she might have been taking off, climbing up, seeing the earth fall away below. Except she wasn't looking down. Instead, on every side it seemed the world was drawing itself away from her. Once, long ago, in a dim Dayton stairwell, her arms beneath her father's arms, dragging him down, flight after flight, fast as she could, she had felt it—in his eyes on her, in the *thud thud thud* of his heels on the steps, in the desperate heartbeats of his departing life—had felt the world withdraw like that. There, on the landing where they'd stopped, he had watched her with such hurt, such hope, so much understanding (*selfish? selfless?*), such loneliness suddenly inside her.

Standing in the hot sun in front of the abandoned house, she set her suitcase down. Hiked up her skirt. Peeled away her stockings. They ringed her shins like thick black shackles. But God the breeze on her legs felt good.

It gusted all the time. Flat fields like runways for the rushing wind, windbreaks bent by its launch against them, the stolid brick house huddled close to the ground, Clara leaning forward, dress and coat and hair afloat behind her, her whole body seeming about to lift off into the sky. These days no more mailplanes flew by. Just clouds and birds and the bellies of DC-4s, their fuselages perforated with passenger windows, their cargo holds carrying the mail alongside luggage now. How high up they flew! How far away they seemed! How fast they grew—Comets and Constellations and Stratocruisers—big as blue whales swimming through the sea above. Sometimes it struck her as strange: the way their shapes—so much larger than the biplanes of before, but so much higher, too—seemed, from below, to stay the same size to her. She hung tobacco in the barn to dry, stuffed advertisers' envelopes all winter, barely scraped by. Even with the checks Abner still sent her. She knew he couldn't afford to give so much, knew she should tear them up, just as the once she'd seen him in Maumee she'd known she should leave him alone. But she had crossed the street to the lunch counter window, watched his shape stiffen at sensing her, his face furrow with the effort of staring into his shake. She'd turned away, gone further down the street, glanced back: there on the sidewalk her still-husband stood, his hat pushed up from his eyes as if to keep the brim from blocking even a sliver of her in his sight.

And the next time an envelope came from Abner it contained not just the usual check but a story clipped from *Life*. *Is he the greatest living painter in the United States?* the caption read. Photographs of splattered paint, scattered color. To Clara they looked like her field when she'd first come home: a bird's-eye view of what nature could do without her. Sometimes at night lying alone in her bed she could hear the airliners droning overhead. Sometimes, mid-day, sunbright rooms would dim for a second, go bright again. Their shadows passed over her there in her field, and she watched them sweep away, disappear, didn't even look up.

But look down. Out that oval window. There, on the ground—what is that?

"I'd like to buy it," the gentleman said. He stood on her doorstep, pinstripe pants aflutter in the breeze, voice like the news on CBS. News of a collector out in California who'd sent this man to hunt out art.

She looked past him to the field, the barn, the shadow of the plane. She'd stitched the tar paper together scrap by scrap, covered it with black painted muslin that wavered, rippled, gave the sense of the shape moving. Though it was nailed down, glued, painted mid-pass atop the barn, the yard, the plowed-under field, its wingspan nine hundred feet long, its fuselage distorted as a real shadow's would have been by the slant of the sun. It had taken her three years.

"The barn?" she asked.

"That too," he said, in his Edmund Chester voice.

Now Chester was off the radio and everyone was watching television instead and her barn was gone to some hangar outside L.A., and she was in a magazine. Some writer spurred by word of the sale had done some digging, discovered a defense department file, photographs of her early '40s shovelings, revealed the message she and Abner had sent the Japanese:

Clouds drift back and forth
Over my fields—I wonder:
Can you see them too?

Clara Lowell. There on the page her name seemed like another person's. She read the story of herself as if from far away, from before she'd taken Abner's name, a Purdy girl again who might tear out a page, pin it to her bedroom wall. She read it all until, halfway, she hit a thing she'd never heard: *soldier, bullet,* how her brother had died. Face down in a ditch, it said. Shot from the air by a strafing ace. Her eyes kept moving along the page, her mind making out the words, but she was seeing Larry again: running, running, engulfed by the onrushing shadow of the plane.

And there went her phone again, ringing, ringing. The Garner Agency, the Fineman Gallery, funding from an arts foundation in San Francisco where she spent the first year of the new decade peering down from the Golden Gate or up from a boat beneath it, devising a way to make the bay look as if the shadow of fuselage and wings had been painted on its waves. Across the ocean, over Pyongyang, jet fighters screamed into the sky. She couldn't hear them. No more than Jackie Cochran, three years later, could have heard the sonic boom she left behind along with all the other aviatrixes still shackled to sound. Clara was in New York City, affixing the faux reflection of an onrushing airliner to the steel and glass of the Empire State—a tragic trompe l'oeil. Haunting, critics called it, heart-stopping. They said her work rang of the grim reaper, contained a sense of the moment made permanent, and yet seemed fleeting, too, as if to offer a possibility of reprieve. And so was also hopeful. And so when, high above the Colorado Plateau a DC-7 struck a Constellation, she was commissioned to commemorate the lost souls, spent the fall of '57 marking the Grand Canyon with two immense shadows facing each other across the chasm, their shapes distended exactly as the sun had stretched them the morning of that last day.

It would be known as Clara Lowell's final shadow piece. Even in the moment, hovering above in the helicopter the Park Service pilot flew, she knew it: the silhouettes were old shapes cut from the woman she used to be, not who she had become. Down in the station everyone else had moved on, too. They were crowded round a short wave radio, listening to a faint, steady beep. *That's it*, one of the rangers said. *It must be passing over us right now.*

Back in Ohio she stood in the spot where her barn had once been and watched the tiny glint arc along its orbit. She had seen pictures of the Soviet's sphere. She wondered what, from that height, it could possibly see down here.

Old ovals found in dusty bureau drawers, age-spotted hand-me-downs, rearviews salvaged from crashed cars, castoff skyscraper panes from construction lots in Cleveland: she collected shards of any size, from all over, carted them back to her small square of earth, slowly, piece by piece, resurfacing her old canvas in glass. Ten entire acres. Half as many years. Hundreds of thousands of seamless fits found from a million broken sides. By the time John Glenn radioed down *Oh, that view is tremendous!* he might have meant the flash of glinting land she'd covered.

Or the sight of all the others who'd come to help. From the beginning she had watched in wonder—these young seekers fleeing their old lives, stopping by on their way to wherever, stepping out of dusty cars, parking in her driveway for a day, a couple, crashing in her guestroom, on her couch, men on motorcycles with their plaid shirts unbuttoned, wind-wild hair, women wearing jeans, scarves in colors more vibrant than anything for miles—but as they crouched by her side, helping find a fit for a piece, holding a glued edge together, she had begun to think of them as somehow akin to her. These kids who were a third her age! Who drove up blaring bands with names like The Del-Tones, The Animals, The Stones. "Can't you hear my heartbeat?" The girls sang it while they worked. Girls who said things like *out there it's trying to bury us alive*, and *can't let it stifle your voice within*, who laughed when she insisted she was still married. *Well*, she said, *it's true I haven't seen him in, let's see, oh jeeze* . . . . And they told her she couldn't continue like that, it was a new era—*all that matters now is what will make you happy, what's the point in living if your life isn't true to you*—an age of self-fulfillment, of our own happiness not just pursued but caught, kept, held perpetually near all our hearts. They could have been her children, her grandchildren, but standing amid a group who'd helped her put the last broken piece of glass in place, she felt as if she had at last found her generation, kindred spirits, a moment in time in which she fit.

Only the babies gave her pause. The ones brought into her home on the hips of girls younger than Clara had been when she'd first entered the house herself. In their sounds she would hear her long-gone husband's late night voice, his telephone pleas. And watching the stare the babies settled on their mothers, she would wonder if Abner—another's husband now?—had felt enlarged by that enamored gaze. She hoped he had. Though whenever an infant was handed to her, she felt the opposite: the child's need tight as its fist around her finger, squeezing her down to fit its purpose, herself made small as the reflection in its unblinking eyes.

Instead, she kept her sights on the work before her. There, in the field of mirrors, the sun shone up out of a sky in the ground. Clouds crept through the grass along the edge, floated into twin squares of blue, followed themselves. Soon, she knew, a contrail would cut across like a line of chalk. A 727 on its way to Chicago, or coming east, a hundred and more passengers peering out their windows. Staring down at the sky beneath herself, she tried to imagine what they would see.

A blinding glare, according to the FAA. Clear the mirror off the ground: the agency's order that at last turned Clara Purdy into a household name. The destruction on the evening news, the documentary about the flood of youth answering the artist's call, the image censored around the world: all that mirror-cleared ground blanketed now by a thousand bodies stripped bare, a ten-acre square of naked flesh flashed upward in a fuck you so communal it seemed to capture the entire decade's mood. By the end of the '60s she had lit an entire rural county's roads, spidering bright veins across the nighttime dark; she made a color photograph of one square mile of the earth, shot from a mile high, then blew it up to actual size, printed it in pieces, put them back together over the spot, so from the air it almost looked like life, but not.

Still, it was her "Long Bright Line" that Clara meant to be her masterpiece. She had convinced the postal service to loan her the antiquated airmail beacons for one night. Coast to coast, every twenty miles, they stood rusting, signals extinguished long ago, last remnants of an idea once pioneering, now obsolete. Until, for sixty seconds on the night of July 20th, 1969, she would bring it back to life. All her funding had gone into the purchase and installation of 140 first-order Fresnel lenses, powerful as any lighthouse beam, mounted atop the towers, aimed straight up. The volunteers who manned the stations wanted only to share in would happen at her signal: starting in New York the first would flare on, followed by a second to its west, and the one that was next, and the one after, a constellation untangled across the country into a single strand of terrestrial stars, a gleaming necklace laid atop the earth's dark breast. Seen only by the moon. And the astronauts on it.

Sometime early that afternoon the TV would show the lander touch down. Around sunset it would show Armstrong or Aldrin stepping onto the surface. By dark they were supposed to be done. And she would call the beacon in New York and start her signal to them.

But in between the landing and the moonwalk, her phone rang instead. She picked it up, heard breathing.

"Wasn't that incredible?" the voice on the other end said.

Even after all these years she knew him. While he talked all out of breath about the surface of the moon seen coming close, and closer, the shadow of the lander growing (*that beep, beep, beep*, he said, *can you still hear it?* and, for some reason, laughed), she slid open the deck doors, let the scent of the ocean in. She stood there trying to smell it, trying not let him hear her inhale. Her old nose. Her old mind. Him? He must have been approaching eighty. He must have been becoming senile: how else could he have just now asked her to come see him?

"I'm sorry," she told him.

"Tonight," he said.

"I live in Los Angeles now."

"Clara . . ."

"I'm busy, Abner."

"I'm dying," he said.

Isn't this something, Cronkite exclaimed.

And it was. It was like nothing she'd ever seen.

From 240,000 miles out there . . .

She sat on the couch, in the salt sticky breeze, feeling it on the loose skin of her neck, her scalp beneath her thinned-out hair, remembering the scent of peanuts, engine oil, the soft fleece of the aviator cap, the warmth of the earflaps—on winter days his fingers had brushed her chin, buckling the straps, just so she wouldn't have to shuck her gloves—how he'd gazed up at her astride him that winter night, his face full of bonfire light, the way he'd looked at his new wife in the picture he'd sent so many years ago to share the birth of his first child. A daughter? A son? She sat in the breeze, trying to remember (*what do you think I do all afternoon?*), listening to Armstrong speak from the moon.

There seems to be no difficulty . . . Definitely no trouble . . .
Gee, Cronkite said, *that's good news.*

And she leaned forward, turned the volume down. She sat in silence, staring. A gray, grainy picture. A pale blur she knew was the shape of a man but might have been anything that moved. The longer she watched, the more strange and beautiful and unworldly, unreachable, it seemed. The longer she looked, the more it broke into its parts—stillness, shadow, something stirring—the more she felt her own shape blurring too. If anyone had looked away from their TVs, glanced up at her window, aglow with the light broadcast off the moon . . . but who on earth would?

She was still watching the fuzz of the screen when, a long time later, the broadcast done, the window for her beacons passed, the phone rang again.

"What happened?" The volunteer's voice came all the way across the country. Some young woman high up in her tower, finger on the switch. "We're waiting," the voice said, crackly with distance, beginning to doubt.

In the hospital she meant to tell him it hadn't been his fault, but stepping into his room, she found herself unable to utter the words *work*, or *self*, or *matter*. Instead, she sat gazing again, this time at her once-husband's face. Someone had turned his sound off, too. When the nurse told her he could no longer speak, Clara asked what his last words had been. The nurse didn't know. She wondered: would they have even been meant for her to hear? She wondered: would she have even be able to? There was just the beeping of the EKG. The blinking of his eyes. Even when they were open, she could tell they didn't see her. But she watched them: blink, blink, blink.

Flying home, she could not stop feeling her own lids opening and closing, even as she leaned toward the window, looked down. The lights of Dayton dwindling. The lights of its outskirts spread as far as she could see. Somewhere down there, it struck her, was what used to be her father's farm. It was smothered by suburbs now, buried beneath the unrelenting burn of each house's separate star, but once it would have been unlit, all of it, house and barns and trees and field and little girl looking up, all indistinguishable, dark as sleep. When the moon went behind the clouds the balloon must have seemed suspended in pure blackness, they must have held the basket tight, peered over its edge, thought *how beautiful!* So strange, she thought now, what we have done to the surface of the world. She shut her eyes—simply paused her lids, stopped them from opening. And, taking in the emptiness before her, wondered how many seconds of each minute she'd spent like that, how many minutes of each day, how many hours, how many years.

ON A TRAIN FROM THE PLACE CALLED VALENTINE

Theodore Wheeler

IT ISN'T UNTIL THE WIND CUTS THROUGH her that Amy actually considers what she's doing. This is December after all and she's riding north on the bed of a railcar after sunset. She nestles into her downy black coat, shoves her hands deep into its pockets, and waits for the train to pass through a town where she can jump into a grassy ditch and roll away from the rails.

She'll have to call her father, wherever she lands, and beg him to pick her up, the way she did in college. A tall man with a dopey mustache, her father would wear gray sweatshirts and blue jeans, if he came for her on a weekend, or a tweed jacket and corduroy pants if he had to take time off from work. He never asked why she needed him, but just came for her, then hummed almost happily as they returned home. "My baby girl," he'd say, as if it were part of an old song. "What has happened to you now?"

Amy isn't scared of riding on the train, even if she should be, and she doesn't mind the cold, the way her nose and cheeks burn from it. She's been schooled in patience and won't jump before she has to. She likes listening to the clink and groan of the cars, and smelling the layers of grease that pervade the train.

She lets the first few chances to jump pass her by, hesitating at the edge of the flatcar, and then the next few until several towns are behind her and she's still standing on the precipice, rogue strands of hair working out from under her stocking cap to whip the back of her neck. She stands on the train bed, serves witness to the abandoned industrial yards of small towns, the timber stands and feedlots unmanned during the night.

Eventually she curls against the cargo she's riding with and watches the dark countryside as she rattles into it. Amy is unwilling to jump. She wants to see where this train will take her.

On the day her father arrived with the rental van, the day she moved to St. Paul, Chadron just kind of hung out and watched as Amy packed up her half of the house. He lay in bed as she filled cardboard boxes from the grocery store, then he sat on the couch eating cereal and watching baseball, then he stood with his back to the sink, slurping cans of Dr. Pepper until the furniture was loaded out and her clothes boxed up.

"Don't you have anything to tell me," she asked when it was time to leave. Her father had already driven the moving van across town.

"No," Chadron said. "I knew this would happen. The kind of guy I am, the kind of girl you are. We both knew this would happen."

From the moment they first met Amy recognized him as a man she could take care of. She fell for him—sweet, malleable Chadron, her dumb-muscle beau. He adored her with such genuine affection and loyalty, a kind of simple gentility that was lost on most of the men and women Amy's been with both before and since. It was so bizarre to her, the way she acted with him—this just months after dropping out of school in Lincoln—but she was a changed woman, no longer the type who promised things to herself. She took charge and told him the way things were going to be, that she was attracted to him, and what she was going to do with him. He listened, guileless Chadron.

"You know it's *me* who's going to leave *you*," she teased. Sometimes she whispered this to him when he held her too closely, if she felt like he really did love her. Amy knew she was running from something, being with him, and Chadron knew it too.

A friend of her father's found her work in St. Paul, as an assistant in the admissions department of Macalester College. She planned to finish the degree she'd begun at NU there. Amy liked the job, but something was still missing. Some vital part of her life was deficient. Her initial months in the Twin Cities were wild, those first loose nights when Amy was let free on the lesser dives of University Avenue, often finding herself in the basement bedroom of some college boy or another, once in the backseat of a car with a woman she met at a dance club, and then there was the man with a red beard from the cigar bar. Even though there was a booster seat in the back of his car, and a wedding band in the ashtray, she still went down on him. Amy never learned the names of these acquaintances. She'd create an alias for the guy then repeat it unprompted throughout the night, refusing to hear his real name. It was a guardedness that nearly masked her melancholy—a mournfulness she transformed into a self-sufficiency of sorts.

These encounters seemed incidental when they happened, forgettable indiscretions. Amy had to reconsider them. Things change, sure, she knew this. Life progresses. It's just that the change you end up with isn't always the one you need. You don't have to accept it. She got to the point where she was an embarrassment to be around for the people who were trying to be her friends. Amy was trashy. That's what happens when you sleep with every guy you know and then hate them afterward. It's OK to be sad, Amy learned, unless people know you are. Then it's bad for everyone. It's untenable.

These were the reasons why Amy backtracked the weeks before Christmas, to reestablish a hold on herself. She found an apartment close to campus in St. Paul, curtailed her drinking, arranged for part-time admission to the college. With her father's help Amy hired a lawyer to draft papers dissolving her lingering marriage to Chadron and she returned to Aurora for the holiday with the intention of having those papers filed at the Hamilton County Courthouse.

This was the one thing she'd needed to accomplish while in Nebraska, so she drove to the old house where Chadron still lived and had a small drink with her husband and his roommates. She should have made him sign at the kitchen table but Amy didn't want to embarrass Chadron in front of his friends. She told him to get in her car and drove to a spot where they could be alone. Even this could have been simpler, but Amy drove out near the railroad tracks because she wanted to be with him one more time. Chadron was attractive. His rangy muscles and sloppy blond hair, the way his face was always red, partly from his sun-damaged cheeks, partly because of capillaries burst from alcohol, and partly from the country bashfulness he couldn't suppress. Amy made things easy for him, she tried to, explaining how there was a folder in her bag that held papers she needed him to sign, and that she was going to screw him one last time before they dissolved their union.

Afterward, he started to object, nearly crying in the Neon, her coat draped over his naked legs, so she took him on a walk along the tracks to give him a chance to talk it through. In times past, Amy would have comforted her husband when he broke down, let him rest his head on her lap to cry out his frustrations, lamenting his struggle to become a man, but she didn't this time.

Then the train rumbled out from the northern edge of town, blowing by as they pushed against its current. The train's noise was stultifying, its sheer power electrified the very air she breathed. Its surging muscle infused itself in her, compelled her body to move on a parallel circuit. It was almost too easy, the way she pulled herself up and flopped onto the railcar bed. She wasn't thinking about divorce papers or doing the right thing or how her direction in life had been so long ago untracked. Amy didn't even think about where she might be headed, to where this line led. It was instinct to attach herself to the rumble, to loose her hair in an astounding wind. Even if the result was painful, she wanted to discover what awaited her at the end of the line.

It's close to morning by the time Amy hops off the train. She has a headache and needs coffee, so she positions herself at the edge of the railcar as it slows into another town, coasting into what looks like half timber yard, half salvage lot. There are long open stacks of lumber. On the other side of the tracks are great mounds of scrap, washers and dryers, the torn-out insides of buildings and wrecked cars ready to be compacted and bound together. Amy hops down, stumbles over rail rock as she lands, her legs shaky from a night of riding ill-spliced rails, then she follows the tracks until she's on the other side of a chain-link fence that edges the rail yard off from the town. The sunlight is orange and yellow in rays that sneak over the horizon, which seems odd to her. The sky usually looks this way only in the evening, or during a storm, when dust rises into a tumultuous atmosphere to color the sky.

Amy realizes that the town is called Valentine by the signs on its businesses. She finds a fisherman's cafe, a small brick building with old men drinking coffee inside. They wear plaid shirts with red suspenders and ball caps with the names of feed companies over the bill. These men resemble her father and his friends from church. Amy orders coffee and sits at a table near the window. The men smell her, she notices, their noses bend in her direction. The odors of the train followed her in, the heavy grease smell, the biting tang of too-fresh winter air that trails those who spent the night outdoors. It doesn't bother Amy if the men stare. She's used to being stared at.

When her coffee is finished Amy decides to call her father. She doesn't really have any other options. The sooner she can get back to Aurora, the sooner she can take care of things and get her car and get back to the Twin Cities. There isn't much waiting for her in Minnesota, but it's what she has now.

A skinny man in a T-shirt is waiting to snap a picture of her when she opens the door. There's a flash from his digital camera, and then she sees the man behind it, standing in the street.

"Don't run," he says, hiding the camera at his hip.

Amy stops to look at him, her body twisted in the doorway, confused as to why anyone would take her picture just then.

"Who are you?"

"I noticed you walking across the street," the man explains, circling as he moves closer. "My name's Aaron Kleinhardt. I'm staying at the motel over there." He points to a brown motor lodge down the block.

"I wanted to take your picture," he says. "You're pretty."

"What are you? Crazy?"

"No," Aaron says. "Why would you say that? We don't know each other."

Amy lets the door bang shut behind her, squaring her body to this man. He's a little older than she is, Amy figures, but he dresses like he's trying to look young, in a yellow Wyoming Cowboys T-shirt and tight jeans, his feet bare. His hair is stringy and needs trimming. The bangs hang over his eyes and, in order to see, he has to flip them to the side of his forehead. He's friendly, has blue eyes, a big smile that projects his straight rows of teeth.

"Listen," Amy says. She turns away. "I have a call to make."

But she stops, nudges at her scalp where the wool cap makes her hair itch, and stares at him again, this man who's still smiling at her, holding the camera at his side.

"If you don't mind my nerve," Aaron says. He moves gingerly, with pantomime steps over the gravel on the sidewalk. His feet must be freezing.

"I wonder if you'd tell me what you're running from."

"Excuse me?"

"You betrayed yourself." That's how he puts it. "It's the smell, your clothes," he explains. "I've learned a few things about being on the run, believe me, and you have the look of it."

"I have—really?" Amy flusters, turns back to this stranger. "I don't know what you're talking about."

"You don't have to tell me. I see what's going on." He slips the camera into the back pocket of his jeans and takes Amy by the arm, trying to shepherd her across the street.

"Don't touch me," she says, pulling her arm away.

"I'm sorry." He takes an exaggerated step back, palms raised.

"What I wanted to tell you," he continues, "is that you can use my shower if you need to. That's all I wanted to say. If you don't have the money for your own room, you can use mine."

Amy turns and walks away from him as he speaks to her, but again she stops to look back. He's kind of pitiful, the crummy clothes, his scrawny limbs. She laughs to herself at the very image of Aaron Kleinhardt, this pathetic man luring her back to his room.

"How stupid do you think I am?"

"You don't get what I mean," he says, pleased that she's listening. "I'll leave while you're there and wait outside while you shower. If that's what you want."

She can't believe how this man's approached her on the street, in Valentine, or the way his voice fluctuates, like he's constantly defending himself. Amy knows it's a bad idea to stick around, to associate with a man who acts like Aaron acts, but she can't help herself.

Aaron has her cornered in the room but Amy knows how to handle him. She guides him to the bed and goes to her knees in order to diffuse the situation. She won't lie in the bed with him, not that, but she unzips his jeans and touches the cold damp tip of his prick with her tongue, then takes him into her mouth relentlessly so that it's over quickly and she can get in the shower. He tries to thumb at her crotch after coming but she pushes him away. He won't insist if he's already had his. Amy understands these diversions.

When she emerges from the shower, a long white towel wrapped around her body, Aaron is still on the bed. He's stripped down to his boxers.

"How was it?" he asks, grinning, brushing away the stringy hair that hangs over his eyes.

"Mediocre," she says. "But nice, still, after the night I had."

"Are we talking about the shower?"

It's the way Aaron asks this, a huckster's smirk on his face, and that he'd even ask if giving head was good, that makes Amy feel again that she's made a mistake. She knew this already, when he followed her into the room and wouldn't leave her alone, and then in the moment she capitulated, Amy felt like what she was doing was wrong. But she's been in situations like these before and understands it's a zero sum game. What can it hurt, that's what she thought. Who will know the difference? If she gets a good shower, it would be worth it.

And she did try calling her father before Aaron convinced her to come to his room, but the call went unanswered. It wasn't her fault if events conspired against her. Standing there on the street, Aaron watching while it became clear that whoever she was calling wasn't going to answer. She couldn't think of another excuse for why she wouldn't use his shower. That is, besides the most obvious, that she didn't like him, that she knew what would happen once they were in his room, that she didn't want to have sex with him.

Amy didn't feel like she could tell Aaron in plain words that she wasn't interested. From the first moment they met she recognized the way he wanted her; she understood it would be easier to satisfy his desires than it would be to avoid them; she didn't have anywhere else to go.

"Listen," she says, freshly resolved to shake him. "Thanks for the shower and everything, but I need to get going."

"Sure." His eyebrows drop. "If you got to leave, I understand."

"It's nothing personal."

"Of course."

"It's not that I didn't enjoy it." They both cringe as she says this, because words like those can only mean their opposite. "You're on your own journey somewhere, I suppose, and I'm on mine. Let's just leave it at that."

Sitting on the bed, hands in his lap, Aaron drops the smile and squints at Amy, as if he's searching for something specific. It creeps her out, standing in a towel while he examines her, even though he isn't looking at her body exactly, her bare shoulders or legs. It's her face he's watching, her hair made curly by the shower steam, the furious glare she feels overtaking her eyes, the way her chin inches back into itself because she's nervous.

It's Aaron who breaks away first, his gaze darting to the door that leads to the street, to her puffy black coat that's hung over the knob.

"You were on a train, weren't you?" The full dopey smile reemerges as his gaze returns to her body. "Not a passenger train, that's not what I mean. They don't run here. I can smell it, the oil, the ozone of dynamos. You hopped a freight."

"I don't know what you're talking about."

"No," he says. "It's OK to admit it. I know about the kinds of things that set folks off into this country up here. I even rode a train like that before. It's a secret, that kind of thing. It's free."

"OK," Amy says. She leans down to snatch her clothes off the carpet. "I'm leaving."

With the bathroom door locked behind her, Amy dresses quickly. She slips on her jeans as she sits at the edge of the bathtub, then refastens her bra, its wires bent out of shape after sleeping on the railcar. It's when she's holding her shirt that she hears Aaron move, noticing the sound of him walking across the old motel shag, his pressing a hand against the bathroom door. It's dead quiet in the morning. Amy stands stock still in the bathroom, listening. The door seems to hum, as if Aaron is sliding his fingertips over its surface, his nails imperceptibly scraping the veneer. She jumps when he speaks because she doesn't know what's going to happen.

"Amy," he says, his voice still earnest and unashamed, a hint of begging in it. "If you're going to hop another train, I'd like to come." She stands with her back to the door, a cold shiver running along her spine. She wishes her father had answered when she called him.

"Would you let me go with you?" he asks.

Amy hesitates, grips the edge of the sink. "I'm not going to jump a train."

"You can tell me," he says. "I'd like to go on one, if you are."

Their agreement is to jump a southbound.

Amy had left the room, she'd dressed quickly and hurried out the door, slipped around the corner and called her father, misdialing twice because her fingers were shaking. She needed to get out of Valentine and should have kept walking, that was her mistake, because Aaron emerged jogging behind her on the street, wearing only his boxer shorts. He jumped in front of her and Amy had to end the call before anyone answered, cutting off the dial tone as she snapped her phone shut. She stuffed the phone in her pocket because Aaron was standing there, practically naked on this small town street where they both were strangers.

Somehow he calmed her again and convinced her that they must catch a train together, his voice jumpy trying to make it sound like fun before he rushed upstairs to put his clothes back on. Amy should have run then, but she hadn't. If she was someplace familiar, Aurora or the Twin Cities, or even Lincoln, where there were crowds of people, or folks she knew nearby, Amy would have run from him. But there wasn't anywhere she could go here. What would she tell them, these people that lived in Valentine? That she'd hopped a train and was stuck here? That she went down on this man in a motel room? Nothing had happened that she hadn't allowed to happen. That's what it would look like—that's what they would think—that she was seeking this weird man's attention. She was a stranger too. She couldn't rely on anyone here to save her. So she agreed to hop a southerly because at least then she would be headed in the direction of Aurora.

When Aaron falls asleep within the first hour it seems like a real blessing, especially when her phone vibrates in her pocket, when Amy sees that Chadron is calling. He's still her husband, she remembers, because they never signed the divorce papers. She left them in her car, then jumped the train and now she's here, wherever that is, somewhere south of Valentine. Amy doesn't answer the call, though, she presses the button on the side that stops the vibrating.

They're passing through another town when Amy notices that her phone is going to run out of battery, and it's this juxtaposition of events that causes her to stand and lean toward the ground rushing by—she's going through a town, her phone will soon die, Aaron's asleep behind her. She nearly jumps. But then she pauses to rationalize with herself.

It seems too simple, that she can jump off the train and walk to town, stop at the library and call her father, that she could escape from Aaron's cloying presence while he's sleeping. And it's while she's thinking of these things—remembering the way her father would softly hum, "Oh, Amy, what has happened to you now?"— that she returns the phone to her pocket, sits back inside the boxcar, and decides to hang on a while longer. *This is what I'm doing*, she thinks. She'll wait until they're closer to Aurora before jumping, so she can walk back on her own.

Aaron sleeps curled in a back corner of the near empty rail car. There's just scrap metal in the car with them, segments of rusty I-beams. *Who is this man?* she thinks again, standing over Aaron as he sleeps, his skinny ankles showing out the bottom of his jeans. He's not particularly attractive, Amy knows this. She's embarrassed that she went down on him, although embarrassed before whom she couldn't say. It doesn't matter. Amy can't think of anyone she's slept with whose looks or personality were cause for bragging.

It's true that Amy hasn't always made her own decisions, she hasn't always been in control of the situations she's found herself in, but if she could help it, she would never let a man treat her like she's a victim again.

Because it's just sitting there unattended, Amy digs in Aaron's bag and carries it to the edge of the railcar. Inside she finds his wallet and some other personal junk that isn't interesting, but her fingers jump when she sees his digital camera in the front pocket, wrapped in a small cotton sack. She wants to see who else Aaron has taken pictures of, remembering the way he'd approached her that morning, his obvious ploy to get her in bed.

The first few photos in its history are of Amy herself, a close-up of her face, then one of her leaving the café. She feels something roil in her stomach before she even realizes what it means, as she finds images of herself walking into the café, and even before then, when she first entered town, long-range shots of her bending over to tie her shoes. It's as if Aaron had anticipated her coming, standing at his motel window with this camera at first light, waiting for a woman to wander into his frame. Amy thought his line was pitiful but she was wrong. These pictures of her coming into town, nearly a dozen of them, showed that he'd planned for her arrival. He'd been waiting to tell her she's pretty.

Amy looks over her shoulder at Aaron, still sleeping, this skinny dweeb who somehow convinced her to go along with him. She wants to hit him, to kick his face in while he sleeps, but she merely closes her eyes, shakes her head in disgust, then turns back to his camera.

There are a few more shots of Valentine and other towns Aaron traveled through, stone-built town halls and decommissioned tanks in municipal parks, then images of a woman lying naked in bed, covering her face in embarrassment, followed by a few of this same woman standing outside a coffee shop; then a different woman tied-up, her breasts squeezed purple in the cinch of a nylon rope, what happened after Aaron snapped her photo outside a shopping mall; others of a woman blindfolded, her ankles and wrists hog-tied, her parts exposed; another of Aaron wielding a knife, biting a woman's nipple as he slices across her belly.

There's a video Amy plays. A big woman lounges in a dark room, the curtains drawn. Her bottom-heavy breasts rest on her stomach as she lies in bed, drinking from a beer can. Her hair is done-up in what looks like an old-fashioned style, even though she couldn't be much older than thirty.

The camera's small speakers distort from the loud music that played in the room, an undulation of hoary blues music, the big woman singing in chorus between slugs of beer, spread out naked on the bed, her flesh sinking into itself.

Amy turns again to look at Aaron, to see if the video woke him. He's slumped in the corner, arms folded over his chest, sleeping.

His voice is under the music in the video. *"The Kellogg Rooming House. June 15, 2010."*

The image shakes, as if the camera had been set on a table, although the woman is still the only one on the screen. She's humming to herself, twisting her legs together as she lies there, her long brown body full across the bed sheet. There's a pop. The sound feeds back in short crackles. Then two more. The woman in the video drops her beer to the floor. Three small holes appear on her body, two in her stomach and one in her breast. The woman cries, it sounds likes drunk wailing, like she's merely confused and lonely. The video plays for a long time after she's shot, the loud music over her moans as the bed sheet blots red. Long after she stops making noise, stops moving, the video freezes on the image of the woman in her bed, the holes in her stomach and breast.

Amy holds the camera for what seems like a short time. The image of the woman dims and then fades to black. Amy still doesn't jump; even the thought of it has left her. Her head buzzing. Her vision fuzzy outside the borders of the camera viewfinder. She can't control it: Amy thinks of simple Chadron, her husband back in Aurora, drinking a morning beer at the kitchen table.

Sitting at the edge of the railcar with the camera in her hands, Amy doesn't think that Aaron is awake while she watches the video. She's wrong about that.

The train is going over a bridge. Amy sees this above her through a dizzying matte of tree branches. She's landed at the foot of the pylons that support the bridge. There are whole minutes of blackness and white noise, the sound of train rumble vibrating through bridge feet. Amy feels behind herself. Her fingers bump the blood-sticky hilt of the knife in her back.

She felt the burning of it before she heard Aaron grunt, the knife needling into the softness of her lower back. It was the crescendo of pain rising in her torso that caused Amy to arch away from him, her body going stiff, legs straightening in shock, the fire of the knife at her kidneys. The camera was in her hands, his bag nestled between her legs at the edge of the railcar. It was only by chance that when Amy rolled away the train was going over a bridge that spanned a wide coulee, and that as she fell the thirty feet through snapping tree branches, clutching to his bag, she curled into herself and landed in the spongy gut of a stream bottom.

It's when she bumps against the knife that Amy understands she's still in danger, that the images on Aaron's camera come back to her, and that she's still holding that camera, she still has his bag—and he will come looking for them.

Amy is unable to stand when she first tries. The pain in her back saps the strength from her legs, the muscles battered, but she manages to gain her knees on the second try, and then her left foot as she leans against a tree. She can crutch herself along, grasping from one sapling to another, his bag slung over her shoulder, moving from the spot, down the coulee to where there's light. It's a narrow snatch of forest she's in, a few acres hugging tight to where the railway bridge spans the gully. It gives her enough of a head start on Aaron, though.

He will make sure she's dead, Amy knows this. That's why she drives herself on, advancing quicker as her legs stretch out underneath, the pain in her muscles abating as she moves them. There's still the blooming shock of the knife in her back, where the blade keeps her wound more or less closed, but Amy can't worry about that. She doesn't want to end up like those other women in the camera.

It's when Aaron's bag slips from her shoulder and dumps its contents to the ground that Amy finds his pistol. The bag tilts upside down as it drops, his wallet and notebook fall out, then the gun on top of them. The glint of its plating flashes a ray of light. Amy checks the pistol and sees it's loaded. She secures the safety and stuffs it into her beltline. She unfolds his wallet, removes his driver's license and sees that his name really is Aaron Kleinhardt, just as he told her. If he planned on killing her all along then it couldn't matter if she knew his name.

At the edge of the woods Amy spies the open country of a farm, long furrows of soil ground in by tractor tires during harvest. The trees edge into a straight line where the field begins, along the right-of-way, so she can see a long distance in front of her. Aaron can see too if he's looking. There's an irrigation shed or something like it, a wooden structure in the clearing, about fifty yards away. Amy can just make out its flat roof, its wood shingles worn the same color as the soil. It's getting cold again. As she hobbles across the frozen clods of dirt she can feel the wind blow through her.

She crouches inside the shed once she reaches it. There isn't much to the structure, one main line that humps in and out of a concrete box dug into the ground, a few pipes that sprout near the door with gauges at their ends, the dripping odor of moss. But there's space enough to settle against the wall planks and wait to see if Aaron will find her. She feels behind herself again, touches the sticky hilt of the knife. There isn't much blood. Even with her fall, the blade's channel hasn't widened.

Amy isn't sure what she'll do when he discovers her. She girds herself, holding the pistol between her hands, and whispers that she can do this, she's shot before. And it's true, she's shot a pistol many times. She knows how to prepare the gun, how to stare down the back of it while loading the chamber and how to flip the safety so that it's ready to fire.

It isn't long before Aaron finds her, a few minutes, as if he was poised at the other end of the clearing, watching as she entered the irrigation shed before circling in.

She hesitates, despite herself, when he opens the door, shocked somehow to see him standing there looking pathetic.

"I'm unarmed," he says, holding his hands up by his face, his fingers outstretched. "Please don't shoot."

Amy slides across the concrete floor as far away from him as she can get before jarring the knife against the back wall. She doesn't shoot. She holds the pistol out, both hands squeezed around the gun so that it looks tiny, in wraps under her fingers, its barrel emerging darkly from her hands.

"I don't want to kill you," she says.

"Give me the gun, please. You don't know what you saw. There's a good explanation."

Aaron inches closer as he talks, kind of leaning, his feet sliding to catch up. His body becomes bigger in the doorway once he clears it, the flimsy door quivering in the wind behind him, his hands still held out in front.

"Give me the gun and we'll wait for the next train to come."

"Stop."

"We both made mistakes today. I'm willing to walk away. Just give me the bag."

Amy feels like closing her eyes, to just black out everything and squeeze until this man is gone. But she holds Aaron in the doorway with her gaze, her jaw stern, eyes flashing a glint of blue above the pistol clutched in her fingers. She sizes him up, determines where she should shoot to wound him, where she can aim to kill. She looks him in the eyes again. It's difficult to look Aaron in the eyes and not falter for an instant, to stifle a flutter of sympathy, because of the way he holds himself. His skinny limbs and bad posture, those ill-fitting clothes made for a younger man. And that half-smile, still he's smirking, like he can't believe that it's come to this. All the while he inches closer.

Amy feels how those other women must have underestimated him, because of the way he looks and acts, like he couldn't possibly get the better of her. But she can see it in his eyes too—in a too-late way like the others—how all this is thrilling him. She knows what's going to happen.

He's started to say something when Amy shoots. She squeezes the pistol until it pops, and then again, hitting him twice in the chest. He still talks even as he tries to pool blood in his fingers. Invoking the train, trying to sell her. The words end as a sort of gulping. He staggers out of the shed and falls into the dirt.

It's ten minutes or more before Amy is certain he's dead. The gasps of his body twitter out into nothing. Slowly she works to her feet, the burn pulsing from the knife in her back, and then she escapes the shed, the pistol poised in front of her, just in case. She has to step over him, to look down at his pale face still smirking, one eye open and one closed. Amy doesn't falter as she looks down at his chest bloat slowly, knowing that he's dead. It's just the mechanics of his lungs working.

She doesn't cry yet because there's the knife in her back, her clothes wet with blood, and she's walking toward what looks like a farmhouse on the horizon.

Amy fires three shots in the air before she collapses, too weak to continue, using the last of the bullets to attract the attention of the farmer and her husband in the house that's less than a mile away. They're the ones who find her.

THIRTY MORE
DISTINGUISHED STORIES

"Sloth" by Charles Baxter. First published in *New England Review*.

"Photographers' by Light" Rosellen Brown. First published in *Antioch Review*.

"Memorare for the Ding Dong" by Michael Czyzniejewski. First published in *Yemassee Journal*.

"Harmony Arm" by Steve De Jarnatt. First published in *Cincinnati Review*.

"Domain" by Louise Erdrich. First published in *Granta*.

"The Abyss" by Rebekah Frumkin. First published in *Granta*.

"Good Riddance" by Jim Heynen. First published in *The Georgia Review*.

"Building Walls" by Dustin M. Hoffman. First published in *Puerto Del Sol*.

"Sawdust & Glue" by Dustin M. Hoffman. First published in *Sou'wester*.

"The Way It Is Around Here" by J. A. Howard. First published in *Glimmer Train Stories*.

"I Just Died" by Evan James. First published in *The Sun*.

"The Weave" by Charles Johnson. First published in *Iowa Review*.

"Remora, IL" by Kevin Leahy. First published in Briar *Cliff Review*.

"The Baby Cage" by Molly McNett. First published in *Crazyhorse*.

"The Future" by Joe Meno. First published in Fifth *Wednesday Journal*.

"Good Faith" by Colleen Morrissey. First published in *Cincinnati Review*.

"A Talented Individual" by Andy Mozina. First published in *Natural Bridge*.

"The Hunter" by Joyce Carol Oates. First published in *Boulevard*.

"Indulgence" by Susan Perabo. First published in *One Story*.

"The Collector of Thoughts" by David James Poissant. First published in *Gulf Coast*.

"Whatsoever" by Amy Sayre-Roberts. First published in *Ninth Letter*.

"The Calendar Ordeals" by Sarah Elizabeth Schantz. First published in *Midwestern Gothic*.

"The Couplehood Jubilee" by Christine Sneed. First published in *New England Review*.

"Clear Conscience" by Christine Sneed. First published in *New England Review*.

"The Collapse" by Sarah A. Stickley. First published in *A Public Space*.

"Come the Revolution" by Emma Torzs. First published in *Ploughshares*.

"The Fighters" by David Treuer. First published in *Granta*.

"Handsome Pair of Sunday Walkers" by Marc Watkins. First published in *Third Coast*.

"Stripped" by Mark Wisniewski. First published in *Stoneslide Corrective*.

"The Carousel Thief" by David Yost. First published in *Cincinnati Review*.

BIOGRAPHIES

Thomas M. Atkinson's novel *Tiki Man* was a finalist in the 2014 Leapfrog Press Fiction Contest. His collection of linked stories, *Standing Deadwood*, which includes "Grimace in the Burnt Black Hills," was a finalist in the 2014 Spokane Prize for Fiction (Willow Springs Editions) and the 2014 St. Lawrence Book Award for Fiction (Black Lawrence Press). His short play, *Dancing Turtle*, was a winner in the *38th Annual Samuel French Off Off Broadway Festival*, and appears in an anthology of the same name. He has won five Ohio Arts Council Individual Excellence Awards and was the 2013 Ohio Arts Council/Fine Arts Work Center Collaborative Writer-in-Residence. His short fiction has appeared in *The Sun*, *The Madison Review*, *The North American Review*, *Indiana Review*, *Tampa Review*, *Fifth Wednesday Journal*, *The Moon*, *City Beat*, *Clifton*, and *Electron Press Magazine*. He and his wife live in Ohio and have two sons.

Charles Baxter was born in Minneapolis and graduated from Macalester College, in Saint Paul. After completing graduate work in English at the State University of New York at Buffalo, he taught for several years at Wayne State University in Detroit. In 1989, he moved to the Department of English at the University of Michigan—Ann Arbor and its MFA program. He now teaches at the University of Minnesota. Baxter is the author of five novels, five collections of short stories, three collections of poems, two collections of essays on fiction, and is the editor of other works.

Catherine Browder's award-winning stories have appeared in a variety of journals, including *Nimrod, Prairie Schooner,*

Shenandoah, Kansas Quarterly, New Letters, and *Kansas City Noir;* and her plays have been presented regionally and in NYC. She has received fiction fellowships from the National Endowment for the Arts and the Missouri Arts Council. *Ploughshares* recently published her novella, *Café Deux Mondes,* in its third *Solos Omnibus,* after first publishing it in e-book and audio formats. Her most recent story collection, *Now We Can All Go Home: 3 Novellas in Homage to Chekhov,* is from BkMk Press (2014). An associate in the creative writing program at the University of Missouri-Kansas City, she serves as an advisory editor for *New Letters* magazine.

Jason Lee Brown is the author of the novel *Prowler: The Mad Gasser of Mattoon,* the novella *Championship Run,* and the poetry chapbook *Blue Collar Fathers.* His fiction has appeared in *Kenyon Review, Literary Review, North American Review, The Journal, Southern Humanities Review, Ecotone,* and numerous other journals. He earned his MFA from Southern Illinois University Carbondale.

Claire Burgess's short fiction has appeared or is forthcoming in *Third Coast, Hunger Mountain, PANK* online, *Joyland,* and elsewhere. Her stories have been listed as "notable" in *Best American Short Stories* and *Best American Nonrequired Reading* and have received an honorable mention in the *Pushcart Prize 2014* anthology. Claire holds an MFA from Vanderbilt University, where she was a founding editor of *Nashville Review.* She currently writes "This Week in Short Fiction" for *The Rumpus,* and you can find more of her writing at byclaireburgess.com.

Shae Cohan is a photographer and videographer out of Illinois. He focuses on weather in his photos and videos with a passion for storm chasing. He is a meteorology major at Western Illinois University.

Peter Ho Davies is the author of the novel *The Welsh Girl,* long-listed for the Booker Prize, and the story collections *The Ugliest*

House in the World and *Equal Love*. His new novel, *The Fortunes,* is forthcoming in fall 2016. His short fiction has appeared in *Harpers*, *The Atlantic Monthly*, and *The Paris Review*, and been anthologized in *Prize Stories: The O. Henry Awards* and *Best American Short Stories*. One of *Granta*'s "Best of Young British Novelists," Davies now lives in Ann Arbor and teaches in the MFA Program at the University of Michigan.

Stephanie Dickinson, an Iowa native, lives in New York City. Her work appears in *Hotel Amerika*, *Mudfish*, *Weber Studies*, *Fjords*, *Water-Stone Review*, *Gargoyle*, *Rhino*, *Stone Canoe*, *Westerly*, and *New Stories from the South*, among others. Her novel *Half Girl* and novella *Lust Series* are published by Spuyten Duyvil, as is her recent novel *Love Highway*, based on the 2006 Jennifer Moore murder. *Heat: An Interview with Jean Seberg* was released in 2013 by New Michigan Press. Her work has received multiple distinguished story citations in the *Pushcart Anthology*, *Best American Short Stories*, and *Best American Mysteries*.

Jack Driscoll's most recent short story collection, *The World of a Few Minutes Ago*, was the 2013 winner of the Society of Midland Writers Award for Fiction and the Michigan Library Award. His stories have appeared in numerous journals including *The Georgia Review*, *The Southern Review*, *Ploughshares*, *Missouri Review*, *Gettysburg Review*, *Michigan Quarterly Review*, and twice in the *Pushcart Prize Anthology*. He currently teaches in Pacific University's low-residency MFA program.

Nick Dybek's first novel, *When Captain Flint Was Still a Good Man*, was the winner of the 2013 Society of Midland Authors Award, a finalist for the VCU-Cabell First Novelist Award and has been translated into five languages. He's also a recipient of a Granta New Voices selection, a Michener-Copernicus Society of America Award, and a Maytag Fellowship. He teaches in the MFA program at Oregon State University.

Stuart Dybek is the author of five books of fiction: *Paper Lantern, Ecstatic Cahoots, I Sailed With Magellan, The Coast of Chicago,* and *Childhood and Other Neighborhoods.* Both *I Sailed With Magellan* and *The Coast of Chicago* were *New York Times* Notable Books, and *The Coast of Chicago* was a One Book One Chicago selection. Dybek has also published two collections of poetry: *Streets in Their Own Ink* and *Brass Knuckles.* His fiction, poetry, and nonfiction have appeared in many magazines and anthologies, including *The New Yorker, Harper's, The Atlantic, Poetry, Granta, Tin House, Best American Fiction,* and *Best American Poetry.* Among his numerous awards are a MacArthur Fellowship, the Rea Award for Short Fiction, PEN/Malamud Prize "for distinguished achievement in the short story," a Lannan Award, a Whiting Writers Award, an Award from the Academy of Arts and Letters, several O.Henry Prizes, and fellowships from the NEA and the Guggenheim Foundation. He is currently Distinguished Writer In Residence at Northwestern University and part of the permanent faculty for the Prague Summer Program.

Abby Geni is the author of *The Lightkeepers*, a Barnes & Noble Discover Great New Writers Spring 2016 selection, and *The Last Animal* (2013), a finalist for the Orion Book Award and a winner of the Friends of American Writers Literary Award. Her stories have received first place in the *Glimmer Train* Fiction Open and the Chautauqua Contest, and her work has appeared in *Glimmer Train, Indiana Review, Flaunt Magazine, Confrontation,* and *The Crab Orchard Review*, among other literary journals and anthologies. Geni is a graduate of the Iowa Writers' Workshop and a recipient of the Iowa Fellowship. She lives in Chicago.

Albert Goldbarth has been publishing notable books of poetry for more than forty years, two of which have received the National Book Critics Circle Award. He is also the author of a novel, *Pieces of Payne*, and a number of essay collections, of which the latest, *The Adventures of Form and Content*, is due from Graywolf Press in early 2017.

Baird Harper's fiction has appeared in *Glimmer Train Stories, Tin House, Prairie Schooner, StoryQuarterly, The Chicago Tribune, Mid-American Review, Another Chicago Magazine, Carve,* and *Printers Row Journal.* His stories have been anthologized in the 2009 and 2010 editions of *Best New American Voices* and *40 Years of CutBank,* and have won the 2014 Raymond Carver Short Story Contest, the 2010 Nelson Algren Award, and the 2009 James Jones Fiction Contest. His first book will be published by Scribner in summer 2017. An Illinois native, he teaches fiction writing at Loyola University and The University of Chicago.

Shanie Latham is an associate editor at *River Styx* magazine and an associate professor of English at Jefferson College in Missouri. She earned an MFA in creative writing from Southern Illinois University Carbondale. Her work has appeared in *Slant* and *Boulevard.*

Rebecca Makkai is the Chicago-based author of the novels *The Hundred-Year House,* winner of the Chicago Writers Association's Novel of the Year award, and *The Borrower,* a Booklist Top Ten Debut, which has been translated into eight languages, as well as the short story collection *Music for Wartime.* Her short fiction was chosen for *The Best American Short Stories* for four consecutive years (from 2008 to 2011), and appears regularly in journals like *Harper's, Tin House,* and *New England Review.* The recipient of a 2014 NEA fellowship, Makkai will be visiting faculty this fall at the Iowa Writers' Workshop.

Lee Martin is the author of the novels, *The Bright Forever,* a finalist for the 2006 Pulitzer Prize in Fiction; *River of Heaven; Quakertown; Break the Skin,* and *Late One Night.* He has also published three memoirs, *From Our House, Turning Bones,* and *Such a Life.* His first book was the short story collection *The Least You Need to Know.* He is the co-editor of *Passing the Word: Writers on Their Mentors.* His fiction and nonfiction have appeared or are forthcoming in *Harper's, Ms., Creative Nonfiction, The Georgia Review, Kenyon*

Review, Fourth Genre, The Southern Review, Prairie Schooner, Glimmer Train, Best American Mystery Stories, and *Best American Essays.* He is the winner of the Mary McCarthy Prize in Short Fiction and fellowships from the National Endowment for the Arts and the Ohio Arts Council. He teaches in the MFA Program at The Ohio State University, where he is a College of Arts and Sciences Distinguished Professor of English and a past winner of the Alumni Award for Distinguished Teaching.

Monica McFawn's story collection, *Bright Shards of Someplace Else,* won a Flannery O'Connor Award and was named a Michigan Notable Book and an NPR "Great Read." Her stories have appeared in journals such as *The Georgia Review, Missouri Review, Gettysburg Review,* and others, and her screenplays and plays have had readings in New York and Chicago. She is also author of "A Catalogue of Rare Movements," a poetry/art chapbook. A recipient of NEA Fellowship in Fiction and a Walter E. Dakin fellowship from Sewanee Writers' Conference, McFawn is an assistant professor of English at Northern Michigan University, where she teaching fiction and scriptwriting.

John McNally is author or editor of sixteen books, most recently the young adult novel *Lord of the Ralphs* (2015) and a collection of personal essays, *The Boy Who Really, Really Wanted to Have Sex* (2017). His short stories, essays, and reviews have appeared in more than a hundred publications, including *One Teen Story, Virginia Quarterly Review,* and *Washington Post.* He is Professor and Writer-in-Residence at the University of Louisiana at Lafayette. A native of Chicago's southwest side, John divides his time between Lafayette, Louisiana, and Winston-Salem, North Carolina.

Emily Mitchell's first collection of short stories, *Viral* (W. W. Norton) was published in June 2015. Her novel, *The Last Summer of the World* (W. W. Norton, 2007), was a finalist for the NYPL Young Lions Award. Her short fiction has appeared in *Harper's,*

New England Review, Ploughshares, and other magazines. Her non-fiction has appeared in *the New York Times* and *the New Statesman.* She is a recipient of fellowships from the Ucross Foundation, Virginia Center for Creative Arts, the Breadloaf Writers' Conference, and the Sewanee Writers' Conference. She teaches in the MFA program in creative writing at the University of Maryland.

Devin Murphy's debut novel, *The Boat Runner,* is forthcoming from Harper Perennial in 2017. His recent fiction appears in *The Chicago Tribune, Glimmer Train, Michigan Quarterly Review, Missouri Review,* and *Shenandoah* and others. He holds an MFA from Colorado State University, a Creative Writing PhD from the University of Nebraska—Lincoln, and is an Assistant Professor of Creative Writing at Bradley University. He lives in Chicago with his wife and two kids.

Joyce Carol Oates is a recipient of the National Book Award, the PEN/Malamud Award, and the National Medal of Humanities. Her short-story collection *Lovely, Dark, Deep* (Ecco, 2014) was a finalist for the 2015 Pulitzer Prize in Fiction. Her national bestsellers include *We Were the Mulvaneys* (Dutton, 1996), *Blonde* (Ecco, 2000), *The Falls* (Ecco, 2004), which won the 2005 Prix Femina, and the memoir *A Widow's Story* (Ecco, 2011). Oates is a member of the American Academy of Arts and Letters and is the 2010 recipient of the National Book Critics Circle Ivan Sandrof Lifetime Achievement Award.

Lori Ostlund's novel *After the Parade* (Scribner, 2015) was shortlisted for the Center for Fiction First Novel Prize and is a Barnes and Noble Discover Great New Writers pick. Her first book, a story collection entitled *The Bigness of the World*, won the 2008 Flannery O'Connor Award, the Edmund White Debut Fiction Award, and the 2009 California Book Award for First Fiction. Stories from it appeared in the *Best American Short Stories, PEN/O. Henry Prize Stories, New England Review, The Georgia Review,* and other places. Scribner reissued the collection in early 2016. Lori has received a Rona Jaffe Foundation Award and a fellowship to the Bread Loaf Writers' Conference. "The Gap Year" is part of her in-progress second story collection. She is a teacher and lives in San Francisco.

Noley Reid is author of the short story collection, *So There!* (SFA University Press) and a novel, *In the Breeze of Passing Things* (MacAdam/Cage). Her stories have appeared in *The Southern Review, Other Voices, Quarterly West, Black Warrior Review*, and *Meridian*. Her next novel is forthcoming from Tin House Books. www.NoleyReid.com

Christine Sneed is the author of four books. Her first book, *Portraits of a Few of the People I've Made Cry* won AWP's 2009 Grace Paley Prize and was chosen as Book of the Year by the Chicago Writers Association. Her second book, the novel *Little Known Facts*, won the Society of Midland Authors Award for best adult fiction 2013 and was named one of *Booklist*'s top ten debut novels of 2013. Christine Sneed's third book is the novel *Paris, He Said* (Bloomsbury USA) and her fourth is another story collection titled *The Virginity of Famous Men*.

Randolph Thomas's short story collection *Dispensations* won the Many Voices Award from New Rivers Press and a Bronze Medal from the Independent Publisher Book Awards. His stories have appeared in *Glimmer Train Stories, The Florida Review, The Hudson Review*, and many other journals. His collection of poems, *The Deepest Rooms*, won the Gerald Cable Award from Silverfish Review Press. He teaches English at Louisiana State University.

Anne Valente is the author of the novel *Our Hearts Will Burn Us Down* (William Morrow/HarperCollins) and the short story collection *By Light We Knew Our Names* (Dzanc Books). Her fiction appears in *One Story, The Kenyon Review, The Southern Review* and *The Chicago Tribune,* and her essays appear in *The Believer* and *The*

Washington Post. Originally from St. Louis, she currently teaches creative writing at Santa Fe University of Art and Design.

Laura van den Berg is the author of the novel *Find Me*, longlisted for the 2016 International Dylan Thomas Prize, and two story collections *What the World Will Look Like When All the Water Leaves Us* and *The Isle of Youth*, both finalists for the Frank O'Connor International Short Story Award. Her honors include the Bard Fiction Prize, the Rosenthal Family Foundation Award from the American Academy of Arts and Letters, the Jeannette Haien Ballard Writer's Prize, a Pushcart Prize, and an O. Henry Award, and her fiction has been anthologized in *The Best American Short Stories*. Beginning in the fall 2016, she will be a Briggs-Copeland Lecturer in Fiction at Harvard.

Josh Weil is the author of the novel *The Great Glass Sea* (a New York Times Editor's Choice that won the Dayton Literary Peace Prize, the GrubStreet National Book Prize, and The Library of Virginia's Award in Fiction) and the novella collection *The New Valley* (awarded the Sue Kaufman Prize from The American Academy of Arts and Letters and the New Writers Award from the GLCA). A Fulbright Fellow and National Book Award 5-under-35 honoree, his writing has appeared in *Granta*, *Tin House*, *One Story*, *Esquire*, and *The New York Times*, among others. He lives with his family in the Sierra Nevadas.

Theodore Wheeler is the author of a collection of short fiction, *Bad Faith* (Queen's Ferry Press, 2016) and a forthcoming novel, *Kings of Broken Things* (Little A, 2017). His work has been featured in *Best New American Voices*, *The Southern Review*, *Kenyon Review*, and *Boulevard*, and in 2014 he was a fellow at Akademie Schloss Solitude in Stuttgart, Germany. He lives in Omaha with his wife and their two daughters.